"Succeeds in magisterially re-creating that woeful and bizarre period of Spanish history that prefigured the discovery and conquest of America. . . . The overall effect is one of splendidly rendered originality and authenticity."
—*New York Times Book Review*

"An extraordinary account of religious persecution in the fifteenth century . . . This is a book of glittering and garish surfaces, teeming with weird incidents and violent fates. . . . The sense of menace and threat that Aridjis conjures up is extraordinary." —*Times Literary Supplement* (London)

"An encyclopedic vision of catastrophic times . . . Among worldwide bestsellers, *1492* is most similar to Umberto Eco's *The Name of the Rose;* both are concerned with the trials of heretics and the violence employed against dissidents."
—*La Jornada* (Mexico City)

"This superb book reads like the wind, like an epic chronicle. . . . Homero Aridjis retrieves, through the miracle of his magical prose, the very essence of the twilight of Spain."
—*La Quinzaine Litteraire* (Paris)

HOMERO ARIDJIS is one of Mexico's foremost poets and novelists. He has published more than 20 books of poetry and prose, and was awarded the Diana-Novedades Literary Prize for his sequel to *1492, Memorias del nuevo mundo.* Twice the recipient of a Guggenheim Fellowship, he has taught at Columbia University, New York University, and Indiana University. He has been Mexican Ambassador to the Netherlands and Switzerland, and is the president of the Group of 100, Mexico's leading environmental organization. He lives in Mexico City.

"A stunning re-creation of the bloody Spanish frenzy to convert the world."
—*Detroit Free Press*

"With *1492*, Homero Aridjis has achieved a novel of exceptional grandeur."
—*Le Soir* (Brussels)

"This highly readable novel about a special and painful chapter in history combines erudition, sensitivity, and poetic imagination. I recommend it warmly."
—Elie Wiesel

"*1492* is a colorful and witty description, swarming with details of a dark era. The novel, by one of Mexico's greatest authors, has breadth of language and sensuality in the description of milieus and characters. Homero Aridjis has created a tremendously strong novel."
—*Nerikes Allehanda* (Orebro)

"Aridjis' depiction of [Juan's and Isabel's] romance is exquisitely handled."
—*Publishers Weekly*

"Not only a heartbreaking account of the human misery caused by the Inquisition, but also a marvelously colorful description of daily life in Spain in the 15th century."
—*Manchester Evening News* (England)

1492

The Life and Times of Juan Cabezón of Castile

HOMERO ARIDJIS

Translated from the Spanish by
BETTY FERBER

Ⓟ

A PLUME BOOK

PLUME
Published by the Penguin Group
Penguin Books USA Inc., 375 Hudson Street, New York, New York 10014, U.S.A.
Penguin Books Ltd, 27 Wrights Lane, London W8 5TZ, England
Penguin Books Australia Ltd, Ringwood, Victoria, Australia
Penguin Books Canada Ltd, 10 Alcorn Avenue, Toronto, Ontario, Canada M4V 3B2
Penguin Books (N.Z.) Ltd, 182-190 Wairau Road, Auckland 10, New Zealand

Penguin Books Ltd, Registered Offices: Harmondsworth, Middlesex, England

Published by Plume, an imprint of New American Library, a division of Penguin Books USA Inc.
This is an authorized reprint of a hardcover edition published by Summit Books, a division of
Simon & Schuster, Inc.

First Plume Printing, October, 1992
10 9 8 7 6 5 4 3 2 1

Originally published in Mexico by Siglo XXI Editores as *1492, Vida y Tiempos de Juan Cabezón de
Castilla.*

 REGISTERED TRADEMARK—MARCA REGISTRADA

LIBRARY OF CONGRESS CATLOGING-IN-PUBLICATION DATA
Aridjis, Homero.
    [1492 English]
    1492: the life and times of Juan Cabezón of Castile / Homero
Aridjis: translated from the Spanish by Betty Ferber.
        p.   cm.
    ISBN 0-452-26914-8
    I. Title.
PQ7297.A8365A61513   1992
863—dc20   92-53559
                                                           CIP

Printed in the United States of America
Original hardcover design by Eve Metz

ACKNOWLEDGMENTS

Above all I would like to acknowledge my enormous debt to those authors who, by virtue of their biographical sketches, chronicles, memoirs, histories, annals, accounts, dictionaries and publication of numerous documents, have made the writing of this book possible. First, the contemporary sources: Fernán Pérez de Guzmán, Fernando del Pulgar, Andrés Bernáldez, Alonso Fernández de Palencia, Diego de Valera, Gerónimo de Zurita, Alonso Fernández de Madrid, Selomó ibn Verga, Antonio de Nebrija, Sebastián de Covarrubias, the biographers of San Vicente Ferrer (from whom I quote on occasion), the travelers León de Rosmithal, Tetzel, Hieronymus Munzer; then the modern scholars: José Amador de los Ríos, Fidel Fita, Henry Charles Lea, Yitzhak Baer, Manuel Serrano y Sanz, Agustín Millares Carlo, Juan de Mata Carriazo, Francisco Cantera Burgos, Pilar León Tello, Luis Suárez Fernández and Haim Beinart, among others too numerous to mention here, whose research on different aspects of the Spain of the three religions, published in the *Boletín* de la Real Academia de la Historia, the *Boletín* de la Real Academia de la Lengua, the *Memorias* de la Real Academia de la Historia, the *Revue Hispanique* and *Sefarad*, has provided me with a wealth of historical detail. Finally, to all those whose precise words have guided me one way or another through the complexities of history, my lasting gratitude.

HOMERO ARIDJIS

The translator also wishes to thank Anne Stainton for her assistance with the Latin translations.

TO BETTY, CHLOE AND EVA SOPHIA

And the captivity of Jerusalem, which is in Sepharad, shall possess the cities of the south.

—Obadiah 20

Ever since the day when we abandoned our homeland to go into exile, the persecution has never ceased; from our youth it has reared us as a father, and from our mother's womb has guided us.
—Moses Maimonides,
Epistle on Persecution,
or Treatise on the Sanctification of the Name
(after Job 31:18)

After many years there will come a time when the Ocean Sea will loose the chains of all things and a huge land will lie revealed; and a new mariner, like that Tiphys who was guide to Jason, will discover a new world, and then Thule will no longer be the ultimate.
—Cristóbal Colón (Christopher Columbus),
Book of Prophecies (after Seneca, *Medea*)

Many kiss the hands they would gladly see cut off.
—Fifteenth-century Spanish proverb

1492
The Life and Times
of Juan Cabezón
of Castile

My grandfather was born in Seville on the sixth day of June in the year of Our Lord 1391, the very same day Ferrán Martínez, the Archdeacon of Ecija, incited the Christian rabble to burn down the gates of the Jewish *aljama*, leaving fire and blood, looting and death in his wake. While my great-grandmother Sancha cried out in the throes of labor, Ferrán Martínez and his followers slit the throats of women and children, reduced the synagogues to rubble and left four thousand innocents lifeless. My father's grandfather watched my great-grandmother on her bed and, through an unglazed window, the rapacious faithful pillaging books and tiles, hides and cloths, lamps and perfumes, furnishings and jewelry, bricks and plates. More than once Ferrán Martínez burst into a house where some woman was shielding her small daughter against a wall, and this man of little learning but exemplary life glimpsed himself in a shattered mirror, saw his reflection heady with death in the bloody shards, and lifted the dagger of faith to plunge it into a little girl whose mother begged for the baptismal waters that could save her child.

Milling around the archdeacon, the mob rooted, raped and ravaged like a thousand-handed beast among collapsing furniture, torn clothes, pockmarked walls and floors. Threats and groans, unheeded words and whispers troubled the air and the sensitive ears of the woman in labor who flinched at the slightest sound, convinced that the fury raging in the *aljama* had entered her own body. Great-grandmother's house stood back-to-back with a Jewish house, and any disaster that befell one echoed in the other, for their rear rooms were secretly joined by a narrow door, which was subsequently blocked with earth and stones.

Great-grandmother gave birth to grandfather in agony, shrieking as if her belly and infant had been pierced by the awful archdeacon's sword, or as if at that very instant one of the many dead littering the *aljama*'s streets had entered the newborn baby's body, condemning itself to live all over again in the world. Great-grandfather picked up his son mournfully, studied him in the blood-red light and, holding him up to his mother-in-law and sister-in-law, gravely announced that the child's name would be Justo Afán, Justified Zeal, since it had been born thirsting for justice. Then, after peering through the window at the dying dragging themselves through the smoldering fires of the *aljama* and at the lurking shadows of the guilty encumbered with the spoils of their crimes, he turned towards the women and said, "I will have no other child than this in my lifetime, for in a world where Cain walks about freely brandishing an ass's jawbone, who wants to put more Abels in his path? I may have learned late, but now I understand that just as seeds scatter over the fields to bear goodly fruits, evil advances through villages, cities and kingdoms to destroy the crops of the righteous."

This said, he laid Justo Afán in his mother's arms, staring into her eyes as if henceforth their conjugal love would exist only in that look, in the other world and in dreams, and without so much as a backwards glance, with only the clothes he wore and the food still in his belly, he closed the door of his house behind him, never to return.

Twenty years later my father was born, although my grandfather never knew him, having succumbed to the plague, with much nausea and vomiting of yellow bile, four days after a tumor the size of a pine nut appeared in his right groin. People said he died discredited by all, because of his excessive dealings with women, and because Doctor Mosén Sánchez had sliced into him and found a gallbladder the size of a pear, oozing green bile. My grandmother was not troubled when she learned of the infidelities that had ostensibly brought about her husband's death. As she explained to her friends and relations, since he hadn't been hers before birth, nor would he be after death, there was no reason for him to belong to her while he was alive.

A rumor spread that he had been infected by Death garbed like a nun, who had thrown a ball of blue flame through the open window of his room; they also said he had caught the disease from a nun disguised as a whore when they made love in the putrid fields near the city dunghills. In fact, there was no time to mourn him, as he was cremated hastily at night to keep the neighbors ignorant, although everyone already knew. My grandmother would have her whole life to lament his absence, so what difference could one night make? However, she apparently never mourned him again and banished him with an inscrutable rigor from her days and her speech to such an extent that when his name was mentioned in her presence she had to make an effort to remember of whom they spoke. Perhaps she was pretending, but only she knew the truth, she, Blanca de Santángel, mother of my father, Ricardo Cabezón.

At that time, Fray Vicente Ferrer—or the Angel of the Apocalypse, as he called himself—driven by an intense proselytizing fervor, swept through the *aljamas* in the cities of Aragón, Castile and Catalonia, converting Jews to Christianity. Crucifix in hand, he preached in churches and public squares and burst into synagogues to consecrate them in the Catholic faith. He was born in Valencia around the year 1350, the son of a scrivener who lived in Calle de la Mar, and it is said that his mother felt no discomfort before he came into the world, as her pregnancy was curiously easy. The town's bishop heard the barking of dogs in her belly several times and interpreted this as a sign that she would give birth to a son "who would be the mastiff chosen to guard the Christian flock and awaken it with his barking from sinful sleep and frighten away the infernal wolves." Thus, from the age of six, he never cared to play with other children, summoning them instead to his side and preaching to them from above like a hoary old man. Early on he acquired the habit of fasting twice a week—Fridays on bread and water—and of listening to whatever preachers crossed his path, however uncouth or coarse they might be.

At the age of eighteen, he entered the Monastery of Santo Domingo and assumed the Friar Preachers' habit. Santo Domingo himself was his model, and he read the sacred books the saint had read, and gestured and walked as he imagined Domingo had done. Three years later he was sent to the Convent of Santa Catalina Mártir in Barcelona, and thence to Lérida, where he devoted himself to the study of theology and practiced the rules of his own *Treatise of the Spiritual Life,* frequently lifting his eyes from his book to focus on the wounds of Jesus Christ, to whom all his reading and learning were consecrated.

After his return to Valencia, while he was praying at the altar of the Virgin or before a crucifix, the devil repeatedly appeared to him in the form of San Antonio or as a hideous black man who exhorted him with threats to abandon the monastic life. One night in his cell, while poring over San Jerónimo's book about the perpetual virginity of the Virgin, he implored Mary to intercede before Christ on his behalf that he might die chaste, and suddenly a voice said to him, "God does not grant to all the grace of virginity, nor will it be given to thee, but rather will it be taken from thee very soon." However, the mother of Jesus appeared to him in glorious splendor immediately afterwards and reassured him that these were the devil's wiles and that she would never forsake him.

Nevertheless, the demon took possession of a woman called Inés Hernández, who feigned sickness so that Fray Vicente would be summoned to reconcile her with God and set a penance for her sins. Once he was in her room, she undressed and would have fornicated with him, but Fray Vicente fled in terror, and when the woman tried to shout, she was bewitched and struck dumb. Her parents quickly brought exorcists to drive the devil from her body, but the demon refused to emerge until the man who had stood in the fire without being burned came back. Fray Vicente returned, and from the moment he crossed the threshold the woman was rid of the evil one. Upon entering his cell on another occasion, he encountered a harlot who tried to seduce him, urging him-not to fear, as she was a genuine woman and not the devil. Enraged, he reminded her so vividly of the endless torments of hell awaiting those who abandoned themselves to the fetid delights of the flesh that the woman repented and renounced the life of pleasure forever.

Meanwhile, the "devil's son," the Aragonese Pedro de Luna, had been elected pope in Avignon under the name of Benedict XIII. He summoned Fray Vicente to be court chaplain and confessor, and Vicente remained at his side until one day, as the friar lay at death's door, Jesus Christ appeared to him in a vision, flanked by Santo Domingo and San Francisco, and revealed that soon he would be cured of his illness, that several years hence the schism in the Church would begin to heal, and that he must go into the world as an apostle preaching against the grievous vices of the time. "Warn them," Christ said, "of the danger in which they live, tell them to mend their ways, as Doomsday is near." Touching His hand to the friar's cheek, He added, "Arise, my Vicente." And that touch was so efficacious that whenever he preached about the Last Judgment, the marks of Jesus Christ's fingers appeared on his face as a seal or signature by which God authenticated his preaching. Fray Vicente, nearing sixty years of age and racked by quartan fevers but impelled by that vision and that command, left the court at Avignon behind to roam the sinful realms of man and the dusty roads of the world, in bloody penitential processions.

Braving sun, wind, rain or cold, he went first on foot, limping, staff in hand, then mounted on an ass which he had caused to be castrated so that the sight of its member would offend no one. He wore a jerkin, a scapular and a cloak, which also served as a blanket, and carried a Bible from which he drew his sermons. He spoke little with those who accompanied him unless it was about doctrinal matters. Before entering a town he would kneel and, turning his eyes heavenward, ask for deliverance from pride and vainglory. Next his people went in two by two following a certain Milán, who wore long robes, carried a crucifix and intoned a litany which the others repeated. Immediately afterwards came the envoy of Jesus, Fray Vicente himself, riding the ass now fitted with boards to keep the faithful at a proper distance on the way to church.

The miracle-hungry rabble thronged after him in solemn procession, chanting religious and penitential hymns, waving banners and pennants, carrying statues of saints, crosses and relics jealously guarded over the centuries. The learned and the ignorant, peasants and nobles, clergymen and merchants, men and women chastely separated by long ropes, all offered him bread, wine, fruit and stews, clasped his hands and tried to tear off strips of his clothes or pluck hairs from the ass to keep as relics. He answered with blessings, greeting them with bowed head, his senses mortified and his eyes fixed to the ground. A legion of clergymen from various nations, empowered by the antipope Pedro de Luna to absolve whomsoever they would, was on hand to confess the fervent multitude. Notaries were available to document reconciliations between former enemies to the death, to record the public repentance of infamous sinners and pardons granted for offenses committed long ago, such as parricides, fratricides or plundering of earthly goods. Fray Vicente furnished portable organs to churches that had none so that people could feel the majesty of the Mass. One young clergyman was specifically charged with teaching religious songs and hymns to the local youth, for them to sing at night instead of the popular ballads that were going round at the time.

Once he was settled in a convent or church and his retinue had been distributed among the townspeople for food and lodging, he devoted several hours to receiving those who came for favors or advice or to complain of problems or illness. The remainder of his time was spent in a cell commending himself to God, contemplating the things of the celestial life and pondering the revelations of the Holy Scripture. In lieu of meat he ate fish, which he received with "great contentment when the stew was seasoned with poverty." He partook of only one dish and drank twice, or thrice if exceptionally thirsty, but the wine was watered down. He was a virgin and for thirty years had seen no part of his body except his hands. No one had ever seen him naked, not even himself, as he changed his clothes in the dark to shield his eyes from the offense of his own nudity. He slept dressed and shod in his daytime attire, and for a scant five hours stretched out or tumbled down on an armful of twigs, a straw mattress, a few planks or the bare earth, with a stone or the Bible as his pillow, in emulation of Santo Domingo who used to sleep at the foot of an altar or on the biers of the dead.

He scourged himself nightly and when lacking the strength for it would enjoin his fellow priests to flog him for Christ's sake with a rope whip, begging them to show no mercy and strike him as hard as they could. There were five men who used to flagellate him: Pedro de Muya, Juan del Prado Hermoso, Rafael Cardona, Jofre Blanes and Pedro Cerdán. On preaching days he rose early, confessed and sang Mass at the pulpit from which he would afterwards preach, but if the crowd was too numerous for the church he would officiate in a public square or in a field from an altar erected atop a scaffold, so all could see him despite his short stature.

When Mass was finished, he would remove his priestly garments and don the cape of the Order of Santo Domingo. Although he was reputed to speak Latin and Hebrew, he preached only in Valencian, which those of the faithful who had no knowledge of that dialect were able to understand "by the grace which God had given him." Some saw angels in human form hovering over his head. Much of his preaching was done at nightfall, when people had concluded their labors and the husbandmen were back from the fields. Great flambeaux were lit in the square, and as the King had so ordained, Jews were forced to listen to the sermons. While he preached he would turn towards them and try to demonstrate, by quoting from the Old Testament, that the Messiah had already come and would return only for the Last Judgment. The Jews and Jewesses of twelve or fourteen years and more sat close to the pulpit so none might disturb them. When the man of God quoted a text from the Scripture he bent down to them and repeated it in Hebrew. "Before the sermon he seemed weak and sickly, but as he became inspired his body grew robust and his face lively. His words and gestures glowed like kindled torches and those far away from the pulpit heard him as clearly as those near to it."

He cried easily, dissolving into tears as he spoke; while describing the horrors of the Last Judgment, his voice became so loud that his listeners were terrified and fell to the ground in fright, believing they had already emerged from their graves to stand before the Supreme Judge. "Mountains, fall upon us and cover us with the Lamb's great wrath," he would shout furiously, and the sinners prostrated themselves before him in repentance, gamesters promising to forswear gambling, thieves, thievery, clergymen, gluttony and greed, whores, lechery and murderers, crime. Voices in the crowd were heard to beg or grant forgiveness, and those possessed by the devil howled, jumped, laughed, cried or sang, prompting him to interrupt the sermon and address Satan directly: "Devil, in the name of Jesus Christ I order thee to be silent!"

He had the gift of divining whatever was hidden or distant, as when in Lérida he claimed that the body of his master Fray Tomás Carnicer had remained intact after forty years in the ground, or when in Saragossa he revealed that his mother had just died in Valencia, or when he said in Tortosa, "Brothers, a fire has broken out among the haystacks on this bank of the river, go and put it out, upon your lives." Forthwith many volunteers set out to smother it but upon reaching the spot found neither smoke nor fire but only a man fornicating with a woman, and thereby the faithful understood that this was the fire of which Fray Vicente had spoken. At the close of his sermon he was accustomed to cast the devil from the bodies of the possessed who were brought to him by their kin for exorcism, and to cure the sick of all manner of ills by blessing them with these words: "*Signa autem eos qui crediderint haec sequentur, super aegros manus imponent, et bene habebunt. Iesus Mariae Filius, mundi salus, et Dominus, qui te traxit ad fidem Catholicam, te in ea conservet, et beatum faciat, et ab hac infirmitate liberare dignetur.*" "These signs shall distinguish the true believers: they will cure the sick by the laying on of hands. May

Jesus, son of Mary, salvation of the world, who has brought you to the Catholic faith, preserve you in the same and make you blessed, and may He deign to liberate you from this infirmity."

After Vespers the penitential procession of men, women and children took place. Like a long, bloody crocodile, nigh upon three hundred flagellants wound their way through the streets, lashing their flesh in remembrance of the scourging Christ suffered and convinced that if the mortification was carried out correctly, God would mix His own blood with the penitent's, who would thus receive valor and merit, but forewarned that those who whipped themselves without faith or out of vanity were merely foolish and despicable priests of Baal.

After confessing and receiving Holy Communion, shrouded in the darkness of night to avoid recognition, their heads covered with white hoods, barefoot, their backs and shoulders exposed, the rich and the poor, laymen and clergy, nobility and commoners, the men apart from the women, all advanced in procession from the monastery of the order or from the church, bearing aloft a statue of Christ and a banner on which the symbols of the Passion were painted. Infants who could barely walk and four-year-old boys carrying crucifixes preceded the men, while girls of the same age went before the women, holding images of Mary with her dead son in her arms.

All paused at the Stations of the Cross, beating themselves with scourges of twisted hemp twined into branches, with iron lashes, thick rods and briars. Some struck their bodies so frenziedly that the great quantity of blood which gushed from wounds wide as fingers made it necessary to take the whips from them, lest they kill themselves. Some had bits of flesh clinging to their clothes or chunks hanging from their irons. Others yet, in imitation of Christ, inflicted such harsh punishment upon themselves that they repeatedly fell to the ground under the weight of the imaginary cross and rose again, until they swooned from the pain. The thirsty knelt as a token of humility to drink the water offered by the compassionate. Everywhere the penitents called to mind the visible signs of the Passion, sang prayers written especially for the occasion by Fray Vicente, clamored in Valencian, *"Senyor Déu, Iesu Christ!"* or in Castilian, *"Sea esto por la Pasión de Nuestro Señor Jesucristo y la remisión de nuestros pecados!"*—"This is for the Passion of Our Lord Jesus Christ and for the remission of our sins!" The townspeople followed and surrounded them, singing hymns, carrying crosses and statues of Christ, the Virgin and saints, banners and lighted candles. The bells tolled an accompaniment to the human serpent in its wretchedness and agony. "The use of this penance was so widespread that wherever Master Vicente went, the silversmiths and other craftsmen set up booths with scourges, as if they were having a whip fair," San Antonio wrote.

In such manner the tonsured Fray Vicente, holding a crucifix in his left hand, traversed the villages and cities of the kingdoms of Spain, haranguing Christians, Jews and Moors alike. The nineteenth day of January in 1411 he entered Murcia, prohibiting dice-playing within the city limits and issuing strict decrees against those Jews and Moors who had not yet converted to Christianity. After dwelling there for one month, he set out on Ash Wednesday to preach in Librilla, Alhama and Lorca, then returned to Murcia. He departed for Castile on the fourteenth of April, was in Ciudad Real on the fourteenth of May, and on the thirtieth entered Toledo, where he preached daily, especially to the Jews, whom he attempted to instruct in the Christian faith.

One day, seeing them unmoved by his sermons, he descended from the pulpit in a rage, left the church followed by a great crowd, strode towards the *aljama* holding his crucifix aloft and entered the ancient synagogue, to cast out those who obeyed the Word and Law of God. In the name of Santa María la Blanca, he consecrated the synagogue in the Catholic religion. From Toledo he left for Yepes, Ocaña, Borox, Illescas, Simancas and Tordesillas, where he suffered from quartan fevers. In Valladolid he not only preached but also asked the city magistrates to oblige the Jews to live apart. In September he went to Ayllón to speak with the Infante Don Fernando and the Queen Doña Catalina, tutors of the child King Don Juan II. He convinced Doña Catalina of Lancaster, who had palsy and was stiff in body and speech, to publish the cruel *Pragmática* ordaining the isolation of the Jews, which was to be proclaimed in his presence in Valladolid towards the end of 1411. Thence he proceeded to Salamanca, where, cross in hand, he stormed into the main synagogue to preach at the Jews congregated there. When white crosses miraculously appeared on their clothing and toques, many were moved to convert, changing their Hebrew names to Vicente and that of the synagogue to Vera Cruz.

King Fernando of Aragón followed Fray Vicente's conversions of thirty-five thousand Jews and eight thousand Moors closely and listened to reports of the sermons in which he insisted not only that Jesus and Mary had been Jews but also that nothing displeased God more than forced baptisms, since "The apostles who conquered the world carried neither lance nor knife! Christians should slay Jews with reasoning, not with the blade!" Nevertheless, a wave of terror swept through the *aljamas* in his wake, as many, carried away by Vicente's preachings, commited outrages and conspired against the Jews, even refusing to sell them food, as occurred in Alcañiz.

Fray Vicente pleaded with the kings to "set the Jews apart in every town and city of your realms, as great harm results from their conversation with Christians, above all with those newly converted to our Holy

Faith." The miracles he wrought among the Christians were as renowned as the conversions he made among the Jews. Throughout the
kingdoms of Spain it was said that Fray Vicente had raised the dead,
made the dumb speak, the deaf hear and the blind see, that he had
rendered barren women fertile, restored reason to madmen and eccen-
trics, healed knife wounds and stanched bleeding heads, cured the falling sickness, swelling in the throat, and pangs in the heart, straightened
twisted mouths and relieved pains in the thigh, belly, back and chest,
cured of kidney stones and caused to urinate a woman who had not
made water for fifteen years, delivered sufferers from the plague and
leprosy, restored breath to those who were suffocating, enabled the lame
to walk, saved sailors from wind and storm, dispelled famine and stifled
fires, conjured up clouds and dissipated storms—all by the mere mention of his name.

My grandmother, who was always more joyous than a saint and more
generous than a king, was wont to sing this song:

> *Trees cry out for rains*
> *and mountains for wind;*
> *so do my eyes weep*
> *for thee, dearly beloved.*
> *And again, what will become of me?*
> *In foreign lands I shall surely die.*

But death caught up with her at home one Sunday, the last day of
October in the year of Our Lord 1434, on the eve of All Saints Day. She
died of a fever in Seville, where she had lived her life, solitary and
stigmatized by the badge, a Jewish widow whom fate had destined to
wear out her bones and her shadow in that city on the plain, the ancient
Hispalis. During the first days of January her quartan fevers began, the
very same ones that afflicted the King, Don Juan II, "weakened by ill
humors, a slave to sensuality, daily surrendering himself to the caresses
of a young and beautiful wife"—or of a constable, whom he found
equally seductive. But my grandmother, Doña Blanca, had no vices in
this world save her own hunger and solitude. It was on Sunday morning,
while teaching my father the first Psalm, which Rabbi Mosé Arragel of
Guadalajara had recently translated into Spanish from the Hebrew, that
she began to show signs of wishing to quit this world:

> *Blessed is the man that walketh not*
> *in the counsel of the ungodly,*

nor standeth in the way of sinners,
nor sitteth in the seat of the scornful.

Suddenly she interrupted the flow of the verses to give my father some mysterious instructions: if he ever went to Tarazona, he should inquire in the *judería*, the Jewish quarter, for a brother of hers by the name of Acach and ask him for a sack of cloth worth some hundred Aragonese gold florins which her father had left in his care in a shop in the city during the persecution of the Jews in 1391; or if his travels ever took him to Barcelona, he must seek out Don Abraham Isaac Ardit, who would instruct him for six years in the craft of weaving veils, providing him with food, drink, shirts and shoes, and one Aragonese gold florin a month. Then, passing her hand over his forehead as she looked at him inscrutably, she said, "I absolve thee from the beginning of the world to this day."

Then she died, huddled in the kitchen, at the hour of Prime, with no judge to take the measure of her fright, without acts or chroniclers, alone with the immensity of death, which is the same size for all. Almost immediately thereafter, the rains began to fall, hour after hour, over Seville. The Guadalquivir River flooded Calle de la Cestería and reached as far as the columns of the causeway, a vast intruder, narrowing and ebbing, then redoubled, raised up on liquid arms, its stomach swollen, its countless tongues lapping at all within reach.

Left alone with grandmother's death, my father built a coffin to fit her body and took her to the fields rather than the graveyard. With the rain pouring down and the quagmire up to his knees, he made his way to a pine grove he knew well. There, soaked to the bone, he dug a grave without pausing for rest, tossing the earth far enough away so that the great rivers of water flowing towards him could not carry it back, as he feared the cadaver would drown in the coffin and the coffin float away.

Once the burial was finished, he knelt down in the puddle that was her unmarked grave, covered it with leaves and branches and searched his memory for her most beloved face, to carry away with him.

He paid no heed to the water running down his body; he was like a ghost that had buried its dead; his head seemed dissolved into rain, his feet flowed through the streams into the river of all, which is no one's.

After dropping the last clods of earth over her coffin, he noticed a peasant watching him from the door of a hut: an old man, clad in rags and tatters with a bony white face and cavernous black eyes. A terrified dog barked nearby but dared not approach. My father knew why: the peasant's hands had no flesh, his cheeks were flayed, and his gaze was empty: it was Death.

He turned away and pretended to have seen nothing. He had seen enough for now and forever. Then he hurried off, as if trying to flee from the very road down which he ran, to leave his feet behind, to outdistance his own body, always with the disturbing feeling that he had left something irretrievable buried there among the pines. Many years later he would remember thinking he had dreamed that afternoon, imagined himself walking in the rain, burying his mother and glimpsing Death and a barking dog.

In Seville, on Friday, January first, 1435, it rained. It also rained on Saturday; all night long gusts of wind whipped through the streets, and at dawn the earth was shaken by a tremor. On Monday the rain continued; the river reached the battlements of the parapet outside the rampart from the Golles Gate to the foot of the hill of Castilleja and the roofs of Triana. The bells tolled throughout the night, water poured into the city through the conduits, and the floodgates of the river had to be caulked. Day after day torrential rain fell; the river swelled like a muddy snake and covered the marble slabs of the gates up to the lower planks, entered the galley-building yards of the King and carried off eight hundred pine trees and timber belonging to some Galician merchants before bursting through the great iron portal next to the Torre del Oro.

The Buerva and the Guadalquivir commingled, Triana was surrounded by water, the roads vanished under newly formed lakes, and the Tagarete broke through the cemetery gates, dragging with it corpses and bones, tombstones and flowers. Soon bread and meat grew scarce in the city, there was no firewood to be found, and the friars in one monastery had to cut down poplars to cook their food. The walls of many houses crumbled, the water reached the first arch of Triana Castle, half an ell below the image of the Virgin Mary, and the nights were blanched by lightning. Rumors spread that the storms were sent by God to destroy Seville, and while the bells of Santa María tolled incessantly the people sought refuge in the churches and at the highest points of the city. And all the while, they prayed for Our Lord to deliver the city from the danger in which it stood.

At eight o'clock one Wednesday morning it suddenly grew dark. Men and women ran to the churches to confess and take Communion, bells pealed and Masses were read. The water reached the road to San Clemente; boats floated through the streets; dogs, cats and fowl climbed onto the roofs of the flooded houses; the inhabitants of Calle de la Cestería and the suburb of Cantillana took their clothes and belongings to the dunghills at the Golles Gate and pitched tents of sails and blankets in the midst of the garbage and ordure. Since there was no bread, people sought eagerly to buy flour or have their wheat ground at any price, going from house to house in search of someone willing to share a crumb. One night, when the moon and stars were shining, my father went to buy a mule, but he could ill afford the fifty-eight Jaca shillings that it cost. Bread was brought to the square from Alcalá de Guadaira and elsewhere, and as part of the anxious crowd gathered there to appease its hunger he purchased a few morsels. Processions with candles and crosses were held in the city; the ark containing the remains of San Servante, San Germán and San Florencio was carried into the streets, as was the head of San Laureán. The following day, my father closed up his house forever and left Seville. He had no kin in the world save the blood in his own body and no brotherhood on earth except the ubiquitous progeny of Cain. He went on foot, taking with him only the clothes he wore and the food he had eaten.

On Friday, the eighth of January, although light rain fell and lusty winds blew, he walked many leagues, as if he were in haste to escape from himself as well as Seville. He walked without stopping, plowing through avenues of water under a sky of water, fearing he might faint from exhaustion after plodding so long in his shabby, waterlogged shoes. He believed himself unheeded as he crossed the flooded fields, the silvery groves, the rainbow arching over the hills, the sunlight in the rain, the tawny earth and the well-washed stones, until he realized that all along Death was pursuing him, following his progress over fields and mountains, through vineyards and orchards, along the banks of streams, from the far side of bridges and beyond the roads. It was the same Death he had spied among the pines while burying his mother; the one who, undoubtedly, was waiting for his collapse in the mire, and his vain efforts to rise, at which point it would make off with him. But he did not fall, he did not stop—he could not stop. To doubt, to tarry for even a moment was to succumb, not so much to Death as to himself. Like rivers, the roads surged forward to meet him, paths sank under unexpected lagoons, and thousands of fleeting, cold, white drops stippled the trees.

The second day he came across a dying she-mule which had tumbled with her load of wood into a ravine. Her legs were broken, but the muleteer lacked the courage to slit her throat and had abandoned her in a muddy puddle that mirrored the cloudy sky.

The third day he knocked at the door of a house where instead of bread a man and his spouse gave him chestnuts, raisins, boiled wheat and water, and told him of the marvels they had witnessed during the storm. A frightful whirlwind had snatched up a pair of yoked oxen and a church bell weighing five hundred pounds, whisking them into the air; the town's water pipes had been laid bare, the walls of a house reduced to rubble and many orange trees uprooted. Two old men who lived a stone's throw away told of having seen in the west at the hour of twilight armed combatants engaged in a tempestuous battle, after which they hurtled across the sky, leaving long strands of bloody light in their wake.

Another day in the early morning he found along the side of the road an ass felled by a great load: a wooden bed weighing a good three hundred pounds, two padlocked chests of two hundredweight each, a cloak-bag, four lengths of rope and two blankets.

Towards noon he encountered a group of cartwrights, day laborers, muleteers and guides conveying the palanquin and carts of a wealthy man across the fields, for they appeared to have lost their way. On twelve mules and seven wagons they transported the furnishings of a bed chamber and a parlor, bushels of dry beans, wheat and barley, chestnuts, wax, and salt. Two carts laden with a birdcage, three Irish greyhounds, four washerwomen and a baker brought up the rear.

The fifth day, as he went to drink water from some potbellied earthenware barrels leaning against a wall, he met a peasant who said his name was Pedro del Campo, and he was truly a man of the earth, plain and well-nigh anonymous. His daughters were with him, four cheerful, sturdy countrywomen who tended five sheep, several of which were gelded, more than a dozen ewes and many she-goats with their kids. His wife gave my father supper and offered him all the hay in their stable for his bed; he thanked her profusely, for he had spent the other nights under the cloudy roof of the firmament or in a damp cave or beneath a wooden bridge, and once, in a wretched inn where the floor was muddier than the road. His pillows had been logs, rocks, shrubs or his own arms.

The sixth day, as the sun was setting, a curricle drawn by two swift-moving, mud-splashed mules came towards him. Within rode a young woman wearing a blue traveling veil of old, torn Dutch linen. When their paths crossed she gave him a wan, distant look, and the light from her intense blue eyes seemed to glow in the air after she was gone. She raced by in such haste that my father had retained the image of a single body composed of woman, curricle and mules, dashing along together in perpetuity. He had glimpsed the shabby lining of crimson satin, the dangling buckles, the unlined cowhide girths and the woman's palpable solitude. Neither postilion nor footmen nor outriders attended her. She traveled alone; the hybrid, sterile animals dragged her into the night along a dark road she seemed to know from long ago. My father could see incipient shadows, trees and mist through the curricle and the mules, as if they became transparent as they sped away. A good ways behind, two nimble-footed peasants fairly flew down the road through a light drizzle, straining towards the orange-tawny sky as if their mission were to catch up with the sun that was always setting ahead of them.

After a surfeit of hunger and fatigue, cloudy skies and rain, deeming

himself a tireless and skillful walker who could make a three days'
journey in only one, he arrived in Madrid several weeks later, staff in
hand, clothes ragged, his face dried out by dust and sun. He had left
behind him El Pedroso, Cazalla, Guadalcanal, Fuente del Arco, Llerena,
Valencia de la Torre, Campillo, Zalamea, Quintana de la Serena, Cam-
panario, Acedera, Caserío del Rincón, Guadalupe, Venta de los Palacios,
the Arrebatacapas pass, Puente del Arzobispo, Calera, Talavera, Cebolla,
Burajón, Toledo, et cetera. He had overcome the pain of his mother's
death; she had become part of his steps and his shadow, or an emptiness
in his eyes.

I, Juan Cabezón, was born in Madrid, the city of red earth, on Calle del Viento one Thursday morning when my mother, who was eight months pregnant, tripped on her way to market and gave birth to a boy.

During my early years they called me Stumbleson, Alleykin or Airborn, and several people foretold by the flight of sparrows that I would pave streets, plaster walls, daub mud on others' floors or on my own descent, but until the moment my fortunes improved I did nothing but pound the roads and pave my porringers with pottage.

Of that infancy I retain memories only of my hunger; meat days and fish days were for me air days and arid days; by night, my empty belly peopled my dreams with feeble forms and spindly striplings who devoured insipid creatures and bitter beasties.

My mornings were also famishing, and so I filled them with images of my mother bringing back Juan de Madrid's best meat from the slaughterhouse on the outskirts of the city, after she had bought sardines and other fish from the perforated troughs set out in accordance with ancient custom in the Plaza de San Salvador.

But while the fathers of other, better-fed sons than I went out to buy provisions and food, my own brought me proverbs: "Beef and mutton, food for the glutton," "Hungry dogs will eat dirty puddings," "To the grave with the dead, and the living to the bread" and other words that spoke of eating and not eating; upon which I would say to myself, "My father's name is Loaf, and I starve to death."

My father, who was a barber and owned a basin of thin, sonorous metal that seemed to reverberate with every blow in the world, was teaching me to read and write one afternoon when a stout, plodding apothecary came to have his beard and locks trimmed, a task to which the author of my needs quickly applied himself, clipping away with his shears at the neck hairs and chin whiskers, until the blood began to flow from the apothecary's jowl. Finding himself more sliced than shorn, he fell to the hair-strewn floor and exclaimed, "Of what use are my gallipots of glazed clay, my ointments and scents, my stores of plum, pear and peach preserves, to whom shall I leave them, now that I die?"

As a consequence of this accidental, or intentional, death, the sheriff came to arrest my father, who in a plaintive voice bid me farewell with this advice, "My son, seek another barber to adopt thee, but keep away from razors and jowls for as long as thou livest."

An infinite sadness came over me upon seeing my father thus apprehended, as if he were one of the common thieves, murderers, blasphemers or ravishers of virgins, nuns, wives and grandmothers who went up and down the highways, fields and houses in the towns and cities of the Kingdom of Castile at that time, cruelly robbing and killing. For days I did nothing but peek through a rent in the curtain between my bed and my mother's, or through chinks in the wall and a hole in the door that led to the kitchen and the street, expecting to see my father come home or go to the barbershop, his pockets full of proverbs and jokes, instead of food. But I saw only Fernando the shoelace maker, Alonso the chandler, Perancho the carpenter, Gonzalo Núñez the belt maker, Master Zulema the surgeon, Simón García the wineskin seller, Pedro de Chinchón the cobbler and many others—why bother with their names and trades now?—who were in love with my mother.

Still young and handsome, she had no thought of offering herself to other men, as I had feared, although her suitors came to the house at all hours of the day and introduced themselves: "I am Alonso the dyer," "I am Juan, the sackcloth weaver," "They call me Juan Malpensado," "My name is Juan Rebeco." My mother accepted no one but me; I lay down by her side and we slept in each other's arms to ward off the chill of our bodies and souls.

She did much with the little there was in the house, pampering me with sweet cakes and puff pastries, delicacies and fruit stewed in sugar and honey. She always managed to appease my stomach, although she seemed not to notice that I roamed the streets with my clothes in tatters and my shoes patched, leading the neighbors to regard me as an orphan, poor Juan, the son of the barber who was drawn and quartered.

After a few months, which to me seemed like years, my mother, to alleviate the pain of losing my father, or to cure a bodily ill which I never understood but which malicious neighbors called heat, began to keep company with a corpulent miller who had a clumsy waddle, flabby flesh and a bloated face, and it was to his house, after she had referred to him for a few weeks as my future father, that she and I betook ourselves, "for shelter and sustenance," she said.

For many months I slept peacefully in the same room with them, sometimes even between them, until one day the miller contrived to wake me from the deepest of sleeps by blowing in my ears and tickling my ribs and the soles of my feet, to whisper to me, "Juan, oh Juan, I hear noises on the roof. Go outside and if you see anyone, stab him with this dagger." Tingling, alarmed and half-asleep, I flailed at the air,

28

pushed away the shadows of night and looked at my mother to see what she might say. After a few moments of silence and doubt, during which she scrutinized the miller's face and mine, she said, "I can hear nothing, for I have a catarrh."

Wrapped in the miller's warm, roomy clothes, I grumpily sallied forth into the darkness to inspect the rooftops and sniff at the wind in search of some hobgoblin hidden among the tiles. Hours passed with no trace of a live object, or even a ghost, and I sat there outside waiting to surprise man or corpse and stitch him with my knife or vanquish him with the sign of the cross.

What I did hear clearly, thanks to the early-morning silence and despite the intervening walls and roof, were rustlings from the bedroom that confirmed my worst suspicions. Taking full advantage of my absence, they did not stint in their fondlings and enjoyed themselves at their ease.

They opened the door for me at dawn, when the miller rose to throw wheat into the hopper at the mill. "Don't worry, Juan, the air will do you good," my mother said when she saw me bathed in dew. "To the love of a father, empty air is all other," I responded, reminding her of a favorite saying of the author of my days. "Cover up, you're all wet," she replied, and carried me in her arms to her bed. But I pushed her away from me, for she reeked of the miller's stench mingled with her own sweat.

He was a tall, bald man with a burly body and small eyes, presumptuous when giving orders, more inclined to malice than affability, cunning and impatient. When something displeased him he went into a blind rage, punching and kicking at the slightest provocation. Sitting with us at the table after dinner, his speech thickened by wine, he used to explain to my mother and me how fleas are begotten from dust and dampness, or that in France there are apples that last all year and are called pendlepates, because when they have withered they resemble the heads of hanged men. Narrowing his eyes, he confided to us that stags stung by venomous spiders cure themselves by eating crabs; that tortoises chew on hemlock as an antidote to snake bites; that the stork heals itself with oregano and the wild boar with ivy; that elephants protect themselves from the poison of chameleons with the leaves of olive trees, bears from mandrakes with ants, and that ringdoves purge themselves with bay leaves. While he spoke my mother's kohl-darkened eyes never left my face, until the moment when he realized we were not listening and rose to bolt the door. Then we all went to sleep, the miller with his drunkenness, my mother with her dreams, and I with my sorrows.

Often when the sun had set, his friends would come to the house—

Don Pero Pérez, an expert in omens and calamities; the Cordovan convert, Acach de Montoro; and an old friar from Toledo, Don Francisco Manrique, who had spent a good part of his life in Rome. They sat with the miller around the table, drinking wine by candlelight and interrupting each other until far into the night. My mother and I listened from a bench built into the wall, unseen and silent, as if we were not even in the same room.

"There have been many portents during the reign of Enrique Cuarto," said Don Pero Pérez, his eyes starting out of his head. "In Seville, a squall destroyed that part of the Alcázar where the King was in residence, uprooted trees from the garden and split them like a sword. A tall, stately orange tree was pulled from the ground, carried through the air beyond the city walls and tossed into an orange grove, where the people picked all its fruit and hacked the tree to bits. A marble statue with a gilded diadem vanished; the walls of the city towers crumbled; the temples lost their roofs; the brick aqueduct fell without a sound to the stones below; tombs burst open and more than five hundred houses collapsed, leaving only one, old and in ruins, still standing. In Segovia, in the King's palace, howling and wails broke out in the middle of the night, terrifying spirits materialized and caused everyone's hair to stand on end, even Don Enrique's, who never loses his aplomb or becomes frightened, and always answers in jests, laughing off in public ominous private confidences. When the sun rose, the Segovians at first believed that all had been a hallucination, a misapprehension, but then they discovered a fissure which had cleft the building down the middle and disappeared into the abyss. In Seville, a girl child was born who had a phallus growing from her tongue, a full set of teeth in her mouth and hairy lips."

"They say," affirmed Don Francisco Manrique, glancing at me to see if I was asleep or not paying attention, "and this is not for the ears of the child or of the respectable lady, that when the sixteen-year-old king, Don Enrique Cuarto, married the Infanta Doña Blanca of Navarre, during the round of tournaments, pageantry and games—in which, by the way, a number of people perished—the courtiers sang couplets and ditties ridiculing his reputed impotence. People said that his member was narrow at the root, wide at the tip and incapable of erection, and that he had to urinate squatting like a woman."

"They say," recounted Don Acach de Montoro, "that on their wedding night, for lack of manly prowess, he left her as she had been born, infuriating all present, but especially the witnesses stationed at the door to exhibit the bridal sheets, in accordance with the old Castilian law which requires the presence of attestants and a notary in the chamber when a royal marriage is consummated."

"I have heard," said Don Pero Pérez, "that at the beginning the King brought another man to the marital bed to take his place in the carnal act and furnish a successor to the throne, but as Doña Blanca saw through the ruse, his loathing for her grew and he sought a divorce, maintaining her in niggardly fashion until he obtained the papal license and returned her intact to Navarre."

"They say," continued Don Francisco Manrique, "and I hope the boy is still asleep and the virtuous lady remains deaf, that he celebrated his emancipation by hunting animals in the deepest forest and fornicating young lads, amongst whom was his favorite, Juan Pacheco, who had been chosen as his page by Don Alvaro de Luna, his father's protegé."

"The same Juan Pacheco used to sit by his bedside singing and playing the lute when the King was at home ill," added Don Pero Pérez.

"Without a doubt, the end of the world is drawing near," said the miller, the first words he had uttered all night.

"And if not the end of the world for all, at least the end of ours," Don Francisco Manrique put in.

"Only the blind fail to see and the deaf refuse to hear," intoned the miller as solemnly as a soothsayer.

"The Messiah comes, and the Last Judgment with him," the Cordovan convert announced.

"Now let us go to sleep, for I must arise at Matins to read the early Mass," said Don Francisco Manrique, taking his leave.

In this way four years passed, during which I little knew whom to blame more for my troubles: the boorish miller for his enmity, my mother for her tribulations or myself for my wretchedness. Be that as it may, the day my stepfather was killed, instead of grieving I felt greatly relieved, as if a weight had been lifted off my days or a wall torn down between my mother and myself. However, with him went our sustenance as well, and his absence brought us hunger and insecurity, for in this world joy and happiness never come unalloyed.

The miller had journeyed to Segovia on business, when he was waylaid by rogues who not only despoiled him of everything he carried loose or sewn into his clothes but also slit open his stomach to see if it wasn't stuffed with gold as well.

A peasant found him dying amongst the bushes and, barely making out that he came from Madrid, had draped the body over his donkey and brought him home, after ascertaining where he lived.

At dusk he was brought to the house, his head dangling and his eyes wide open, as if he had been observing the dust of the road. His face was purple, his belly gaped open, his sleeves drooped over his hands, which had been scratched by stones, and he had no shoes on.

"It won't help him to say, 'Though they cut off my skirts, they left me the sleeves,' " remarked the peasant, as he asked for a drink of water before exacting his fee and returning whence he came.

The night before that day had been Shrove Tuesday Eve, and my mother and I went to one of the city squares where bonfires were lit and there were processions, dancing, bell ringing, dart games with sharpened reeds, and throwing of blown eggs filled with foul-smelling water, all for the amusement of the throngs milling about in the streets and hanging out of the windows in pre-Lenten celebration.

Strumpets shaking tambourines pranced out of the bawdy house, followed by two servant girls feeding tidbits to a donkey dressed up as a lady. Three of the harlots were crammed into one garment, their hands and feet sticking out of various holes. The procession was led by a garishly painted giantess swinging through the air a dwarf who she claimed was her husband, who had three humps, two heads, four arms and as many feet.

Behind them capered a squadron of fools wearing long, misshapen, starched robes of black, green and flesh-colored buckram, holding out chamber pots to beg for alms. One fool dressed as the pope, surrounded by cardinals and friars brandishing torches and scepters, was conveyed in a wagon, followed closely by another fool dressed as a king, in silks and gold and a crooked crown, escorted by horsemen in white or crimson suits and liveried minstrels playing Jew's harps.

Next came a wedding party of peasants, riders on asses preceding the rustic bride and groom, who were accompanied by a priest, a sheriff, the town mayor, the groomsmen and a drummer in goatskins heralding their arrival. Several yards behind came the villagers in shirts and white pantaloons, short stockings and shabby shoes, and a group of women on foot, some pregnant, others with their children. A young girl carried apples tied to poles, and an old woman fished out tripe and pizzles from a crock with a pothook, while a scrivener waved a bloody sheet that testified to a girl's maidenhead.

Close on their heels, to the sounds of trumpets and snare drums, came a procession of inquisitors on horseback. The gonfalon of the Holy Office was carried by a sallow friar wearing a white velvet habit, a crimson cowl and shoes and stockings trimmed with gold, silver and precious stones. Officers, horsemen and sumptuously dressed torch-bearers escorted them.

Other friars led to the scaffold a condemned man coiffed with the red hood worn by those sentenced to hanging. Behind them rode a headless horseman holding his head in his hands, with no notion of which way to turn.

At the tail end of the procession were seven blind men representing the seven deadly sins. The first held a black banner painted with white eyes; the others waved rags and sticks and kept jostling each other.

In the middle of a broad street, the King's marshal had hung a square canopy emblazoned with his master's arms, and had erected a dais four steps high, covered with colorful carpets. Street musicians illumined by rushlights played on shawms at the foot of a tower. A mounted, black-garbed mace-bearer rode his lance at a ring hanging from a rope but twice failed to hook it and splintered his lance against a wall.

Another mace-bearer in scarlet snared the ring three times in a row. The judge was made of straw, the witness another straw man propped up in a window. The prizes included mirrors, baubles, gauntlets, red buskins and both live and stewed capons.

A group of illustrious noblemen and their ladies emerged from a tower and ascended the dais, their way lit by cressets, to the sound of shawms, trumpets and minstrelsy. A band of mummers in lambskins began to dance. They feigned fear of everyone they met, grimacing and hunching over and freely dispensing their quips and sallies.

Having grown weary of dancing on the dais, the gentlemen left with their ladies between Compline and Matins. Out of a dark alley darted a mummer disguised as a cock, with bright red wattles and comb, white membranous ears and long neck feathers, which bristled and ruffled as he strutted and boxed with his own shadow cast on the walls and ground by the rushlights. As he drew near us he raised his eyes to the heavens to see if it might rain, fanning out his tail feathers, his cockspurs sharp as rowels. Guileful and lecherous, he threw himself at the women, cock-a-doodle-doing and crowing as if day were about to break.

"He heard the cock crow, and knew not on what dunghill," a toothless hag screeched at him, pulling his feathers.

"Eat up all your sausage, for tomorrow is Lent," another one hissed in his ear.

"Today is Shrovetide, a night of feasting and revels, of decency and abstinence from fornicating flesh, a time to castrate lascivious cocks like thee and lock up women and hens, who otherwise are lost by gadding about," a man rebuked him.

And then a cock was buried up to its neck and a blindfolded mummer came from afar and struck at it with his sword and chopped off its head.

At about that time, Don Enrique Cuarto died at the age of fifty in the Alcázar of Madrid—according to some, because his entrails were ravaged; according to others, from an excruciating pain in the side; and according to his own people, from being poisoned in Segovia during conversations and festivities with his sister. Weakened by copious discharges of blood, he succumbed in two days' time, his limbs contorted, bare-legged, clothed only in a ragged hair shirt and a pair of Moorish

slippers. As he lay dying and casting languid looks of farewell at his
intimates, the prior of Santa María urged him to die as a Christian at
the altar he had placed in front of him; but without uttering a single
word of contrition for his licentious reign, while his limbs convulsed
and his mouth twisted, he expired during the second hour of the night
on Sunday, the eleventh of December, 1474.

Even more wretched than his death was his burial: laid out on some
rough planks, his barefoot body—which had been neither washed nor
embalmed—wrapped only in a torn sheet, he was carried unceremon-
iously on the shoulders of hired porters to the Monastery of Santa María
del Paso. My mother and I were standing in the street, and we saw his
corpse go past the meager crowd that had gathered out of curiosity.
Don Acach de Montoro, Don Pero Pérez and Don Francisco Manrique
were among the gapers.

"We miss him extremely much," said Don Acach de Montoro, referring to the miller.

"He was no lover of insignia or court ceremonies," said Don Pero
Pérez, referring to the defunct king. "He used to wear a red fez upon
his head, somber greatcoats, pointed hoods and cloaks made of dark
wool; he covered his legs with coarse leggings and his well-worn buskins
would fall to pieces on his feet."

"They say the blue of his eyes shone with violence, suspicion and
greed, and that 'wherever his gaze fell, he looked long and hard,' " said
Don Francisco Manrique, who had supposedly met up with the King
once. "He was an ill-formed, fleshy man, tall, with strong limbs, and
large hands, which he was loath to have kissed, and not out of humility
or discourtesy but for reasons less pure."

"He had a broad forehead and cheekbones, arched eyebrows, sunken
temples, a flat, squashed nose, and he was long in the jaw; he often
ground his teeth. His friends used to say that his big, round head was
like a lion's, while his enemies likened it to a monkey's," added Don
Pero Pérez.

"He was malodorous, and I have heard tell that he enjoyed inhaling
the sickly sweet aromas of pestilence and putrefaction, and was partic-
ularly excited by the stench of severed horses' hooves and burning
leather," remarked Don Acach de Montoro.

"It is common knowledge that when the hirelings of Pedro Arias
attempted to take him captive, he escaped in his nightshirt, leaving
behind in his bed a certain Alonso Herrera, who was mistaken for the
King; also, that he gave the priorship of the Order of San Juan to Juan
Valenzuela, the dissolute youth who powdered his face white like a
whore's and used to go incognito as a courtesan, mounted on a mule,
to the masquerades and jesters' revels, accompanied by two cronies

playing the parts of a ruffian and a drunkard, and when people ridiculed him in the street, he would answer with obscenities and low jokes in the worst taste," recounted Don Francisco Manrique.

"He loved to hear Alonso Pérez, 'the Horrible One,' reminisce about his misdeeds, for as they passed this or that place together, the Horrible One would boast, 'This is the very spot where we assaulted a wayfarer; we robbed him and fearing he might denounce us, we murdered him. Then we scraped the skin from his face with our swords, so none might recognize him and thus have evidence which could attest to our crime,' " said Don Pero Pérez.

"When he wed Doña Juana, the King of Portugal's sister, before a populace eager for ceremony and celebration, there was no joy in his face nor gladness in his heart, nor did he even remove his cape or the bonnet worn low on his brow," continued Don Francisco Manrique.

"Without delay he seduced her into making love with another man to furnish him with an heir to the throne. That man was Don Beltrán de la Cueva, and their issue is known as Juana la Beltraneja," added Don Acach de Montoro.

"Ensconced in the heart of the loneliest and most umbrageous of forests, he solaced himself with the contemplation of a menagerie he had assembled during his wanderings over the years. He had a house built in a walled-in part of the woods where he could indulge himself with his friends in practices so nefarious that the child's presence prevents me from enumerating them," confided Don Pero Pérez.

"His privacy was ensured by a fierce Ethiopian dwarf and a band of ruthless armed men who patrolled the roads to frighten off anyone of illustrious lineage or remarkable wit who might disturb him in his retreat," said Don Acach de Montoro.

"Weary of these outrages and of his crapulous life, the grandees of the realm resolved to overthrow him," said Don Francisco Manrique. "Some suggested he be tried on charges of heresy, as he had already prompted the Marquis of Villena and the superior of the Order of Calatrava to convert to Islam; others proposed he be condemned as an apathetic and licentious tyrant. Although they quibbled over the charges, all were agreed on the actual dethronement, and they went so far as to erect an uncovered wooden scaffold on a plain outside the walls of Avila, where it could easily be seen by the throng, and brought to it a rag effigy of the King, complete with crown, scepter and throne. The grandees mounted the scaffold and a crier read aloud the petitions presented in vain by the downtrodden, the list of burdens he had imposed on the populace and an account of his evildoings, depravity and unbridled corruption. Next the King's deposition was decreed, the Archbishop of Toledo removed the crown, a marquis snatched the scepter from the rag doll's right hand, the Count of Plasencia seized the sword, the superior of Alcántara, with the help of the Counts of Benavente and Paredes, divested him of the royal insignia and then kicked him off the platform to the ground, as the flabbergasted crowd almost seemed to lament the symbolic death of the dethroned king. Then the King's eleven-year-old brother, the Prince Don Alfonso, was raised up to the royal seat, and as trumpets blared and the multitude stood agog, he was declared King of Castile. The people offered him obedience, shouting, 'Castile, Castile for the King, Don Alfonso.' The boy died in Cardesoña at the age of fifteen, of the plague said some, from poisonous herbs baked into a trout said others.

"Once the nine days allotted for the decomposition of the body of King Don Enrique Cuarto had transpired, and the mourning period for his death had passed, a wooden stage, open on all sides so the crowd might see without impediment, was erected in the main square of Segovia, and a young woman of average height, fair and blond, with blue-green eyes, a gracious, honest mien, a joyful and beauteous countenance and modest carriage, dressed in sumptuous finery and bedecked with jewels of gold and precious stones, mounted the steps to the sound of snare drums, cornets and trumpets. The royal pennants fluttered in her wake as the heralds sonorously proclaimed to the gentlefolk, aldermen and clergy of the city the Princess Isabel as the new Queen of Castile and León. All the dignitaries kissed her hands, acknowledged her as their queen and swore fealty to her on the Holy Gospels. Her brother Enrique's major domo delivered to her the keys to the city's strongholds, the staves of justice and the King's coffers, all of which she returned to him, bidding him keep and administer them in her behalf. Then the company set off for the Church of San Miguel, the nobility preceding the Queen, who was mounted on a richly caparisoned horse and followed by immense throngs."

In our little world, now that the miller had been buried, my mother became most melancholy, as the future seemed to close in on us and our provisions diminished. I, however, being pubescent and my mother's sole begotten child, was not displeased to become, once again, the center of attention for the creature who had given me life. It was a short-lived gladness, for a few months thereafter my still-handsome mother took up with a lame baker, slender of build and fiftyish, who had a long nose and a startled expression, a sallow, elongated face, curly hair and penetrating eyes, and who, to my surprise and annoyance, began to call me "my son."

This man, who understood more than he admitted to, knew Latin and had read several poets, was fastidious in his manners and dress,

in his conversation and his reasoning. At first he would visit our house
only at the hour of Prime, on the pretext of bringing bread fresh from
the oven, but as he had risen at Matins and was drowsy, he stayed on
to sleep in my mother's bed until midday. As the days passed his routine
changed and he began to appear empty-handed between Vespers and
Compline, rising at cockcrow to bake the bread. As I watched him vanish
into the midnight cold and darkness I envisaged in his person the promise of that bread I was to eat sooner or later, and whether it would be
of wheat, barley, rye or millet, its weight, size and fragrance palpable
in my fancy.

My mother awoke me from this daydream one day by confiding to
me that before long I should be eating frosted bread, by which she meant
that a wedding day was near. These tidings filled me with jealousy,
suspicious as I was that she had shifted her affections to him and wished
them to remain there forevermore. And although the marriage never
took place, I ceased scowling at the baker and never again broke into
their chamber with the intention of surprising them in shameless copulation.

While we sat together under the eaves the baker not only taught me
to write correctly but also led me through each of his books, pointing
out the properties of the various animals, plants and stones. Desiring
to make me a baker like himself, he would wake me at dawn to accompany him to heat the oven, which I prepared and warmed after throwing
in the kindling to light it.

"Be careful, for loaves, like passion, must rise in a single baking," he
used to caution me when he saw me shoving the ring cake into the
mouth of the oven, which was shaped like a vault, with a large vent for
air.

At times we went together to visit the butcher, who displayed cows'
heads and hides on a table, and we heard him boast that he never
pumped up his meat nor was it rotten, nor from ailing animals, and that
he was always heedful of the prices set by the council; or we went to
the blacksmith's house and heard about all the beasts he had shod that
day, using naught but good horseshoes and sound nails; or to the shoemaker's, who employed quality leather to make his shoes, eschewing
the skins of horses and asses, or to the weaver's, who had woven much
sackcloth at only one copper *maravedi* a yard.

He was a serious man who was wont to listen more than he spoke
and could perceive what caused others anguish or vexation. I grew to
be fond of him and began to help him when he neither asked for nor
expected it, shooing away the flies that speckled his cakes with filth in
the summer, buzzing and buzzing around in the sunlight as if they had
conspired to come in a swarm from the city dunghills.

"You look like the Emperor Domitian," he said, "amusing yourself by killing flies."

For although I dispatched most of them with a whisk, I pulled off the six legs of the ones I caught live and then quartered them; or I plucked off their filmy, leaflike wings and held them against the light to see the little veins, or examined the brownish down covering their bodies.

"Most of us will swallow a camel and strain at a gnat," he added, laughing, and went into the house.

It was about then that my mother met a Flemish merchant who had brought trunks crammed with coarse cloth from Bruges, fine cloth from Mechlin, scarlet stuffs from Ghent, woolens of worsted warp from Ostend and sheets from Holland. Early one Wednesday morning she took me to visit him at Alfonso's hostelry, where he was lodged. There, in a dimly lit room, whose windows he opened only to count his money, I saw him give my mother a gown from Mechlin and a pair of Valencian chopines made from tinseled kidskin with soles of new cork and oxhide, gifts she blushed to receive, asking herself and me what the baker would say when we returned home.

The Flemish merchant had set out five trunks on the floor of his chamber, with the prices of the cloth by the yard written on each one. A tall, slender man with a narrow, honest face, long nose and straight hair, he never failed to mention his native city each time he spoke, beginning his sentences this way:

"In Antwerp, lengths of linen cloth stretched on tenters in the fields are sprinkled every hour until they are pure white . . . In Antwerp, there are loaves of milky wax as large as mill wheels . . . In Antwerp, flea sellers carry the fleas in little boxes, and the fleas have tiny chains of gold and silver tied to their necks . . . In Antwerp, the chimneys are built of narrow bricks . . . In Antwerp, we say that children are like swallows who never fly away; that the young are peacocks; those in their thirties, lions; and old people, doctors versed in the preservation of life . . . In Flanders, there is an herb with yellow flowers, and when a cow is barren she is brought to graze upon this herb, and soon conceives, and the Flemish women drink water distilled from this herb when they, too, wish to be with child . . ."

Some time after this visit, towards the ninth month, when Sagittarius is in the ascendant, my mother's belly ballooned out. The baker, fearing the worst, thought it was dropsy, as he knew of three misers in her family whose thirst had never been quenched. He began feeding her remedies against that sickness, until one cold night, after considerable affliction and a quantity of blood, she presented him with a son and me with a brother. But as the child was pale and blond—the baker had jet-black hair, and when he dressed in white he looked like a fly in the milk—my mother explained how she had used sweet incense and sand-paper to bleach his skin and hair when he was born.

"Do you remember that Flemish merchant who told us how in his country the women take waters distilled from the yellow flowers of an herb to get with child?" she asked me once, summoning me to the bed where she lay resting with her baby. "I drank of that very water, from a mug my friend from Antwerp gave me to quench my thirst; once I had drunk, I broke the mug and hid the pieces in the courtyard, lest the baker find them, for the people there say that many men, upon learning that their wives have partaken of this cordial with a stranger, grow as jealous as during the midsummer moon, waxing so wrathful that they turn mad."

Gossip spread all over Madrid that my mother had lain with the Flemish merchant, but neither this tittle-tattle nor the absence of any physical resemblance between the child and himself diminished the baker's enormous devotion to his son. It was such that he never left the red-faced little nubbin's side by day or by night, for whenever he disappeared for a few minutes to knead the bread, the bantling would call out to him, and at once he came running, as if he had heard the cries in his own heart.

This misleading life came to an end the following spring, when the merchant of Antwerp returned to the city and invited my mother to Alfonso's hostelry to show her the woolens, Flemish stuffs and Brabant laces he had brought, for "Never has there been cloth so fine in this land," he boasted. In a leather-covered trunk divided into compartments, he kept black goatskin chopines overlaid with green and white brocade, "of twenty-four layers of cork, tall as a lady herself, or more discreetly, of a mere four layers, to elevate gracefully the figures of maidens and small women," as well as blue and Castilian-red velvet stockings embroidered with myrtle sprigs or laced with silver cords.

Solicitous neighbors informed the baker of this and other visits my mother paid to the merchant, until one afternoon, bristling with suspicions, convinced that she had transferred her affections elsewhere, he waited for her behind the door, hidden among the gathering evening shadows. And, as love, being jealous, makes a good eye look asquint, he stabbed her until she was bathed in blood, exclaiming in his frenzy, "The merchant shod you in chopines, the merchant gave you vermilion hose, he made you a present of the most costly Flemish woolens—but I shall put you in your grave."

Spattered with her blood, his mouth contorted, his fingers splayed out as if seeking the merchant's neck, he staggered from room to room repeating, "Some jealous husbands bolt the doors or brick up the windows, others break their wife's leg or cloister the life of the woman they love . . . but I, tranquil and trusting fool that I was, I went off to make our daily bread."

After so saying, he carried the child to a church and left him on the steps as a foundling. Once the bells had rung Compline, he returned home and locked me in a room, for he imagined I would run away to accuse him of my mother's murder. Through the wall I heard him cry, curse and smash pottery, then bang his head against some hard surface. In a barely audible voice, he spoke to my mother and the Flemish merchant as if they were standing before him, and he struck the furniture and threw knives at the floor, door and walls, as if the two of them were taunting him by moving about the room. And I believe that in the end he would have wounded himself as well if an armed sheriff had not appeared to arrest him.

Next day the scene was set in the cemetery, whither I went with the Fleming and a few curious neighbors to bury my mother. The resurrection of the flesh, the pardoning of sins and life eternal were words the friar spoke over her inert body, for we gave the pious woman a church funeral.

The merchant, a man with gray eyebrows, hair and mustache—which I had seen blond just a few months before—seemed inordinately gaunt, as if the grief of seeing my mother slain and myself left an orphan had desiccated him, like a man buried in sand whose flesh has been leached of all moisture.

Contrary to my expectations, once we had left my mother to her eternal repose, the merchant gave me neither food nor even one single *maravedi*, nor did he offer to take charge of me in any way; he merely patted me on the head, wished me good fortune and uttered these comforting words: "Death is but a sleep; your mother is dreaming in paradise. One day you shall see her, when you, too, go to rest from the travails of this world, there where wealth and want are of no import."

I remember the fixed stare of his eyes as he spoke, how his voice choked in his throat, the extreme pallor of his face, his tremulous chin. I thought his knees would buckle, that he would cast himself into the grave and embrace the dead woman's corpse, but he only said to me, in a sententious voice:

> *"The mad follow the mad, the blind the blind,*
> *as we seek our fortunes to find:*
> *The more we have, the less it seems,*
> *much like the moon's shadows of our dreams."*

After obtaining mules for the journey, he left in the greatest possible haste, but not before filling his trunks with Castilian woolens, cumin, almonds, grapes and raisins. I returned home, feeling as though I had spent that day, and the day before, and all the days of my life, in a dream.

The chamber where I usually slept seemed as confined and empty as a tomb, and I felt as if the ceiling, floor and walls were splashed with blood which I would never be able to scrub off.

For hours my mouth tasted of ashes. I was distraught, I touched things aimlessly, I looked about me, I might have been groping at clouds, passing through walls, lifting up air. Enveloped by the hushed darkness, I rested my body in the abyss, I abandoned it to bottomless melancholy.

Left alone with my fate, I sensed myself changed. I confronted a person who was I but with brittle hair, withered cheeks and hands that could not feel each other. My wearied eyes roamed through the night of my room, which seemed to extend beyond the roof, beyond space, into the world's unending nothingness . . . and into the stinking yard where one lone sheep was bleating.

I awoke suddenly at midnight and saw my mother in the flesh; her green eyes were joyful in her comely face. I remembered her during the days of her widowhood: peaceable, honest, bearing her grief without complaint, despair or anger. Now, beneath her arched brows her eyes were blackened by kohl, and her cheeks were rosy; standing there in nowhere, she called out to me, offering me the chick-peas and stew, the meatballs and fried fish that I liked so much and that she knew how to make so well.

For days on end, perhaps even for weeks, I watched the sunlight on the wall, with nothing to do but go to the square fronting San Salvador's and listen to the crier proclaiming the news to the people. I found my sustenance in the kitchen in the chimney stack, where the baker had hung some blood puddings and sausages to be cured and dried by the smoke. I drank water from the well and nourished myself on fantasies until sleep began to confound my eyes, and menacing shadows crept off the floor and ceiling and spoke to me. To my astonishment, clothes lying on the floor began to slither across it like wrinkled snakes, flies as big as my hand chased hairy spiders along the walls, a table moved about with no human help, and a blood-drenched woman wept behind every door. Each crack was a grimace, each crumbling wall seemed like a fallen creature, wormholes in the wood became gnawed faces, holes gaped like graves, and every dumb beast seemed to be dismembered, disemboweled and defenseless. The universal enemy who deceived our mother Eve tried to enter my body through my mouth, flapping its great wings around me, scratching my shoulders with its talons, attempting to nest on my chest. In terror I fled from my nightmare corner and went to sit in the doorway for the rest of the year. Then all at once gripped

41

by a mysterious inspiration, I went to the kitchen and other rooms and rummaged through the chests, clothing and storage jars, until fate would have it that I found a pot filled with Castilian gold coins beneath my mother's bed.

Dawn came, ray after ray; the light lifted the firmament, dissipated the mists, opened up dark roads and gilded the stones, tiled roofs and bodies of the early risers off to their labors in the town or the fields. The clock over the Guadalajara Gate struck the hour for three leagues around. Seated once again in the doorway of my house, I gazed at the wavy peaks of the Sierra de Guadarrama and the flinty walls of the city, struck by the sun's blades, sending back golden sparks into the sky, as if an invisible magician had suspended in space the music of the spheres: the dialogue between stone and light.

Down the road came an ugly, red-haired blind man who had a long, florid face, broken nose, shaggy beard and pointed ears; he was gaunt, and he jabbed his staff at the air and the ground, embraced walls, kissed doors and fell down to rest on steps. A stone's throw from me he inquired into the void, "For the love of God and the sainted Virgin Mary who bore us and almost made us equal, tell me who lives here. . . . I beg for alms at the Church of San Francisco, to whose convent the unfortunate Doña Juana has retired, to a room over the old porter's lodge, which has two latticed windows looking into the church and one window looking into the chapel of San Onofre, to be precise. . . . I was blinded by the Caliph of Córdoba, Muhammad ben Abd al-Rahman, who sired forty male children, without counting the females, and who crushed the renegade Omar ben Hafson and crucified Ixen betwixt a dog and a pig. But to whom am I speaking? Is there someone here?"

Then, as if he had glimpsed me out of the corner of his eye, he came up and smacked my knee with his stick. "What shape are you? Are you man or maid? Moor, Jew, Christian, Portugee, Segovian? Are you at odds with Madrid or with me? Why are you standing there? If you are not a beast, speak."

"I am sitting here at the scene of the crime," I answered.

"Were your parents murdered by the rogues who hide under cover of night at the Culebra Gate to rob and kill?" he asked, drawing his face close to mine.

"My father was a barber and he slit an apothecary's throat and the sheriff took him away to be executed. My mother was slain by a baker because she bore him another man's son."

"I cannot comprehend so much death. You say that an apothecary slit a barber's throat because he gave him a baker's son?"

"You have made it all into a muddle," I remarked.

"I have understood nothing," he said, sitting down by my side on a stone. "Tell it to me more slowly."

"The memory of so much crime mortifies my soul and pains my stomach," I protested.

"I begin to understand," he said. "A baker slit an apothecary's throat because a barber gave him a son."

"Better be silent," I begged him.

"You shall tell it to me another time, when the sky is not so cloudy. Can you reason? Did your parents teach you aught of usefulness or discernment, or merely to grow old and perish?"

"My father taught me proverbs and my stepfathers led me through various books," I answered.

"I am glad you are not a donkey, but quickly, tell me, what do you see at this very moment?"

"A light the sight of which would cure you of blindness, could you but see it."

"To see that light I would lead a parade of geese through the streets of Madrid, or guide an army of fools through hell," he sighed.

"Now I spy a creature which goes on two legs, has two arms, two eyes and a red mouth," I said.

"Has it a dagger or a scabbard? Is it a gentleman or a lady?"

"Sir, I believe it carries a Toledan blade, and it is the most like a man that I have lately seen."

"Is that a mule passing by?" he asked next, straining his ears to make out the clip-clopping.

"It is a scrivener who has a wooden leg," I replied.

"Let us be on our way, for we must hasten to the square in front of the church where I make my living, and there we shall meet a fine company. . . . Afterwards I shall take you to the baths, for you have a great fetor."

"And what might that be?"

"Many odors together."

"I have not bathed since my mother died."

"That is as I thought, for I first perceived you from afar by your stink. I perceive men through my nose: some smell like dead dogs, others like wet crows or drainpipes or sweat, or of the road. Now gather up your tatters, we must hurry along."

"I do not wear rags," I said with annoyance.

"Then I am sorry, but from your smell I perceived you as a trampled and downtrodden thing, whose flesh peeks through his clothes in a dozen places, who presses the bare soles of his feet against the ground when he walks and sits down on naked buttocks. Is it not thus?"

"Not in the least."

"How can you be of service to me?"

"I have a pair of fairly new eyes which can see the sun during the day and the stars at night; I can make out drakes, pigs, dogs, stone walls, puddles, hills, doors and every living creature in this town," I responded.

"For me the sun is dark and the moon but a shadow," he said.

And he stood by my side, staring into the distance as if he could see it.

"Have you eaten?" he asked after a lengthy silence.

"No."

"Have you slept?"

"Like a dead man."

"Have you committed any misdeeds?"

"Not yet."

"While you are making up your mind to it, do not come too close to my pouch, for in this woolen sack I carry one hundred coins stamped with the *Agnus Dei* which were minted by Don Juan Segundo."

"I have never stolen from anyone," I protested.

"I have already been left once without sustenance, when I allowed a wench who said the same to fondle me."

"You can trust me."

"That's what the other one said."

"If you don't believe me, farewell."

"Are you not alone in the world like myself?"

"Yes."

"Well, now you have father, brother and friend; you shall see how we will amuse ourselves in these blind alleys."

"Blind?"

"Because I cannot see them."

"If the blind lead the blind, both shall tumble into the ditch," I said.

"Do not trust those old saws, which never befall a cautious person like myself."

"My father knew many."

"That is why he killed a barber."

"It was my father who plied that trade; he killed the apothecary."

"It is all one. Bring your things, as we must be off."

"I have no other things in the world than those I am wearing."

"Have you food in your house? Did not those people who met their deaths eat well, did they not leave some blood sausages behind for pilgrims?"

"I ate them all."

"All by yourself?"

"My soul helped me."

"Is there any water? I am thirsty."

"Not a drop, for the well ran dry," I said to tease him.

"With so much water in Madrid—in the fountains, flowing under the ground, running down the walls—that one has only to dip one's hand into any hole to find it, you have none?"

"I have told you that the well ran dry."

"Then let us be off; we will fill the jug at the first fountain we pass, as we must attend to an urgent business before Evensong," he said, grabbing me by the arm.

"How can you tell the time?" I asked.

"By feel, by certain calculations I know how to make. I sense heat and cold in the air, the warbling of birds gives me counsel, the snorting of mules signals nightfall to me. . . . Now, get on with you."

"Uphill or downhill? Shall we take Calle de los Tintes or Calle del Espejo?"

"Take whichever way you will, only go, for I am in a great hurry to get anywhere."

But after a few steps he stopped, as if dubious of my company.

"What is your name?"

"Juan."

"Juan what?"

"Cabezón."

"Father's name?"

"Ricardo Cabezón."

"Mother's?"

"Juana Morales."

"Married?"

"Unwed."

"Smooth?"

"Hairy."

"Christian, Jew or *Converso*?"

"Descendant of converted Jews."

"Anyone guilty of heretical depravity in the family?"

"No one."

"How did your father die?"

"The neighbors told my mother that he had been executed for slitting the apothecary's throat in his barbershop, but I never sought him out after his arrest."

"You did well," he said, turning his face skywards, as if he were addressing someone on high.

"And your name?" I asked him.

"Pero Meñique, born in Jaén in the year of Our Lord 1438 . . . I learned to walk by myself, I played in the Plaza de la Magdalena and the Plaza de San Ildefonso; I drank from the fountain of the Pilarejo and I knelt

before the jasper-and-rock-crystal cross in Santa María's. As I was a
fervent believer, I yearned to follow in the footsteps of Fray Vicente
Ferrer and preach evangelical doctrine and fear of the Last Judgment,
but to the damnation of my soul I met a clerk's wench who wore a
vermilion canvas badge three fingers wide on her toque . . . Moreover,
I was disappointed because the strumpet soon presented me with the
amorous clerk's bastard, so I fell in love with a devotee of Nuestra Señora
de la Concepción whom I met not far from the Church of San Pedro el
Viejo as she went, in her white tunic and russet surcoat, to Saturday
Mass."

"What happened next?"

"It happened that Don Juan Segundo, father of Don Enrique Cuarto
the Humble, had his favorite, Don Alvaro de Luna, beheaded—the very
man who, thanks to his nefarious liaison with Don Juan, was held in
greater esteem in Castile than the King himself, distributing towns and
villages among his kinsmen and friends."

"Was he your friend, your protector, your father?"

"Not at all, but his disastrous end changed my mother's life. Visited
by the grace of God, she retreated from this century, abhorred worldly
matters and fled from vice, to spend her days in fasting, vigils and
prayer, going so far as to dress in coarse cloth and lead a life of extreme
poverty, such as was formerly practiced by the Order of the Humiliati.
One fine day twelve paupers and other bashful beggars came to the
house for food, and she served them their portions at the door, even
taking the bread from her own mouth to feed it to them. A short while
later it chanced that on her way down the street to church a poor wretch
approached her to beg for alms, and having naught else to offer, she
made him a present of her gloves and the book in her hand; as another
starveling who had been ill used by the world appealed for her help,
she took off her mantle and gave it to him. Furthermore, when in the
square a lewd woman begged for some old clothes to cover her half-
naked skin, my mother asked permission to go into a house where she
could take off an intimate garment with which the woman could cover
up her privy parts. Thenceforth she took up hospital visiting, hovering
over the beds of the most grievously ill to feel their pulses, examine
their tongues and tidy their bedclothes, taking especial care that they
should lack for nothing that was within her reach. And my mother was
so taken with the vice, or virtue, of charity that there was no thing she
owned in this world which she did not yearn to give to the poor, until
one day when my father had journeyed to Seville, when she had ex-
hausted all the provisions and monies in her keep, she held a public
sale of all our goods, excepting only the table and the beds, and that

was because the auctioneer took pity on us and refused to knock down our last remaining possessions, though he had even sold the mule which enabled us to get away from town and to transport heavy objects.

"But just as she loved the poor, she loathed the brawny, strapping vagabonds who, albeit fit for work, went from door to door taking bread and clothing from the truly needy. 'He that will not work shall not eat,' she would say whenever she came across such a young and healthy fellow. What pained her most were the blind men who could not earn an honest living, being unable to move about alone although sound of body, until one day she devised a way to employ them—to blow the bellows for blacksmiths, since this required hands rather than eyes. Reasoning thus, she sent every blind man she encountered in the streets to a blacksmith acquaintance to be put to work. Next it occurred to her to save bawdy women from perdition of body and soul, and she would go at night to the brothels to collect them and, by dint of wheedling, cajolery and money, bring them to our house, where there was still a room with beds and an altar consecrated to Nuestra Señora de la Aurora, so that they might meditate and pray when they were so inclined. Each morning a chaplain would sit before them and lecture them about the horrors of vice and the beauty of the soul, the transience of life and the eternal torment awaiting them in punishment for their devotion to the deadly sin of lust."

"Is your mother still alive?" I asked.

"She was not satisfied to seek for lepers outside the towns and off the King's highways. When she heard their little bells and clappers—for they are forbidden to cry out so as not to infect the air with their sickness—she took pity on the clawed hands and hunched backs of the most severely stricken, as the disease not only rots their bodies and gnaws at skin and flesh but even shrinks the nerves in their extremities, and they are totally excluded from all human commerce. One Sunday, after a priest had sung a Mass *pro infirmis* and sprinkled her with holy water at the church door, she was escorted in a procession to a fenced-in hut outside the city walls, ashes from the cemetery were strewn over her feet, she was prohibited from answering questions to prevent her putrid breath from contaminating the air, and she was vouchsafed to touch things only with her stick. 'You are dead to the world,' they told her, 'but you shall live forever in the Kingdom of God.' She died amongst the lazars, her bedclothes were burned the day of her burial, and people took her hair, her fingernails, her garments, what remained of the wax tapers and earth from her grave to cherish as relics. They say she has performed many miracles, except for my father and me."

Hurrying along, we arrived at the Church of San Salvador, whose tower is known as the town's sentinel, and where the council of Madrid meets in the small chapter house above the church portico. We came across a number of citizens headed that way as well: Rodrigo de Cidillo riding a light chestnut horse, Juan de Alcalá astride a dark chestnut, Rodrigo del Campo on a gray, Pero de Pinto mounted on a chestnut which was not his, Luys de Buendía straddling a strawberry roan and Pero González Cebollón on foot, as he had tethered his horse by the riverside. They were all going to answer the summons of the King's attorney, Ximón González, who had convoked them.

Behind them a man was driving a wagon loaded with building materials from the demolition of one of the city gates. Walking behind him, we entered the newly enlarged square lined with arcades of shops built at the behest of Enrique Cuarto, who had also charged that a number of houses be torn down and leveled so that henceforth every Thursday the market which had hitherto convened in the suburbs could be held here, with special areas provided for the fishmongers, bakers, gardeners, fruiterers and cobblers. The voice of Diego, the town crier, resounded from amidst a throng of men and women: "In Madrid, Monday, the twenty-fourth day of the month of November, in the year seventy-seven, this day, the council, being gathered together by the pealing of the bells with the Honorable Juan de Bovadilla, Corregidor, or chief civil magistrate, and Doctor de las Risas, Regidor, or municipal councillor, in the Church of San Salvador, of the aforementioned city, gave as an annuity estate, in perpetuity and forever anon, to Alonso Ximón, citizen of this aforementioned city, a terrain to build houses, which terrain lies at the Hontanillas fountains, bounded by the yard and house which belong to Doña Antonia, and has for limits on the one side the aforementioned yard and house, and on the other side, the brook, and on the other side, the street which goes past the Alzapierna Tower . . ."

"Who hearkens to the crier?" Pero Meñique asked me.

"Diego de Yllescas, silkman; Pero González, silversmith; Diego Sánchez, glover; Doctor de las Risas and his servant Gonzalo Mexía; Juan de Sevilla and Juan del Campo and many other men and women whose names I will not mention."

"Has Doctor de las Risas seen me?" he asked. "He is a great friend of mine."

"Yes, at this very moment he is paying you his respects," I told him, as the portly doctor bowed towards us, a wide smile on his froggy face revealing all his teeth.

"Let us make haste, as I am in a hurry to attend to some business in another part of town before nightfall," Pero said, striding off so vigorously that he seemed in danger of falling down flat on his own shadow.

"What sort of blind man are you, virtuous or sinful?" sneered a friar who had grabbed Pero's beard as they collided with each other upon turning a corner.

"There are only two kinds of blind men, the rogues and the rueful," retorted Pero Meñique. "I am a mixture of both."

"I only acknowledge two sons of man, the milk drinker and the meat eater; which are you?" the friar scowled, clutching at my chest.

"I am feeble, footloose, randy and in need," I answered quickly.

"And are you really blind or only feigning to be so?"

"People say I am blind, and in truth, I begin to believe them," said Pero Meñique. "And what are you?"

"I would be a snake if I were not a pig," the other man muttered.

"I can believe that too," replied Pero Meñique, laughing.

"You are passing ugly, but you don't laugh about that," snapped the friar as he walked away.

"Once there was a time when you could go about the world showing the whites of your eyes and nobody made mock, there was a time when you could walk through walls and no one paid any heed," said Pero Meñique after ruminating for some time about the churchman's insult.

"Don't vex yourself over the friar's words, for there are worse things than being blind, such as being dead," I reasoned.

"The worst thing about being blind is that you fall into the same hole and you bump into the same man twice," he sighed. "At times I wish I were something more than a sightless man roaming the streets of Madrid. . . . Oh to be a Cid Campeador, a Marquis of Santillana or a Doña Urraca."

"You know this city well, its many secrets and its many puddles, its many smells and its many churches, its many stones and its many chamber pots," I insisted.

"I walk in a private Madrid, made of unalloyed night," he said. "I am a lost soul on any street, and there are days when each body jostles me, when all obstacles seem very hard. . . . One must have ready hands and a brow of stone to be blind on such days, my dear Cabezón."

"You have not told me yet how you became blind, whether by infirmity, ill fortune or punishment."

My words seemed to stop him in his tracks and cut his breath short. I felt as if he were looking at me through a tiny slit in his eyes as he drew his face close to mine and said, "A matter of ten years ago, after I was expelled from the preaching friars' monastery, I wandered unhindered from town to town in the kingdom, until I had carnal knowledge of the daughter of a supremely vengeful Moor, who threw in my face the indignities he had suffered from a legion of Christian youths who

had lain with her since she was but a girl. One night he surprised me
half-naked with her in a doorway, and in his frenzy he chased me
through the streets of the Moorish quarter, as if he recognized in one
single man all those who had trifled with his honor. Rage lent him wings,
and after a brief race he caught up with me in front of Doña Fátima's
house, where he wrathfully blinded me with his dagger, although I was
miraculously saved from castration and having my mouth slashed by
the opportune appearance of a sheriff, who came to my aid when he
heard my groans. . . . You had best not laugh at me, for as Catullus
says, there is naught so foolish as a foolish laugh."

"I am not laughing, I am only locating obstacles on the road so that
you shall not bump into them," I said.

"Were we not so far from the dunghills, I could believe you were
leading me beyond the city walls to where the night soil and filth are
dumped, for you have nearly tumbled me into a ravine from whence
the stench of chamber pots arises," he said, poking me with his stick
as we passed the Church of Santa María, in olden days a Moorish mosque
until the King, Don Alfonso VII, had it cleansed and consecrated.

We walked past the narrow entrance of the Vega Gate, from the
highest point of whose antechamber is suspended a great iron weight
ready in the event of necessity to be dropped upon any enemy who
might find himself beneath it. We continued along Calle de la Ventanilla
and Calle de Ramón, down Calle de Segovia, past the mint and the
Vistillas vacant lots. Parish churches, crumbling ancient walls, large
ramshackle houses, steep riverbanks and the barbicans and towers of
the city walls loomed up and disappeared. We took the Cuesta de los
Caños Viejos and the Cuesta de los Ciegos, and walked alongside the
stream, which seemed to be following us with its mud and its watery
murmur.

"This street is going upwards, Juan. Are we on the Cuesta de Ramón?"
Pero Meñique inquired, breathless and seemingly faint.

"We are on the Cuesta de los Ciegos," I answered.

"I knew it, I knew it—that is why the road rose up before me," he
said, stopping to rest.

A number of Madrid's citizens, all by the name of Juan, were coming
down the hill: Juan Calvete the glover, Juan Catalán the baker, Juan de
Yllescas from the gully, Juan Toro, Juan Laredo, Juan Béjar, Juan Romo,
Juan Malpensado, Juan González, Juan Madrid, Juan Rebecó and Juan
the sackcloth weaver.

"I hear puffing nearby," said Pero.

"It is the Juans coming down the Cuesta de los Ciegos," said I.

"I know many of them by heart, so if any should nod or raise his hand as he goes by, tell me straightway so I may answer his courtesy."

"They have already passed," I declared, although the last of them was just making him a great bow.

"I perceive the fragrance of a young girl's hair, unblemished skin, vermilion lips, long heron's neck, is it not thus?" he asked me, suddenly sprightly. "Paint me a picture of her in the flesh, for it pleases me to hear talk of brave wenches."

"This is no brave wench but rather Doctor de las Risas, who is striding down the hill laughing and salaaming."

"Where is he? Quickly turn me towards him that I may greet him," entreated Pero Meñique, who was facing a wall.

"He is gone," I said.

"So he has. . . . Now I hear the footsteps of a woman who walks wiggling her hips. . . . Tell me if she is broad-beamed, wears a white headcloth, has a comely face or a mouthful of bad teeth."

"It is a toothless old hag, bearded and mustachioed, her countenance disfigured by recent wounds, who has the bilious eyes of a harpy, wobbly legs and buboes in her armpits," I said, to hoodwink him.

"And the other one who comes after, is she not more blithesome of face and shapely of body?"

"She has the thick, hairy neck of a peasant, the wantonness of a fourteen-year-old and the blossoming breasts of eighteen. By her way of walking I conjecture she is from the stews, although she is dressed in widow's weeds. Perhaps she is a virgin nun," I said, although no girl of any sort was coming down the street.

"When she passes by us, say pleasing things which will flatter her," he whispered.

"I am embarrassed to speak to her."

"It is a stinking man, I can smell him from afar. It is no girl at all," he cried angrily.

"She turned the corner at Calle del Factor and I couldn't catch up with her."

"We passed that street long ago. I have the whole city in my head and I walk through it in my mind better than you can seeing it," he said. "You may trick me because I am blind, but take care when you look skywards, for if a swallow's droppings should fall into your eyes, they will be blinded too."

"You said swallow, and a swallow flew by," I said.

"It must be May," he gasped incredulously.

"Are you still there?" I asked him after he was silent for a while.

"Is a mule coming towards us, has a pig grunted or a hen clucked, did a goat cross our path, that you disturb me thus?" he asked me in turn, much annoyed.

"The sun blinded me," I said.

"I'm blind, you're blind, all the world and his wife is blind," he sputtered. "Since when do you talk dim-sighted gibberish?"

"Swiftly have I learned to pull the wool over your eyes," I replied, "and my teacher is not far off."

"You will be struck blind in earnest before that happens," quoth he, spurning my assistance, as if the probing of his staff and the chain of smells could lead him where he wanted to go. And so by taking the gallery of the Church of San Andrés we soon found ourselves in the Plazuela de la Paja.

"Here comes the beclouded one," said a tall, strapping man who had a pockmarked face and wore the raiment of a raggedy king: no shirt, scarlet breeches, brocade doublet and taffeta-lined cape.

"Since I hear you, I must assume you are here," retorted Pero Meñique.

"Where did you happen upon this fledgling?" asked a one-eyed man, malevolently winking his good eye at me.

"I found him in his nest," answered Pero Meñique.

"Your face is flushed, so I conclude you have eaten," remarked a gluttonous-looking woman seated on the ground who held her hand outstretched lest some invisible being get by without giving her alms.

"Whence come you?" asked the regally attired man, pacing back and forth.

"I am come from the Humilladero, the Wayside Cross, where I prostrated myself humbly before the image of our Redeemer, overwhelmed as I was by the burden of my sins and the weight of my imagination, for man has but to think and he becomes troubled and weary."

"I believe he comes from watching the women waggling their behinds as they scrub clothes at the riverside washery," said One-Eye.

"You look like a pelican, a bird better known by renown than by sight," said a jovial well-proportioned woman with an ample belly, great eyes and hair dyed black.

"Are you blind as a buzzard as well?" the old glutton asked me, thrusting her foul-smelling face into mine.

"He's a lambkin," said the jovial woman. "Do you not see how tender he is?"

"Don't play the blindling with me, for I cannot abide the sightless," growled the man dressed in royal tatters.

"I recall that when Dionysius went blind, his sycophants fell all over each other feigning blindness as well," said Pero Meñique.

A man walked past the gluttonous woman without dropping anything into her hand.

"In these tightfisted times, the only openhanded man on earth is the beadle who drives the dogs out of the churches," she said, watching him go on his way.

"Don't despair," said One-Eye, "for the curmudgeon gives more than he that has naught."

"Who are these people?" I asked Pero Meñique.

"The peevish, violent one is King Bamba, a most valiant thief who claims to be descended from monarchs, dresses like a deposed sovereign and goes barefoot through the world. One-Eye, who always wears black breeches and a wide leather belt, thinks he owns the walls of Madrid, but he is only proprietor of the ditches and dunghills outside them. The old glutton sitting on the ground is Babylonia, and she comes from Seville. They say she was so fair in her youth that the Madrid bear who was wont to go about on all fours would rear up on his hind legs to watch her walk by. The short-haired woman in the saffron coif, who has deep-set eyes, a thick, downy neck, a long fleshy snout, dark skin under the powder, bare arms and a neckline so low that her nipples show when she bends over, is the Trotter. A dexterous dancer of the chaconne and teller of jests in catches, she roams the streets and knows the churches and squares better than anyone in town. The saying may go, 'Hop whore! Pipe thief! Hangman lead the dance,' but here we say, 'If you're hot to trot, then follow the Trotter.' The other one, who has not spoken yet but who I infer is among them, a man who has hair clipped round, a long beard, a yellow band about his right arm, and who wears a mended gray tabard which covers poorly his fleshy parts, is the Moor. He claims his forebears were the Mussulman masons who built the tower of the Church of San Pedro, the Alcázar and the Guadalajara Gate."

"My alcázar is neither of brick nor of stone; its gates are of water, its floors of earth, its walls of air and its roof of light. Time, the master builder, raised it up, and its mornings share equally in its magnificence," the Moor said, after overhearing Pero Meñique. His bruised face approached mine, the forehead furrowed by wrinkles, sweat, blood and grime, with one pale protuberant walleye staring elsewhere.

"Have you nothing further to say?" asked Pero Meñique.

"I was born in the Zafayana fields four leagues distant from Granada, and in Almería, the City of Mirrors, I espoused an azure-eyed lass from Belmar, the daughter of a wealthy sarcenet seller. But I repudiated her by reason of the four causes for divorce among us: folly, adultery, drunkenness and bad breath. I was wounded in the face by a Christian lance when I was muezzin in the Alhambra, where every day from the pinnacle of the minaret two hours ere sunrise, at midday and in the evening I proclaimed, 'Allah is great, there is no God but Allah.' I was loud beyond

54

compare. Nowadays I am fraught with humility and suffering and must beg for a dog's portion to survive in the *aljama*."

"I'll bet you sang out loud and clear, you're a real canary," said One-Eye. "Where's the wine?"

"No wine today," said King Bamba, "for there's work tonight, and we need our wits about us. I have heard tell of a most solemn wedding in town, and the procession will pass this way. Let's see who we can catch napping."

"How many coins did you get?" the Trotter asked One-Eye.

"Thirty-four."

"Pinched?"

"No, cadged," he replied sarcastically.

"What's that slash on your face?"

"A knifing."

"When'd you get it?"

"They gave it to me last night for climbing walls, well-nigh took out my other peeper as well."

"Had you no lookout?"

"Aye, a first-rate ladder man and footpad too. I thought the knave knew his business, but he died like a dog."

"Didn't he defend himself at all?"

"Nay, for they stuck him like a pig as he was going up the wall."

"I foresee that you will swing from the turning-tree, with a crier in attendance," remarked the Trotter.

"I shall never die on the gallows," One-Eye protested angrily.

"She is an augur, I can see the signs," said the Moor.

"Your words are superfluous," One-Eye fumed.

"Whist, I have a splitting head, and I begin to turn mad and fidgety as though trumpets were blaring in my brain," growled the Moor.

"Watch your step, or I will mash your face into a bloody pulp and take the measure of your renegade ribs," menaced One-Eye.

"Never!" roared the Moor, struggling to draw a dagger from his tabard. "From this day hence you will be hamstrung."

One-Eye seized him by the neck and tumbled him to the ground as if he were a sack of chick-peas. He thrust his patched shoe into the Moor's face, pressing the muddy sole against his mouth, and said, "On your knees, son of Allah, for your Mahomet cannot save you from this filthy puddle. Kiss my hands."

"Many kiss the hands they would gladly see cut off," said Pero Meñique from elsewhere.

"Twist his hands like a candlewick," bade Babylonia.

"Take heed, for I am a respectable captain," hissed the Moor between his teeth as he lay flattened on the ground. "The spies of the King's guards are coming down that row of houses to seize you . . . Mercy, I desire to piss, I feel mangled, and little by little I become speechless and witless, like a dying sparrow."

"Silence," ordered King Bamba. "I hear the stomping of beasts."

One-Eye gave yet another kick to the Moor on the ground, took him by the head, squeezed it mightily and said, "You are full of airs, so I shall press them out."

"Why are you doing this to him?" asked Babylonia.

"So he may understand how hard-hearted I am and be pacified," One-Eye jeered.

"I can smell you well enough from afar," said the Moor, "you need not suffocate me in your reek."

"Bad scissors made my father wry-mouthed, but it is evil deeds and evil words that left you one-eyed, and before long I shall break your crown," King Bamba warned, shaking him.

"Let me go, I will be still," One-Eye pleaded.

"Yes, release him," said Babylonia. "Even if nobody else wants him here because he has only one peeper, I love him. For his sake I would doff my duds."

"You are the kind who sheds her clothes on the way to the bedroom," King Bamba scoffed.

"In my youth I was a cockatrice and a wag-tail, I was wild for booze and bawdry," she admitted.

"Dazzle me with your beams, show me your world, night is falling over me and I would cloak you in darkness," said One-Eye, making as if to embrace her.

"All in good time I'll drop my drawers, I'll show you my gams, I'll bare my bum . . . after my flowers have bloomed," said she.

"Throw open your casements, and I'll climb inside your smock," said One-Eye.

"Keep your paws off my paunch, that's where I keep my purse, and I know all about filchers," she said, brushing away his hand.

"The mare's kick does not hurt the colt," One-Eye declared.

"You think you're the cock of the walk," remarked Pero Meñique, who had been following the sounds and the voices.

"In the kingdom of the blind, the one-eyed man is king," One-Eye said to him.

"Ahh, there's no jest like a true jest," sighed Pero Meñique.

"Do not grieve overmuch, for another world comes after this one," the Trotter consoled him.

"The crow cannot be blacker than its wings," replied Pero Meñique.

"Why are you all atremble?" Babylonia asked the Trotter.

"I inherited the quakes from my mother, who died of the phthisis," the Trotter answered.

"My mother left me these shoes patched with holes and these clothes mended with air, which have made me master of the winds," said One-Eye.

"For you I would die," said the Moor to the Trotter. "I would give you a red camisole and a petticoat lined in blue so you might go about disencumbered morning and night, in little more than your shift."

"Pay him no heed, he's a coarse feeder, he eats his lentils and broad beans right off the ground, without a table," One-Eye snorted.

"Also bread of millet and other loaves of sundry sorts with raisins, figs and honey," added the Moor.

"Pay him no heed, for he sleeps on the floor like a beast, under the kitchen benches," One-Eye went on.

Meanwhile, a small man came skipping towards us with short, brisk steps. His arms and legs curved into an arch, a hump protruded above his gnarled spine, and his codpiece covered not only his private parts but his whole belly as well.

"The human seraph has reached Madrid, the glorious Father Don Rodrigo Rodríguez," Pero Meñique hailed him.

"My friend exaggerates a bit," said the small man, blushing as a broad smile curled his mustache.

"Do you bring us kneaded ring cakes, puff pastries, stew or a casserole of fish?" Babylonia asked him.

"No."

"Then why have you come?"

"To palliate the nightmare of his body, for nature chose to make him the butt of jests, a regurgitated abridgment, with only the head in correct proportion," said the Trotter.

"It is said that Pliny called this abridgment a misfortune in the days when the Romans played gladiatorial games with dwarves," said Pero Meñique.

"Who is this wizened child?" asked King Bamba, offended by his presence.

"I, sir, am Don Rodrigo Rodríguez, born in Toledo; I studied grammar, the arts and theology in Alcalá de Henares."

"Beggar or thief?"

"Beggar, thanks be to God, but if it is your wish, tomorrow I shall turn thief."

"What has brought you here?"

"I came in search of my friend, Pero Meñique."

"For what purpose?"

"A female by the name of Doña Flor Domínguez, a native of Segovia,

57

of whom I was most enamored, is come to Madrid with a Dominican priest."

"Can you pick a lock with a hook?" One-Eye asked him in turn.

"No," answered the dwarf, smiling shyly.

"Can you lose yourself in the crowd?"

"That's child's play for me."

"Then you shall be my lookout, halfling," said One-Eye.

"Please, call me Don Rodrigo, for my father was a brave, stouthearted knight, an excellent horseman, skillful at his weapon and a beloved friend of Don Alvaro de Luna."

"A friend to Don Alvaro de Luna, whom the King Don Juan Segundo beheaded as a traitor?" asked Babylonia.

"Yes, the Constable of Castile; the criers proclaimed his death."

"My father was a bungling doublet maker," said the Trotter, "for the only thing he mastered in his lifetime was the riddle of the doublet, which goes like this:

> *Arms and bodies have we*
> *but no head, hands or feet,*
> *we all have necks, but cannot eat;*
> *And though our eyes are open wide,*
> *we cannot see a thing outside."*

"My father, on the other hand, had more than one thousand men in his house to work and shear the cloth. He was a rich and respected man, and not a poor wretch like that woman's," boasted Babylonia.

"Mine was a renowned thief," said One-Eye. "The Marquis of Villahonda offered a reward of one thousand *maravedis* for his capture and when a traitor sold him, he confessed to the murder of fifteen men. The day he was executed they wheeled him out in a barrow lashed to an iron ring on a pole, with half his body dragging in the mud, so that as they went past a certain street several blacksmiths came forth brandishing red-hot tongs and tore off his ears, which they impaled on the pole. In the square he was beheaded and quartered."

"Doubtless an exemplary death," said King Bamba. "My father was so strong and nimble that when, just for sport, a horse was stood in the square and one man spread his arms out over the crupper and another spread his arms over the first man's shoulders, my father could leap over them both and land standing up on the horse's saddle. When he went off to war, so great was his courage and ferocity that any enemy who crossed his path got such a stab in the chest that he could not live to count to seven. One day at dawn in a battle against the Moors, when he would have rescued a friend besieged by many lances, he was shot from behind by an arrow and died.

"My grandfather, who was so poor that he lived by spreading dung on the fields and buying up broken-winded sumpter mules which he nursed back to health and then sold, took me in and carried me with him when he turned to cony-catching and preaching by the wayside in the company of a woman friend dressed as a nun. For many a long year we traipsed on foot or muleback from village to village and town to town, tethering the animal close by the church where my grandfather would deliver his sermon, while the counterfeit nun, medals dangling from her neck, sold heart-shaped *bullae* wherein saints' names were inscribed, for folk to wear on their breasts as a remedy against envy, ague and gout, or merely to remind them that they were mortal and destined to die. With these charms in our bags and hands, we beat the fields, took on the hills and scoured the streets, through heat waves and rainstorms, starving or sated, although to tell the truth, we more often bit upon the bridle, like the *bulla* seller's horse, than ate our fill, and many a time, as we stood in the middle of some wretched village square, my grandfather would conjure the kinsman figured on his ring to furnish us with aught to dine on and a place to sleep. Perhaps this errant existence might have lasted forever had not a spiteful clergyman who coveted my grandfather's paramour caused him to be arrested as an impostor and delivered over to the Dominican reverends to be tried as a heretic. And that is how I found myself in the streets of an unfamiliar town dressed as an acolyte and hungry, not knowing if I should eat roots or stones, clothe myself in animal skins or shadows, until I became King Bamba, and I am who I am."

"Speaking of scurrilous clergymen," said the dwarf, "they say that one evening a Franciscan friar in the confessional of a church in my town asked a comely virgin if she had clipped her nails, to which she replied, that there was no need to clip them in order to confess to a priest. He insisted there was, and that he had some scissors for her beneath his cassock. The maiden stretched out her hand, only to pull it back posthaste, exclaiming, 'Oh, Father.' 'Have you trimmed your nails so quickly?' he inquired. And as she laughed, he chortled, 'Praised be Saint Francis.' "

"I have heard that on Calle de Puebla in Palencia, a cleric's wench gave birth to a freakish girl child with a smooth, hairless face, and instead of a nose it has a fish eye with no lid, and a minute rabbity snout like a round hole with teeth where the mouth should be. Its ears stretch halfway down its neck, and the rest of its body is like any woman's, with little dugs, cunt and bum," said One-Eye.

"In Toledo, a nun had a monstrous kind of creature with the head, hair, face and ears of a lion, bats' wings instead of arms, a horn growing from its brow and toothed lips beneath its left nipple. A lock of hair not unlike a mustache sprouts above its navel, and its privates are male and female both, the male parts like a dog's and the female like a seashell. Its right leg is a man's, but the left one is covered with scales, for running in the fields or swimming in the water, so they say, whichever takes its fancy," affirmed Don Rodrigo Rodríguez.

"With no offense meant to my friend Don Rodrigo Rodríguez," said Pero Meñique, "I should like to relate how several years ago the Portuguese brought to these precincts a bearded dwarf about thirty years of age who was so tiny that he measured but three spans high, feet and head included. Two men carried him easily in a cage on their shoulders up and down the village streets, earning much money from the crowds which thronged to see him. The manikin was so quick-witted and sensible that he cried like a babe when they taunted him, and when they caressed him through the bars of his cage he played with the people. But on account of the very misfortune of his body, or because nature did not equip him to live for many years, to the great chagrin of the rapacious Portuguese he died one Sunday at the fair in the sight of a large crowd he was entertaining with merry conceits."

"I feel no pity for your body nor does your skimpy size amaze me," said the Moor to Don Rodrigo Rodríguez, "but you are in need of a barber to snip your beard. . . . How many *maravedis* do you have?"

"Why, none to speak of," the dwarf stammered.

"What, your gallant father didn't leave you a fortune?" Babylonia asked him.

"He left me the streets of the towns and the landscape of the fields," he answered.

"His clothes are good," One-Eye noted.

"I inherited this doublet from my grandfather, it was one he wore as a child."

"With that body he could earn his keep as a money-box," Babylonia declared.

"Or as a pilferer, for he can easily slip through a breach in the bricks or waft under a window like a gust of wind," King Bamba observed.

"I fancy him in women's veils or dressed as a little girl, keeping an eye out, hidden in a hole or sitting on some stone," said Babylonia.

"He has sharp lights and crafty paws, I see him as a ponce's pawn or a sponger," the Trotter suggested.

"I shall do as I am bidden, and even as I am not bidden," said Don Rodrigo Rodríguez, turning scarlet. "I thank you with all my heart for having uttered so many noble sentiments about my humble person, but I know I am so dull at gaming, so cuckolded in wooing and so wont to lose in strife and combats—on top of which, the crowds are always trampling me in the squares—that I greatly fear I shall not accomplish the glorious tasks to which you would destine me. For rather than clamber up towers and station myself on rooftops or squeeze through windows and cut off people's clothes, I prefer to spend the day in bed watching the figures my fancy draws on the wall or counting my fingers over and over again to make sure one has not been lost during the night."

"I could tell this one was all talk, and at the first turn of the rack I warrant he will squeak," sneered One-Eye.

A centenarian clad in caterpillar green crossed the square leaning on a small girl's head. He halted in front of us, opened his mouth to gulp for air or exhale his last sigh and stared at the ground gripped by the anguish of old age and death. I feared he might commence ranting, but a moment later he was on the move again, seeking a doorjamb to lean against, as if he'd gathered all his courage up to give himself a push.

Two kempt and cleanly Moorish women passed by after him, wearing wide pleated linen trousers tied below the navel and long shirts, likewise of linen, beneath their woolen tunics. They were festooned with bangles and black bead necklaces and their breasts swelled upwards under the green lining of their camisoles. They turned down the street into the Moorish quarter and I was able to see only their eyes, for their heads were veiled by white cloths. Next came a married woman in a devotee's coif and drawn claws, followed by a barefoot Moor with a pruned beard and hair parted down the middle. A clergyman in a pointed hood, buttoned tunic and rabbit fur mantle, carrying a golden staff, brought up the rear.

"One day they served Queen Isabel a garlic bulb wrapped in parsley, the which she spat out, remarking, 'The clod came clothed in the color green,'" said Pero Meñique, oblivious to the people bustling about in the square.

"They say that the King of Macedonia had several servants who were charged with reminding him that he was a mortal man, and it is reported of our own Queen Isabel that when she is present at royal entertainments and solemnities, there is always a lady by her side who pulls on her plaits to admonish her: 'Remember that one day you shall die,'" Don Rodrigo Rodríguez added with alacrity.

"I like to dine plainly in the mountain fashion, and I am content with a rye loaf, watered wine and a roasted cheese," the Trotter declared.

"Better a humble meal than a funeral feast in the treacherous hospitality of a scaffold," remarked One-Eye.

"San Jerónimo recommended to the poor not to eat of dishes which they were unable to digest, nor should they desire those which are beyond their reach, for there is considerable wisdom in a mess of herbs and pulses, and a meager meal preserves a man from sickness," said Don Rodrigo Rodríguez.

"There are foods which do harm to the stomach and the soul, such as eggplants, which induce melancholy; broad beans, which cause forgetfulness; and mushrooms, which contain a deadly poison. It is greatly to his detriment for a man to carry a mouthful to his lips if he has not first swallowed the preceding one and to lean overmuch into his porringer when hunger is fierce," cautioned Pero Meñique.

"You know much of matters that pertain to the filling and emptying of the body," said the Trotter. "I vow there was a physician Acach or Yucé among your forebears."

"When the King would dine on mutton, partridge, fish and the finest white bread, a table is laid for him with a cloth of golden brocade in a hall in the palace, his tasters sample the dishes before he eats of them to prove them free of poison, he has a basin by his side for the leftover bits and bones, and within easy reach are ewers of water scented with mint and vervain, as well as divers kinds of knives, Venetian three-tined forks and ornate spoons. I eat with my hands, bolting down the fatty parts of bacon and an ill-kneaded loaf while seated on a stone or leaning on air, beneath the blue roof of night," said King Bamba.

"Hunger is a whore," One-Eye complained.

"Open your eyes, you look like a beetle," the Moor scolded me harshly as he squeezed my jaw in his rough hand. "You keep wincing while you listen, as if the light bothered you or you were ducking a blow."

"Surely you know that blindness is also an affliction of hens and chickens," Babylonia blurted out.

"Just as dwarfishness is also a deformity of oranges and apples," added Don Rodrigo Rodríguez.

"He that will be rich before night may be hanged before noon," the Trotter said to the Moor.

"Why must he hang?" King Bamba asked the woman brusquely. "If nobles and gentlemen live by stealing and seizing the land; if it is said that, once inside these realms, not a soul is suffered to set foot out of them without being forced to bite his lips at any of the borders on account of the greedy, uncouth and surly toll takers and tax collectors who strip travelers down to their very undershirts searching for hidden monies, with no thought of whether what they may have left is for the return journey."

"We live betwixt urine and feces, which is why San Isidoro of Seville ordered the monks to say their prayers aloud when they visited the privies," Don Rodrigo Rodríguez said from beneath the Trotter's skirts.

"When he bent over he could see your mutton," Babylonia warned the Trotter.

"No matter, for the law forbids hunchbacks to be gentlemen or husbands. He may look beneath my skirts as much as he likes."

"Here comes a Moorish girl in her linen veil," said the Moor.

"Her hair hangs loose, her shoes pinch, her stockings droop, and her tunic is too tight," observed Don Rodrigo Rodríguez.

"Doña Toda is approaching, the wife of Iñigo Arista, Gutierre Díaz, Diego López and who knows what others in the dark days yet to come," said King Bamba.

"Why mention so many names when the first husband will be her master in hell?" Babylonia argued.

A tall, swan-necked, broad-beamed woman wearing a headcloth over her long hair appeared in the square. As she went by her deep hazel eyes stared boldly at King Bamba, who, as if bewitched, followed for a long time the disappearance of her body down the emptiness of the street.

"Did you see the gleam of sincerity in her hazel eyes?" he asked Pero Meñique, who was standing next to him.

"I saw a shadow cross from one side of my head to the other, but I made out no gleam in it," answered the blind man.

"Here comes a fine, rich lady dressed in fancy brocade," One-Eye announced.

The Moor began to bawl, "For the sake of Santa Casilda, who was so merciful to the captive Christians as they lay dying of hunger and thirst in the dungeons of her father, King Aldemón of Toledo, alms for the love of God."

Babylonia clamored, "For the sake of San Isidro Labrador, who was born in this very town to poor but honest parents, and who worked many miracles, such as restoring the sight of a blind boy whom he named Domingo, alms for a hungry old woman."

The Trotter beseeched, "For the saint who never turned to dust, whose shroud was still whole and immaculate forty years after burial and whose incorrupted body was carried in solemn procession to be interred amidst clouds of incense in a sepulcher adjoining the Apostles Peter and Paul, a bit of bread in the name of God."

The Moor rejoined the pack. "Beware if you give no alms and then pass through the Balnadú Gate, beware, for it is the devil's own gate, and if you venture farther and reach Xerez, know that it is a land of misfortune. If thence you return to Madrid, I see signs that you will be walking on clods of fire."

"Have done, you smoky Moor, for your howling is driving away those who would come into the square," cried King Bamba, grabbing him by the tabard.

Meanwhile the woman walked past without turning around and seemed not even to hear them. She was followed by a great noise: trumpets, shawms, snare drums and tambourines. After them came masked buffoons; maimed, crippled and humpbacked revelers; crossbowmen dressed in blue velvet doublets, green shirts and yellow breeches. Behind rode the groom, wearing a black hat studded with costly gems, a doublet embroidered in gold and a crimson jacket with gilded braid on the shoulders, mounted on an egg-colored horse whose mane was plaited and tail docked. Eight highborn men and four pages in hoods accompanied him, garbed in brocade doublets, short green cloth jackets and shirts so long they had to drape them over their shoulders.

The bride was next, very young, very gracious, her eyes demurely downcast. She wore a sumptuous gown of fine green brocade trimmed with gold passementerie beneath a cloak of black damask. Her black hat was of the newest fashion; her necklace, precious stones. The white mare she rode had black velvet embellishments on cruppers and withers.

Women of divers rank and manner followed her on foot into the square. All of them were maidens save one elderly lady. A man clothed in showy brocade with a rapier over his shoulder led a horse into the square, and then came a hooded page.

Night fell. The square lost its colors and angles. Beggars, thieves and townspeople were muffled in the selfsame darkness. All became quiet, empty, mournful, as if at any moment the blurry figures would be transposed to a dream.

Suddenly a straggling couple, splendidly dressed, appeared in search of the others. The man wore a riding coat of yellow cloth over a scarlet doublet and a blue cape with a hood of the same color; a twisted gold chain glinted at his throat. The woman wore a blue brocade gown beneath a golden mantle, and her hair was softly dressed. Together they crossed the square as if they were traversing an ancestral dominion inherited in perpetuity, not only on earth but even beyond death.

When he saw that they were illustrious gentlefolk, King Bamba made a sign to One-Eye and the Moor.

"Shall we be on our way?" asked the Moor.

64

"What is to be gotten on the way?" asked One-Eye.

"Gold *castellanos*, finery and jewels," answered King Bamba.

"How shall we proceed?" asked the Moor.

"Hard on their heels," answered King Bamba.

"Keep an eye out for Death," the Trotter warned.

"I have no fear of the reaper," said King Bamba, hurrying off, keeping close to the walls, concealed amongst the shadows.

A stone's throw away One-Eye and the Moor followed him.

Pero Meñique slowly crossed the square. He probed the emptiness, the ground and the walls to right and left, above and below, as if he were testing hardness and softness, distance and proximity with the tip of his cane.

We left behind the spectral towers of the Moors' Gate, the cramped, shuttered houses in the *aljama*, Calle de Yeseros, Calle de los Mancebos, Calle del Toro and many others, winding, uneven and steep.

The light shed by smoking torches and oil lamps revealed through open doors and windows the insignia and tools of blacksmiths and patten makers, tailors and mercers, wax-chandlers and carpenters and other craftsmen.

Here and there Pero Meñique conjectured the shape of a rock, the length of a wall, the earth's dampness, an unexpected hole, ever alert to the chamber-potfuls of urine and excrement tossed from the windows of houses. More swiftly than I had thought possible for a blind man, he walked with the resolute gait of those who are hungry and know where the food is waiting for them; at times he nearly fell, more often through his own impatience than because of the hazards of the road.

"It is deepest night," he declared, "and because we dawdled in the square talking with our friends about matters of small comfort to the spirit, we did not hear the bells of the clock above the Guadalajara Gate chime Vespers, and now we are tardy in taking our ease at an inn known to myself where the wenches are given to lewdness. You will know when we are drawing near, for you will see along the street sundry monks and nuns furtively entering and leaving darkened houses. Before the door stands a man known as the Clapper, who rocks back and forth on his crutches while he informs the bawdy-house keepers of who comes and goes without. When you espy him, you must say to me, 'This basin is as miraculous as the one in San Millán de la Cogolla.'"

Nevertheless, we still had a long way to go up hills and down alleys where nothing moved but ourselves and no steps echoed but our own, frequently returning to the same place when we missed the way.

"I can see the man called the Clapper," I said, when I had made him out swinging to and fro in front of the house.

Pero Meñique knocked at the door with his cane, and a small head in a saffron wimple appeared at a window concealed in the dark wall.

"Who may you be, and what do you seek at this hour of the night?" the woman asked, in the manner of one looking for something which has dropped to the ground amongst the shadows.

"I am Pero Meñique," he whispered, as if the street were peopled with invisible bodies curious about his presence before the brothel.

"Who?" she asked again.

"Pero Meñique, the blind man," he answered more loudly.

"I hate blind men," she snapped.

"Lower your voice, for the ears of the law might hear us and have us whipped or set naked in the pillory," he begged.

"In that case, away with you."

"I am looking for Francisca Hernández."

"The one with no nostrils?"

"This one has them, and big ones, too."

"Then they must surely be like a man's privates, which disappear during the day and grow out again at night," said the woman.

"Open the door for me now," he pleaded.

"Tell me, who is that with you?"

"A son I found along the way."

"Can he be trusted?"

"I would put my hands into the fire for him."

"And promptly singe them."

"If need be."

The door opened and closed so fast that we scarcely had time to slip inside. We found ourselves in a cold, damp passage with a low ceiling, narrow walls and a sloping floor.

"That door seems as cunningly fashioned as the door a Spaniard made in Flanders through which one could enter but never see open," said Pero as he put his foot into a basin of water someone had left on the ground.

"A blind man walking along a dark corridor is doubly blind," I commented cheerfully.

From a few paces beyond in the darkness a woman's voice inquired, "What has Pero the blind man brought us?"

"A son I encountered on the way," he answered.

"A foundling?"

"No, a stripling."

"What does he have in his pouch?"

"Who? Juan Cabezón or Pero Meñique?"

"Pero Meñique, what does he have in his pouch?"

"Provisions."

"Has he no newly stamped golden *castellanos*?"

"In his imagination."

"Any *excelentes*?"

"No."

"*Enriques*?"

"I dream of them every night."

"Does he at least have some silver coins fresh from the royal mints?" persisted the woman's voice.

"I have coins struck elsewhere."

"Show them to me."

"No, for you might keep them."

"Then you shall not pass."

"I will display them in the pouch," said Pero Meñique.

"No, take them out that I may see them."

"There is a danger that one may stick to your fingers."

"I shall not touch them."

"Where the devil are you?"

"Over here."

And by the light of a candle a woman older than her voice had suggested materialized, seated on a wooden bench. There was a black hole where her nose should have been and arches drawn with soot in place of eyebrows. Her tongue came and went between her toothless gums and rounded lips. Her withered, battered, scarred flesh was visible through the tears in her saffron skirt. When she saw that Pero Meñique was standing before her but did not show her the coins, she began to insult him in a resounding but unintelligible voice, as if she were sucking on the words in her mouth. While she spoke her right lid closed over the eye, although the other one remained open, staring at us.

"Have you found a new way of talking to yourself?" Pero asked her.

"Wait, you haven't heard anything yet," the old woman retorted.

"Quickly, slip your hand into the pouch and take out an eighth of a piece of eight, which is square, with an *F* topped by a crown on one side and on the other side an *I* with a crown over it as well," he whispered to me.

I grabbled among the coins in the pouch, seeking with my fingers the one he had described, but when I drew out a different coin, he asked me with alarm, "What does it look like?"

"The royal coat of arms is on the face, and on the reverse the yoke and bundle of arrows, emblems of the Sovereigns; on the border of both sides is written: '*Fernandus et Elizabeth Rex et Regina Castellae et Legionis et Aragonum et Siciliae*': 'Fernando and Isabel, King and Queen of Castile and León and Aragón and Sicily,' " I said.

"That is a silver royal—put it back immediately."

I plucked out a gold coin bisected obliquely by a band whose extremities disappeared into a dragon's mouth.

"That is a doubloon," he said. "Has she seen it?"

"No."

"I will search for the coin myself," he said, quickly finding the one he wanted.

"Just what are you up to?" the old woman asked gruffly, for she suspected we were gulling her.

"The coin I am putting in your hand is one fourth of an *excelente*," Pero said to me. "Note well if the foreside bears the faces of the Kings looking at each other, with the motto *'Quos Deus conjunxit homo non separet'*: 'Whom God has joined together let no man put asunder,' and the reverse the royal coat of arms. If it is the one I say, show it to her without relinquishing it and put it right back in the pouch."

"Enter," croaked the old woman in a hoarse voice after I had showed the coin to her in the blink of an eye, leaving her in doubt as to what she had seen.

"Don't stand there like a dog barking at thunderclaps," a mannish woman who opened a second door for us admonished Pero Meñique.

"I do not dislike this blind man's body, but his eyes disturb me: they stare with such white fixity," said another woman, hidden behind the first.

"Who brought this beggarly starveling, this sand-eyed satyr, this thirsty fellow of no fortune?" asked yet another denizen from within her room.

"I brought myself," answered Pero, swiveling his head towards the voice.

"Beware of this man, for he is a dog with those he loves not," said a woman of considerable size and weight whose head was festooned with colored ribbons. She had been spying from behind a door.

"Francisca Hernández?" asked Pero Meñique.

"The fat lady that nobody loves," she replied.

"Francisca!" he exclaimed.

"This woman is too big for you, she will smother you in her embrace," I told him.

"I am not afraid of her," he answered, "for I prize females for their corpulence, I judge them by their bulk, and I subdue them by force so they cannot escape from my clutches."

"Do not fret yourself over this man, he walks through the world sinning," she assured me. "I wager that if he were privileged to see two moons in the sky, he would take them for breasts and stretch out his fingers in the night to fondle them."

"And if the gibbous moon is lit up by the sun, why shouldn't I draw near to its warmth?" replied Pero.

"It must be midsummer moon, for you are at the height of your madness," she said.

"Show me your crescents presto."

"First take off that black cloak, you look like a crow mimicking a man."

"Thus is my night, I am mourning for the deceased," said Pero Meñique.

"Since when do you have dead?"

"I mean that I am mourning for the deceased in myself that has not been able to see the light of day, for whosoever is deprived in his lifetime of the sun's marvels is like a dead man," he explained.

"Don't be so gloomy."

"Very well then, let me feel the lay of the land."

"Have patience until we are in the room."

"As the saying goes, women, wine and dice will bring a man to lice," said Pero.

"Who are you?" asked one of the voices again from the darkness.

"The first man to laugh when he was born."

"Liar," said the voice.

"And who may you be?" Pero asked in return.

"An honest woman disposed to be a whore, a whore who longs to be a mother and a grandmother," answered the voice.

"It is better to marry than to burn," said Pero as he began to walk on.

"Give me a cake of Neapolitan soap to turn my hands white, give me some of the marrow of cows, sheep and deer which the town grocers have brought from Saragossa," Francisca Hernández requested of him.

"Is this not the same blind man who stands on the pavement singing in the atrium of San Andrés?" asked a tall woman in the dun-colored dress of a peasant, with dark chestnut eyes like dry tinder and short hair under her saffrony headcloth.

"It is not the same one, for that blind singer is lame and his breath stinks of the bowels of the earth and of his own body, especially of his own body," he retorted.

"Don Pero Meñique knows all about physicking and pandering to public women," boasted Francisca Hernández, as if she were bragging about her own son.

"Blind by birth?" the other woman asked.

"Blinded by a dagger wielded by an evil hand," said Pero.

"Are you a man or a monstrous Cyclops?" the other woman continued.

"Man is the best monster in the world," said Pero.

"And just what is your loutish face looking at?" she spat at me when she realized I hadn't taken my eyes off her. "Are you perchance the son of a horse and a jenny?"

"He's a paschal lamb," said Francisca Hernández.

"Throw that bone to some other dog," the woman replied.

"Aren't we ruttish tonight," Francisca snorted.

"I catch a whiff of skirt," said Pero Meñique as he sidled up to the strumpet in the yellowish coif.

"No sooner do you sniff her out than you would have her," Francisca scolded him.

"I am like the King, Don Fernando, who loves his wife but lavishes himself on other women," said Pero.

"Do you really love this friend of yours, all gray, wrinkled, bent and bleary?" the woman in the yellow headcloth asked her.

"Love is blind, the same as hatred and fortune, as a trull like you who consorts with a goat-bearded monk who burns Jewish women and small boys' mothers should know," retorted Francisca.

"There's no doubt about it, when you fuck in the muck, Peter's the same as Paul," the other woman shot back.

"She should know, who has rubbed her rump in every bordello in Andalusia," Francisca jeered.

"I was daughter to goatherds, the last of four children, and made much of by my cousins, the cowherds. Having been brought up in the bosom of our Holy Mother Church, on my wedding night as I lay on the nuptial bed in my nightshirt about to celebrate the communion of the flesh with my husband, the shepherd from the hill, an archbishop had me abducted, and it was he who held me in his arms that first night," recounted the woman in the saffrony headcloth.

"*Jus primae noctis, droit du seigneur*," remarked Pero. "And what happened next? Did the archbishop give the bloody sheets to the witnesses to show to the crier?"

"My husband the shepherd repudiated me, and I spent the following night in a monastery tucked between two elderly monks who slept stark naked, using me as a bed warmer."

"And is that how the daughter of goatherds became a hedge whore?" Pero Meñique inquired.

"Nay, for a company of Moorish horsemen who rode about with the guard of Don Enrique Cuarto, ravishing youths and maidens throughout the towns and countryside of this kingdom, snatched me away from the monks and after having their way with me for several days gave me to an Ethiopian dwarf in the King's retinue, from whom I escaped to fly with an esquire I encountered by the roadside. That base fellow abandoned me at the first inn where we spent the night, and thence I made my way as best I could to Madrid," said the woman.

"They say that rapeseed oil helps loosen the chest," said Pero Meñique.

"Who asked for your advice, you bleary-eyed bumbler?"

"A blind man gropes at the world with his hand because he is in the dark, but he is no fool," said Pero, "and if I could see your flabby face I would not come within an arm's length of your body."

"You ought to be in church praying to Santa Lucía to give you eyes so you could walk upright on the thorny paths of this kingdom instead of wantoning your way through the world," chided the woman.

"I won't go there, for they would rather close my eyes under a tombstone than show me the light," Pero shuddered.

"Then God give you good luck, my child, you already know the way to the privy, a good ways from the bedchambers. Within, it is dark and airless, but there is an opening onto the stream," said the woman.

"You've swallowed enough henbane for tonight, now it's time for humping," said Francisca to Pero.

"You mean hemlock" he said, tilting his head to one side as if her words dropped down from the ceiling.

"That's what I said. Let's go to my room."

"We shall both lie with Francisca," Pero muttered into my neck, mistaking it for an ear. "Her body, being so large, shall be yours from the waist down and mine from the waist up."

"You will both take a fall. That woman is like a winged cow when you mount her," said the peasant woman behind us.

"Have no fear. Loving makes me forget I am blind, and I shall fly holding fast to her flanks," Pero crowed.

"Follow me this way; someone has blown out the candles and the corridor is passing dim," Francisca warned.

"I will guide you, for I know my way around in the dark," said Pero.

"The ground is stamped earth with an occasional patch of tiles which are easy to stumble over," said Francisca, leading Pero by the hand as she jabbed her fingers into my neck.

"A lathered beard soon dries in bed," mumbled a toothless beldam from within a doorless room.

"Good even, Doña Urraca," Francisca greeted her. "How is it with you?"

"I am worse off than a whore in Lent," whined the old woman.

"May I ask why?"

"Though we shall all be bald one thousand years hence, there's no catching of old birds with chaff."

"Truth may be blamed, but cannot be shamed," said Pero.

"They are not all men who piss against the wall," the hag retorted angrily.

"She comes from the boneyard and asks about death," jeered Pero.

"I already died and saw who cried," the old woman sputtered.

"Who has neither fools nor whores among his kindred was born of a stroke of thunder," said a woman looking out of a window, the lantern she waved beneath her chin making it seem as if smoke were rising from her chest.

"Speak of the devil, and he appears," snapped the old woman.

"An ass is known by its ears," said the woman at the window.

"Beware of me, for I am spare at the spigot and let it out at the bunghole," threatened the old woman.

"What can you expect from a hog but a grunt?" the window woman parried.

A bearded woman grabbed my arm through a broken door and beckoned, "This way, you great hobbledehoy."

"Leave my son alone, you furry female. Like a nanny goat's, your knobbles betray your years," said Pero Meñique.

"Water is medicine to the sick man who is destined to live," she sniffed.

"If you seek love for your son, I can offer him my fragrant white lily," said the woman at the window.

"Shave it off, shave it off," hissed the toothless hag.

"Too much painting has scoured the shine from your face, ruined your teeth, wrinkled your hide and given you bad breath," the bearded woman railed at her.

"Rub it in, rub it in," growled the old woman.

"The rouge you daub on your cheeks and breasts to make them rosy has turned you ashy black," the bearded woman went on.

"How you can say that to Doña Urraca, when your own color is feigned as well," said the woman at the window, "in addition to wearing that beard which almost reaches your testicles."

"Thus was I born, testiculate and hairy," she began. "As a child my stones were so heavy I could barely walk. In my girlhood I played at thimblerig, catch-as-catch-can, bumblepuppy and quoits. No boy dared kiss me, on account of my hoarse voice and my fists. When I was full-grown I came here to vanquish men and my hunger, and I have surpassed myself. Wouldn't you like to come with me?"

"I have no use for a virago," answered the woman in the window.

"If I had *castellanos* to pay you, you would come with me," said the bearded woman.

"Were you to lie swathed in gold in the street, no one would pick you up," the other one sneered.

In the next room we came upon a carefully washed and combed Moorish girl wearing large hoop earrings and a red linen blouse.

"Zaina the Shammer does it salaaming," said the bearded lady when she saw us staring at the Saracen.

"This Moor professes to be a geomancer and claims she can see into the bowels of the earth, through stone walls and inside closed coffers," Francisca whispered to us. "She swears she can make out distant objects in the night and see through clothing. When she walks abroad, she says, she knows where there are underground springs and what people who pass her are thinking. Her real name is Zaida, and she is as graceful as her namesake the egret. Her father married her off at the age of eleven, and her husband repudiated her for being barren. She wandered alone and rejected through Andalusia, until she took up with a Christian who had carnal knowledge of her and then brought her to this house."

"Tell me, sister, how you can mortify me thus by divulging my secret, when I have done you so many services?" cried Zaina as she disappeared into her room.

"I should never have betrayed her secret, for she hears and knows everything, even if it is spoken in a soft voice on the other side of town," said Francisca. "I shall beg her forgiveness anon."

"Walk on," said Pero Meñique. "It is almost midnight."

We entered a room. A wooden bed was flanked by a Moorish rug and a chamber pot; a termite-ridden bench and a dilapidated chest stood against the wall. A little stool was placed before a small table covered with glass vials, gallipots, cosmetic lotions, nail enamels, tooth whiteners, scissors, a saucer filled with kohl, a comb, a hand mirror and a cake of soap. No curtain covered the window, and the door that led to the privy was off its hinges. The room was lit by three candles impaled on a copper pricket.

Francisca immediately set a jug of wine on the table and put a candle in my hand to illuminate her while she removed her shirt. The blind man's tremulous voice seemed to pierce her stout body as he sang, *"The game is worthy of the candle, let us burn it at both ends."*

With no modesty whatsoever, just as if she were alone in the room, before my eyes she unloosed her big breasts, big thighs, big buttocks. Not yet satisfied with her nakedness, she took off pendants, bracelets, earrings, the curved comb that held her part in place and something that looked like wooden teeth. Nevertheless, she still seemed to be dressed, by virtue of the abundance of rouge on her cheeks, civet on her eyebrows, gum resin in her hair and oils and perfumes anointing her body.

"You are the only man I know with whom I can feel comfortable without blowing out the candle," she said to Pero.

"I grieve in my very soul that my eyes are deprived of this prodigious fleshiness," he sighed.

"Don't stroke my back with your raspy hands, as it is somewhat chapped," Francisca cautioned him.

"I had a lovesick brother whose lips were chapped, and the girls in Jaén did not care to kiss him on the mouth," he said.

"You look like a deer with lopped antlers, your member calls to mind a bone out of joint. Were you a flagellant, did they flog your flanks, or are these strokes from the goddess Venus?" she asked after undressing him.

"The mere recollection of monastic life makes my hair stand on end. I grew thinner and thinner, but my fasting was never sufficient: to feel truly virtuous my body had to disappear entirely from the world," said Pero Meñique. "There was a superior who took great pleasure in whipping me with a knout, until the blood spurted from the wounds. The more cowed and sore I was, the more he scourged me, spattering the walls as if he were slaughtering a sheep in my cell. I can still see him standing behind me, foaming at the mouth, his cowl like a hawk's hood shielding his eyes as frenzied and unrelenting he chastised my poor flesh with holy discipline, interposing neither surcease nor clothing between his furor and my pain. I clenched my teeth and wanted to weep or pray, but the whoreson never let up in his lashings, and when he saw me turn pale and faint he had at me even harder."

"He nearly finished you off with all his penances, for he was on the verge of turning you into a martyr of sacred Spain," said Francisca.

"I give thanks to heaven that in his enthusiasm he did not draw and quarter me, for afterwards I learned that prior to becoming a monk he had been a trooper of the Holy Brotherhood, one of those who unhinge your jaw to dislodge secrets and chop off a hand to brand the robber. The man merely dusted me off, and to my good fortune he never knew that the disciple he mortified by day succumbed to temptation at night and caressed imaginary wenches on the walls. At last I escaped by counterfeiting sickness when weakened by such a great loss of blood that beneath his very eyes I fell into agony. The predatory monk grudgingly released me and vouchsafed me to go to the hospital."

"You're dazzling me with that candle, fuzzyface!" Francisca said as she took it from my hand and set it on a rickety table. "Just hearing about the monk makes you shudder."

"He reminds me of Garci Sánchez Trémulo, the son of Don Sancho and Doña Urraca, who always trembled before entering the fray but once on the battlefield fought like a lion," Pero mused.

"Show me your nutmegs," she coaxed, undoing my clothes. "I want to see if they quake as much as your hands do."

"He's still very bashful and has to be taught to plunge," he said.

"I think I have found the corn silk," she said, fishing more with her hands than her eyes.

"Your breasts are shaped like Greek letters," he said. "Show them to the boy so he may learn the tongue of shadowy Heraclitus."

"He has already been weaned," she said, "but he has yet to couple."

"Even now Matins are ringing," he complained.

"Your hands are pincers," she protested.

"Imagine yourself stretched out on the pavement in the atrium, given over to prayer," he said, pushing her towards the bed.

"I have come here for dalliance, not for blasphemy," she frowned.

"Hee-hee-hee, the boy has just dug his claws into my rump," said Francisca, referring to me. "He is drawn to the smell of warm meat with the astonishment of a man who marvels because the cunt is cleft, and who puts his hand to where the path divides."

"Paint her for me in her entirety," he begged me. "Is the black rose between her legs? Is her belly roomy and slack? Are the moons on her chest round and milky white?"

"She has in abundance all that you mention, but the Castilian tongue would not suffice for me to describe her curves," I said.

"Will you love me as much when my breasts are sagging, when I no longer have teeth or hair, when my eyes are bleary and two walnuts could fit into the sockets?" Francisca asked him.

"I shall love you somewhat less than now, but more than yesterday," he said cautiously.

"Well then, come here," said the woman.

"Let us go together," Pero said to me, "but be careful, for entering her is like going into a damp room—you may come out with a cold."

"Show me how."

"Take the woman naked, starting at the root, as if she were a tree which lies down beneath your body, or clasp her all in your arms, swathe yourself in her, storm her flesh with great bites, but enjoy her slowly," he advised me.

"You do learn quickly," she said, "only mark out your boundaries between the peaks, and avert the candle's flame from my face."

"Our flesh is soft, our union perfect," Pero crooned.

"So it is, but you put me in mind of the physician from Orgaz who felt for a pulse in the shoulder: what you seek is in front."

"Do you have enough?" he asked me.

"What I have is much for another, but little for me," I answered.

"Before you bite into her, are your teeth clean?"

"And my hands washed," I replied.

"Then the rest is simple: if two goes into one, Pero will be left," he said.

"I shall leave you the whole cow," I offered.

"I am crazy about cows," said he as he turned towards her.

"Be careful you don't fall to the floor in your ardent abandon," she warned him.

"We always fall into the hole we dig," he declared.

"Today is a good day and the morrow will be better," she murmured.

"By this beard that no one ever tweaked before, which not even the wool carders of Castile can untangle, I long to love you openly, imagining that, just as at the wedding of Isabel and Fernando, there will be a witness to wave the testimonial sheet stained with blood to the sound of tabors and trumpets at daybreak," said Pero.

"How did you come to this house?" I asked Francisca.

"I was a daughter of lechery, my father a gentleman who lay with a peasant woman. I grew up as a servant and became a streetwalker. The man who brought me to this inn was a sharper who had paid with his thumb after he was caught gaming in taverns. All I have left of him are a few cards from the fresh deck he gave me when the law publicly proclaimed him a villain. I never saw him again, for the night before, he had tried his luck until he was stripped of all he ever had and ready to wager his mother, had she been there at his side."

Pero's face peered out from between her legs, resembling a severed head displayed in an iron cage, and he began to sing:

> "Three Moorish girls ensnared me
> in Jaén:
> Axa, Fátima and Marién."

"Every cock crows on his own dunghill," she said, slipping away from him.

At the same instant Pero tried to grab her, groping in the air, but he encountered only a table, the wall, emptiness in her stead.

"I heard no door open nor steps walking away," he said, trampling the clothes scattered on the floor, "so where can she be?"

"Hungry hands flutter in the air but cannot find their morsel," said Francisca from elsewhere in the room.

"My friend, where are you? Have you made a study of those magical arts whereby Don Enrique of Villena rendered himself invisible to the human eye?"

"You can paw over here where I am, but you won't find me," she answered.

77

"It wearies me to lurch about blindly in this bulk of a body, I want to get hold of you. Stand still."

"Pat the air more slowly, you might hit on something over there," she hinted.

"Stay where I hear your voice," he pleaded.

"Keep close to the wall, for I am yonder."

"Come down to earth; you're teasing me and the void tastes of gall."

"Hate makes love grow worse and grow better," she said.

"It is cruelty to trifle thus with a blind man. But perhaps you are trying to inveigle the son I found on the road today into favoring you?"

"Tush, old mollycoddle, you are as broken-bellied as you are jealous. I am not gamboling with the paschal lamb, I am in the arms of a shaggy, big-footed lummox who just came into the room."

"The second cock has already crowed and soon we must depart," he complained.

"Unravel this enigma and I will be all yours," said Francisca, thrusting her breasts at Pero as if they would be his prize for solving the riddle.

> *"My lady, I will speak*
> *words of great comfort:*
> *it came when you were wed*
> *and pushing it to and fro*
> *affords you much sport;*
> *when you see it I know*
> *you always feel pleasure*
> *and grasp it in your hand*
> *to insert this fine treasure."*

"Now is not the time for games or riddles; moreover, the opposite is always the right answer. I give up," he said as he swiftly shot out his hand towards the place whence came the voice, only to meet with a wall.

"The answer is a ring," said Francisca, pushing him to sit down, but as there was no chair, he remained folded over in the air, as if suspended in time. "Are you content now?"

"Oh, very much so," he answered.

There was a knock at the door.

"Who is it?' she cried out.

"Me," said a familiar voice from the other side. "Don Rodrigo Rodríguez."

"I know nobody of that name," replied Francisca.

"It is my friend the dwarf, Don Rodrigo Rodríguez," said Pero Meñique.

"Here I am, very like the spirits that materialize at night," he announced when I opened the door.

"Whence come you at this hour of the morning?" Pero Meñique asked him.

"I took no notice when you left the square, and I have walked half the night in search of you throughout the town," said the dwarf. "I am only saddened to see more persons in the room than beds. But do not trouble yourselves over me, for I can sleep leaning against the wall or lying on the table."

"At this time of night all you will get is a bed of bricks, rags or stones," said Francisca. "Choose which befits you and be off at once."

"I am a humble fellow who does not mind having bare earth for his couch, a rough stone for his pillow and the sky's vault for his roof," said Don Rodrigo Rodríguez.

No longer attending to his words, Francisca stretched the rough soles and jagged toenails of her bare feet towards me. Sitting on the bed, I examined her thighs, whose hairs had been plucked with little pincers, I smelled the sour saliva she had used to burnish her skin, I touched the pearly mass of her belly. Pero Meñique lay down between us, resting his head on her stomach as if he wished to sleep or be stroked.

"If the Moorish woman who is dozing next door would care to rid me of fleas as well, I should not take it amiss," said the dwarf, his back to the wall, like a lackey sitting on a stool.

"Zaina is wearing her smock and she durst not shift it while she has her courses," said Francisca.

"If she would deign to shift her smock, she would be clean enough to bed down and breakfast with me," Don Rodrigo Rodríguez insisted.

"Zaina is not only wearing her smock but she also has her hempen rag on, and when in that condition she has a great abhorrence of men," replied Francisca.

"I would take her no matter how bloody," said Don Rodrigo Rodríguez, "for in my short life I have yet to find someone to love, and there are nights when my loneliness is such that I think I am living there where there is no one and not here where I am."

"I do not understand you clearly, but I am sure you are right, by reason of the great sincerity of your words," said Francisca.

"Do not mock me, for if I had been my own creator I should have done otherwise: a few more inches in the leg and a few less in the shoulder, arms less long and chest less prominent, eyes less bulging and mouth smaller, more smiling. Moreover, as I was fashioned by another, I often forget who I am and the burden I bear, and I muddle what I should say, mistaking myself for the Cid Campeador, Bernardo del Carpio or even Doña Sancha."

"From the size of your body I would infer that your mother was a hen . . . an honest hen," said Francisca.

"I never thought of that," said Pero Meñique. "Come closer so I may feel whether you are at all like a chicken."

"Bend down a bit and I shall give you much pleasure, for I am as yet untried and yearn to be quickened, body and soul, in this squat figure which perambulates the earth," Don Rodrigo Rodríguez said to Francisca.

"If you think that you will share a bed this night with Doña Francisca Hernández, you are perfectly wrong," Pero Meñique exclaimed.

"I have had my fill of talk tonight but we have yet to go to bed," she said. "Let this halfling stand guard at the door, and give me your son as if he were my own."

"So be it," cried Pero Meñique, rushing at her as if she were an exquisite delicacy he would stuff into his mouth with both hands.

"First scratch me," said Francisca, her kohl-rimmed eyes ablaze, "for my belly and bum are itching me to death."

"Close your eyes and jump in, you whited sepulcher," Pero Meñique muttered to himself as he pressed his face against her naked buttocks and clutched at her breasts.

"Have a care! Instead of caressing, you claw at me, you give blind man's buffets and wild punches," Francisca screeched.

"Where is your body's red spider, where is your fathomless mouth?" he moaned as he tried to penetrate a patch of flesh with no hole in it.

"It pleases me to feel a man's bottom while he is yoked to a female," Don Rodrigo Rodríguez said, fondling Pero's fundament and panting in his ear. "I am a capon, for as a child my mother squeezed my testicles between her fingers until they became soft as wax, but she did not mutilate me for vice, as that Lydian king did his women, to have greater use of them, but for virtue, since we eunuchs can go among nude women without any danger."

"Go stand by the wall, for the straining of your heart beating with the force of a man engaged in love's combat perturbs me overmuch," Pero Meñique said to him with an odd smile.

"I must confess that, due to the state of my privates, I cannot love man or maid and am only able to satisfy myself using my eyes and the figures of my fancy," the dwarf admitted.

"I understand you well enough, but I request that now you move over there, very much over there, for you are inhibiting the current of my desires and the flow of my passion," said Pero Meñique.

"Love her as if I were not present, as if I were not at your side," urged Don Rodrigo Rodríguez.

"I am asking you one more time to station yourself farther away, next to the wall or the door, for here we might kick you or cuff you, since lovemaking waxes more hectic as the flames are fed," Pero Meñique warned him.

"I suggest that instead of turning to the strumpets in this house, who are too hard-hearted to coddle cracked nuts, go rather to the convent founded by the followers of Santo Domingo, beyond the Balnadú Gate, near the lower enclosure wall of this town, where there is a well the saint caused to be dug whose sweet water, when drunk devoutly, is a remedy against fevers and other ailments of the body," said Francisca.

"But for now, stand facing the wall and imagine the posturing of frogs, for considerable instruction can be gotten therefrom," said Pero Meñique.

"Snuff the candles and the oil lamp and puff yourself out of the room," she said, nestling the blind man's head between her breasts as if she would bury it there.

"Awaken me when the bells ring Lauds, no matter how deep asleep I may be. We must be on our way before daybreak, as everyone knows me in this town," Pero said to me.

And then, from the other side of the bed, I freely perused the naked woman, I stroked her arms and thighs and even kissed her neck. The perverse dwarf took advantage of the blind man's darkness, and without blowing out the lights he followed close at hand the jiggling and plunging of the embrace, his small body repeatedly dodging the slaps. It began to rain and a stiff wind crossed the dawn, battered the rooftops and whistled through the streets. In my dreams the earth turned tawny, was besprinkled from the sky, and a million white seeds lulled me to sleep.

When I awoke a bluish light coming through the cracks in the door was filling the room. Pero Meñique was sitting on the bed wearing a string of onions around his neck, peeling and eating the layers of a bulb with hungry diligence, as if at any moment an invisible being might snatch it out of his hands and mouth. Francisca slept, splayed out and uncovered, wet within and damp without. There was something wounded and withered about her whitish flesh, and her face beneath its daubing was pale and ashen. Last night's intoxication seemed far away in the past.

"Those onions will do you much harm," I said to Pero.

"She set me to eating them because she claims they augment virility and increase the sperm," he explained.

"The bells already rang Prime and we did not hear them, as we were all asleep," said Don Rodrigo Rodríguez, virtually unnoticed in a corner.

"We must leave right away, for I am too well known in Madrid," said Pero, jumping out of bed.

And so we left the sleeping house, apparently unheard by all. The lights burning in the white morning saw us take leave of Don Rodrigo Rodríguez in the street and proceed down a hill pocked with puddles which reflected a long wall and bits of sky.

"Have they tilted the town?" Pero Meñique asked me, still drunk from loving and sleep.

"Your imagination is tilting it," I answered.

"That is what so humiliates blind men. When they think the path is dry they step in puddles; when they are sure the road is flat they topple into a ravine," he grumbled, his waterlogged shoes sloshing in the wet.

We bid each other farewell anon, vowing to meet again.

The clock over the Guadalajara Gate had just struck the hour of Nones one day when Pero Meñique came to fetch me. He looked like a blind peacock, his faded hair fanning out in the sunshine in a wheel of colors as, without uttering a word, he strode off, his staff extended like a drawn sword, since for him walking down the street was to enter into a skirmish where there were enemies lurking within walls, snares on the ground and wayward pillars just around the corner.

"To sniff is to live," he exulted, altogether drunk on smelling, busy waving, gesticulating and grimacing at the invisible beings he imagined were saluting him as they went by, until he stumbled over a faceless lump of a woman so thoroughly shrouded in gray garments that only the tip of her nose and the knuckles of her fingers, which clutched at a long wooden rosary attached to her waist, were to be seen.

"Accursed clumsy blind man," she muttered.

"I perceive the scent of a virgin maiden," Pero said.

"You may be right as to the virgin part, but as to the maiden, I am not sure whether it is a girl or a grandam, child or ghost that lies here, shut off from life and in retreat from the world, its body imprisoned in a cell of cloth. The heat of day makes us all sweat, which is why I cannot comprehend a creature like herself wrapped in this heavy apparel on which the sun beats leadenly down. I do believe that since the day she was born no one on earth has seen her naked, not even herself . . . save her mother, in the first hours after she was delivered," I said.

"Many of these maidens who live cloistered in the streets spend their nights unclothed in convents, coupling with lewd clergymen," Pero remarked, pausing when he heard the tinkling of a little bell that a young thief with an iron ring about his neck wore on his head to make his presence known.

Eyes popping with greed, the crafty knave stared hard at Pero, ready to pounce on him at any moment, but when he realized that Pero was waiting for just that, he limped down the street looking every bit a dog driven away.

"Within the enceinte, near the royal stables, stands the Campo del Rey Hospital, dedicated to the Immaculate Conception of Our Lady and

endowed with twelve beds for the care of ailing dowried women; the
King Don Juan and the Queen Doña Juana founded a brotherhood there
for burying the dead who lie unsepulchered in the streets and fields, as
well as the unclaimed victims of justice and those who are struck down
by loathsome diseases,'' said Pero Meñique when the little bell could
no longer be heard, already far away in his own darkness.

"The sight of that pilfering lad has saddened me greatly, for I felt as
if I were looking upon another boy much like myself, but who goes
through life contented, whereas I must make my way in the world
hapless and hungry,'' I complained.

"Both of you may be nothing more than phantoms walking the
streets,'' replied Pero Meñique, "as alien to the ground you tread as a
sailor who disembarks in a foreign port.''

We followed the poplars along the river and, once beyond the walls,
took the Segovia Bridge down as far as the San Lázaro Hospital, climbing
again with the walls up the Cuesta de las Vistillas and the Narigues del
Pozacho Tower, until we reached the Church of Santa María, the Caños
del Peral and the tower that bears the name of Gaona. In a ravine a
woman, believing herself unseen, had hoisted up her chemise, display-
ing her privy parts among the branches to every passerby.

"This little church nestled against the *alcázar* is called San Miguel's,
and along with Santa María's, it is one of the oldest in town, and was
dubbed la Sagra when they built the other San Miguel's—San Miguel
de los Ocotes, that is,'' said Pero, just as if we had passed in front of
the church.

"Can't you tell we are on the Cuesta de los Caños Viejos? Don't you
perceive how rugged the path is, how difficult to walk upon, how la-
bored our breathing?'' I asked him, when I read in his face that he
thought we had taken another way.

"Whatever lies within and without the walls of this city is merely an
extension of my own person,'' he replied. "Its precincts are my limbs,
and if we happen to be going down one street and I speak of another,
I am not mistaken, for I carry about in my breast that street down which
I walk *in absentia*. Its history revolves in my mind; I open its doors
and I peer into its past and future windows, thinking to see the street
I dream I am walking on.''

"Be it in the future or in the past, in reality or in dreams, I know
naught of wherever we are going,'' I admitted.

"My nostrils are filling with an odor of sanctity, by which I surmise
that we are near the stream of San Ginés,'' he said. "I perceive in all its
clarity the odor of these waters which hark back to antiquity. I give ear
to their murmur of yore. In the olden days there was nothing here but

the Guadalajara Gate and the suburbs of San Ginés, where the Mozarabic Christians dwelled, and San Martín's quarter."

Just then a withered old man appeared wearing the tabard and scarlet badge of the Jews; his beard and white locks, by virtue of the prohibition he was under not to cut them, were long, ragged and bushy. With an air of eternal resignation he trudged down the street, not like someone who goes from one part of town to another, but like a man crossing space and time. Thrust into that caftan of coarse cloth and roomy sleeves, long, wide and very like a laborer's, his body seemed to be imprisoned, affronted, aggrieved. He was talking to himself, soundlessly moving his lips with the expression of one who is carrying on an immemorial, uninterrupted dialogue between himself and God. He was a physician who by virtue of his science was allowed to leave the *aljama* and enter Christian houses to care for sick children. His Castilian aspect was as pronounced as that of the other inhabitants of the Kingdom of Castile, and he would not have been distinguishable from them had it not been for the signs. When he passed near me I thought I heard his voice emerging from my own body to say, in the soft archaic timbre of the poet from Tudela, "All my bones cry out: Adonai. Who is like unto Thee?"

Meanwhile, oblivious to his presence, Pero Meñique stroked the thick trunk of an oak tree with both hands, touching the bark and leaves as if this would increase his knowledge of it; something about its hardness fascinated the blind man, who was so like a human tree himself with his rootlike feet and hair thrusting branchlike towards the sky.

"Jewels contrived by divine wisdom are these leaves which I cannot admire in their entirety. As far as I know, no tree in the world is the twin of another in size, shape and color, and if the most minute details differentiate sister leaves on the same branch, how much more so between one tree and the other, between one oak grove and another oak grove," he mused, tracing the veins of a leaf with the tip of his right index finger.

He ambled on during this marveling discourse without paying much heed to where he walked, staff tucked under one arm and stepping carelessly, so that several times he would have fallen into a hole or smacked his face against a wall if I had not swiftly grabbed him in midair or thrust my hand between his nose and the bricks. Never once did he notice any danger or give thanks for my watchfulness, until at last, upon turning a corner, he tripped over a half-naked dead man who he must have thought was asleep.

"Beg pardon, Your Worship," he said to the stiffened mass.

Behind a crumbling wall a couple was making love dog fashion. Her kohl-rimmed eyes and whitened thighs revealed her to be one of those women whom the rabble call hedge whores, because they frequent the ditches and river basins to ply their trade. The man was merely a bearded rustic used to making the outdoors his home, the stream his bed, a tree his door and the ground his table.

"For trying to save themselves the price of an inn, the law will exhibit these bawdy ruffians in the pillory, and should they relapse, it will give them a year chained up in the fortress," said Pero when he heard their panting.

Farther on, two fierce geese waddled out of a house to hiss at a passing vagabond so covered with patches that his rags seemed fused to his body.

"Ho, you whoreson, there's no better bait than your own buttocks!" Pero Meñique exclaimed, stopping short at the sound of someone being pursued by the geese.

But my eye was drawn, more than to the savage geese, towards the peaks of the Guadarrama, which at that moment were overshadowed by red curdling clouds, and towards the somber holm oaks flanking a road which led I knew not whither and came I knew not whence.

Keeping close to the walls of the tall houses whose roofs drooped like old hats, my blind friend seemed to have the city in his head, to walk along its streets from memory, to cross the yards and squares by hearsay, for he was almost never mistaken as to the particulars of houses and shops or the identity of noises and smells that emerged from the doors and windows behind which craftsmen were concluding their daily work. Occasionally, it is true, the streets did not match the names he gave them, and once he even collided with a mule and begged its pardon, as if it had been a man.

"I heartily forgive Your Worship, albeit you have badly bruised me on one foot and battered my ear," the mule driver replied, giving the beast a voice.

"Stop proffering apologies, for the person standing before you is a quadruped, the offspring of a stallion and a she-ass, or perhaps of a mare and a jackass," I said to him, since he persisted in excusing himself. "A fat muleteer rides upon it backwards, using the tail as a rein, and he is laughing at your expense."

After finding himself thus ridiculed, Pero trudged on pensively, asking me questions that were mortifying to him, such as whether blind men were ugly to look at, whether his body was grotesque when he walked, whether people we met in the street often laughed at him, whether he was unwittingly the butt of many jests, whether his hair and beard were hideous, whether he did not breathe out a fetid smell when he opened his mouth, whether he frequently spoke in error in the presence of situations and persons that were not what he believed them to be, and other similar matters, which I was especially cunning not to answer with truths but rather with examples from fables or with riddles, stammerings and misunderstandings.

My responses did not satisfy him; he took them for mockery as well and began to rebuke me, striking out blindly with his stick and squealing like an infant or a pig, until he heard steps coming towards us. Three beggars approached with outstretched hands. Clad in patches with bandaged wounds, they wore shoes so thin that when they walked the soles of their feet touched the ground. Through the multiple eyes, ears and mouths of their torn doublets the bare caked flesh of their desiccated bodies was visible. They had neither shirts nor breeches, and dirty bits of once-white stuff barely concealed parts of shame more akin to sores and little stalks, withered figs and grape skins than to men's privates. The motley stockings they wore doubtless came from the best hosier in the Kingdom of Castile, the blue, yellow, green and black pieces having been collected in riverside laundries, backyards and the rubbish heaps of towns through which they had passed. Their heads had a blackish cast, hair cut short like sooty stumps of a wood ravaged by poverty, and they appeared to have pods of lice behind their ears. The man in the lead was lame, his shrunken limbs stumbling over each other as if he would fall down at any moment. An earless man came next, puffing as he walked and keeping his balance with great difficulty. Deaf as a post, he staggered like a sailor newly come ashore. A knife or stone had slashed his upper lip in two and sliced his right nostril.

The man in the rear was a weedy spindleshanks stuffed into tight clothes too short for his long extremities. Wedged beneath an arm stiff as a log, the unsteady crutch he leaned on had a broken crosspiece. He was of no particular age, and his chest seemed to be furred with woolen dross or something equally wispy and insubstantial. His milky eyes swiveled in all directions, the pupils like spilled egg whites. This man bereft of sky, for thus alone could his misfortune be described, had no feature in his face on which the eye could rest in pleasant contemplation; all its parts eluded the canons of human beauty. Like his companions, he roamed the world angry with one and all, seeking on the highways for victims to satiate his wrath and assuage his woe. Unaware of other indignities, from time to time he stopped to address the earless man, believing he had the lame one before him, and when he received no answer he cursed between his teeth, lurched forward and cuffed the air, lest the world should slip from beneath his feet and escape from his grasp before he could pummel it.

Seeing them near was even more deplorable than observing them from afar. I had the feeling that whole days went by during which they

put no bread in their mouths, not even a dog's portion for their sustenance. Most likely they had been sleeping in the dust among brambles
and had lain upon stones and been cudgeled by peasants and pelted
with rocks by young rowdies, for every part of their bodies seemed to
have been trounced, mistreated or thrashed.

"This creaky crutch is a bad mount," grumbled the blind cripple.

"Don't let that thing whose stinking miasma has announced it from
a distance come too close to us; it reminds me that the stomach's dregs
are also called horse dung," said Pero Meñique, warding off the lame
man with his hand to forfend any physical harm from the reek of his
mouth, which gaped open as if it had jammed.

"Do not scoff at my lameness, for I toil through the world in a body
bound by invisible cords which hamper all movement from my feet up
to my shoulders," he said in reply.

"Know that there are waters passing miraculous which can straighten
a cripple's nerves; you need only find them and bathe in them," Pero
Meñique called out to the departing hobbler's back.

"Does Your Honor know where they are to be found?" he asked,
turning towards Pero's voice.

"As a child I knew, but I have since forgotten for lack of needing
them."

"Should you ever remember, seek me out on the roads of Castile, and
I will tell you about a place where there are powders which, when rubbed
upon the eyes, restore sight instantly," the lame man parried before
vanishing forever.

"This luckless fellow doubtless thinks he is more fortunate than his
traveling companions, but in truth he is the most wretched, for he
measures his misery on all sides when he observes the world's splen-
dors," said Pero Meñique testily as he angled his face slightly towards
the setting sun and resumed his progress.

The limping blind man, who had lagged behind indifferent to the
dispute, suddenly began to howl in the middle of the street, his voice
erupting from his innards:

> "Henceforth you need not go to Flanders
> but can remain here and soon shall see
> the stock I have brought of buboes and glanders."

Struck by the truculence of the blind vagrant, who seemed like a living
travesty of himself, Pero Meñique immediately strove to make a distinction between his person and the other sightless men in the world,
declaring all of them to be comrades in misfortune but not in chicanery.
To mark an even greater difference between the stranger's insolence and

his own civility, he recalled with pleasure the sheen of leaves bathed in light during bright spring mornings when the trees on the hillsides share in the sky's beauty with their own resplendency.

"Tell me today, at the hour of dusk, whether the flint in the ramparts gives off golden sparks when smitten by the sun, and whether you have the feeling that a waning ray encompasses the city as night approaches. I remember as if in a dream the fire glowing silently over the city walls as afternoon draws to a close, the mute battle waged on the watchtowers between the fugitive shadows and the sober glints. They say that just as the Guadarrama River flows betwixt the hushed orchards and the gray sloping banks of night, the ramparts of Madrid enter darkness corruscating like a fiery snake," said Pero Meñique.

His face became gilded, his hair and beard were shot through with gleams, his feet trod on light, his hands clutched at transparency, while with all the words at his command he tried to grasp the ungraspable substance of the imagined afternoon, he sought to understand the ethereal Martian red at the hour of both crepuscules, he desired to be here and be gone at the same time, like the river with its waters, its poplars and its ghostly willows. We arrived in the Plaza de San Salvador just in time to hear the crier proclaim:

"In Madrid, Monday, the twenty-second January of the year fourteen hundred eighty-one. This day, the council of the aforesaid city being assembled in the Church of San Salvador by the pealing of the bells, as is usual and customary, the Commendary Juan Zapata and Doctor de las Risas ordered and commanded the aforesaid gentlemen that of all the Jews in Madrid and it precincts, save Rabbi Jaco, physician in this city, none should be suffered to go about without badges in the aforesaid city, save within their own confines, under pain of paying one hundred *maravedis* the first time they are caught without it, two hundred *maravedis* the second time, and the third time, of handing over the clothing they wear on their backs, and that this decree shall take effect after the proclamation has been made in this city and its suburbs.

"Within their own confines, even though they go about without badges, no fine shall be levied against them, and as to the clothing which in keeping with the aforesaid sentence is lost on the third occasion, the overclothes are understood, that is, the robe or the cloak or the hood, but not the other garments in which they are dressed; and if any Jew shall come from foreign parts, no fine of any sort shall be levied on him, save were he to be three days in the aforesaid city, during the which he can well become acquainted with the ordinance. This shall not extend to children, the which need not wear badges. Furthermore, demarcation has been ordered of the places in which the Jews and Moors must dwell in the city of Madrid: for the Jews, it shall be the place where they have their synagogue, and for the Moors, where they have their mosque. The crier Pero Buentalante made the proclamation."

"Who has listened to this proclamation?" asked Pero Meñique.

"Amongst the crowd I can make out the *alguacil,* the officer of justice Rodrigo de Sant Estevan, Pablo the miller, the laborers Juan and Pedro Palomino, Juan Sánchez the mason, who is very old and deaf, Maestre Pedro, the smith who was given permission to build a wooden rack, and Juancho the painter, who paints all things that are wanted for Corpus Christi, and countless people whom I know not," I told him.

"Bad tidings have I heard today for the Jews, and worse will I hear tomorrow," said Pero Meñique as he started to walk away.

Babylonia sat on the ground and began to take stock of her money, plucking it from amongst secret bags in her clothes, as if it had been buried for a long time. After making a count she clenched the cash in her left fist, squeezing it like a chicken's neck, and then stealthily stashed the bags close to her chest. With lowered eyes she had already slipped the coins she was counting into the purse of her eyes and the strongbox of her body, as though convinced that others could steal her gold merely by looking at it.

"Have you been ailing?" the Trotter asked her.

"No," she answered, "only envious."

Next to Babylonia was a fat, frog-faced man whose eyebrows were longer than his hair and thicker than his mustache. He wore a monk's habit splotched on the sleeves and chest with vast grease stains. At that moment he was engaged in building a fire on the ground, brandishing in his right hand a hog's pudding which looked more like a male organ than a blood-filled pig's gut. It was her brother, Agustín Delfín, who had set out from Seville in a litter borne by running porters, but as they collapsed in Cazalla under his great weight, he was obliged to continue his trip on a young mule, who broke down in Fuente del Arco, whence he proceeded in an old handbarrow lined with green bombazine which had once belonged to an infanta. He reached the pass of Arrebatacapas in a short-legged folding chair, seated like a woman, his back and arms cradled in its leather straps and a pillow cushioning his head, his habit raised above his knees, revealing his thighs and navel. However, the handbarrow broke apart in Cebolla, and he entered Madrid in the middle of the night on an ass, both it and he dying of hunger.

Now as he leaned toward the fire he had lit after several unsuccessful tries, he bared buttocks white as eggshells while dragging across the ground a string of tiny dead birds which dangled from his habit like a rosary.

"Don Enrique de Villena was wont to say that the flesh of man is good for fractures; dogs' flesh, to wedge the teeth; old badgers', to banish fear and dread from the heart; kites', for the itch; hoopoes', to sharpen the wits; horses' flesh, to make a man valiant; lions', to make oneself

feared; frogs', to refresh the liver; snakes', for the falling sickness; grass-
hoppers', to quench thirst; and the flesh of crickets, against strangury,"
he said, as if talking to himself, or reciting a litany, or chatting—although
his back was turned to her—with his sister.

On the ground his fire called to mind burning grubs and death that
sparkles and crackles as one by one he threw onto it the birds on his
string, stripping off their feathers and tearing them to pieces once they
had changed color before his eyes.

"Take off the feathers but not the tail when it is roasted; slice up the
breast without removing the legs so that, the body being so small, there
will be something left to chew on. Cut them into four and eat them
before they grow cold—now that is the art of eating birds."

"What is that noise, and whence comes that smell so near to my
nostrils?" asked Pero Meñique.

"It is a friar who is eating roasted birds," I answered. "Even when
his mouth is empty he does not stop chewing."

"That friar is my brother, Agustín Delfín, who has come to Madrid
to spend some weeks with me and then return to Seville when he has
had enough of seeing me, for he says that he has urgent business in
that city concerning an inquisition which the Holy Church wants to
establish against the Judaizers," said Babylonia.

"Or when he has had enough of sponging on us, for it is plain to see
that your brother lives only to gobble and gorge," Pero Meñique remarked.

"Hand over that little snotnose, so I may drink his eyes out of my
hands and suck his marrow with my lips," Agustín Delfín said to frighten
me, clutching one headless bird and about to put another onto the fire
with the tongs, uncovering as he moved a crimson wounded knee, which
looked like a chancre, covered with soiled gauze.

"Beware of a half-kindled fire, for many have been suffocated to death
by the vapors from a brazier," cautioned Pero Meñique.

"Everything turns to smoke," said Babylonia, who held in her hand
a pig's trotter she had extracted from a money bag.

"So be it, and may God furnish us with peacocks, pheasants, cranes,
ducks, partridges, pigeons, swallows, cocks, sparrows and turtledoves
to eat," sputtered Agustín Delfín, crossing himself, his mouth busy with
a bird he was gulping down, whose bones crackled between his teeth,
for he was swallowing it whole: flesh, eyes, feathers, wings, feet.

"May God give us four-footed beasts to devour: oxen, fallow deer,
hares, mountain goats, sucking pigs, kids, rams, ewes and bucks," par-
odied Pero Meñique.

"Conger eels and turbots, crabs and prawns, salpas and tunnyfish,
salmon and trout," added Agustín Delfín. "But now I must quickly take

a drink, for a thrush has stuck in my throat on its race to my belly, and I am afraid I will choke."

He drank greedily, the wine ran from both sides of his mouth, and his left foot trod on a skull which he carried about in an open bag and used to illustrate to the crowds he preached to the equality of death, which carries off king and peasant alike, pope and mountebank, virgin and churchyard strumpet.

"You have roused my appetite considerably, and right now I would fain eat many greens together: lettuces, turnips, onions, garlic, strawberry pigweed, carrots, parsley, celery and fennel; procure them for me or I shall cut off your beard," snarled Agustín Delfín at Pero Meñique, grabbing him by the whiskers.

"Your habit is dirty and threadbare, as if you had not changed it for many years and slept in it every night, which is the custom of monks," King Bamba said, trying to make him release Pero.

"I, like your King, Don Fernando, who is reputed to be the most avaricious man in these kingdoms, do not change my worn-out apparel until it falls off in pieces. Also following his fashion, I replace the sleeves three times for each doublet and mend my shirt before and behind. . . . But who are you, that you address me thus?"

"I am a descendant of that Bamba, King of the Goths, who was chosen after King Recesvinto's death and was crowned in Toledo by the hand of San Ildefonso, but having reigned for eight years, he was given potions which caused him to lose his memory and go mad, and so he relinquished the kingdom and entered a monastery, where he lived for seven years and then died."

"Bamba is what we call a foolish fellow, a tongue-tied simpleton," Agustín Delfín sneered at him.

"Join together with me," the Trotter bade King Bamba, who replied:

> "You stout and I stout,
> who shall carry the dirt out?
> Booby me and booby you,
> no one knows just what we do."

"The river of lechery has no banks," said Pero Meñique to the Trotter.

"Psst, psst, psst," Babylonia hissed at a sparrow as she threw it a few weevily grains of wheat.

"They say that this little bird is most lascivious, that on account of his lewdness he lives only for one year and that the male has a beard like a billy goat under its breast," cooed the Trotter, making as if to crush the sparrow against her half-bared breasts.

"They are good for giving warning about the plague, for as soon as they sense noisome air, they fly away immediately, and wherever they abide, there is a safe place," said Pero Meñique.

"These finches make delicious eating; you can easily find them in crannies in the wall, near taverns, in yards, wherever cattle feed and in ravines," said Agustín Delfín, smacking his lips.

"The male farrow is deceitful," Babylonia declared as she threw the bird more grain.

"It's sparrow, not farrow, and it won't eat the wheat you're throwing because it's weevily," One-Eye scoffed.

"The king picked the rose, but the laborer picked the wheat," said Pero Meñique, quoting Ramón Llull.

"The king did not want to eat acorns, because that is pigs' fodder," added Don Rodrigo Rodríguez, whose voice had not been heard until that moment. Shod in tight buskins, he tried to conceal his hump, stubby legs and long arms. There was something doll-like about his body with its green breeches, yellow doublet and red cape.

"It is well known that our King, Don Fernando, is a great eater of testicles," stated Agustín Delfín without missing a bite.

"Your brother does not concern himself with the mere nourishment of his stomach, but with cramming into it day and night all the plants, meats and preserves in the Kingdom of Castile," said King Bamba to Babylonia. "He doesn't eat, he attacks with his teeth, he devours as if he would ravage and cause severe suffering to the birds he wolfs down. No matter if they are already stiff, there should be greater discretion in the manner of eating the animals man kills for his sustenance, and he should not eat them ravenously or disdainfully, or while making grimaces, hiccoughs or farts."

"Perchance tomorrow we will no longer be able to eat or stand up, or digest or dream, but we will enter into the eternal repose of the grave," reasoned Agustín Delfín between two gulps of wine.

"All the birds who are singing here put together will not give a single warble next year in the graveyard," said Babylonia, "so why don't we just eat them all now and be done with it?"

"Oh Babylonia, where is your glory? Where are the terrible Nebuchadnezzar, the mighty Darius and the fabled Cyrus? Where are Regulus, Romulus and Remus? The pristine rose is only a name; only names remain, when cities and men have disappeared," cried Pero Meñique.

"Where are Solomon, Samson and Absalom, who lived in this world amidst such splendor? Where are those beauties of yore whose shapeliness and laughter gladdened their ashen existence? Have they not vanished like day into the setting sun or fire into smoke, have they not made the fields fecund like the dung of beasts? The centuries have left us nothing but words, words in dead tongues," lamented Don Rodrigo Rodríguez, standing on tiptoe to make his body appear larger and more dignified.

"All empires are but powers in the dust," said King Bamba.

"Dust is the great leveler and light the most evenly allotted commodity in the world—except to me," said Pero Meñique.

"We will be skeletons with naked shinbones, rotten corpses whose mouths and entrails crawl with worms," Don Rodrigo Rodríguez cried out almost triumphantly.

"The shapely thighs and rounded breasts, the broad hips and billowy stomach, the sable armpits and matted braids, will fall from our hands like so many fleshly flowers," King Bamba said in a savoring yet stricken voice. "How horrible! Once her flesh is gone, of the beloved woman only voluptuous worms streaming from her cold belly will be left, and I, in the dark night of the bed, will nervously lift up her shift only to discover her nothing. As I stroke her hair my fingers will bring away handfuls of ashes, and when I lie down with her in the death position I will make love to both bodies, while making love to myself. Amidst the vague lights and evasive shadows of my spectral embrace I will hear the double carcass say to me as it falls apart, 'It is you that you are embracing; the fleshless body of the beloved is your fleshly body: look at yourself in that mirror.' "

"A little thing is man," Pero Meñique concluded, "for once the nine days of decomposition are over, only bones and a memory remain."

"Let us speak no further of decomposition, just thinking about it takes away my appetite," said Agustín Delfín. "To me, as to that poet who relished the macabre, the mere thought of death makes me tremble and blanch, puts my nose out of joint, twists my veins, puffs out my neck, slackens my flesh, swells my joints and stretches my nerves."

"We must chastise ourselves, scourge our flesh until we overcome the fear of death," Don Rodrigo Rodríguez exhorted.

"I am no flagellant from some order of dogs that I should eat cowering and drink on my knees, then arise at midnight and lash my back, for in my darkness the moon looks like a breast and in my dawn I suffer the pangs of hunger. Day is punishment enough for me and night is sufficient desire," said King Bamba.

"For me, it suffices to propel through the world the bewildered legs of a blind man which seek for warmth but stretch out in dampness and shadows," said Pero Meñique. "Truly, a blind man's life is like the silence of snow."

"I shall be a torch-bearing penitent; they will expose me to public shame," the Trotter declared.

"I shall carry a strap and be whipped by the constabulary, and the best jeweler in Castile shall fasten my ankle bracelets in prison," boasted One-Eye.

"Your furnace is always stoked, your body stinks, and your clothes are soiled; your smell is an ancient one," Pero Meñique reproached Babylonia.

"After the manner of our good Queen Isabel, I neither change my clothes nor eat off tablecloths; I wash my hair only on Saturdays by the riverside before I dine with my brother," she said.

"You don't wash clothes, you throw them away when they are worn out," replied One-Eye, barely parting his lips.

"For ten *maravedis* per year commencing Saint Michael's Day next first of September, I can lease you a plot of land which should be more or less big enough for a *fanega*'s worth of sowing, that is, a bushel and a half, and which is bounded by the Toledo highway on one side and the Umanejas brook on the other," Agustín Delfín said with a yawn to King Bamba, gazing into the distance as if divining his future in the evening clouds.

"I want no more land than I can stand on, nor more day than my body can live through," King Bamba answered without looking at him.

"I heard Pero Buentalante in the square of this city proclaim that Pero de Madrid said he did give a lease in perpetuity forever anon, commencing Saint Michael's Day the month of September next and henceforth, of five hundred *maravedis* for a plot of ground under the vault of the Guadalajara Gate," said Don Rodrigo Rodríguez.

"I heard it said that an ox shits more than one hundred sparrows," said Pero Meñique.

Meanwhile the Trotter sprawled on a rock, her loose clothing revealing bare hips and a dark curly cunt. Languidly moving her arms and legs, she abandoned herself to an invisible lover, her behind like a voluptuous white pitcher balanced on the stone.

"You remind me of a rock dove, for the sun on your breasts makes them glimmer with gemlike colors," King Bamba began.

"The world must be a-changing," she replied, "for never have I heard such cajolery."

"Recall my fair words that night when we made the animal with two heads and eight limbs," he went on.

"Lust does not recollect the bodies it consumes, it lives only in pleasure's present; forever hungry, it is nostalgic only for what it had and for what it cannot have," she affirmed.

"Perhaps," mused Pero Meñique.

"Desire gnaws on itself," grunted Agustín Delfín.

"Let me delve into you," King Bamba said to the Trotter as his quick hands swarmed up her stomach and like two small, rapacious animals grabbed at her breasts while she dug her nails into his neck and back and thrust her tongue into his mouth, her eyes hidden beneath their lids in the intimacy of a kiss.

"Man is the fire and woman the oakum, then comes the devil to blow on and stoke 'em," Babylonia intoned.

"Don Alfonso Martínez of Toledo, whom my father knew well in the days of King Don Juan Segundo of Castile, taught that lust is a final and efficient cause of weakening the human body, that it deprives a man of sleep, makes him age and turn gray before his time, causes his limbs to tremble and alters the five senses," said Don Rodrigo Rodríguez.

"That very same archpriest, who was a friend of my father's as well, delighted in telling of a woman who lopped off the privities of a man who was enamored of her, who was called Juan Orenga, a maker of sword guards from Tortosa, because she learned that he was bedding another. She seized him one day, twisting his parts in her hand, and sliced them off with a razor, crying, 'Traitor, neither to you, nor to me, nor to any other will they ever be of use!' She plucked them and cut them and straightway she fled, and he was left miserable and bleeding," Agustín Delfín recounted.

"Furthermore," Don Rodrigo Rodríguez continued, "he spoke of a married woman who bit off her husband's tongue with her teeth, for she made him put it into her mouth in jest and she clamped her teeth together and so she cut it off and he was left dumb and maimed. The woman escaped posthaste to a monastery of Minorites. She was questioned by the law as to why she had done it. She admitted she had seen him talking in secret many times with a woman she suspected. She had said to him, 'Nevermore shall you betray me in conversation with this one or any other.' "

"I am like Tamburlaine's camel, who would graze wherever he desired unabashed," murmured King Bamba into the Trotter's ear as his hands fondled her breasts.

"I can't understand what attracts you to that woman. She's skinny as death, her breasts are wizened, her neck is like a bull's, and she's as dirty as a pig," said Babylonia.

"Hold your tongue, old gossip. How you wish you were in my place,' she snapped.

"God forbid I should break His seventh commandment by copulating in public," retorted Babylonia.

"If you use her as is fitting and right, it is impossible to commit the crime of fornication with your own wife," said Agustín Delfín. "The appetites which excite your lust are not attributable to mortal sin, only to venial sin."

"The sin of carnality is so vast that even those who couple in matrimony are sinning mortally," argued Don Rodrigo Rodríguez.

"Rein in," the Trotter said to King Bamba. "You have yet to sit in the saddle and you are already galloping."

"I had best withdraw," he replied, "for feeling as I do now, I could make you thirty sons, all of good Spanish stock, with name, property, fame and lineage."

"Speaking of ancestors, my father told me that the Sephardim, who are descended from the tribes of Judah and Benjamin, arrived in these realms in King Solomon's day and founded cities whose names evoked those of the Bible," I made bold to say.

"The Jews have violated professed nuns in exchange for gifts; they have profaned the sacraments of Holy Mother Church, they have performed witchcraft with the Host, they have flogged statues of Jesus Christ, and they have thrust crucifixes up their behinds to mock him even further," said Agustín Delfín indignantly.

"In their arrogance they boast that no better a people exists in the world, no more discerning or sharp-witted, or more honorable than themselves, since they are of the lineage of the tribes of Israel," One-Eye sneered.

"They are most diligent when it comes to acquiring honors, royal offices or favors from kings and lords," said Babylonia. "Some of their number have intermingled their sons and daughters with Old Christian gentlefolk and have been taken for good Christians on this account and much honored for it."

"They always spurned the trades of plowman or digger, or to raise cattle in the fields, nor did they teach them to their children, but only town trades and how to sit and earn their livelihood with little work," Don Rodrigo Rodríguez complained.

"They have always been gluttons and voracious eaters of pipkins of Saturday stew, of onions and garlic fried in oil, but will touch neither bacon nor lard nor bloody meat. They eat no pig unless it cannot be avoided, and they secretly dine on meat during Lent, vigils and the four ember weeks," said Agustín Delfín.

"The reason the Jews stink is because they Judaize and because they are not baptized," Babylonia exclaimed. "They are a godless and lawless people."

"Even if they are baptized, they are still Jews. They shun Church doctrine and Christian customs; they cause Jews to be brought to their houses to preach to them on the sly, especially to the women; and they have rabbis who slaughter the cattle and poultry for their meals," declared Don Rodrigo Rodríguez.

"The Kings of Castile and Aragón welcomed the New Christians with open arms, duped by the professed sincerity of their conversion, and the Santa Marías, the Santa Fes, the La Caballerías and other questionable believers rose to high positions in church and state; why, even Hernando del Pulgar is a descendant of Jews," fumed Agustín Delfín, now thoroughly outraged.

"In 1473 the sea played a cruel joke on the Cordovan converts, who, upon being informed that along the Portuguese coast some sailors had killed a whale two hundred paces long by one hundred paces wide, believed that cetacean to be the Leviathan foretold by the prophets as a sign of the imminent coming of a Messiah on earth, and they sent their servants to fetch them chunks of the monster as proof, but the monster was only a whale after all," Don Rodrigo Rodríguez recounted.

"Four years ago the clergymen and Christians of Seville, under the leadership of Alonso de Hojeda, a friar bent upon the destruction of Judaism, informed Isabel and Fernando that many *Conversos* were performing Jewish rites in secret, that they did not believe in the Christian faith or baptize their offspring, and that they had risen to positions of consequence in the ecclesiastical ranks and the royal palace, for which reasons they implored Their Majesties to punish the transgressors.

"The Sovereigns were greatly troubled to learn that there were so many heretics and apostates in the kingdom, and they ordered the Archbishop of Seville, Pero González de Mendoza, to make them a catechism in which he would speak about the beliefs and duties of Christians. And then, when the Kings had proceeded to Córdoba, Fray Alonso de Hojeda caught up with them to report the news of a terrible evil: In Seville on Maundy Thursday a certain Guzmán had overheard six Judaizers blaspheming the Catholic faith while they were paying court to a female Jewish *Conversa*. Without delay the Monarchs petitioned Sixtus the Fourth to issue a bull contemplating the establishment of the tribunal of the Inquisition in Castile, the which was granted to them so they might lawfully proceed against the Jewish heresy with death by fire," said Agustín Delfín.

"Here in Madrid they have complied with the ordinance issued one year ago by the Cortes, the parliament, of Toledo, which the Catholic Kings decreed as law in the Kingdom of Castile, commanding all unbaptized Jews to wear upon their garments a token whereby they may be known, to dwell apart in a walled-in quarter and withdraw from the rest of the population to their *juderías* before nightfall. It also forbade them to practice the profession of physician, surgeon, barber, apothecary and tavernkeeper among Christians; and any of them who were found making their abode outside the *aljamas* would have all their goods confiscated. Those who chanted at burials wearing linen vestments over their clothes shall be stripped of them," Babylonia recited as if by rote.

"As I am but a gadabout, I cannot condemn anyone in this world; death by fire horrifies me, and I take pity on whatever creature must endure it," declared the Trotter. "One day when I was a child wandering famished in the streets, an old Jew gave me bread to eat, and I took no notice if his hand was Hebrew or Old Christian, for goodness and evil have no lineage, they are only known by their fruits."

"You, gluttonous friar, who steal tiny innocent birds from their nest to crush them in your tireless jaws; you, foul frowzy Babylonia, who drag your body over the ground like soiled clothing; you, botch of nature, who bear on your back a great shell you cannot take off day or night, like a conspicuous caterpillar—tell me, when you are face-to-face with a comely maiden or a fair child or a physician who is curing you of your ills, do you feel more worthy of life than they who are Hebrews? Do you feel more blameless, or more handsome to look upon?" demanded King Bamba.

"I simply believe what the pious Franciscan brother Fray Alonso de Espina argued in his *Fortress of the Faith*, to wit, that if ever a true inquisition were carried out in our time, countless numbers of those put to the stake would be found out as Judaizers, and that it is better for them to receive their punishment on earth than to burn in the eternal fire," said Agustín Delfín sanctimoniously as he stretched out on the ground, squeezing half of his body into a barrel.

"I wander the streets of this world blindly, and I have no wish to open my eyes to see the fires of death that will be kindled all over these realms to burn innocent people. I prefer the peaceable ignorance of my night to the hate visible everywhere," Pero Meñique sighed.

A gaunt, pallid man with grizzled eyebrows, hair and beard crossed the square, his coarse seaman's clothes more like a gray cuirass than wearing apparel; he was barefoot, and so thick and rough was the skin of his feet that he seemed to be shod with shoes made out of his own soles. His aspect was choleric, despairing, hunger brimmed in his eyes, and he advanced in conversation with himself as if an unseen interlocutor walked by his side.

"This is the reckoning of the creation of the world according to the Jews. Adam lived one hundred and twenty years and then he begat Seth. Seth lived one hundred and five years and then he begat Enos. Enos lived ninety years and then he begat Cainan. Cainan lived seventy years and then he begat Malalchel. Malalchel lived sixty-five years and then he begat Jared. Jared lived one hundred and sixty-two years and then he begat Enoch. Enoch lived sixty-five years and then he begat Methuselah. Methuselah lived one hundred and eighty-seven years and then he begat Lamech. Lamech lived one hundred and eighty-two years and then he begat Noah. Noah lived five hundred years and then he begat Shem. And Shem was one hundred years old when the flood came. Thus from the creation of the world until the flood one thousand six hundred and forty-six years passed . . ." He moved his ashen lips rapidly, figuring up the world's accounts, just as I later was to hear Don Cristóbal Colón do.

Suddenly, like a phantasmagory, he vanished from sight. I was about to ask the others if they, too, had seen him, or if I had been the only one to mark his presence, when a mad dog came tearing down the street chasing its own shadow, attempting futilely to bite it, but the sharp and elongated shadow always ran ahead of its paws, eluding the snapping jaws.

In a flash the dog disappeared down the same street the gray-haired man had taken, leaving behind only the echo of his bark.

"The bark of a dog is its shout, and the shout of a man is his bark," Pero Meñique intoned gravely.

In the twilight silence the day's final shadows crept along the ground or leaned against walls, like the elusive spoor of an ephemeral splendor that was ebbing away. Agustín Delfín had fallen asleep, mouth agape, his head resting on his right arm. And as he slept his jaws began to move, chewing in a dream, while his hands opened and closed as if squeezing a woman's breasts or other fruits of nature. Full of noises, his body spoke in whiffles, hiccoughs, farts and all manner of abdominal movements.

"This fellow even feeds in his sleep; he keeps the fodder in his mouth and ruminates on it over and over again," King Bamba observed.

"My brother Agustín Delfín is so lazy that just to shit is an effort for him," said Babylonia, baring her teeth in a laugh.

"People who eat many silver-tongued thrushes piss blood-colored urine, and if people lie down after eating, their bellies fill with water," said Pero Meñique.

"But my brother lives at prayer, so he is safe from all ills," replied Babylonia.

"But not from death," countered One-Eye.

At that moment sundry bands of mummers came singing and dancing down the street towards the square, as at Shrovetide. A pasty-faced princeling sitting in a chair went before, wearing a torn cap and carrying a broom in his hand as a scepter; his cart, on mismatched wheels, was pulled by a monk and pushed by a peasant. They were followed by blacksmiths, cobblers, barbers, physicians and bespectacled tailors feigning blindness, all of whom mimed the motions of their trades, squabbling for precedence and swatting each other with their tools. They burst into confusion, making a mass of mistakes: the tailor measured a mule, a blacksmith shod a physician, and the physician held the barber's pitcher of wine to the light instead of the sick man's urine. Some had painted faces and besmeared bodies and wore on their heads hoods or caps shaped like animals, vegetables and fruits. Others wore masks and goat-skins. The rest did not cover themselves, flaunting their faces and their deformities.

Next came giants whose scanty dress exposed their navels, knees and elbows. Lame, maimed and blind men, beggars and juggling Moors ringed the giants. Divers wagons trundled by, conveying a mad knight hugging a tree trunk, proclaimed by a buffoon who declared, "Whom God would forsake, He first makes mad"; an archer aiming a crossbow as if to shoot, proclaimed by another buffoon crying, "It's a bad bowman who shoots at his own"; a nun with red face and hands flapping her habit while a dwarf nun trailing a long wooden rosary on the ground declared, "Nun's love is like a fire of tow, no sooner kindled than dead." Next came a skinny old woman who resembled a scrawny bird and held on her lap a donkey. She was announced by a buffoon wearing a lizard's snout who said, "In vain was the crane giving suck to the ass."

Then a raggedy, cadaverous peasant playing a tabor announced Death, who rode as a charioteer on a wagon dragged by an emaciated horse. Death held an extinguished torch in one hand, an invisible rein in the other. Four lesser Deaths on the wagon were trying to make a gentleman, a lady, a cleric and a peasant fit into four open coffins much too narrow for them, for now a head hung out, now the arms, then the legs. Suddenly the horse's knees buckled, and it fell to the ground. The wagon overturned, and the human beings escaped, pursued by the little Deaths. Death the charioteer attempted to right the wagon, a drunkard approached to give assistance, then a red angel and a white devil, both winged, came from opposite ends of the square to set it straight. The lesser Deaths caught the people, put them in the coffins and laid them down with their heads, arms and legs doubled up, just as two barefoot vagabonds arrayed in patches entered the square, fighting over a piece of bridge.

"I say that this bridge is mine; it was I who first descried its curve, I touched the void beneath its arches before anyone else, before any other I walked over it," one of them said.

"The bridge belonged to my grandfather, who was the oldest vaga-bond in the city. He was the first to lie down beneath it when they had just thrown it across the river," the second replied.

"My great-grandfather slept on the waters, stretched out in the air, with his feet on one bank and his hands on the other; people passed over him, and rains, winds, suns and moons," said the first.

"I say that the bridge is mine; it was I who first glimpsed its breastwork. I saw its wood when it was still a tree, I walked on its footpath when it was only dirt," insisted the second.

"The bridge belongs to the town, it has no owner save the years," said an *alguacil* who was eavesdropping, and he took the piece away from them.

Pero Buentalante reached the square, stood up before the considerable number of people assembled and began to proclaim aloud:

"In Madrid, the twenty-second October in the year fourteen hundred eighty-one, Doctor de las Risas expired, Doctor de las Risas will expire, Doctor de las Risas is expiring!"

The bands of mummers clambered onto a platform that had been erected in the square and began to dance amidst torches, drums and fifes.

Thus was the night ended.

O nce the papal bull for the establishment of the Holy Office throughout the realms and dominions of Don Fernando and Doña Isabel had been obtained, the Dominican friars Juan de San Martín, Miguel Morillo and Doctor Juan Ruiz de Medina, a priest from San Pedro's, had set out for Seville in possession of a royal order commanding all officials to give them lodgings and nourishment during their travels. Upon their arrival in that city they were received at the chapter house, and the following Sunday, clothed in black and white, they paraded through the hushed streets in solemn procession to the Convent of San Pablo, of the Order of Santo Domingo, whence a few days later they dispatched their assistant, Diego de Merlo, to apprehend the town's most upright and wealthy *Conversos*.

On 2 January 1481 in the cathedral, the edict containing their appointment was read, and it was declared that the Duke of Medina Sidonia, the Marquis of Cádiz and other Andalusian nobles, upon pain of excommunication and prosecution under the charge of harboring and protecting heretics, must arrest the families of those New Christians who had escaped to their lands in fear of the Inquisition. They must then sequester their possessions and deliver them up as prisoners within a term of fifteen days. In response to this exhortation, the local nobility straightway sent to the Dominicans so many bound and fettered Jews to be judged that the Convent of San Pablo was too small to hold them all, and they had to ask Queen Isabel for Seville's fortress, the castle of Triana, and remove there with their prisoners, their *alguacil*, their prosecutor and their notaries, causing these words to be writ upon its walls: *"Exurge Domine; Judica causam tuam; Capite nobis vulpis"*: "Arise, O Lord; Judge thine own cause; Take us the foxes." And henceforth they held their audiences, inflicted torture and sentenced to death in its gloomy chambers.

On 6 February the first auto-da-fé was celebrated. Six men and women were escorted by a lengthy procession from the Convent of San Pablo to the cathedral, where Fray Alonso de Hojeda tediously preached at them, before they were conveyed to the Campo de Tablada, the Burning Place, where four hollow plaster statues known as the *four prophets* stood at the corners. The condemned were placed, still alive, in these to be roasted to death in a slow fire. Several days later the three richest *Conversos* in Seville were sentenced to die on the pyre: Manuel Sauli, Bartholomé de Torralba, and Diego de Susán, whose fortune was estimated at ten million *maravedis*, and who was said to be the father of that beauteous maiden who was dallying with the Castilian who had denounced to the inquisitors a secret meeting of the *Conversos* at the parish church of San Salvador, on account of which they had been apprehended by the assistant Diego de Merlo, brought to the Convent of San Pablo and thence transferred to Triana Castle.

Terrified by the arrests of Benadeba, of Abolafia "the Perfumed One" (also known as Abolasía, Abosasia, Abolajia, Abolafria) and of the other foremost and moneyed *Conversos* whose wealth and favors had been of no avail and whose confiscated possessions served to swell the coffers of Isabel and Fernando, numerous New Christians tried to escape from Seville and its archbishopric to Portugal or France, or to the lands of nobles and Moors. The inquisitors stationed guards at the city gates and decreed the death penalty for those who were captured, for so many were caught in their attempted flight that nowhere remained to jail them.

Moreover, just as the Dominican fathers were diligently and zealously placing spies everywhere (one young prior going so far as to climb upon the roof of San Pablo's every Saturday morning to espy whether smoke issued from the chimneys of the *Conversos'* houses; if no smoke was seen from any one of them, its inhabitants were detained on charges of observing the Jewish Sabbath), multiplying the arrests and sifting through proofs against their next victims, the Lord scourged Seville with a pestilence so terrible that in every corner of Andalusia the dying were to be seen dragging themselves through the streets and fields, and the dead went unburied, for thousands perished.

When the *Conversos* saw the Old Christians fleeing the city, they themselves sought permission to leave from Diego de Merlo, who granted it on condition that they present safe-conducts to the guards at the gates and leave their chattels behind. Upwards of eight thousand left for Mairena, Marchena and Palacios, and the Marquis of Cádiz, the Duke of Medina Sidonia and the other lords received them willingly.

Fearing the plague, the inquisitors also abandoned the city, taking with them their families, their servants, their spies and their jailors. They halted at Aracena, where, not wishing to be idle, they burned twenty-three persons, both male and female, as "wretched heretics" in an auto-da-fé, and doomed to the fire many bones belonging to dead people whom they believed to have died in a state of heretical depravity.

When the epidemic ceased to rage, they returned to Seville, where they continued their inquisition, condemning seventy-nine persons to

perpetual imprisonment and an equal number to the wearing of large
red crosses on their clothing all the days of their lives, rendering them
and their children ineligible for any public position of trust and forbidding them "to dress in or wear silk, gold, or camlet, upon pain of death."
Hundreds more, having become reconciled with the Church, were paraded on Fridays barefaced and in solemn procession, flogging themselves in the streets in public penance. During the remainder of the year
they burned nearly three hundred souls, among whom were several
clergymen and a friar from La Trinidad, accused of eating meat on Good
Friday after preaching the Passion. They also burned an infinite number
of bones belonging to corpses disinterred from the courtyards of La
Trinidad, San Agustín and San Bernardo for having been buried in the
Jewish fashion, and they proclaimed and burned in effigy many of the
Jews who had fled. Their children were deprived of the right to trades
and benefactions, and their possessions and inheritances were made
over to the King and Queen's exchequer. "The fire has been kindled,"
wrote the palace priest, "and will burn until it reaches the end of the
dry wood, for it must blaze until all are consumed and slain who are
Judaizers, so that not one remains, not even their children who are
twenty years or older, and should they be tainted with the same leprosy,
even those who are younger."

At midyear the inquisitors published a second edict, which they called
the Edict of Grace, wherein they exhorted those who had committed
errors of apostasy to give themselves up, for if they did so in a spirit of
genuine contrition, they would be absolved and their goods left untouched; otherwise, if they were denounced by others, they would be
apprehended and tried as heretics and apostates and turned over to
secular justice. Nevertheless, although many responded to the call, they
were denied absolution until they had furnished the name, trade, residence and description of all those persons, be they family, friends or
acquaintances, whom they might have seen, heard or understood to
apostatize. Thus did the inquisitors in Seville come to know about Jews
in Córdoba, Valencia, Toledo, Segovia, Burgos and other parts, violating
ecclesiastical secrecy for their own convenience.

And so, out of nearly twenty thousand *Conversos* who responded to
the edict to confess their faults and be received back in the fold, more
than three thousand were sentenced to wear the *sanbenito* and four
thousand more were burned, not counting the bones of the deceased
who were burned in effigy.

The Term of Grace having expired, a new edict was published commanding all the Church faithful, under pain of mortal sin, to denounce
whomever they knew to have exercised heretical depravity, warning
that if they allowed six days to pass without doing so, they would be

eligible for excommunication. Also, in order to enlighten the ignorant about Judaism, a list was published of thirty-seven articles of accusation by which it could be proved that a man was Judaizing, such as: if he was awaiting the Messiah; if he kept the Sabbath; if he donned a clean shirt or gown on that day; if he lit no fire in his house and abstained from any work commencing Friday afternoon; if he removed the suet and fat from his meat and sprinkled earth over the spilt blood; if he ate meat during Lent; if he fasted on the days prescribed by the Jewish fasts; if he celebrated the Festival of the *matsah*, the Feast of Tabernacles and the Feast of Lights; if he blessed the table and drank *kasher* wine; if he made the benediction called the *baraha*; if he ate of animals slaughtered by Jewish hands; if he recited the Psalms of David without saying at the end *"Gloria Patri et Filio et Spiritu Sancto"*; if a woman did not go to the temple for forty days after giving birth; if a man had his son circumcised and gave him a Hebrew name; if after baptizing his son he shaved or washed his head on the spot where the oil or chrism was applied; if he caused his son to be laved on the seventh day after his birth in a basin containing gold, silver, seed pearls, wheat, barley and other things; if he made a *Hadas* ceremony for his newborn child on the eighth night, convening maidens and kinswomen to dance, sing and feast in the white-robed baby's presence the eve of his circumcision; if he was married according to the Jewish rites; if he prepared a *ruaya*, a supper of separation, for a friend or kinsman the day before a long journey; if he wore *tefillin*, the Jewish amulets; if when kneading the bread he set aside the *hallah*, the priests' portion, and burned it as a sacrifice; if on his deathbed he turned his face towards the wall; if he gave orders that a corpse be washed with warm water, its beard and other body hair shaven, that it be wrapped in a shroud of new linen, with britches and a folded cape placed upon it, and that a pillow filled with virgin soil be put under its head and a coin inserted in its mouth; if he keened over the deceased and spilled out water from pitchers or jars in the dead person's house; if as a sign of grief he partook of fish and olives while sitting on the floor or standing behind a door; if in mourning he did not leave his house for the space of a year; and if he buried the deceased in untilled soil or in the Jewish cemetery.

One evening in Madrid, as we were returning from the Plazuela de la Paja, Pero Meñique asked me if I could shelter in my house two friends of his from Ciudad Real, the children of a physician, an intimate of his own father since infancy. "For a long road and a little inn, show a man the company he's in," he said.

They had been hidden, he told me, in Francisca Hernández's house, which, being public and lewd, was not a proper place for a lady of Doña

Isabel's quality, or of her brother's, Don Gonzalo. To tell the truth, they
were in flight from the tribunal which had been installed at midyear to
serve Ciudad Real, its bailiwick, the Campo de Calatrava, and the Archbishop of Toledo. In keeping with the procedures of the inquisitors
Francisco Sánchez de la Fuente and Pero Díaz de Costana, upon their
arrival in the town they caused to be read aloud in the Church of Santa
María an Edict of Grace exhorting all those persons in the said city and
its vicinity who had fallen into and practiced the Mosaic heresy to confess
to them their errors within thirty days, renouncing the heresy and de-
livering themselves up to the Church; promising, as in Seville, to receive
them with as much mercy and compassion as possible. Similarly, they
gave warning to those persons who would not avow their sins, and to
those who had fled in fear of the Holy Office, about whom they had
ample information, for they had already been testified against and were
being sought after by the prosecutor, the inquisitors having issued a
letter of summons and an edict against the infamous and suspect persons
who had taken themselves away.

Sánchez de la Fuente and Díaz de la Costana themselves had instructed the faithful on how to detect those who were Judaizing and
falling into errors against the Church, prevailing upon them to make
denunciations in the ward of San Pedro where the inquisitors had ensconced themselves while they gathered information about the Jewish
community in Ciudad Real, with which the New Christian Ferrán Falcón
and other spies and informers were providing them.

Furthermore, since the Sevillian "absolutions," the ensuing trials and
autos-da-fé had become public knowledge, and since the designation
on 17 October 1483, by the Catholic Kings and Pope Sixtus IV, of Fray
Tomás de Torquemada, the Dominican prior of Santa Cruz Monastery
in Segovia, as Inquisitor-General of Aragón, Valencia and Catalonia,
with the power to appoint his subordinates, it had become exceedingly
dangerous for Pero's friends to remain in Ciudad Real, and they, like
other *Conversos* and Jews who were able, had escaped.

It was going to rain at any moment; clouds had invaded the sky and
moisture saturated the air, announcing the imminence of water. The
streets seemed narrower, darker, more forlorn, pervaded by an earthi-
ness, a grief-stricken silence at once aching and sepulchral. Pero Meñique walked with his head cocked and his staff atilt, in readiness against
invisible attacks or inquisitorial shadows rushing at him, the din of
accusations in his ears, his fancy lurid with countless fires burning terrified men and women.

A man of sickly, unwholesome pallor standing in a doorway stared
strangely as we approached. He might never have seen a blind man in

his life, for when he caught sight of Pero Meñique his countenance contracted into a sneering claw.

"Even in his dreams a man cannot change history, cannot modify the course of his life, cannot alter the past which gives shape to the future," said Pero Meñique.

There was thunder, lightning. The gray peaks of the Guadarrama flashed in the distance, and closer by, the poplars on the riverbanks and the city walls of chipped flint scintillated. On all sides hitherto unnoticed dogs barked at the thunderclaps. Someone ran down a shadowy street. There was a bang on a rooftop, a disembodied voice wafted through a crumbling wall. The bells chimed Compline with a muffled sound, as if from the bottom of a well or reverberating from the waters of a lake.

"Don't turn your head around towards the windows, lest the people watching us from them take you for a stargazer," I said.

"Pay no heed if I should act strangely, for at times this murkiness makes me go mad," he said, seeming newly awakened from a dream.

"What do you mean?" I asked.

"Nothing."

"You did say something," I insisted.

"I was putting you to the proof to see if you were still with me, if you had not died, for I was far away, truly far away, and your voice brought me back again."

A smell of meat stewed in oil, of onions and fried garlic escaped beneath the closed door of a darkened house, betraying the *Converso* in the kitchen. The smell made me hungry and sad because it quickened my appetite and made me think of my mother, now turned to ashes.

A short way ahead, a coarse, bearded fellow slumping in a doorway looked us up and down with a bygone anger, as if we had become enemies in a past life and the sight of us now reminded him of forgotten affronts.

Suddenly I felt the rain on my face, bloated drops, swift and chill, like the myriad fingertips of a remote and elusive animal touching me all over my body simultaneously.

"Water is running down my cheeks, I smell and breathe the rain," said Pero Meñique.

"The rain is pelting our backs," I pointed out.

"Be careful the water doesn't get into your lungs, which are the spongy parts of the body, and swamp the bellows that receive the air to cool the heart," he cautioned me.

"Be careful the water doesn't get into your mouth, and hurry your steps," said I, drenched to the bone.

"Sssssshhhh," said he.

Heavy drops the size of a *castellano* spattered on us, and Pero Meñique started to run, cackling in a loud, grating voice.

"The goose is loose, the goose is loose," I cried, going on with the jest, but he stopped immediately to reproach me.

"Hush, not so loud, or the people who hear the shouting will want to catch me to play at goose-grabbing at Shrovetide, for on that day they bring them out for sport, tying a line across the street with a goose hung in the middle, and people riding under it endeavor to pull off its head."

" 'Twould have been better had I shouted, 'Run, run, Pero Meñique, for the maiden, the nun, the butcher wife—the unspeakable one—is hard on your heels,' " said I, to pacify him.

" 'Twould have been better had you not shouted at all," said he.

And again the rain beat down on walls and rooftops, streaking the streets with silver tracks, and we stood still for a moment, not knowing which way to go.

Here and there lightning flashed on the city walls; a riderless white horse passed us at a bewildered trot, turned the corner and reappeared in the square. A man who looked like a fish draped in clothing attempted to stop it by grabbing at the reins, but with a neigh the beast eluded him.

We continued along Calle Sin Puertas, then down streets and more streets whose names were no longer of any import. Our bumbling feet plowed the puddles, we rowed through the thickened air and bumped into trees distorted by darkness.

Suddenly, Pero Meñique bent over to pick up a sparrow stiff with cold which must have fallen from a branch. He carried it a long while, cuddling it in his hands, unmindful of the cold and the rain.

He, who was always dusty, seemed to have become water: silvered drops slid down his hair, forehead, nose, beard, ears. He trod on twigs and slippery stones, he flowed over them, until one foot sank into a deep, muddy puddle.

Across the street a man in shabby clothes pissed against the wall, arching over to shield himself from the gusts of wind. Not too far off another man seemed to lean against the darkness, as if he were part of it or a physical extension of the rain.

The bells rang Matins. Their tolling penetrated countless walls, unknown faces, millions of drops of water, mantles of night and doubt. From an open window at our side a woman's voice called through the rain, "You're all disheveled and damp—where have you been?"

"In the village—where else should I have been?"

"Why are you so late?"

"Because the bridges are out and the roads are blocked."

"Especially near Juana Gómez's inn?" said the woman.

"Indeed, not far from Juana Gómez's inn," said the man.

"The next time I see you talking to her I'll cut out your tongue, and if you lie with her I'll wring your prickle."

"I can run away before you do."

"Not fast enough to keep me from catching you."

"I can run away from you," the man insisted.

"But not from Death," countered the woman.

We left behind the voices and their endless bickering. Through another window I glimpsed a girl's face, yellow in the light of a torch. A woman's soft footsteps in another street drew near invisibly and then were smothered behind a door.

Someone ran up behind us . . . a patched vagabond with a mute, lipless grin in a permanent laugh. His head and feet were too large for his puny body, his face was tired and wan, with bushy eyebrows and pendulous ears. He was missing an eye and dragged a black gunnysack behind him, almost a continuation of his feet. He stretched out his hand.

"Who is following us?" Pero Meñique asked uneasily.

"It is nobody, only a vagabond," I said.

"Vagabonds are troublesome; in many lands they force them to work, they whip them or send them to the galleys," he said.

"I have naught to give," I told the man. "You are wasting your time."

"A copper, give me just one copper."

"Look for a knight or a rich man," Pero Meñique muttered. "Follow us no farther."

The vagabond took no notice and trailed along behind us until we reached the house. As I was taking out the old key, Pero Meñique whispered, "Go in quickly."

The vagabond lingered outside by a tree, like a dog without a master, protecting his head from the rain with his hands and swiveling his good eye from side to side in a droll manner.

After a short while Pero Meñique departed, on the understanding that he would return later with the two de la Vegas in such wise that, under cover of dawn, no one might see them entering my house.

Reappearing as stealthily as he had gone, he tapped on the door to let me know he was there, although I was on my guard and had been watching for him from the moment he left.

And so, upon the opening of the door, three figures muffled up in cloaks entered wordlessly. I led them to an inside room of the house where the candlelight could not be seen from the street.

There it was that Pero Meñique introduced me to brother and sister, both of whom were dressed as men. Isabel was a maiden of middling stature, harmonious in her person and the proportion of her limbs, very white of skin with large, smiling, almond eyes, long hair, long lashes

and a handsome, merry face; she understood with a glance and responded with a look; she must have been twenty years old or there-
abouts.

Gonzalo was a tall youth, well made and vigorous, with a pale face,
black eyes and curly hair and beard. With his unruffled movements and
straightforward mien, he appeared to reason more than he spoke.
Brought up since childhood to book learning, Pero Meñique explained,
he desired to become a physician like his father and to minister to the
lepers who were perishing untended and unloved by the waysides of
the royal highways of the Kingdom of Castile, and notwithstanding that
he mounted a horse ably in the Castilian fashion and the Moorish way,
he was fonder of playing chess and devoted more time to this game
than he ought. Above all he prized his sister Isabel, and they were like
two boughs of a single tree, for if one was hurt, the other suffered, or
if she was moved to laugh, he became joyous as well, and both man
and maid mirrored the gleam in each other's eyes.

When Pero Meñique had finished speaking, they remained silent, their
eyes riveted on the door to the room, as if danger could penetrate or a
way out could be found in that slab of wood. The yellowish candlelight
gave an air of faraway tranquillity to their faces, and standing there
they seemed suspended in time, not belonging to any specific year or
country.

"Is something the matter?" Pero Meñique asked Gonzalo, perplexed
by his muteness.

"I have a toothache," he replied, blushing.

"If the pain results from the cold, smear a bit of garlic on the gums;
if it is of another sort, you must squeeze four or five drops of watercress
juice into the ear closest to the tooth. If the pain still does not cease,
drops of hot oil should be put into the ear," said Pero Meñique, who
had wrapped a rag around his own head. He was sodden from feet to
whiskers and sported buttons and hose of various colors.

"Does something ail you?" I asked him.

"My body is soaked through, and I have a headache as big as all
Madrid," he said.

Shafts of light flashed in the window facing the yard: someone holding
torches had run by. We heard the rain drumming on the roofs, the walls,
into the well. Gonzalo wanted to say something, but did not, his long
silence seeming to flow from another silence. He looked tired and
drowsy; behind him the green stump of the candle had almost reached
the socket of the candlestick, signifying that a day, or a life, was about
to end. Isabel watched me from the wooden bench on which she sat,
her legs crossed, a worn but steady smile on her face.

"This is the room where you will sleep, on two hard, narrow wooden beds with pillows like rocks. As you can see, the walls are peeling and the ceiling exudes water from the sky, but it is all I have, and you will be safe here as far as it depends on me. In this room my mother slept before she was murdered by a jealous baker, but you must not be startled if you hear murmuring and groans, footsteps on the roof and knocking on the wall, for she was a good woman and will do you no harm. And now, sleep easy. . . . One thing more—the room is not so gloomy and cold as it appears by night; in the morning a bright light comes in, and outside the window there is a large, leafy tree," I said.

It was then that Pero Meñique departed. Wrapped in darkness and drizzle, his stick leading the way, he disappeared down the street, which at that hour resembled a watery tunnel.

I went to my own room; I sat down on the edge of my bed; I listened to the rain, I listened to my visitors' silence, above all to Isabel's, for, I knew not why, I was already taken with her. Weary but wakeful, I closed my eyes and a man clad in black holding a lantern, who was neither wholly real nor entirely a dream, walked past me several times. Finally, hearing only the rain, I fell asleep.

The light on my eyelids aroused me. But it mattered not to me whether it was the hour of Prime or Sext, I tarried in bed, postponing the moment of rising, as if the longer I lay there, the closer Isabel would be to me. It was her voice that made me leap up and go in search of her; I had no need to dress, having lain down fully clothed. The morning was clear and sunny, the rain had blown over, and there was not a cloud in the sky. How rightly my father had once said that each morning is the first day, and all the ages of the world are present in a day, for that one, in particular, was like a day in paradise.

Isabel was in the kitchen, her elbows propped on the table and her head cradled in her hands. Sleep had made her youthful again, transformed her into a blither and more trusting maiden. As I came in she fixed her large almond eyes on me, although her thoughts were elsewhere, far from Madrid and my house.

"Gonzalo has gone," she said. "He had to leave. Ever since the Dominicans arrested several of our kindred he can no longer sleep or remain in one place, for he feels on his shoulders the menace which weighs on us all. At any moment the entire Kingdoms of Castile and Aragón will turn into a gigantic auto-da-fé."

"Even the most imbecilic, vile and murderous inhabitant of these realms believes he is entitled to attack, despise and kill Jews," I said.

"No person ought to slander and condemn another, be it only talk, whatever their race or country or religion, for in the blink of an eye we can find ourselves facing the Divine Being and we will have to bare ourselves, our thoughts and our deeds to Him," she declared.

"It is better to die an innocent victim than to live on as a guilty executioner," I said.

"It is better," she agreed, and said no more; and the morning light became all eyes, its incandescence suffused her gaze, conferring on her face a childish repose.

Then I ventured forth into the street in search of provisions. In the balmy autumn warmth people came and went on foot, on horseback, with laden mules and carts filled with building materials. With no further ado I reached the Plaza de San Salvador.

A crowd was gathered around the crier Francisco de Valladolid. On his right, a stout woman with a dark, fleshy face and thick, bulky legs, pendulous white breasts and broad, flabby arms wheezed loudly as if she had bellows instead of lungs in her chest. On his left was a wan-faced dwarf with straw-colored beard, sunken temples and ears set close to his head. His hands were so filthy it seemed the dirt was glued to his skin, and he was clad in a faded doublet and green hose. Behind these three, a maiden swathed in clothes revealed only the tip of her nose and her knuckles clutching a long wooden rosary. Standing apart from the rest, as if plague-stricken or leprous, an aged boy or a boyish old man gaped at the crier, looking like one of those birds that freeze when stalking their prey, so that they appear to be sleeping, stuffed or dead, until suddenly they stab with their beaks.

The crier announced, "In Madrid, the first day of November of fourteen eighty-three. On this day, being assembled the gentlemen of the city council within the Church of San Salvador, in accordance with their custom and usage, along with the honorable knight Rodrigo de Mercado, Chief Magistrate of the said city of Madrid and its environs, by command of the King and Queen, determined that, in order to avoid the unpeopling of the city of Madrid, when by following the orders of the King, Don Fernando, a separation into New Quarters of the Jews and Moors is made, as these New Quarters are very distant from the public squares wherein the commerce of this city is carried on, the King himself has caused a writ to be issued whereby they must be allowed and permitted to maintain their shops and wares and trades in the aforesaid public squares, provided that the aforesaid shops are not overlarge and are not their dwelling houses, save in the New Quarter or their *judería*. . . .

"Moreover, it is bidden that the decree of the Kings be obeyed and enforced, which made public the taking by certain of our knights of the city of Alhama, which is one of the principal cities in the Kingdom of Granada and situated in that place, and notified that our subjects who are there do wreak great destruction, and ordered that the city of Madrid come to their assistance with one thousand bushels of wheat, two thousand of barley and the persons necessary for their conveyance.

"Furthermore, every Jew in the *aljamas* of Madrid and its bailiwicks and the jurisdictions of its archdeaconry who is married or widowed or a widower must contribute one gold *castellano* or its equivalent of four hundred and eighty *maravedis,* requisite for the continuation of the war at Granada.

"The crier Francisco de Valladolid delivered the proclamation out loud in the afternoon, in the Plaza de San Salvador, many people being gathered there together."

Amongst the crowd, which dissolved, I caught sight of the physician Rabí Jacó, whom the councilmen had petitioned the Sovereigns to allow to remain in the city, where he had formerly dwelt, beyond the bounds of the *judería,* so that the inhabitants of Madrid might have better use of him at night, the *aljama* being shut up and he being forbidden to leave it then, obliging the sick to summon him from the New Quarter where he resided, which was far removed from the city and its outskirts. He, who drew a salary of six thousand *maravedis* and had broken his leg in a fall, was exempted from wearing a badge like other Jews in Madrid and its environs. With him was his son Ozé, also a physician.

A few steps away from them I saw a sort of multiple animal breaking apart into separate limbs and heads and going off in several directions at once, and recognized the *alguacil* Gonzalo de las Risas, the taxpayer Juan de las Risas, Pedro de las Risas and the ghost of Doctor de las Risas. He had been a judge of appeals, charged also with inspecting and setting a price upon provisions and determining the chief civil magistrate's salary, and empowered as an alderman to bequeath the office to his son or some other person. I saw Juan Rebeco and Juan Redondo, Juan Ricote and Juan de la Porqueriza, Juan Pingarrón and Juan Perales, Juan Lagarto the gamekeeper, and Isabel Palomeque, heiress to the mills of Mohed; I met Antonio the barber and Juan de Asensio the butcher, the watchmaker Juan Arias and Pedro de las Comadres, the taxpayer Juan de las Hijas, Gonzalo de las Monjas and Juan Honguero. I was about to leave the square when I came upon Don Rodrigo Rodríguez, who passed me by as if he had never seen me before in his life; he was dressed as a Dominican friar, and there was something toyish about his appearance.

"Don Rodrigo," I exclaimed when I saw he meant to snub me.

"These days you must not call anybody by their name in the streets, in the square or even in church," said he with displeasure, glaring so fiercely that I feared he would humiliate, wound or murder me. His face was smeared with white stuff, as if it had been bathed in flour.

"I crave your pardon, for I have no knowledge of the dangers besetting your person," I replied.

"These days news travels swiftly enough to the most distant corners of these kingdoms: on foot, horseback, muleback, in the gossip of laborers, merchants and travelers or through the post situated at intervals so that letters may proceed without delay. Jihan Garrido, Gonzalo de Salamanca, Salvador Daguas, Johan de Valencia and the couriers such as Juan Aragonés, who journey all the day long on foot or on horseback, come and go in five, ten, twenty days from one end of this realm to the other," he said. "What has transpired in Seville and in Ciudad Real has reached me from many mouths, it has been told to me in much detail, and one cannot claim ignorance when the venerable fathers call upon one to testify against those who stand accused of heretical depravity."

"But it is I, Juan Cabezón, friend to Pero Meñique," I protested, ignoring his lengthy explanation.

"Ah," he grunted.

"We met in the Plazuela de la Paja."

"Oh?"

"We were together in the house of Doña Francisca Hernández."

"Hmm."

"We spent the night with her. Pero Meñique and I shared her bed, until dawn broke."

"Ah," he said again, turning away.

"Don Rodrigo, you do know who I am?"

"Only too well," he answered.

"Have you seen your friend Pero Meñique?"

"That fire is good which consumes and burns heretics, wrote Ramón Llull," he said.

"Who is a heretic?" I asked.

"The son of *Conversos* Pero Meñique, who practices the Mosaic depravity," he declared.

"As far as I know, his mother was a most pious woman who died among the lepers on account of her prodigious compassion," I said.

"That fire is good which consumes and burns heretics," he repeated.

"Do not forget that Ramón Llull himself was nearly put to the stake by that blessed devil Nicolaus Eymerich, he who wrote the *Handbook for Inquisitors*," I reminded him.

"I am well acquainted with the book and with the fire wherein heretics burn," he said.

"Don Rodrigo, why are you dressed up as a Dominican friar?" I asked, my hand on his arm.

My question disturbed him deeply. His face beneath the white daubings took on a bluish cast, and he shifted his hump somewhat as he spoke. "An Old Christian like myself must go about garbed as a friar to demonstrate the purity of his blood, to keep Jewish depravity from tempting him in the streets and squares; with all the strength of his soul

he must banish from his being every *Converso* he has ever known, spoken
with or frequented in the weakness of his faith; he has to root out from
his body the Jewish grandfather who engendered his father, draining
him drop by drop from his own blood until the Kingdom of Castile is
cleansed of them."

"Do you mean to say that you are disposed to burn Pero Meñique at
the stake?"

"Without the shadow of a doubt," he answered, turning his back to
me as if he were shutting a door in my face.

"Are you in such a great hurry?" said I, detaining him again.

"I have urgent business with the Inquisitor-General, Don Fray Tomás
de Torquemada, son of the gentleman Pedro Fernández de Torquemada,
who from earliest childhood donned the habit of the Dominican Order.
That saintly man of most zealous faith has need of my wise counsels,
and I must depart forthwith for Segovia to join him. . . . We are brewing
something, Juanito Cabezón, something that will dazzle you ere long
with its flames," he gloated, smiling dryly and then clamping his teeth
together as if that were the first time he had ever smiled.

As he left, he unclenched his fist to drop a stone I had not noticed
he was holding all the while he spoke with me. He passed between two
Moors wearing cloaks with moon-shaped badges who continued to stand
listening even though the crier had finished his proclamation and left.
They squinted at us without turning their heads.

Behind Don Rodrigo Rodríguez walked a runty peasant with dirty
yellow hair, untrimmed beard, bruised face and overlarge hands, like a
great giant's. He was wearing a green doublet which had probably belonged to a man four times his size. As he went by, he scowled at me
rancorously, leading me to believe he held something against me after
overhearing my conversation with Don Rodrigo Rodríguez. Then, in a
perverse parody of the latter, he puffed out his chest in an aggressive,
defiant manner. Perchance they had nothing to do with each other, but
to me it seemed that he was the dwarf's guardian, following him closely
wherever he might go.

The sun died on the horizon, leaving behind blue shot through with
night and darkness clothed in clarity. It was the gloaming, when a man
cannot make out if the nebulous figure he glimpses in the shadows is
angel or demon, when the face of evening is stained by red clouds and
wounded by lights.

In minutes the street seemed filled with invisible spirits, which were
jostled, trampled and breathed upon by the people this All Saints' Day.
We passed the rich on their way to church, bearing bushels of wheat,
gallons of wine, baked breads and honey, in honor and memory of their
dead ones. Some brought wax torches, flambeaux and candles to burn

during services for the souls of the departed. They put them into wooden and silver candlesticks in the chapels where their kinsmen were buried; in the churches choirs sang Psalms for the souls of the dead and the living, who contemplated their destiny as if the future had already passed and the present were only a memory.

Suddenly the great sky lake was filled with clouds and dusk alighted on roofs and walls. A little girl in flames of light ran behind her glowing mother; a Moor carrying a pannier heaped with raisins for sale turned the corner as if plunging into ancestral darkness. Taper in hand, two high-bosomed maidens went by; an ancient woman crept across the square with her dangling bunch of keys and a great sack in which she seemed to carry all the days of her life.

Upon returning home with meat, bread and wine, I feared, because of the silence and dark in the room, that Isabel had gone. It was not so. I found her at the window facing the street, sitting as still as a stone.

"Here I am," I said.

"There you are," she echoed.

Moments of muteness, of uncertainty.

"It would seem that all the phantoms in Castile are here this night bewailing in the wind the injustice that has been wrought," she said.

"You have taken the words from my lips, for this entire evening I have been sensible of ghosts in the street."

"I understand what they say, they converse with my blackest dreams, and in their silence I hear the growling of my own fear," she shuddered.

"I will light the fire and heat the kettle to cook the meat I have brought. I am hungry," I said briskly.

"It is all one to me whether I eat or die of hunger," she replied, going into the kitchen to make a fire and hang the kettle from the chains over the hearth.

"I will draw water from the well. Give me the bucket, the rope and the pothook."

"Do not throw the bucket in after the rope," she remarked with grim humor.

"Nor will I throw myself in either," I answered, also unsmiling.

I went, I cast the bucket into the well, I drew out water, I lit candles in the other room and returned as quickly as I could, so that Isabel was surprised to see me back so soon.

I felt at ease in her company, finding with her a harmony I had never before experienced with a woman. To amuse her I carried the bucketful of water hobbling on my heels, not mincing like a harlot but as if my ankles were broken. I walked with grave, measured steps, like a sage and prudent man; I lunged and skipped haphazardly; I thrust out my chest, bent my knees and wagged my head back and forth, like a coxcomb; I walked knock-kneed; and I paused occasionally to listen, as if there were someone else following in my shadow.

Later we sipped hot broth out of porringers, we ate meat and stew, bread and wine. The moon appeared in the kitchen window, a glowing target amidst the white clouds which drifted away like ships into the immensity of the night. A dog howled in a house, the bells in the tower atop the Guadalajara Gate chimed Compline, and out in the street several men ran by as if chasing someone.

"They are after my brother," she exclaimed, startled.

"It is the nocturnal silence that makes us imagine noises, or hear our fancies," I replied, leaning out of the window to see whether the inquisitors were not indeed running after him.

"I have passed this whole day picturing to myself a thousand ways to die. I have envisioned my brother imprisoned, hostage for a ransom, shackled and chained in damp dungeons, in dark wells, on torture racks . . . I have watched him escape, be recaptured, be brought to trial and tortured over and over again . . . and burned at the stake."

"Sitting over there you are like a snuffed candle in the darkness."

"The floors in this house have not been swept for years; there are spiders on the walls, mice in the holes, ants in the corners and swarms of dead flies in the kitchen," she said, coming so close to me that I could feel her breath and see myself in the lambency of her eyes.

"After my mother died I left all as it was, partly out of melancholy and partly out of slovenliness and sloth," I admitted.

"I swept away a ghost in that room," she said.

"Doubtless my father's or my mother's, for both died a violent death."

"I swept it away without knowing whose it was."

I stood still next to the window in the moonlight, until I saw her nearly naked in the other room, clad only in her headcloth and the hoops in her ears, her arm curving beneath her breasts, her nipples showing, her belly uncovered, her thighs like white fishes.

Her body by candlelight, *languidus ignis*, was a fountain of honey and gold over which the candle's yellow quivers danced, while her clothing, shift and gown, lying on the bench, obliquely attested to her nakedness as the outer coverings of her intimate contours.

For a long while I observed her with unabashed concentration, trembling at the discovery in myself of a desire I had not known to be so ardent in my body. I followed every movement, I listened for each of her heartbeats as if it were my own. My imaginary hand cupped her breasts and kept them from spilling over into the darkness. The folds, the wrinkles, the marks her clothing had left were scarcely visible, they scarcely interrupted the continuous line of her flesh, the ebb and flow of her hip, the bowed curve of her thigh.

As I moved closer to the wall to shorten the distance separating me from her I held my breath, I held in my gaze, which seemed to make noise; then I looked again and saw her whole body turned frontwards to me, as if surrendering itself to my eyes. The dark rose of her sex, like a soft mouth, opened in parallel lips, an upside-down pyramid.

She turned her back to me, showing her buttocks in all their sensuous weight, their rounded fall. She sat down on the bench. She called to me.

"I will show you a fire more beautiful than your first love," she said.

I emerged from my trance with her body before me still stirring in my fancy, while beyond myself, in its visible splendor, that body became real and accessible. Imagination cannot be seen, said Ramón Llull, but at that moment I could have sworn it was dazzling and palpable.

Sitting on the bench, she removed her earrings, golden eels, unfastening the little tail from the hollow mouth, and threw off her headcloth. Then she stroked my hair tenderly, ran her hand over my chest, my stomach and my private parts.

My eyes followed her, attentive to every undulation, every flicker of candlelight on her body, as if my gratitude to life would flood every inch of her skin and the open abundance of her belly. With artless candor she pulled me down to the bed, resting my head on her breasts, like Leda about to receive the swan between her legs, and extended her arms along her hips, her stomach sunken in the center. She engulfed me, not with her sex alone, where our activity converged, but with her eyes as well, which took in my slightest movement.

And thus were our bodies reconciled, not in the church of the inquisitors but in love, if not in a single flesh, then in a shared desire. The mute language of our limbs faltered only in their sweating, fatigue and hesitations. And the maiden who had never known a man became a woman in my arms; a woman, not a goddess with brief breasts, delicate ankles and wrists, not a virgin painted in a church or dreamed of in a cell, a true woman.

"A thousand monks have died without knowing the flesh, and thousands more will die without even imagining it, roused solely by a body that has turned to ashes, is bathed in blood or lies beneath a stone," I said.

"Make haste, but come slowly," she murmured, submerging me within her oval, as with timid longing I admired the soft spreading of her spilt moons.

She dragged me down into her whirlpool, biting as she kissed me, her body adhering to mine, bending and stretching; she sighed into my ear, as if life abandoned her as she did so.

The wind sang at the dawn watch.

While the inquisitors were burning Isabel in effigy in Ciudad Real, and their *alguaciles* and familiars sought her flesh and blood in all the towns and villages of these kingdoms in order to roast something more than a statue, my passion left me no doubt about accompanying her to prison and to the stake, for the supreme bliss of dying at her side.

We were scarcely apart daytime or night, and soon the days of our love became weeks and the weeks became months. Each time we snuffed out the candle, her body became tangible in the darkness, her face bathed in black light was radiant, and her lips parted to receive me. So vulnerable was I lying upon her, so naked, that a shout from outside, a knock at the door, a wrathful face, could have killed me.

Our bodies joined together partook of the silence, the repose of objects, the quietude of gratified love.

"It is at night that our face is most ours, for thus will we look on the brink of death," she once said to me as she was standing near the window.

"Perhaps, but our body is also real treading the threshold of light in the morning," I replied.

"In the dark the distance between things is abolished by grace of the bodies that love each other," she said on another occasion, her hair loosed, breasts bare, her feet unshod.

"Or else the separation between them becomes even more profound," I said.

However it may be, silence, separation, obliviousness to the world had taken hold of the house; for days on end we heard naught but our own footfalls, breathing and voices, as if they belonged to a third person we had fashioned from our two beings.

The city reached us through the bells, the unseen cocks who heralded the dawn and the winds and rains that swept untrammeled down the streets.

We had no other tidings of Christmas save the church bells at Matins summoning the faithful to early Mass, or of the New Year or the Feast of the Circumcision except the torches and festive lights glimmering far off in the night to the sound of trumpets, tabors and bells.

The bells were always calling to Mass. At Epiphany and Candlemas we found diversion gazing at the stars from the dark courtyard or watching the lengthy procession of candles on the road to church headed for yet another Mass.

We knew it was Ash Wednesday only because of the sooty heads that filed by in the street window as if on their way to the grave. We spent feast days strictly cloistered; the more noise in the street, the more hushed were we; the more bonfires lit in the square, the greater the din or shouting penetrating our walls, the more alone we were.

It made no difference to us whether we were shut in or not; we loved each other as if all the forsaken spirits in Castile had converged in our embraces, all the incorporeal dead who floated in the air with no fixed abode in space, all the souls who for centuries had been seeking their birth, unable to take shape in any body.

Each night Isabel was there, naked, open, urgent, with no longings save those of her own desire, no triumph beyond love accomplished. And all the while perhaps our bodies became ashes in the minds of the inquisitors and dust in the memory of the dead.

"This is my kingdom, this is my span, I have no others," she said to me one morning, her eyes shining as she pointed to her belly and her milky-white breasts.

"Let me kiss your kingdom, let me plunge into your span, I have no others," I answered.

"Then I shall go astride you, albeit to the stake," she said as I lifted her in my arms.

Nevertheless, after long months of captive existence there came an afternoon when she yearned to walk by the river's edge, and so, arrayed in tattered hose, torn doublet, dirty face, bristly mustache and short hair, in the likeness of a man, she ventured forth into the street.

So effective was the camouflage that none who knew her would have imagined, had they met her, that here was the notorious Isabel de la Vega, the *Conversa* so eagerly sought for by the *alguaciles* and familiars of the Inquisition to carry out the sentence passed by a tribunal which had more in common with a stinking ditch brimful of corpses than with the justice of God.

At that time the sun had entered into the sign of Capricorn, the air had shrunk from dampness and cold, the days were shorter and more overcast, and the sparrow hawk flew close to the city walls, hugging the ground in search of prey. Days came and days went in their wintry colors, but even yet, like hidden treasures of nature, here and there petals shone like rubies, and dry leaves gleamed on the ground, their small shadows crackling beneath our feet.

We paused by a willow tree, we touched its drooping boughs, its

springy and lanceolate leaves, its green tresses; we halted at the foot of
an aspen and raised our eyes to its tall and frondent crown as if to a
temple of triangular leaves. Afterwards we kept close to the gullies,
looking our fill at the houses, the black poplars, the stout walls and the
long shadows they cast. The sun setting on the horizon streaked the
sky with red and gray. A half-plucked hen chased by a dog scurried out
of a backyard, as if narrowly escaping from a pot of boiling water. On
the road a gaunt and scowling laborer appeared. His face, his hands
and his clothing blended with the dust; his forehead was bound with a
dirty rag; perhaps he had just been wounded, or anointed with holy
oil. When he passed us by he mumbled unintelligible words, and we
saw a mask of mud moving its lips. Soon he was far away, the same
color as the landscape and the road.

Heading in the opposite direction, an infantryman approached riding
an ass and carrying a mewing cat in a gunnysack. They went by in a
great hurry, as if the man were long overdue for a skirmish against the
Moors, and his companions in arms found themselves in grave straits
on account of his absence.

At the edge of a ravine a number of children, like so many colored
shadows in the afternoon, were jumping up and down on a pig's blad-
der, meaning to burst it open explosively. As each one jumped, the
others covered their ears; there was something fantastical and old-
fashioned about their appearance, in their elongated shadows, which
as they skittered across the ground seemed like figments of the twilight.

Not far off other children played at priests and penitents, a short
procession of habits and bare backs moving in a circle, eyes downcast,
chanting hymns. With rods and straps they scourged themselves in
imitation of adult sinners. A stone's throw away four lads had strung
up a lopsided swing from the branch of a tree on which they pushed
to and fro a puppet dressed as a man.

An old woman crouching in the bushes purged her guts, as if seated
on a hidden stone. On the ground next to her lay the buckled leather
pouch of a pilgrim, for keeping alms. She might have been alone in a
privy or parading her street clothes in some square as she waved her
chilblained hands at us by way of greeting.

We trod the dry leaves, the pebbles, the burgeoning darkness. In the
distance the day's last gleams dimmed over the peaks of the Guadarrama. Beneath our feet the shadows began to fade.

"When I think of the sentence hanging over my life and I see myself
walking along these dusty roads, I say to myself that it is better to dine
on a coarse loaf than on a clod of earth, to dress in tatters than to be
air, to sleep on the ground than to rule among the clouds, to grieve for
everything than to have nothing to grieve for," Isabel said.

On the way back we saw Pero Meñique at the door to my house. He had come to tell us that some *Conversos* recently arrived from Ciudad Real had related to him how in that town, during the month of February, in the course of various autos-da-fé, the inquisitors had burned alive more than thirty persons, among whom were María González la Pánpana, Alonso Alegre and his wife Elvira, Alonso de Belmonte, the tailor Juan de Chinchilla, alias Juan Soga, Rodrigo the Jailor and Rodrigo Alvarez, Juan de Fez and his wife Catalina Gómez, Juan González Pintado and Juan González Deza, Juan Galán and his wife Elvira González, Rodrigo Marín and his wife Catalina López, a woman known as La Perana and Gómez de Chinchilla, the son of Juan de Chinchilla. During another auto-da-fé Isabel and Gonzalo de la Vega, Juan de Ciudad and his wife Isabel de Teva, Constanza González and Constanza Alonso, the cobbler García de Alcalá, the tanner Juan Calvillo, the spice seller Juan Falcón, Sancho de Ciudad and his wife María Díaz, among others, had been burned in effigy. Marina González had been consigned to the flames for having washed and wept over the bodies of the dead; and the bones of her husband, who had been prosecuted posthumously, were disinterred and cremated. An ailing old woman, Juana González, under arrest by the Inquisition for having kept the Sabbath, had thrown herself into the well of the private dwelling to which she was confined before the Holy Office could bring her to trial. Nonetheless, she was prosecuted in death and condemned to the fire, as by taking her own life she had admitted herself guilty of heresy.

Isabel was badly shaken by this news. "If someday I should have to flee from Madrid," she said, "seek for me in Saragossa, at the home of my aunt, Luna de la Vega. If I am not there, I will surely be in Calatayud, Teruel or Toledo. Somewhere or other you will hear news of me, you will meet kindred of mine who can tell you what has become of my person. I foresee that the day is not far away when the hounds of the Lord will discover my hiding place and ferret me out, to throw me for life into an oubliette or put me to torture, tied to a trestle, stripped naked before the inquisitors, who will chastely cover me with the cloth of shame to keep their virginal eyes from sinning.

"Their informers listen behind walls; they peep through chinks in doors; they watch from church towers and from under rocks. I have seen their spies in the ditches, amongst the corpses of dead animals, waiting to discover anything suspicious in the raiment of those who pass by the edge of the ravines. . . . Before long you will have to go to Mass on Sundays and feast days, to confess whatever is needful and to take Communion whenever necessary, for there are many invisible eyes vigilant to see whether you as a descendant of *Conversos* perform the duties of the Catholic faith. If you do not, one morning they will seize you and carry you off to a secret prison where you will be told what your sins are."

"Shall I kiss the hand of a Dominican priest?" asked Pero Meñique.

"Many kiss the hands they would gladly see cut off," she replied.

"If you go to buy sardines in the Plaza de San Salvador, or find yourself at the Christian butcher's, take great care answering the innocent questions they may ask. Order swine's flesh, mention your fondness for bacon, for in this city the person you least suspect can denounce you as a Judaizer. Above all, be on guard against the neighbors who have known you since childhood, who, out of hatred for your parents, will want to revenge themselves on you," Pero Meñique warned me.

"The other day," I admitted, "when I went to the money changer's with a gold *castellano*, he admonished me for changing too many coins. 'Keep them for your old age, Juan Cabezón, for he that saves his dinner will have more for his supper,' he said to me. 'If I don't take it out for an airing, Don Lope, my gold will turn to coal,' I said to him."

"And now there is something you must tell me, no matter how cruel," Isabel entreated Pero, searching his face. "Where is my brother? Have the inquisitors taken him?"

"I have no news of Gonzalo," answered the blind man. "I ask every *Converso*, merchant or traveler I meet on the road about him. As luck would have it, no one knows aught of him."

"Often the inquisitors bury the accused in secret prisons, and nothing is heard of them until they are brought out of the dungeon dead or sent to the stake in an auto-da-fé," she said.

"Alas, I know," murmured Pero Meñique.

"I cherish the hope that he has escaped alive from these realms and is now far from the inquisitors' terror," said Isabel.

We sat down to eat hogs' pudding and lambs' stones, which Pero Meñique in his blindness mistook for pignuts, asking whether it was already springtime, prodding them to determine if they were raw or cooked, as if they really were the round roots which have neither stem nor leaf.

"I am looking for a coin hidden in a truffle, like the one Plinius bit upon in Cartagena," he declared. But when he discovered by the flavor that what he had been chewing with enjoyment were sheeps' testicles, he called them ballocks and cods, and wolfed them down in great mouthfuls.

After he had gone, at first cockcrow, Isabel led me by the hand to the bedchamber and began to embrace and kiss me ardently, as if that night were to be the last of our nights and she were breathing out her soul in those kisses.

While I kissed her I took off her chemise, I freed her breasts and her belly, until, totally naked, with love in her eyes, she abandoned herself to my caresses.

Then I parted her thighs, and she was surprised by my determination, by the way I held her and pressed her to me. I feared she would vanish from my arms, leaving the tangible and the visible for a world of phantoms and loss.

Later, seeing me poised on the verge of her body observing the candlelight on her face and her hair strewn over the pillow, still hesitant to enter her warm vortex, she drew me to her and swept me away in her embrace.

"You will go farther slowly, do not be in a hurry," she whispered into my ear.

"I am taking my time," I replied, and I loved her until we became still, on the edge of sleep, and she, believing I had succumbed, blew out the candle and went barefoot in the darkness to the kitchen.

All around me the shadows turned to stone. I felt as if I were being walled into a tomb, and I hurried out of bed to follow her. I found her holding a piece of bread. She looked at me musingly and said, "Sometimes in the night I think I hear them breaking down the door, and I go to the gate to see what is the matter, but there is no one there. On occasion I become aware of a man staring at me through the window, but as soon as I approach him, he disappears. Perhaps it's the silence, perhaps it's fear that makes me picture noises, hear imaginings."

"And I, when I lie in bed at night, walk about outside myself. My eyes comb the doors and walls, the shadows in the yard and the crannies between the roof tiles, and every stone and tree, to see if any familiars of the Inquisition are hunting for us. After a brief stay in bed I go out of the chamber, my eyes and ears alert, holding my breath, and room by room I inspect the emptiness and scrutinize the shadows in search of signs until, having found all in order, I return to your side and, without making the slightest sound, I fall asleep again," I said.

"In my dreams I often see myself walking down a forgotten street pursued by all the demons in hell, but I resolve to confront my enemies, who then vanish, only to reappear moments later, eternally indestructible," she said.

Indeed, not so far from Isabel's dreams the inquisitors continued to arrest, prosecute, torture and burn their victims. She was as threatened by the honorable clergymen of the Holy Office in Ciudad Real as the day they had condemned her to die at the stake for heresy and burned her effigy with a symbolic torch. Nevertheless, her days, her weeks and her months went by with no apparent greater cause for concern than the news I brought back after roaming through the squares, markets, churches and suburbs of the town with Pero Meñique, King Bamba, the

Trotter or by myself. The Moor and One-Eye had set out for Málaga to fight alongside Alí Muley Abenhazan, while the pure-blooded dwarf, Don Rodrigo Rodríguez, Babylonia and Agustín Delfín devoted themselves to assisting the inquisitors in the discovery, arrest and conviction of Judaizing *Conversos*.

I always told Isabel what Juan de Orgaz had proclaimed in the Plaza de San Salvador, the decrees and ordinances prohibiting any person in Madrid from allowing his swine to roam free from ten in the morning until sunset, upon pain of paying ten *maravedis* for each pig the *alguacil* might capture walking about town; forbidding any knight or squire to be so foolhardy as to carry a sword, under risk of losing it; or the council's decision permitting Alonso the chandler to sell a pound of candles for eight *maravedis* and two of the new *blancas* until New Year's Day of 1485. . . .

The days came and went, set apart from each other solely by a date or our modest, intimate and uncomplicated doings. Monday 17 January, Wednesday 2 February, Tuesday 29 March, Friday 8 April, Wednesday 11 May, Monday 23 May, Friday 3 June, each day remarkable only for the color of the sky, the cold at night or rain in the afternoon. There was no change in Isabel's forced captivity, and her fear did not diminish.

From my vantage point at the window, I narrated to her as best I could the procession of blood on Good Friday, as if the crowd were escorting Jesus the Jew to an auto-da-fé; I counted for her the number of steps, of wax candles, of penitents of blood and penitents of light in the tormented serpentine file in the street. I spoke to her of the feast of Corpus Christi, of the tradesmen in town who had brought out their games and their playacting, upon pain of otherwise paying in perpetuity three thousand *maravedis* every year to defray the cost of the aforesaid feast day; I described to her the opulence of the crosses, the bustling streets, the profusion of banners, the poor fatherless children brought up by charity, the sundry brotherhoods, the fools in motley cutting capers and playing upon instruments, the parade of saints carried out of the churches and monasteries, the solemn priests bearing the Blessed Sacrament on their shoulders in the company of gentlemen and ladies from town, to place it upon an altar in the midst of dancing, shouts and music. I related to her how at the very end came the Moors and Jews, who were forced to dance under pain of a perpetual fine of three thousand *maravedis*; the Jews were led by a rabbi holding a Torah, representing the synagogue and its ancient laws which had been overcome by Christ and the Church.

"They say that all our limbs belong to Christ, and thus whoever commits fornication makes his limbs turn into a whore's," she said.

On one of those deep dark nights when we were at home, Pero

Meñique came, warily and wrapped in shadows, to inform us that a *Converso* had told him now on 10 May last, in Saragossa, where the Inquisition had only recently been established, having been installed as well in Valencia and Catalonia, many *Conversos* had been seized as heretics; their properties had been confiscated and they had been marched out in an auto-da-fé at the cathedral in that city. Among them were Leonora Elí, who, whenever she heard the most holy name of Jesus being uttered, would respond, "Hold your tongue, name Him not, for one of that name has been gibbeted"; Felipe Salvador, alias Santicos, and his wife Leonor Catorce Valenciana, for eating meat on a Friday and in Lent and for keeping the Sabbath and the fast of Yom Kippur; Isabel Muñoz Castellana, for the same crimes and because when she recited the *Credo*, upon reaching the words *"et in Jesum Christum,"* she said, "Here is where the ass stumbled." On another day, in the courtyard of the archbishop's palace, after Pedro de Arbués had preached the sermon, two men were condemned to death as Judaizers; and for performing Jewish rites and having clothed twelve poor Jews in honor of the twelve tribes of Israel, Aldonza de Perpiñan was burned in effigy, *post mortem*.

With misgivings we heard noises far off in the murky night, and we feared someone had been following Pero Meñique, had seen him enter the house and had notified the inquisitors; but after a silent wait we could hear only the hammering next door in the brazier's shop, for he was a man who liked to rise at Matins and set to work. Through the window facing the backyard, the three of us saw a fat friar run to the privy tucked out of sight in a distant corner of his house. Then in the street we glimpsed a corpulent figure dressed in black lumbering through the night like a brawny ghost, and tagging after him a slovenly beggar in filthy, torn clothes made of dangling strips and ravelly threads; suddenly the corpulent shape turned on the beggar and dashed him against the wall, so that his head echoed like an empty nutshell, and he was left doubled over in pain, a rag doll stammering incoherencies in a spray of saliva.

"By fire and blood, we shall do away with heretical depravity by fire and blood!" swore the fat one, who was merely an armed familiar of the Holy Office patrolling the streets.

When Pero Meñique had departed, as surreptitiously as he had come, Isabel and I played at Pyramus and Thisbe, conversing through the door and the chinks in the wall, and we agreed to meet by a tree in the yard, pretending we had arrived from the remote suburbs of Madrid to our meeting place. But unlike those two legendary lovers, a lioness did not attack my beloved Belilla, forcing her to take refuge in a cave where she dropped her veil, nor did I, mistakenly believing her dead, take my own life with a sword; rather I carried her off to bed and love, ready for her sake to confront all the inquisitors of Castile and Aragón, Valencia and Catalonia.

Soon afterwards the sun entered Cancer; the trees were covered with leaves and the fields with yellow, purple, white and red flowers; the swallows flew out from under the eaves of houses and churches; and Isabel's desire to escape her confinement became acute as if outside in the street real life were surrendering itself freely to all passersby. As the days grew longer and more sultry, the air warmer and more subtle, she felt deprived not only of the season but of life itself. Soon enough autumn would come, the sun would move into Capricorn, and once again the trees and fields would denude themselves of colors and fruit; chill rainstorms would swoop down over the city from the frozen peaks of the Sierra Guadarrama, and we would feel weather in our bones and cold-stiffened limbs as fiercely as we felt the cloistered solitude in our eyes and hearts.

It was, I remember, towards the middle of March: Pero Meñique had come to pay us a visit. The city of Madrid had suddenly acquired a reddish hue, as if a bloody light from the sky had flooded the streets with shadows and cosmic dread. Partially deprived of the solar rays by the intrusion of the moon, the townsfolk had become afraid, the astrologers had prophesied misfortune, the dogs had bayed and birds had fluttered in their cages and coops. We had gone into the backyard to watch the eclipse, without telling Pero Meñique what was happening, since he couldn't see it. All of a sudden he asked, "What is occurring that so alarms both man and beast?"

"It is an eclipse of the sun," answered Isabel.

"Haply some prince will die on whose life not our betterment but a great portion of our ills depends," he remarked, turning his face towards the wrong part of the sky, where the celestial phenomenon was not taking place. "I have heard tell these days past that in Rome dreadful comets have been sighted which presage great disasters, but I fear that the columns of smoke from the bonfires kindled almost daily by the pious Dominicans, which have already reached the skies over the pontifical city, augur even more horrific evils.

"Even yesterday, Sunday, to be precise, in Ciudad Real, the inquisitors Pero Díaz de la Costana and Francisco Sánchez de la Fuente held an auto-da-fé in the public square, committing to the flames Ruy González de Llerena and his wife Elvira, Fernando de Adaliz, Inés Belmonte, Pedro González Fixinix, Gonzalo Díaz de Villarrubia and others besides. . . . Also yesterday Pero Díaz de la Costana, with God as his witness, declared and pronounced Juan Martínez de los Olivos, Diego Pinto the tailor, the Bachelor Juan García de la Plaza, Alfonso Martínez the stammerer, the silversmith Juan González and his wife Beatriz, Antón Ruiz de las Dos Puertas, Ferrand García de la Yguera, Marina Gentil, Juan González Escogido, Ruy López and many others to be heretics and apostates, guilty of having incurred the sentence of major papal excommunication and other spiritual and temporal punishments, condemning them to the loss of their property; and because no heretic or apostate or excommunicate may or should be interred in hallowed earth, he ordered the bones of the aforesaid persons dug up from their graves and the consecrated ground where they had been, and burned to ashes in public, so that they and the memory of them might perish together."

"Obviously, pardoning the dead plays no part in the piety of these preaching friars, who seek only to pursue them beyond the tomb and prey on their remains," I said.

"Amongst the instructions issued by Fray Tomás de Torquemada in the fall of 1484, in which he announced the establishment of the Inquisition in every town and required that a heretic confined in a secret jail, upon being reconciled to the Church, should have his penance amended to perpetual imprisonment, was one stipulating that if, by book or by trial, there should be discovered any heretic deceased thirty or forty years earlier, a case should be brought forward against him until he stood condemned, his remains should be exhumed in order to cremate them, and his estate confiscated from the heirs; ordering that on the day of the auto-da-fé an effigy representing the dead person should be stood on the scaffold, clothed in a miter of condemnation and a *sanbenito* bearing the insignia of the condemned on one side and the dead man's name on the other, which effigy, after the reading aloud of the sentence, is to be relaxed to the arm of secular justice and the man's bones disinterred to be publicly burned; and if there should be an inscription on his grave and if his coat of arms is displayed in any place, they should be erased in order that no recollection of him shall abide on earth, save that of his sentence and the execution of it by the inquisitors."

"This may not be the most propitious moment for speaking of the future, but I believe that I have conceived and there is a living creature within my belly," Isabel announced.

"I guessed you had a surprise in store for me," said I, torn between joy and grief.

"I shall pass these months swiftly, I shall not tire even though I am with child," she vowed. "The expectation of soon seeing my daughter or son will lighten the days for me."

"We are already wearied when we come into the world, our death begins in our mother's womb, on the threshold of life we start to wither;

130

it is only the ancient who take such time in growing old and dying,"
said Pero Meñique.

"A wise man says that the woman who carries a babe in her belly is
privileged, as she counts for two," Isabel remarked, "but I feel more
like a wall sprouting a stomach and in danger of collapsing."

"My spirit will also swell during your term, for I shall be filled with
cares and worries until the birth," I added.

"I am the only man who burst out laughing when he was born," said
Pero Meñique. "You seem very perturbed for a future father."

"I only hope I have been my own Holy Ghost," I replied.

"What if Torquemada overheard you," he cautioned, his face turned
towards the wall, as if the Inquisitor-General were imprinted there.

"May Torquemada, the enemy of all life, never overhear us," Isabel
and I cried out together, rubbing him off the wall with a ritual swipe.

"That man is invisible; even when he's present, he's absent; even in
flesh and blood he's a corpse; even breathing in the sultry summer air,
he is icy," said Pero.

As if increased fear magnified desire, no sooner had our blind friend
departed than Isabel lay down naked on the bed as naturally as any
woman who would indulge in a moment's pleasure to counterbalance
the world's miseries and the ephemeralness of human possessions.

"The eyes saw a beautiful lady who was wearing sumptuous clothes,
but the imagination pictured her chemise," I quoted from Ramón Llull's
Proverbs from the Vegetal Trunk."

"The imagination imagines whatever it can't find daytimes or night,"
she answered.

"According to the same author," I went on, "when a man cuts into
meat with a knife, he feels what softness is, and when he cuts into bone,
he feels hardness, but I say that when a man enters the flesh of his
beloved, he feels its hardness, and when he has penetrated it, he feels
its softness . . . and when it is entirely his, he feels its emptiness."

"If you believe that philosopher, imaginings are never visible," Isabel
reasoned.

"But you can touch and suffer from love's imagination," I replied.

"Only if it is of my doing," she said.

"We shall be married this very night," I declared.

"You will drape the veil like a cloud over my face for our wedding,"
she murmured, covering her countenance with her hand.

"I shall go before you carrying the flambeaux, and the heart of pine
will feed the fire of our love," I said as I placed the candles in front of
her.

"The unbidden guest knows not where to sit," she said.

"A wedding is not made with mushrooms," I said, throwing two gold *castellanos* on the floor.

"We have chosen each other for ever and anon," she vowed.

"In life and in death," I replied.

"In the name of the Lord Our God, a marriage has been contracted and by Divine Grace celebrated between Juan Cabezón, inhabitant of Madrid, on the one hand, and Isabel de la Vega, maiden daughter of Rodrigo de la Vega, deceased, inhabitant of the town of Ciudad Real, on the other hand," she recited, in imitation of the wedding ceremony, "acting as witness on behalf of the maiden the said spirit of her father and on behalf of the twain, all the kindly spirits of the world past and yet to come. To this marriage the said Juan brings all the bodily and spiritual possessions he has ever had or will have in any place. And the said maid brings three hundred nights of love, of which she pledged to deliver one hundred and fifty at the present time and one hundred and fifty during the rest of her life. And the said Juan Cabezón and Isabel de la Vega vowed never to take another woman besides the said maiden and never to take another man besides the said Juan. And it pleased both sides that the present marriage was arranged between themselves and ordered as was customary among the Jews and Christians, and they made their *kinyan*, accepting their betrothal, in the presence of Rabbi Abraham de Funes, whose testimony is inscribed below, promising to abide by the aforesaid and never to contravene it. Witnesses: Pero Meñique and King Bamba, by proxy, inhabitants of Madrid."

"I will serve and honor and govern and rule over you, following the laws of the male Christians of this country who serve and honor and govern and rule over their wives," I replied. "I will give to you what is just, and in dowry for your virginities I swear never to take another woman nor oblige you to quit this city, unless it be by your order and wish, or on account of dire necessity. In the name of the Father, the Son and the Holy Ghost. Amen."

"And now, let the bride come forward and the bridegroom enjoy her," she said.

Another day, oppressed by the summer heat, which made her feel a continuous veil of sweat on her skin, Isabel wanted to take a walk in town. Until that moment prudence had made her refrain from appearing on the street (save one time), being ever mindful of the sentence hanging over her and of the risk she ran, since the inquisitors never abandon their prey no matter how many years may go by, making it a point of honor that no heretic should ever escape punishment. In her case, a long time had elapsed without Pero Meñique or myself having inadvertently betrayed the secret of her sojourn in my house, or her having given herself away by a heedless act. Therefore, when she begged to walk abroad in Madrid, her words did not find much favor with me; I would have preferred to keep her in total seclusion, taking no chance whatsoever. But Isabel was becoming melancholy with the light on the wall, the grain of the ceiling beams and the holes in the kitchen floor as her sole study day after day. Finally, she cried out that she wanted to be herself again, even if it meant arrest.

"What crime have I committed against the Kingdom of Castile, save to absent myself from a city where the Friar Preachers daily commit the worst atrocities in the name of the Catholic religion?" she asked me, asking herself.

"None," I answered her, answering myself.

We went on the street. A bird passed by in front of us, flying low between the thick walls of the old houses, as if disoriented in the noon-day heat. A busybody watched us from her balcony, before withdrawing into a room. The town seemed deserted, as at daybreak, when it is laid bare by light but no one is yet abroad.

"Do you realize that we will never again walk down the very same streets we travel in 1485?" Isabel suddenly exclaimed.

"We scrutinize the tides of history, never suspecting that we are riding on a wave," I replied.

"If we didn't forget the moment just gone by, we could never live in the present," she said.

"That is true," I assented, my eye on a harlot prowling by the riverside outside the city walls in search of a man.

She saw me and signaled I should come to her side, ignoring Isabel.

"Do you see that fat squire riding on a puny horse? Look how he beats the animal's flanks, not caring one whit about the pain he inflicts," Isabel said, distracting my attention from the harlot.

"Where?" I asked.

"Over there, among the black poplars." She pointed to a cloud of dust.

"I don't see anything," I said.

"It's too late, he's gone," she declared.

"Isn't that woman coming towards us Babylonia?" I asked Isabel, as if I were in doubt about what I saw but my companion could recognize her more easily from my description alone.

"All I can see is a kind of hobgoblin dressed in black from head to toe. Is that your Babylonia?"

"That is she, the one with the peeling face. . . . Her moulting has been for the worse."

"I don't want to meet her; something tells me she shouldn't see me. Let us turn back or duck around the corner," she said.

"Come quickly, for you are right not to trust her."

But she saw us nonetheless, and her mouth gaped open as if she would bite at the air with her resinous false teeth; she roughly pushed back her soiled headcloth, exposing her rusty hair.

We fled in such haste from her probing stare that we failed to notice, standing in the street, a stout, ugly man wearing a greatcoat of sackcloth, such as executioners wear, whom we met face-to-face.

"What are you running away from?" he inquired, blocking our way.

It was a familiar of the Holy Office, one of those men who, giving proof of their religious zeal in exchange for material privileges, served the inquisitors as unpaid spies, accompanied them to protect their persons and executed their orders, poised to enter into action anywhere at any time. All the familiars were licensed to bear arms and empowered to arrest heretics, and they constituted a small, turbulent army that was dreaded by all and immune from justice.

Without answering him Isabel quickened her steps, and I followed as she urged me to vanish from the street. Meanwhile the man strove to appear inoffensive, strolling behind us at a leisurely pace, although he never took his eyes off us.

"We shouldn't have bolted like that," I told her several streets later. "The rashness of our flight only aroused his suspicions, and now he will persist until he finds us."

"I saw Death in the gleam of his eyes," she said.

"How could you have seen his eyes?" I asked her. "We had scarcely encountered him and you were already running."

"Our eyes met for an instant. That sufficed for me to know everything about him. And then, when I turned to take another look, I saw Death again, in his gestures and his gait, in the malevolent scowl on his face . . . and I shivered all over, as if from a premonition of losing my life."

"I saw no eyes, only dark blotches, matted hair, muddy features, rumpled clothes," I said.

"I even saw his shadow creeping over the ground," she insisted.

Now, to add trepidation to fear, there was Pero Meñique waiting at the door to tell us how the inquisitors had transferred the tribunals of the Holy Office from Ciudad Real to Toledo, where, as was their custom, they had proclaimed a Term of Grace for forty days, to enable the *Conversos* to come forward and confess their errors; but no one had done so in the first two weeks. On the contrary, during the procession of Corpus Christi on 2 June, several *Conversos* had attempted to murder the inquisitors. The plot being found out by the Regidor of Toledo, Gómez Manrique, some of them were imprisoned, and six were hanged.

In that same city, in the course of an auto-da-fé on 25 July, upwards of four hundred dead had been burned in effigy, convicted of Judaizing while alive. In the meantime, the Inquisitor-General, Fray Tomás de Torquemada, had ordered the inquisitors to convene the rabbis and require them, under pain of death and confiscation of their property, to pronounce an anathema upon those Jews who refused to inform on *Conversos* who might have reverted to heretical depravity since their baptism. According to the inquisitors, it was these very same rabbis who could furnish them with the most information.

In Segovia an incensed Dominican friar, one Antonio de la Peña of the Convent of Santa Cruz, was threatening the Jews with the erection of pulpits in the *aljamas* so as to foment, in his words, "a scandal of such magnitude that the entire city would be unable to quell it," for the rabble, aroused by his preachings, was primed to heed the call to arms and attack the Jews.

"Is that all for today?" I asked Pero Meñique when he had given us his bad news.

"I want to know everything that is in store for the harried souls in these godforsaken kingdoms," Isabel said.

That night, sometime between Matins and Lauds, she awoke screaming in the darkness and recounted her nightmare to me.

"I went out for a walk among the poplars by the river to look at the stars. While I was looking at them the moon waxed larger and brighter, as if it were hurtling towards earth, and I said to myself, 'The moon has a face.' At that very moment I became aware of three women inside my body who were breaking off from me, leaving me alone with one very weak and tiny woman, myself. I, walking down a narrow, twisting street, wearing the distinctive Jewish garments my grandmother had worn in Saragossa. And not knowing whether she was in me, or I in her, I gazed at her as at an infinitely tender, kind and generous person. 'Why must you wear these special clothes when your spirit has no size or shape? Who can be so evil as to dishonor you thus, when you are so righteous and beautiful?' I asked her.

" 'It is the devil who has requested it of us,' answered a meek voice behind me, 'a devil who has a great relish for the ashes of the dead and has asked his Dominican disciples for more Jewish bodies to feed the flames.' 'Ah, now I understand; so that was the secret . . . I shall go and divulge it to all the righteous on earth,' I said.

"With that a goat-bearded *alguacil* of the Holy Office appeared of a sudden in the street and, grasping me by the arm, forced me to undress before a crowd of people, because he had discovered that the Jewish badge was missing from my clothes, for it had vanished as if by magic. Violently he ripped off shreds of my skin—my chemise was sticking to my body—and the bloody rays from his eyes pierced my breast as if he were stabbing me in the heart with daggerlike crosses. 'If you were nicer to me, I would become a good Christian,' I said, 'but how can I believe in your mercy if you persecute me so grimly?' 'I'm not interested in your beliefs, I only want your blood, for I have become very fond of it,' he answered. And then he slashed at my belly, just where I am carrying my child, and I was afraid he would discover it and do it harm. So I ran quickly towards myself, who was waiting for me at the door of the house, pursued by the mocking stares of a crowd of riffraff which had gathered to witness my suffering. And even though I am awake now, I am still running."

I held her in my arms in the darkness until she fell asleep again.

A knocking at the door startled me. It was the familiar of the Inquisition whom we had met in the street the day before. In a honeyed voice he explained that he was passing by the house when he remembered that a friend of his lived there, a man from Torre Quemada who was wont to rise at dawn, and so he had dared to knock. When I said no, that nobody from Torre Quemada lived here, he examined me from head to foot, brimming with suspicions and hypocrisy, trying to insinuate his prying gaze into the house.

"Are you a Christian?" he asked.

"Yes."

"And were your parents as well?"

"They lived and died as good Christians," I answered.

He mulled over my words and looked at me coldly.

"Beware of lying to Holy Mother Church, or one day our preaching fathers may furnish you with enough wood to singe your feet," he said.

"I am grateful for your warning, but I have nothing to fear from our Holy Mother Church," I replied.

"All the better for you," he said, staring at the floor.

I shut the door. I ran to Isabel to reassure myself that she had not overheard, that she was still asleep.

There was more knocking.

It was he again.

"Did you not tell me that you are an orphan?" he asked.

"Yes, sir, my parents died many years ago."

"Can you recite the *Credo* and the *Pater Noster*?"

"From beginning to end, and other prayers as well."

"Does someone else live in this house?"

"No, no one."

"A moment ago I thought I heard footsteps other than your own."

"I live alone, sir, but as the house is very large, I often converse with God, the Blessed Virgin and myself as I walk through the empty rooms. That is my way of warding off the evil thoughts which, being a young man, might perturb me, sir."

"You would not be hiding some fugitive heretic?"

"God forbid, sir."

"Keep in mind, I could burn you one day for talking to yourself, along with the shape that keeps you company in sin," he said.

"If it is God's will, sir, but before her death my mother taught me to be a good Christian."

"So were many heretics as well, and now they have been turned into ashes."

"*Memento homo quia cinis es, et in cinerem reverteris:* Remember, oh man, that you are ashes, and that to ashes you will return," I countered.

"In my mind's eye I can already see you marching in an auto-da-fé," he added, ignoring what I had said.

"Oh sir, may God deliver me from the fire of your good intentions."

"Farewell, and pray, for I am worse than I seem," he snarled, not bothering to look at me any further.

"I can see, sir, that you are more wicked than you say, and infinitely more nothing than you imagine yourself to be," I said softly to myself as he dawdled dissemblingly down the street, punishing the cobble-stones with his shoes.

Around then it was rumored that in Saragossa several *Conversos* had murdered Pedro de Arbués, who had been employed as an inquisitor for a salary of one thousand *sueldos*. Juan de Esperandeu, whose ancient father had been seized by the Holy Office for eating meat in Lent as well as *matsah* and *hamin*, Saturday stew, and for keeping the Sabbath, working on Sunday and fasting on Yom Kippur, was one of the assassins.

On the night of Thursday, 15 September, Vidau Durango, Juan de la Badía, Mateo Ram, Tristanico Leonís and three masked men whose identity remained a secret had assembled in Durango's house, and together they proceeded to the cathedral, some entering by the principal door of the church and others by the chapter door, which had been left open for Matins.

The inquisitor Pedro de Arbués was on his knees in prayer, intoning *"Benedicta tu in mulieribus"*: "Blessed art thou among women," midway between the high altar and the choir, where the canons were chanting. Hidden beneath his cassock he wore a coat of mail, and under his bonnet, an iron helmet; he had propped his short lance against a pillar, to have it within reach in case of need, and not far off he had set down the lantern that had lit his way to the cathedral. Upon seeing him, Juan de la Badía and Vidau Durango went around behind the choir. "Give it to him, for here is the traitor," cried Juan de la Badía. Durango stood behind him and drove his sword clean through from the nape of his neck to his chin, and then ran away. Pedro de Arbués staggered to his feet and sought refuge in the choir among the canons, but Juan de Esperandeu pierced his left arm with his sword, and then Mateo Ram thrust through his body past the coat of mail.

The inquisitor fell down, mortally wounded; the assassins fled in such haste that they had trouble finding the doors to get out; the canons rushed from the choir and carried Pedro de Arbués to a nearby chamber and thence to his own house, where for the space of twenty-four hours he wavered between life and death, praising God all the while. His soul forsook his body between one and two in the morning of 17 September. Juan de Anchías, a notary of the Holy Office, bore witness to his demise: *"Die XVII Septembris anno a Nativitate Domine MCCCCLXXXV Cesarauguste. Eadem die:* On the seventeenth day of September in the year of Our Lord 1485, at Saragossa. On that same day, in the chapter house of the cathedral of the aforesaid city, where there was a bench, was slain the Most Reverend Pedro de Arbués, alias Epila, canon of the aforesaid cathedral and Inquisitor of the heretical depravity in the Kingdom of Aragón, in my presence, notary. Maestre Prisco Laurencio and Maestre Johan de Valmaseda, surgeons, attested and declared that the said Inquisitor was dead of the said wounds, and especially of a stabbing through the neck from the nape to the chin, which had severed the organic veins and the throat."

Saturday, at the hour of Vespers, he was buried on the spot where he had been wounded, and it was said that at the very instant they were laying the body in the tomb, the spilt blood began to boil. Immediately thereafter the miracles that proclaimed his saintliness were noised abroad: on the night of the crime the bells had sounded the alarm of their own accord; the blood, which had splashed the choir and the high altar, stayed fresh, boiled up, dried out and liquefied, so that the faithful were able to moisten their garments and scapulars in it; when the assassins were taken, their mouths were blackened and their tongues roughened and so thickened that they had to be sprinkled with water before they could speak during their interrogation; it was even said that before their capture they had been struck dumb by the hand of God. He performed one further miracle: by reason of his death, many more *Conversos* were discovered to be heretics, put to trial and burned alive.

The morning of 16 September the news of the crime spread like wildfire, and before the sun had risen crowds of people swarmed through the streets of Saragossa, intent upon razing the Jewish and Moorish quarters, and shouting, "Burn the *Conversos* who have killed the inquisitor!" The Archbishop, Alonso de Aragón, rode on horseback through the city calming the most impetuous and promising swift and terrible justice. The three municipal magistrates asked other towns for help in capturing the assassins; they issued proclamations and put a price of five hundred florins on their heads. The royal outrage was immense, and orders were given to proceed immediately towards the canonization of the martyr of the faith. The Inquisitor-General Fray Tomás de Torquemada dispatched Fray Pedro de Monterrubio and the canon Alfonso de Alarcón to execute the punishments, empowering Fray Juan Colivera of the preaching order, Fray Juan de Colmenares, Abbot of Aguilar, and the aforementioned Alfonso de Alarcón, by virtue of a decree of the King Don Fernando, to remove the Holy Office from the houses of the Council of the Estates, on the banks of the Ebro River, where it had established its tribunals and jails, to the Aljafería fortress.

The inquisitor's death stupefied Isabel, who foresaw that it could serve as a pretext for new and terrible persecutions of Jews and *Conversos;* that the hunt for those who had been sentenced *in absentia* by the *Suprema* would intensify, since the Catholic Kings had sought from Pope Innocent VIII the seizure and surrender to them of all those fugitives sheltering elsewhere in Christendom.

From that day on, Isabel stopped eating and ceased to take pleasure in life; nightmares tormented her by night and horrors by day; she cried out in her sleep, or during long hours of insomnia imagined noises in the street and pictured to herself the *alguaciles* and familiars of the Inquisition bursting into the house to carry her off. Whenever she saw me going out, she worried that I would be followed or betray myself in some chance encounter with an informer, by blurting out our secrets or seeming unduly agitated.

Thus did I watch my son grow in her belly and see him near the day of his birth, and at times I believed her to be in labor before her term, and I was on the point of summoning the *Conversa* midwife who Pero Meñique had assured us was trustworthy. But it was only the autumn shivers and her sudden fears that occasioned her intense pains and caused her to weep uncontrollably.

We still made love, we tried to forget the world outside, blotting out as much as we could the ubiquitous menace of the Friar Preachers and their holy hatreds; but the imminent birth of our son rendered us even more afraid of the danger we were in and prevented our making plans and dreaming of the future. There were times when we felt so disheartened that we had no desire to even think of a name for the child until we saw it alive and delivered. The mere mention of a name for it drove Isabel to anguish and despair, as if any creature God might cast upon the earth had more chance of bearing it than our own. For which reason she used to say that if it befell her to give birth during the last days of the world, when all mankind was dying around her, she would feel less ill fated, since it would then be a question of universal destiny rather than a sentence passed on a single child.

"I know my pains will not cease with my confinement, for in the course of her life a woman gives birth to her child many times over," she said one November night.

"All I hope for is that it be without blemish, that it may be born whole and able to defend itself with sturdy arms in the war of the living, as human creatures are not endowed with perfection in this world," I replied.

"Beneath the common light we all defend ourselves against death, but even on the verge of dying many still strive to kill their fellows," she said.

That was the last time I saw her in Madrid, because the next day when I returned home at nightfall she had disappeared without a trace. "I hope she escaped in time," I said to myself, certain they had come to arrest her.

Nonetheless, I searched for her in every room and in the neighboring houses. In the kitchen there was cold soup in a porringer, uneaten stew in a pot.

Our bedroom was clean, the key to the door lay on the floor, and her white headcloth had been tossed onto the bench. I tried to imagine what had happened to her; I stretched out on the bed and closed my eyes, but nothing came to mind, everything seemed barren.

I felt as if there were no one in the house, not even myself. My body had become part of the void and was no longer animate, fashioned in the image and likeness of God. "If they were to burn me right now, I would not feel the flames," I thought.

All night I waited for her return; I listened to the noises, voices and footsteps in the street, as if any one of them might herald her homecoming. Lighting neither candles nor fire, I lay still, mute, hanging on a dog's bark, the darkness shrouding me as it did all the other solid objects. In a spirit of complete indifference I heard the bells ring Compline, Lauds, Matins; they might have been ringing inside of me or far away. I arose at Prime and discovered that she had covered over the windows and that the backyard door was ajar.

I went out to seek her in the streets and squares of the city, my heart turning over each time I spotted a woman.

The sight of beggars, cripples and vagabonds gave me hope of finding her; she was cunning enough to disguise herself with clothing, makeup and soot, or to counterfeit bowed legs, to sport a hump and raveled threads, to feign blindness and penury.

Wearied and wistful, I glanced at stout or ruddy or straw-haired women who had pleasing demeanors or high-bridged noses or sensible expressions; I saw flat-nosed girls with thin lips or jutting chins, short necks or dumpy bodies, long legs, sunken stomachs, high shoulders, strong hands; well-shaped girls with agreeable mien, fine figure, serene gaze, passing gay and impetuous.

I went down Calle del Viento, Calle de los Tintes, Calle del Espejo, Calle de la Ventanilla, Calle de Ramón, Calle de Segovia; I passed in front of the Vega Gate, then by the stone piers and foundations on the road near the San Jerónimo mills; I searched the Pozacho orchards, the Vistillas clearing; I scanned thick old walls, portals, fountains, barbicans; I skirted the city walls and the river. I ascended the Cuesta de los Caños Viejos. I descended the Cuesta de los Ciegos; I looked in the stream, among the rocks, behind trees. I saw a horse with a blaze on its face, a drove of mules, roving hens and swine, Juan Malpensado and Juan Rebeco, the apothecary and confectioner Juan de Guadalajara, Alonso de la Porra *el Cojo*, Doña Fátima and the mason Abrahén de Sant Salvador, and a crone in a gown full of mouths, eyes, noses and ears, with so many gobbets of mud stuck to her body that to bury her it would suffice to lay her down and she would become one with the earth. When I reached the Calle Sin Puertas I headed for the Church of San Andrés and from there to the Plazuela de la Paja, where I found no one; where there were many, but Isabel was not, there was no one.

I walked on. I climbed up and down, I came and went. My steps led me to the Plaza de San Salvador, where the crier Juan de Orgaz was making a proclamation to a throng which had gathered round him. I pushed on. Behind me I noticed a stutterer whose bared teeth were like a laugh stamped on his face. He was talking to himself, or he was talking to me, but it was all so garbled that after pausing to listen, I paid no further attention to him. All I remember is that in his right hand he carried a lantern to light his way through Madrid.

I peered into Pedro de Heredía's butcher shop, and into every fishmonger's, chandler's, church, wayside chapel, draper's and market I came across on the way. I scrutinized the Toledans who dwelt in the city, hoping to read some news of her in their faces, and stared hard at the crier Juan de Portillo and Pedro the barber, who were returning from the square in the suburb, as if something they knew would be revealed in their eyes.

Just when I had resolved to storm the first Friar Preacher, *alguacil* or familiar of the Inquisition to be found in Madrid, I met Pero Meñique sunning himself on a stone bench. Bemused, he was passing his hands over his ears, cheeks, eyebrows and lips, chest and legs, to prove to himself that he was real and that he was there, that the invisible ensemble of his body really existed.

"Pero Meñique, what are you doing?" I asked him.

"My sense of smell has become jaded, so I am touching my features and limbs to make sure they are in their places and still entire," he replied.

"They are, and exceedingly ugly to boot," I told him.

"Running my fingertips over the lineaments of my face affords me such knowledge of them that I can almost see myself," he said.

"I have searched for Isabel in all Madrid without finding her," I announced.

"The other day I learned that a draught of radish juice on an empty stomach is an uncommon remedy against jaundice, and that coriander juice can strike people dumb and make them swoon," he went on, paying me no heed, as he turned his face towards the wall in search of shade.

"I said that I have looked for Isabel throughout the city without finding her," I repeated.

"Isabel? A sharp-witted and prudent girl who has read with understanding the Marquis of Santillana and Don Juan de Mena, Salomón ibn Gabirol and Yehuda ha Leví . . . What is that noise?"

"Only women drawing water from a well," I answered. "You are not listening to me. Isabel has disappeared."

"What's that? Isabel has disappeared?"

"Yesternight when I returned home, she had gone, or the inquisitors had taken her away."

"Have the inquisitors apprehended her?"

"Perhaps, but I think that she gave them the slip."

"Sssshhhh, someone is coming," he warned.

"I see no one."

"I say that someone is coming, ssshhh."

And in fact, an old man appeared, walking so slowly he seemed not to move at all.

"It is an old man," I said.

"Yes, I know. Would that he were gone quickly."

But the fellow seemed to divine our wishes and drag his steps even more, lifting his feet leadenly off the ground. It was wonderfully quiet, and the man made no sound, as if in a dream.

"Are those turds you are carrying, or charred rashers of bacon?" Pero Meñique inquired when his nose told him the man was near.

"I have here broth made of hooves, which all have eaten of, and many plunged their hands into it. I know several vagrants who would drink thereof as if it were holy water," answered the old man.

"Is that so? I thought it might be colostrum, the cream of your wife who has recently been brought to bed," said Pero.

142

"Marry sirrah, my wife has been dead since the days of Don Juan Segundo of Castile, and I have no recollection whatsoever of her first milk."

"Are you as ancient as all that?"

"I was born when Ruy Sánchez de Orozco, being charged with the keys of the Balnadú Gate, gave entrance to Vasco Mexía, who is long since imprisoned, to Lope Ferrández de Vargas, Ruy García and sundry men and women of the common folk that they might wreak destruction and despoilment and death and mischiefs, which they did do, in the *aljama* of Madrid."

The old man plodded on as best he could, pausing after each step, his stick planted in the dust.

"Are you blind in earnest, or is it false feigning for beggary?" he squealed at Pero Meñique.

"Unfortunately, I am really so."

"Woe is you, my worthy fellow."

"Woe is you, my good gaffer."

"I kiss your feet and your hands," he said, standing in front of us.

"May God go with you," I said to him.

"May God go with you, noble blind man," he echoed without moving.

"Has he gone?" Pero Meñique ventured after a few moments of silence.

"He is still standing there," I answered.

"Why doesn't he go on his way?" he asked impatiently.

"I no longer have the strength and the courage to walk any farther," said the old man.

"Then help him," Pero said to me.

"Yes, do help me," he begged.

And so I helped him, grasping him by his scrawny arm.

Flimsy and almost weightless, he was smaller and frailer than I had thought. His face was a wrinkled fist with darting eyes. Then suddenly he was off again, standing very upright on his heels, spry and nimble, as if at any moment he might fly into the air.

He departed without a backwards glance, tiny and sere, a century of history squeezed into one human body, uncomplaining and imperturbable.

"I feel certain that Isabel has gotten away," said Pero Meñique.

"I must find her," I said.

"Find *them*," corrected Pero. "But now you will have to be on your guard against the inquisitors who will want to seize you to learn where she is."

"They have no reason to arrest me."

"Under torture they will force you to reveal that you have lain with Isabel and to denounce every *Converso* you have ever known, amongst them a certain Pero Meñique."

"I shall never inform upon anybody, even if they subject me to the water torture and tie me to the rack, scald my feet with hot oil and twist my limbs with a cord," I boasted.

Pero Meñique raised his face, surprised at the bravado of my words, aware I had been speaking lightly of torments unknown to myself which had already broken and driven mad far fiercer men than I.

It began to rain, and it was as if all the rain in the world were pummeling our heads, and we hastily took leave of each other. I returned to the house to see if she had come back. Alas, she had not. She would never return to Madrid. The rains lasted for six weeks, and the earth was left so sodden that it was difficult for travelers to go on the roads and for husbandmen to plow the fields. Innumerable men and women, asses, cows, mules, deer, hens, mares and wild boars were drowned. Countless estates were lost, houses without number tumbled down, and the avenues of water swept away bridges, trees, vineyards and mills alongside streams swollen into rivers and rivers swollen into arms of the sea. In many places, it was said, the granaries were damaged and the grain spoiled; a bushel of wheat came to be worth three *reales* and one of flour, twenty *reales;* out of necessity people ate boiled wheat, raisins and chestnuts.

One day, just before Christmas, it ceased to rain and the sun shone on the muddy earth. All through the following months there was a great pestilence, and many children perished on account of the fevers that began to spread throughout the kingdom. The old King Alí Muley Abenhazan, it was learned, died in exile in Salobreña, and his body was brought to Granada on the back of a mule.

Over dry and stony roads I made my way to Saragossa, the city built upon the fertile plains of the spacious Ebro River and defended by towered ramparts of great thickness. I entered the town through the Angel Gate, opposite the seven soaring arches of the Piedra Bridge, left my pack mule at the Ebro Hostel and went straightway to the Seo, the brick cathedral on whose pavement Pedro de Arbués had been murdered months before.

The great bell was tolling for the consecration of the Host, alerting the inhabitants of the city to make a demonstration of faith wherever they might be. The vicar-general was in the midst of giving Communion to the faithful, who knelt before the altar and its imposing reredos of polychromed alabaster, which Maestro Ans d'Ansó had recently completed, depicting in high relief the stories of the Magi, the Transfiguration and the Ascension of Christ.

At the conclusion of Mass the faithful began to leave by way of the five naves, some becoming lost among the columns and others pausing to cross themselves at the place where the first inquisitor in Aragón had been attacked by *Conversos*.

In the square, priests and officials of the Holy Office were raising two scaffolds for an auto-da-fé to be celebrated the following day—one for the culprits and those who assisted them, the other for the inquisitors, familiars and secular and ecclesiastical authorities. There where the green cross would later be planted, the priests and officials were decking the scaffold with carpets, hangings, torch brackets and candlestands.

The windows in the neighboring houses overlooking the square had already been allotted to the town notables and their families for the spectacle. Two Friar Preachers were dealing out candles to the participants in the procession of the green cross, which would take place that evening. Barriers to restrain the excited crowds had been erected, and the transit of wagons and mules through the streets was forbidden. The entire city was officially in the hands of the inquisitors.

The scorching wind from the east had brought the dog days to Saragossa: houses, streets and people seemed bleached by the heat, and no one but the somber friars, muffled in their habits, their faces concealed, ventured beyond the square.

Not too far off stood the temple of Nuestra Señor del Pilar, on which spot, as legend has it, the Apostle James the Greater had spent one night, during which the Virgin, always a worker of miracles, had appeared to him in a vision. Some said that she in the company of many angels had bestowed upon him a pillar of jasper bearing her image so that he might install it in the church she commanded him to build; others said that he had made the image after the chapel was built. Be that as it may, the crypt was illuminated day and night by a myriad of silver lamps, and it was forbidden to put out garbage in the neighborhood of the temple, for upon occasion the Sovereigns were wont to lodge in the canons' houses. In the nearby streets, craftsmen fashioned fancy needles, knives, iron grates, cordovan leathers, well-tempered swords and all manner of cloth.

Now wending their way towards the square on which stands Nuestra Señora del Pilar came the familiars and notaries of the Holy Office in procession, to the sound of drums and trumpets and bearing the standard aloft, to proclaim for the second time the auto-da-fé to be celebrated the next day. The first proclamation had been made at the gates of the Aljafería, the ancient Moorish stronghold beyond the city limits that the inquisitors converted into a jail, care having been taken to ensure that the condemned prisoners could not overhear the proclamation in their cells. There *Conversos* of both sexes and divers ages lived in fear of being led out on the road to market for the next auto-da-fé, although at times, it was rumored, the burnings took place in the second courtyard of the castle itself, above which, at that very moment, white clouds were drifting.

It was in the square of Nuestra Señora del Portillo, twenty-four days into February of this year, that the Dominican friars had put to the torch the elderly currier Salvador Esperandeu, father of Juan; Gumien Berguero, for performing Jewish rites; Ysavel de Embon, for giving oil to the synagogue; and the effigies of three absent heretics. In that same square, to the blaring of four trumpets and the ringing of a bell, the crier now proclaimed, "Know all ye dwellers in this city that the tribunal of the Holy Inquisition, for the glory and honor of God and of our Holy Catholic Faith, will celebrate a public auto-da-fé tomorrow, Friday, the twenty-eighth day of July in the year of Our Lord one thousand four hundred eighty-six, in the cathedral square."

To get as far away as possible from the criers and the familiars of the Holy Office, I plunged into the winding brick streets leading to the avenue of San Gil, which was truncated by the tanners' yard, and to the *judería*, which was girdled by the ancient Roman walls along the Coso, the principal thoroughfare.

Access to the *judería* was controlled by various wickets, located at the Rabinad Gate, in Hiedra Lane, near Don Mayr's and at San Andrés, where the Bienpiés Synagogue stood, its parapet jutting over the wall; I entered through the lightless arch of the gloomy portal near the Castle of the Jews.

The so-called castle had seven stone turrets, walls of hewn stone and one crumbling tower above the entrance; it served as a jail for Moors and a refuge in case of an attack on the *aljama*. The butchery was close by, with its six shops and two yards, a larger one for the bullocks and a smaller one for the offal. In these shops, the meat for sale was displayed on five slabs, with a sixth counter for receiving the tax levied on foodstuffs. The meat came from beasts slaughtered by Jewish hands, the throats having been slit with an unnicked knife by the *shohet*, the ritual slaughterer, Ya'acob Franco. There were castrated rams, headless and hoofless and cleansed of suet; the boned flesh of ewes, does, and he-goats; hearts, kidneys, dewlaps, tongues, tripe, shins, shanks, udders, hooves, heads and lungs were for sale. Before me appeared the narrow alleyways of the Acequia, the Medio, the Toro and the Sin Salida and the lane that leads to the Argentería, where the silversmiths worked. I saw the synagogue of the turners, the Rotfecede Hospital, the squares, walls, towers, patios, overhangs and private quarters of the *judería*.

I looked for the Great Synagogue, which is known as the *Bikkur Holim*, the society for visiting the sick, and I knocked at a small door.

"Who is it?" asked a man's voice from within.

"Juan Cabezón," I whispered.

"Informer or familiar of the Inquisition?" asked the voice on the other side of the door.

"Neither the one nor the other; I am a friend of Isabel de la Vega's," I replied.

"We know no woman of that name," the voice declared.

"Open the door, and I will explain it to you," I pleaded.

The door opened to reveal a man of some fifty years with a long beard and locks, wearing a loose-fitting tunic with hanging sleeves on which was sewn the scarlet badge required of the Jews; a white cloth was draped over his head and body. He made a cursory inspection of me, as if one look sufficed for him to read the secrets of my soul on my countenance, and then I went inside.

Behind the door a wooden settle leaned against the wall under a candelabrum with seven bowls for burning oil. A book in Hebrew lay open on a table. Five men, their hands upon a Torah scroll in a case of gilded silver lined with tin and surmounted by a crown bearing the royal arms, were taking an oath: "Swearest thou, Nathan the Jew, by that God who made Adam, the first man, and put him in paradise and commanded him not to eat of that fruit which He forbade him, and because he ate of it, He cast him out of paradise. And by that God who is powerful over all and who created the heavens and the earth and all other things, and said thou shalt not take My Name in vain. And by that God who received the sacrifice of Abel and refused the sacrifice of Cain, and saved Noah in the ark at the time of the flood, and also his wife and his sons with their wives, and all the other living creatures which He placed there that the earth might be populated. And by that God who saved Lot and his daughters from the destruction of Sodom and Gomorrah . . ."

No sooner had they marked my presence than one of them exclaimed, "Now we are lost, this man will give us away!"

"I am not of the sort to denounce anybody," I said promptly.

The man who had opened the door for me whispered something into the other man's ear to reassure him, and he, after examining my face carefully, as a tailor might a bolt of cloth, rejoined the others: "And by that God who told Abraham that all those of his lineage would be blessed, and who chose him, and Isaac, and his son Jacob to be patriarchs . . ."

From there we proceeded to a narrow, low-ceilinged side aisle lined with pillars and thence to the central nave whose carved and vaulted roof had gilded plasterwork. An ark decorated with mosaics was built into the wall facing south; across from the ark there was a painted candelabrum with seven candlesticks, and above the candelabrum, a smallish, raised pulpit for reading the text and services. Along both sides were six small doors, through one of which I had entered. Pews deeded to various members of the community stood along the walls. Large red and blue Hebrew letters were painted throughout the interior.

An alert, serious woman, who was arranging a sash of worn silk and a leather strap adorned with silver disks and tips on a table in an adjoining room, drew near when she saw us.

"Blanca, wait upon my pleasure; betake thyself to the house of Luna de la Vega, and say unto her that with thee is come Juan Cabezón, who is husband to Isabel, her niece," the man said to her.

"Keep close to me," she replied.

I followed her down a corridor and through several doorways until we found ourselves in the bowels of a huge apothecary's shop crammed with utensils, drugs, clay vessels, scales, ladders, strainers, burins, red and green boxes, balances, goblets for sweetmeats, spatulas, hempen bonnets, honey pots, pine caskets, little vials, firkins of oil, books about physicking, pepper boxes with four jars each, glass ewers, ladles, molds for pastes and sulfur, ground rouge, Castilian perfumes, syrup of roses, powdered German madwort, extract of lily, Egyptian ointments to cure gangrene, the sleeping potion *confectio requies, confectio naquardina,* potion of nard, to aid the memory, steel filings for thin-blooded women, *sigillum beate Marie* or blessed Mary weed, *radicis mandragore* or mandrake root, *semen berberis, corni cerbi combusti* or ashes of deer's horn, like the pulverized deer antlers mixed with tender viper's flesh which was administered to Fernando VI on his deathbed, soap from Cyprus, pepper, mustard, pine nuts and almonds, a pitcher of ink, mercury, a store of the aureate pills made by Nicolás Mesué, Jew's stone, sugar syrups and honey comfits.

When we emerged on the street, two men crossed our path, and she said to me, "That is Juan d'Embrun, a counselor to the King and commissary of the *aljamas* of the Jews and the Moors; the man at his side is Samuel Baru, who serves as his crier. The women behind them wearing badges are the sisters Sol, Reina and Orovida Lunbroso. Those men who are on their way to the silk market—the finest of its kind in all Aragón— are Jucé Ardit, the cobbler, his son Mossé, a purse maker, and Jucé Abembitas, a hosier in Santa Catalina Lane. The others who are walking somewhat apart from the rest, deep in conversation, are Jucé Chamorra and Mossé Hardit. The man who just came out of that door is Juan de Zaragoza, a *Converso* whose brother lives in the Castle of the Jews. The cripple over there, with the matweed rope girdling his flesh, is Antón, and it is Fray Nofre who makes him go about in this wise as a penance for attending a Jewish ceremony."

Suddenly Blanca's attention was distracted by a group of half-naked children in front of a squalid hovel down an alley who were taunting a deaf man with words he could ill understand. I took advantage of the moment to inquire whether she knew Don Luis de Santángel.

"Luis de Santángel is a prisoner in the fortress of the Aljafería, where the inquisitors have installed their tribunals and jails; he stands accused of conspiring in the assassination of Pedro de Arbués, and the fate which awaits him is most cruel," she answered with dismay. "With him are the *Conversos* Francisco de Santa Fe, Juan de la Badía, Mateo Ram, Sancho de Paternoy and Jaime de Montesa, who they say have been tortured by tying stones to their feet and hoisting them off the ground by a rope fastened to their wrists, to extract from them a confession of their part in the death of that so-called martyr of the faith. Even Jaime de Montesa, who as magistrate ordered all the windows in Jewish houses facing the Coso to be bricked in, and who imposed the infamous red badge on the

Jews, has been unable to save his own skin from torture or his impending misfortune, despite having always sought to ingratiate himself with the Christians."

"I have heard that some among those guilty of the inquisitor's murder have themselves come to a terrible end," I managed to put in.

"On the day of the auto-da-fé held on Friday the thirtieth of June, in the cathedral, when Fray Juan de Colmenares, Abbot of Aguilar, preached the sermon, Juan de Esperandeu was drawn alive through the city to the principal door of the Seo, where his hands were cut off; thence they dragged him to the marketplace, decapitated him on the gallows, quartered him, nailed his hands to the doors of the Council of the Estates and scattered his pieces over the highways." Her voice faltered, as if sensible of the victim's fate in her own flesh. "His Gascon servant Vidau Durango, or Duranso, or perhaps it is Uranso, was also drawn through the streets, to be drowned in the cathedral square, although as a special clemency for having confessed to what he knew, his hands were not lopped off until after his death, upon which his remains were dragged to the marketplace, quartered, the parts strewn over the roads, and his hands nailed to the doors next to his master's. As for Juan de Pero Sánchez, who fortunately managed to escape, he was drawn in effigy with a bag hanging around his neck and then burned in the market-place."

"They say that the Santángel family is a large one," I said.

"But not as large as the hate the inquisitors feel towards it," replied Doña Blanca, "for many descendants of the Chinillo family—one of the most ancient in all Aragón, which changed its name to Santángel at the beginning of this century—have been penanced. The sisters Brianda and Leonor Martínez de Santángel were brought to trial for visiting the *judería*, where it was their custom to enter into the houses of the Jews and accept fruits and sweetmeats of them, for spurning bacon and never putting any into the stew pot, and because, upon occasion, they had given alms to poor Jews who came to their house."

And then, as if she visualized a vanished city, and ghostly creatures who had perished many years ago but still strolled the streets, she said, "In these alleyways, gripped by dread and death, you may not perceive the absence of those who have departed for other realms, you may not hear the screams of all who have succumbed to torture and the stake, but the presence of the Turi, the Lunbroso, the Alazar, the Baco, the Benvenist, the Rabat, the Amado, the Ponz, the Trigo, the Bivaz, the Sánchez, the Eli, the Franco, the Abella, the Silton, the Zaporta and the Caballería families, who have dwelt in Saragossa since time immemorial, is manifest in the emptiness of the squares, the silence of doors, the darkness of rooms, the deafness of walls. Of this *aljama* which you see before you, perhaps not one stone will endure: tailors, peddlers, weavers, parchment makers, cobblers, curriers, barbers and physicians, all those badge-wearing Jews struggling for a miserable corner of the city to call their own, will have gone, not a one among them will remain."

Just then four men clad in long black gowns came towards us. Doña Blanca explained, "They are Maestres Pedro Monterde and Francisco Ely, doctors, and Maestres Pero Puch and Juan, surgeons, and by order of the Inquisition they are charged with inspecting the members of the Jews, young and old alike, for proof of circumcision. And when they do discover a circumcised man, they invariably declare that owing to a defect common to the skin over members and penises, the head may be exposed in some measure, but as they cannot determine whether the defect springs from nature or man's handiwork, they leave the answer to the inquisitors, who invariably incline towards man's handiwork."

We reached a house whose windows facing the Christian street had been walled up, and whose narrow door onto Acequia Lane was hanging on its hinges.

In front of the house an ancient man was trying unsuccessfully to raise himself off the ground. Clad in earth-colored garments, he lay across the threshold, forgotten by all, no longer in a hurry and beyond boredom. Toothless, with blue eyes like flickering lanterns, he was more akin to an elderly child than to a man who had traversed the century, from the massacres of the Archdeacon of Ecija, the preachings of Fray Vicente Ferrer and the pragmatic sanction of Queen Catalina, to the advent of the Catholic Sovereigns and Fray Tomás de Torquemada's appointment as Inquisitor-General.

"Don Jucé Santamaría was baptized during one of the preachments of Fray Vicente Ferrer in Saragossa," said Doña Blanca, "but now, with one hundred years at his back, he sits at the door of his house humming songs in Hebrew."

The old man turned around when he saw us and reared up on his hands and knees for help.

"How is Doña Orovida?" asked Doña Blanca as we lifted him to a vertical position.

"She is with her mother in Calatayud," he answered, after first catching his breath.

"And how are your parents, Don Isaque and Doña Jamila?"

"They have gone to Barbestro to give a guerdon to Don Mossé, who has already received many *reales* on account of his son's circumcision," said the old man in a deep, hollow voice.

"And your daughter, Doña Brianda?" she asked.

He did not answer but doddered into the hushed darkness of his house as though into a tomb where the living and the dead were contemporaries.

A few steps away in the street, a man stopped to glare at us awkwardly through the bushy tangle of his eyebrows, hair, mustache and beard: it was a certain Acach Funes, a sycophant and false witness in the service of the inquisitors, who had already whipped him once for being an agitator by trade.

We entered the dwelling of Doña Luna de la Vega, aunt to Isabel and mother to Clara, who had escaped to France, and to Juan, a *Converso* who used to visit her on Saturdays bringing food and to pass the day in her company.

The two-story building consisted of a portico, a main hall, a privy, two bedchambers and a kitchen; the rooms overflowed with painted coffers, footed bedsteads, tables, enameled white cots, barrels, fire irons, earthen pots, kettles, frying pans and porringers. Nevertheless, the entire house opened up before us like a vast cupboard reeking of stale air and emptiness.

"Luna, are you home?" Doña Blanca asked, her voice probing the silence.

No answer.

"Luna, where are you?" Doña Blanca ventured into the main room and poked at the pine bed built into the wall; she bent down to go through a low, narrow door which seemed to have been made for dwarves or children, or to force the human body to humble itself.

A wan face appeared against the wall, broke away from it with a shy twitch of the head and began speaking to an invisible someone in the room, perhaps an inquisitor: "I confess that a Jewess whose grandmother learned her arts from Na Ceti, the female physician from Valencia, gave me potions to get with child; I confess that when I was about to give birth to Clara, the rabbi came from the women's synagogue and prayed by my bedside; when Donna, the midwife, handed me the girl child, she said, 'God who is most goodly, take three clove gillyflowers and open three doors and pluck the living from the living and snatch two souls out of danger.' I confess that my mother rewarded me with a hen for the good news and anointed the child with myrrh on the palms of her hands and the soles of her feet; that upon arising from childbed I changed the sheets, I put on clean clothes, and I abstained for forty days from setting foot in the temple; that I did not baptize her and that on the eighth night after her birth my husband and I made a *Hadas* ceremony and we laid the baby in a basin of water into which we put gold, silver, seed pearls, wheat and barley, and we recited the holy words. I confess that after dressing her in white garments we invited our kindred and friends to partake of sugared comfits, rusks with honey, almond paste, grapefruit, stewed fruits and *Kasher* wine. Maidens and matrons played cymbals and sang, '*Hadas, hadas, hadas*, may they bring you good fortune,' and I swept the house so they might not stumble or injure their feet, as they danced barefoot. I confess that when my milk dried up, a Jewish wet nurse by the name of Oro suckled the baby in my bedchamber, roasted porged, defatted meat in the kitchen, baked me unleavened bread and kept the fast of Yom Kippur with me. I confess that I am a Jew in body and soul, and I care not a whit if the inquisitors kill Jewish mothers like myself, for our children will live on afterwards."

Framed in the white nimbus of her hair, Doña Luna emerged from the shadows and showed her face; the rest of her body was covered by a tabard with winged sleeves marked with the red emblem. She was no longer any age: in her world of madness she had lost count of the years.

"Awaken, awaken, little Clara, dawn has already broken and the birds are twittering. Awaken, awaken! Our enemies are saying that tonight I shall die for your sake," she cried, standing in front of Doña Blanca.

"She believes her daughter lies there asleep, that it is morning and she won't get up," Doña Blanca explained.

"Give this man a light, give him a light, for my father was always most generous," Doña Luna said when she noticed me.

Doña Blanca took hold of her arm. "This man is Juan Cabezón, husband to your niece Isabel."

The woman glued her eyes to my face, as if seeking Isabel among my features.

"One Monday she departed from here to visit my brother Noé in Calatayud. . . . That's all I know. . . . Now I must be on my way to meet Jucé at the hospital in the *judería*," she said, readying herself to go outside.

"Her husband Jucé was a physician renowned in Saragossa, a past master in the art of bandaging wounds, bloodletting, slicing, extracting bones, cutting up, prescribing physicks and curing cysts, bunchy excrescences, palsies and gouts in the feet. One day he went to Teruel, just when the inquisitor Fray Juan de Colivera was wreaking havoc there, and he never came back. No one ever heard of him again; perhaps he is languishing in a dungeon of the Holy Office. Every day she goes out to look for him in the hospital, the marketplace, the Castle of the Jews, at the butchers', in the synagogues, alleyways and squares, and every day she thinks he comes home with her. But what is most likely is that he will end up in an auto-da-fé one day at dawn."

> *"The river flows on,*
> *the sands remain,*
> *love is burning,*
> *ah! your heart feels the pain,"*

sang Doña Luna, gay as a young girl keeping a love tryst.

"Now she will leave her house to roam the streets until her servant Oro brings her back tonight, accompanied by her invisible husband," said Doña Blanca.

"If you should see Oro, pray tell her the Sabbath lamps are behind the door, not to move them and to see that they are clean, with new wicks, and to light them tomorrow before sunset; above all, she must be sure to light all the wicks, for as Jucé says, each one stands for a book and a prayer in Hebrew. Caution her not to add more oil, nor trim nor extinguish the flame," she instructed us before setting out.

A group of starved, ragged children were waiting in the lane for Doña Blanca to give them slices of bread, honey cakes and other edibles she had in her bag.

"These are the offspring of the prisoners of the Inquisition; King Fernando has confiscated their monies and property, and they live in want, lacking home and sustenance, and all trades and benefices are forbidden them. Ahead of them lies a future filled with fear and persecution under the vigilant eye of the inquisitors, who may summon them at any moment to bear witness against their parents and brothers or, if they are old enough, to stand trial themselves."

The orphans drank in her words and devoured the bread and honey cakes. Doña Blanca drew them close to her breast, and, running her fingers through the hair of one young maiden, added, "This little girl reminds me of the Jewess of Saragossa who became blind from weeping over others' misfortunes. She watches over the rest and leads them through the alleyways of the *aljama* in search of food and clothing."

I took my leave of her to return to the Christian city, where the procession of the green cross was already in progress. They marched with measured step alongside the Ebro River: the preaching and parochial orders, the familiars, notaries, consultors and censors of the Holy Office and all the others who had been invited to take part in the ceremony.

The familiars carried the standard of the green cross; they were followed by monks escorting the white cross and others bearing the cross of the Seo. Next came the Dominican prior and his friars, conveying the large green cross. All chanted the *Miserere*, advancing amidst a forest of torches. Behind them the prosecuting officer hove into view, carrying

a standard of crimson damask embroidered with the royal coat of arms
with a green cross rising out of the crown, an olive branch and a naked
sword, representing justice and forgiveness.

In this wise the procession emptied into the cathedral square, where
the green cross was to be set upon the altar. The white cross would be
carried to the burning place, there to be watched over all night long by
soldiers and Dominican friars.

I heard tell that within the cathedral the *sanbenitos*, the insignia, the
effigies of the absent and the bones of the dead lay in readiness for the
auto-da-fé. Shrouded by night, the inquisitor arrived with a scribe to
notify each condemned heretic that these were his last hours. With the
alguacil and several familiars in tow, he descended into the dungeons,
to put little green crosses into the prisoners' hands and exhort them to
dispose their consciences as befitted men and women who were about
to die, and then he left with each of them two friars to assist them on
their final night.

I slept poorly, and, reclining on the hard bed of the inn with the
candles snuffed, I waited for the jailer to bring light into every cell in
the Aljafería two hours before dawn so that the condemned might arise
and clothe themselves to be led to a secret courtyard, where each would
be adorned with the appropriate insignia and lined up on a bench in
the order he or she would occupy in the procession to the cathedral
square. First came those guilty of the lesser crimes and at the end, those
who were to be burned at the stake.

My night swarmed with dreams of smoldering silhouettes who clamored in the wind at the injustice committed. A little girl terrified by her
flaming shift, her blazing hands and her feet of fire appeared before me
to show me her fingers giving off sparks, her scorched white skin and
her long fair hair turned into ashes.

"The inquisitors took away the key to my house, they took away my
house, they took away my parents, and they brought me to this pyre
where the fire I dearly loved is so terrible," she said to me in the darkness
of the room, her eyes like suns.

I arose when the soldiers who were guarding the white cross in the
square beat their drums to awaken the officials who would take part in
the simulacrum of the Last Judgment. Oblivious to the trees, the water
and the dawn, all along the Ebro River hundreds of peasants and other
folk were hurrying towards the cathedral square, outpaced by a short
woman with emaciated limbs who kept stopping to rest.

"Whosoever witnesses an auto-da-fé earns indulgences for her soul,"
she assured a grimy man.

"The *Conversos* who will perish today are relapsed; I don't know what
that means, but it sounds very bad," he said.

"I should not like to be one; they say that anyone who is sins as much as a person who gives shelter to a heretic," said his neighbor.

"A relapsed is a heretic who, having abjured his faults, incurs them anew, bringing upon himself, once he is discovered, surrender to the secular arm for burning," the skinny woman stated.

"The hatred felt for those wretched creatures when they were Jews has redoubled now that they are Christians," said a wizened elder whose face I could not see.

"I have been making amends for my sins since the day I was born," grumbled a fat man at his side.

"Death is on a rampage throughout the realms of Castile and Aragón; it gallops from town to town, kindling bonfires," said the shriveled ancient, still faceless.

"Death wears the habit of a bloodthirsty Dominican," declared a villain whose ear had been cut off.

"Have a care, for the *Suprema* has its eye on you!" warned the rickety female, looking over her shoulder.

When they reached the cathedral square, the grimy man asked a friar of the preaching order whether the heretics would be burned there, near the Guerba River, or on the outskirts of town. The monk did not reply but glared at him so malevolently that the man interpreted his look as the worst possible answer and edged away towards the crowd.

"As soon as our brothers the venerable preachers have celebrated Holy Mass before the green cross, which is the exalted symbol of the order, and they have taken their breakfast, the prisoners will be brought from the castle of the Aljafería to this square," a sickly friar told me, as if it was I who had asked the question.

"The brother prisoners take breakfast as well, but in their cells," said yet another monk.

"Only thus can they find the strength not to swoon during the penancing and the fire," added the haggard friar.

The swallows soared above the ramparts beneath a spotless blue sky. "Today is a perfect day for something else, for anything else, save an auto-da-fé," I thought to myself.

The procession entered the square: first the halberdiers, then the cathedral cross shrouded in a black veil and immediately afterwards an acolyte ringing a bell lugubriously to left and right, heralding the ceremony. Then came the penitents in their *sanbenitos* and miters of condemnation, yellow candles in hand, escorted by the halberdiers and the familiars of the Holy Office. The porters followed, carrying aloft on poles the half-length effigies of the absent also arrayed in *sanbenitos* and miters with painted flames. Other porters brought the black boxes containing the bones of the dead which were to be burned symbolically. Still others paraded *statuae duplicatae*, double effigies of married couples with one face before and one behind, as of a single deceased heretic. Flanked by pairs of friars, those destined for the secular arm advanced with somber steps, clad in *sanbenitos* on which were writ their names and the words "Condemned Heretic" and miters emblazoned with flames. Their hands, tied with cords across their chests, clutched snuffed candles. They were pale and trembling, about to faint.

The secular officials followed them into the square on horseback, then the familiars two by two, and the prosecutor of the Holy Office, Francisco Sánchez de Zuazo, carrying the standard of the faith, a green cross on a black field, accompanied by two horsemen in habits, each holding up one tail of the standard. Next came the two inquisitors of heretical depravity in the Kingdom of Aragón, Alfonso Sánchez de Alarcón, Master of Holy Theology, canon of the church of Palencia and chaplain to the King and Queen, and Fray Miguel de Monterrubio, Licentiate of Holy Theology and prior of San Pedro de las Dueñas. Bringing up the rear came Maestre Martín García, Vicar-General of the Holy Office and canon of the Seo of Saragossa; Fray Juan de Colmenares, Abbot of Aguilar, of the Cistercian Order; Diego López, *alguacil;* Juan de Anchías, notary; Martín Martínez de Teruel, assessor; and other friars, noblemen and private citizens invited to the auto-da-fé, all making their way through the dense throng.

Several of the condemned heretics staggered painfully, having only recently emerged from the torture chambers where they had been subjected to the pulleys and water torture. Terror was etched on their faces, and the torturer's marks, on their bodies. Two or three were talking to themselves, as if bereft of their reason, or praying, or reciting some charm to ward off fear. Others mumbled Psalms. The men went first, the women behind, in order of their crimes.

The bells were tolling as they arrived in the square, where a great multitude awaited their coming. Rooms with a view of the platforms were packed with the notables of Saragossa and their families. One by one the culprits were ranged on the scaffolding, the inquisitors taking their places on the other side. The prosecuting attorney of the Holy Office sat down upon the topmost step, holding the standard in his hand on a level with the feet of the senior inquisitor, flanked on either side by the horsemen who held aloft the tips of the standard. The consultors, referees, prelates of other religious orders, gentlemen and further persons of note sat on the lower steps. The chief *alguacil* took his seat, staff in hand, on a chair at the entrance to the passageway joining the inquisitors' platform with that of the condemned; he was accompanied by familiars and a porter provided with ropes and gags to bind and silence those who might cause a commotion after hearing their sentences.

As soon as all were in their places the auto-da-fé began: the chief *alguacil* rose from his chair and made a sign to Fray Martín García to preach the sermon. The latter spread his arms out as if he were being crucified, and with an air of carrying all the sins of the world on his soul, save his own, he started to speak.

When the long and tedious sermon was concluded, a secretary ascended the pulpit and requested aloud that all those present swear the customary oath to the Holy Office and pledge their active participation in the persecution of heretics and heresy. All answered "Amen."

The sentences were read out alternately from two pulpits. As his name was pronounced, each culprit was led up two steps to a low platform by the *alguacil,* in order to hear the verdict. Standing with his face upturned towards the inquisitors, he listened to the interminable list of his offenses against the Catholic faith, after which he was made to kneel and receive absolution.

As the sentences against the absent and the dead were pronounced, the porters placed the effigies on poles and the black chests containing the bones to one side of the scaffolding in readiness for their conveyance to the burning place. The living heretics were lined up on the other side.

Clergymen, beggars, cripples, pious women telling their beads, pickpockets, blind men, dwarves, peasants and other common folk made up the restless mass of plebeians enthralled by the intricate procedure, each one of them seeming to confirm in his own heart the sentence meted out to the heretic, indifferent to the humiliation and agony suffered by the victims, who had no witnesses to their innocence but themselves. The doomed were neither saints nor heroes, merely ordinary men and women aghast at that monster of a thousand faces and twice as many fists, that crowd which goaded on the ruthless priests who transformed parables of love into instructions for death, and the promised paradise into hell on earth. And as if I myself were a Jew standing in the cathedral square, for the first time in my life I saw the hostile faces turned towards me, I was aware of my own face, of the weight of my body, and like any animal pursued by butchers or relentless hunters, I felt fear of man.

Castile and Aragón had ignited the fires, and Spain was ablaze. The cries of the *Conversos* were shrill in the sunny Saragossan morning, cries that would be stilled as the days went by, only to resound accusingly across the years and the centuries, there being no rain, wind, silence or night capable of stifling them.

Suddenly a gigantic man stood in front of me, preventing me from seeing the auto-da-fé. He might have been a blacksmith, for he occupied the space of three men together and was as tall as three dwarves standing on one another's shoulders. At first I thought he was a hallucination, a fleshly aberration sent by the inquisitors to block my view of the ceremony. Everything about him was big: head, neck, arms, hands, legs, feet; the other men around him seemed insignificant, diminished. I stepped to one side.

At that very moment the inquisitor presiding over the auto-da-fé from one of the scaffolds, at whose feet was seated the prosecuting attorney, shot me a look like needles piercing my eyes. The man had a jutting chin and black beard, predatory nose and icy lips; his eyes were sunken and red. His bejeweled hands resting on thighs spread wide apart made him resemble a woman at stool. Blind to the harrowing humility of a man who dies martyred for his religion in the sincere exaltation of his own God, the inquisitor followed with cruel satisfaction the slightest details of that man's death in the exquisite loneliness of a crime cloaked in legality, whose only judge is the perpetrator's own conscience.

The second inquisitor had an outsized head balanced on a feeble body, his mien suggestive of the moonlit punishment of his privates to mortify a body tempted by lust. His eyes were popping as he greedily drank in the sentences imposed on the prisoners, and his mouth opened as if to chew while his tongue darted in and out savoring the victories. He looked like the kind of person who cannot stop eating, although he forgets what he is eating in the very act of swallowing it, captive to a spiritual rather than a bodily hunger. He was the opposite of the other inquisitor, who for a few fleeting moments sought in the distance the memory of a childhood candor sullied forever, as if in the midst of the tumult, above the crowd of executioners and victims, his eyes saw and his ears heard the echo of an infinite joy that was singing unrestrainedly in a bygone dawn, an infinite joy from which he had excluded himself by joining the forces of darkness.

The list of offenses charged to the culprits seemed trivial when read out by a stammering friar, but their gravity in the eyes of the inquisitors left no room for doubt as to the fate awaiting the victims. The sentences of the penitents were heard first, followed by those of the effigies, and at the last, those of the prisoners relaxed to the secular arm. At times a profound emptiness yawned between one sentence and the next, as if the words had fallen into a soundless void.

The crowd turned more hostile as the most terrible sentences were being pronounced, the faces became distorted, and there were shouts of grisly delight. The chief *alguacil* and the familiars kept order, being responsible at all times for conducting the auto-da-fé with the solemnity of a religious service. They were successful in this until the moment

when Pedro de Exea, Violante Ruys, Bernard de Robas, Galcerán Be-
lenguer, Gabriel de Aojales, Guillén de Bruysón, Gonzalo de Yta and
Maria Labadía were abandoned to the secular arm and handed over to
the *alguacil* to be conveyed to the burning place, for then the mob began
to bay like a savage beast at the defenseless culprits.

"It was in Calatanzor that Almanzor lost his tambour!" roared a man
with a goatish face, invoking the devil himself.

"There's a woman who knew the *Credo* only as far as *patrem omnipo-
tentem*, and she had chickens slaughtered for her use and blessings were
said over her dresses, in the Jewish fashion," yelled a friar, indicating
one of the penitents.

"That *Converso* is going to get his Messiah," jeered the thin woman,
who reappeared in the crowd.

"I have accepted my torments on this earth since the day I was born,
and I will accept them until the Judgment Day," declared an old heretic
who was condemned to the stake.

"There goes the only Christian among all these Jews; they pierced his
tongue with a reed for blaspheming God and Our Lady the Virgin,"
canted a woman holding a rosary. Her features were hidden by a hood
as she pointed to a fellow who was making obscene faces at her.

"That pig was given a penance by the Dominican fathers for denying
that he was circumcised," sneered a man with a small, wrinkled head.

"Take a look at this one, they tortured him so much with the cords
that his arms and legs seem smeared with Saragossan plum jam," said
a bushy-browed peasant.

One of the condemned cried out, "Where art thou, O city of blessed-
ness, Jerusalem of the almond trees?"

"Today we shall enter into the Kingdom of God," said one of the
Conversos.

"Today we shall become ashes," retorted another.

"May you be blessed in paradise," a woman in the crowd shouted to
one of the prisoners.

"I am not dead yet," the man in question shouted back.

"The corpse of Torquemada shall be like dung spread over the face
of the land in the fertile fields. He who fashioned Adam and gave to
man the form of dust on the earth, blowing into his nose the breath of
life, will undertake to make it so," proclaimed a hoary old man in a
quavery voice.

The soldiers fired off their arquebuses in the square, surrounded the
condemned heretics and mounted them on donkeys to protect them
from the rabble. The friars made one last attempt at saving their souls
before they were conveyed to the burning place beyond the town limits.
The clergymen removed the black veil from the cathedral cross and,

escorted by secular officials and armed familiars, the Dominicans carried the green cross away, singing hymns all the while.

For their part, the penitents, dishonored by wearing *sanbenitos* and miters, were returned to the castle of the Aljafería; the next day they would hear once again the sentences condemning them to the galleys or to perpetual imprisonment, or to being paraded through the streets by the *alguacil*, to receive publicly their punishment of flogging and shame.

I departed from Saragossa, seeing as I passed the Madrid Gate two men strung up by their feet with their genitals tied to their necks, for having committed the crime of sodomy.

Through mountainous regions I journeyed to Calatayud to see Noé de la Vega. His house was on a hilly street, and the rocks loomed over the roof, or perhaps it was the wall that seemed to climb the rock. Beyond the houses hewn out of stone, martins were flying above the fields. The castle looked like a man-made extension of the stony landscape, and even the afternoon was tinged with the tawny hue of the brick towers and buildings.

When I knocked at the door of Noé de la Vega's house, a woman came to tell me that the *mosén*, Master Noé, was unable to receive me because he was dying. As he was slipping away from life, I felt that Isabel was slipping through my fingers, and I begged to see him before he departed this world.

In the courtyard a roan gelding with a lame right foreleg whinnied; four earthen pots, five caldrons and three wooden porringers lay on the kitchen floor. In the hindermost and principal bedchamber, amidst iron candelabra, massive dining tables and pine chests, with one half of his body in the shadows and the other half in the dark, the stranger I had come to visit was giving up the ghost.

Gathered around him in silence were his wife, who had dark brown hair, dark brown eyes, plump lips and an ample bosom, his still-maiden daughter, who had dark brown hair, dark brown eyes, plump lips and an ample bosom, two young but brawny men, already full-grown, so like each other they might have been twins, and seven other men, the notaries and witnesses, sitting in a row on a bench against the wall.

Ignored by the group, which so far had not heeded my arrival, I observed what was happening in the room: Noé de la Vega, lying prostrate on his bed, the anguish of death reflected in the pallor of his face and the tremor of his hands, asked his wife for some cushions to lean upon and, amidst the great sorrow of all those present, began to speak.

"I, Noé de la Vega, a Jew dwelling in Calatayud, being advanced in years and on my deathbed, but of sound mind, firm memory and coherent speech, do hereby make my will and testament, and once it is done may it remain so forever after, be it on this day or in the century yet to come, notwithstanding we be present or no to witness its arrival.

Of death I already have a glimmer, and I do not speak of something
vague and distant but rather of what I can see here now before me.

"As I was coming down the Calle del Barranco one Tuesday, between
eight and nine o'clock at night, I know not who threw a stone at my
head and made all the world go dark, and because I know not with
certainty, nor can I know from any visible evidence, I forgive all those
who were in the street where I was wounded and who are in the house
wherein I do lie, whether Christian or Jew or Moor, in all their three
Laws; and because God had ordained that I should perish from this
stoning, I desire that neither my lord the King, nor the *alguacil* of Calatayud, nor the justiciary of Aragón, nor any other judges or persons
should in any way lay the blame for the aforesaid stoning on anyone.
And it is my wish that all the things I have just said be made public
knowledge.

"I give thanks unto my God, creator of all the world and of the generations of men, who deposited my soul into this body of flesh and
blood and who now dispatches my days into the most uncertain night
of all. I give thanks unto Him who sustains us, that He did not make
me foolish or wicked and ignoble but rather a goodly man who dies still
hungering for life, for my promised land has ever been this earth, and
my glory was always love in this world. For this reason I order you to
not bewail my body, nor should anyone weep for me; not even you,
Doña Reyna, must mourn me overmuch, for I would rather that after
my death you think back on the times and the years when we took
pleasure in each other and when we were as one, for husband and wife
are we, both in life and in death.

"Before all else, I wish, order and command that my body be laved
with warm water, shaving off my beard, the hair under my arms and
on the other parts of my body, that I be dressed in a winding sheet of
new linen, clean hose and clean shirt, and my head laid upon a pillow
filled with virgin earth; that I be interred in the cemetery of the Jews in
the city of Saragossa, wherein lie my fathers and my fathers' fathers,
and their fathers before them, may Adonai give them glory. I do not
wish to be buried in barren soil but in earth which is untouched and
untilled, and in the grave a small chair must be placed facing the east,
so that, when they set me down, my eyes and my countenance will be
turned towards the rising of the sun.

"To my wife Reyna I do bequeath the house in Calatayud in the Calle
del Barranco and the house in Saragossa on the Carrera de San Gil; the
silver plate and the metal dishes, as well as the rope of pearls and the
rings of silver, turquoise and sapphire which I had given her, in addition
to the white silken gown from Sicily, the red shawl from Mechlin, the
green gown from Camprodón, the long veil of carmine linen and the

cushions of old-fashioned cloth that belonged to my lady mother; moreover, I leave to her the movable goods which are mine, and her own dowry, all of which she may give away, sell or do with elsewise as she pleases.

"To my sons Jacob and Isaac I bequeath, equally to each, to wit, forty Jaca *sueldos* and ten gold florins. To Jacob I do leave a gold ring set with a trifling stone, a silver saltcellar, a vineyard situate in Carra la Mata and two tunics from Kortrijk trimmed with silk, with sleeves. To my son Isaac I do leave a silver cup, a golden ring with no stone, a bed of pinewood, a gown of black shantung, three pairs of buskins, an iron roasting jack, a large dining table and a vineyard situate in the Ginesta of Calatayud.

"To my other son, Juan, who fights the war against the Moors in Granada with my lord the King Don Fernando, to be kept for him until he returns by his mother Doña Reyna, a house situate in the city of Calatayud; and I bequeath to him, seeing as he is an avid player of the game of chess, a chessboard with squares made out of jasper and mother-of-pearl, similar to one the King Don Martín of Aragón used to have, along with a pouch of white leather containing thirty-two chessmen, sixteen of one color and sixteen of the other, the eight lesser pieces or pawns of which, according to our King Don Alfonso, were made in the semblance of common folk going off to war. All my three sons, Jacob, Isaac and Juan, may do what they will with whatever I bequeath to them.

"To my daughter Orovida, who has reached the age of twelve, I leave, as a mark of especial favor, a house I own in the *judería* of Saragossa, situate in the Callizo Medio, and forty thousand Jaca *sueldos*, which I desire be given to her upon her bestowal in marriage, and she must marry according to the wishes of Doña Reyna, her own mother, who needs take care that she neither marry nor be gotten with child by any man who has a broken foot or hand, or who is crookbacked, dwarfish or mad, or mangy, scrofulous or reeking of rotten eggs, nor one who has a film over his eye; for little by little young Orovida will flourish, until one day she shall become a beauteous maiden the like of whom has seldom been seen in Calatayud or Saragossa.

"To my brother Salamón, who dwells in the *judería* of Saragossa and, having fallen into great poverty, has naught in this world save the clothes on his back and the weight of his many years, for he possesses neither *castellanos* nor silver, nor Jaca *sueldos* nor any one thing that God has vouchsafed him, and being grievously sick he begged Don Mair Alazar to take him into his hospital, as he was likely to die, but he did not die; he who is so poor that I would not even ask him to obey the commandment of our Jewish law to marry the widowed wife of his deceased brother, that is, Doña Reyna, nor require that he put his right foot into a leathern shoe with twelve laces and twelve knots so that she might untie the bond and obligation of the said marriage, my wife Reyna being in any case too old to have a child by him which could bear my name; to him, to my brother Salamón, therefore I do bequeath my black cloth tabard, a crossbow, an old pair of men's red breeches, a touchstone, a candelabrum made from deer antlers which is missing its chains, a bench for washing clothes, a leather bottle and a wineskin, some tongs for carrying about live coals, a lance and a cot, a pair of shoes somewhat spotted, a green shantung doublet which has seen service, a hood of black cloth, two old doors, an old mattress stuffed with wool, a white quilt for his bed, two wooden plates and a saltcellar.

"To my brother Santiago, whom I have not seen since the day he turned Christian out of melancholy, because once in a synagogue the rabbi gave him a slap and he became vexed and dejected, I bequeath one hundred Jaca *sueldos* to be claimed by him if he should ever return to Calatayud, for I know nothing of his fate, partly because I have not wished to know and partly because he has kept it from me.

"This is the way my wife Reyna, my sons Jacob, Isaac and Juan, my little Orovida and my brothers Salamón and Santiago shall inherit all my possessions, being assured that they will receive them without lawsuits, wrangling or deceitfulness, for on this hindmost article my advice is that you make no quarrel amongst yourselves nor have angry words about my goods once I am dead, because there is no people on earth which is merciful nor any man with a loose tongue who is worthy; for you are verily my children, as Adonai is my witness and your mother who carried your weight in her belly."

Thus did Don Noé de la Vega make his testament, and it was witnessed by the Rabbi Yocef Hazán, notary; Mossé Costantín, physician; Sento Anayut, elder; Salamón Alazán, rabbi; Mossé Abayut; Yucé Lupiel, surgeon; and Yaque Pazagón.

"May God lead you along the just path to the Garden of Eden, Noé my friend, and may He give you a goodly posterity in His glory, for you have dwelt on this earth as a wise man, righteous and free from covetousness," intoned Mossé Costantín. "You, my son," he said, turning towards Isaac, "take up your brick, set it down before you and build the city of Jerusalem upon it. And you," he said to Jacob, "rend your garments, as Jacob did in days of yore, and put sackcloth about your loins and mourn your father for many days . . ."

"Oh my father," moaned Jacob, "I shall not forsake you in this world nor in the next."

"See to it that any person who raises his hand against Doña Reyna and the little Orovida be cast away from amongst his brethren and accursed by the Lord for all eternity," ordered Don Noé de la Vega.

"I will never abandon either of you, mother and sister of mine; I would sooner die or become infected with pestilence than permit any evil to befall your bodies or your souls," Isaac vowed.

"Now I shall leave this world," said Don Noé, whereupon he turned his face to the wall and calmly breathed out his last sigh.

"May God keep him in His glory, for he is dead," Sento Anayut said at once.

"Just as the Exilarch Hezekiah turned his face to the wall to lament his sin, so has Don Noé departed this life," said Rabbi Yocef Hazán.

"He has expired after the great flood on the third day of the month of Marheshvan in the era which began with the Creation of the World, in the year five thousand two hundred and forty-eight, in the city of Calatayud," said Rabbi Alazán.

Towards the rear of the room where Don Noé de la Vega had just died, stacked on a wooden bench against the wall, were divers parchment books, among which could be made out a Bible and several tomes in Hebrew, while in a corner, as if waiting to be parceled out, a great quantity of shiny objects had been piled up, and cloth arms and legs hung out of a pine chest in which clothing had been heaped.

"Were you a friend of my father's?" Isaac de la Vega asked me.

"I came to Calatayud to see your father, but I fear I have arrived too late," I answered.

"Who has sent you?"

"Doña Luna de la Vega."

"For what purpose?"

"I am seeking Isabel de la Vega, your cousin and my wife, who has fled Ciudad Real on account of the Inquisition."

He looked hard at my face.

"My aunt Doña Luna told you to come and see my father? She did not know he was at death's door?"

"I am afraid that your aunt is not too well informed about the misfortunes of this world."

"So you are searching for my cousin Isabel?"

"Yes."

"Is she your wife or your concubine?"

"My wife."

"She went to Teruel after spending several months with us."

"Do you know any more?"

"Nothing more," Isaac said as he turned towards his dead father, at whose side Rabbi Yocef Hazán was keening and reciting from Jeremiah: "For the mountains will I take up a weeping and wailing and for the pastures of the wilderness a lamentation."

"O Lord, whose wrath is everlasting and whose mercy is great, let my lamentation be heard and my funeral chant be wailed in a suitable cadence," said the other rabbi, Salamón Alazán.

"For thus sayeth the Lord: 'In the return to dust and repose shall you find salvation; your strength will lie in quietude and faith,' " added the surgeon Yucé Lupiel, " 'for the strong in spirit shall be like a wind that knocks down walls.' "

"Daniel said of the tree in Nebuchadnezzar's dream: 'Just as the beasts of the field found shade under it, and the birds of the air dwelt in its branches, in thy heart will be heaped up the recollections of thy life on earth when thou art as nothing in the realm of ashes and oblivion,' " the elderly Sento Anayut intoned.

"Farewell," I said, but no one cared whether I stayed or went.

However, when I was already stepping over the threshold of the principal room, Isaac caught up with me and laid his hand on my shoulder.

"Isabel came from Saragossa with a baby boy a few months old and dwelled awhile with us," he said. "Her heart was heavy and her face filled with sadness, but my father made much of her so she would not feel a stranger among us or our people, and she lived as a daughter or a sister in our house, free to obey her own will within the restraints naturally arising out of her dual condition of fugitive and recent mother. She spent her days and nights in silent seclusion in that room, emerging only on occasion to stroll in the orchard; restless and despondent, she scarcely spoke to us or to the *Conversos* who frequented our house. It was her wish to remain aloof and alone in the company of her son, and neither merriment nor festivals could rouse her from her reverie. I do not think she ever looked out of the window or the door, nor did she show any desire to do so; neither did she complain of her confinement. During the last weeks she passed in our midst she seemed gravely perturbed, talking aloud to herself and in her sleep, and at times she would come out of her room uttering strange words such as we had never heard before. She would sit in the dark all night long, wholly indifferent to all conversation or any human activity, her eyes fixed upon her child or staring into some corner of the room. At dawn we would find her in the same position we had left her in before going to sleep. Even the church bells which keep time for the city, chiming Matins, Lauds, Prime, Terce, Sext, Nones, Vespers and Compline, failed to quicken her, insensible as she was to any sound or summons from the outside world. She often repeated one single sentence to herself, 'Death is an empty shape,' as if invisible figures were hovering before her or she was answering out loud a question which someone in her own mind had put to her, not necessarily that day but at any moment during her past life or in an imaginary situation in her future. Finally, one evening after sunset, she announced to my father that she would be leaving the next day. When my mother learned of it she begged to keep the child, but Isabel did not consent, arguing that she feared losing him if she left him behind in the Kingdom of Aragón, for after visiting Brianda Ruiz in Teruel she had thought to go to Flanders, where the Jews suffered less persecution than here. She said that although she and her son did not dwell in the same body, they did inhabit one soul, and if he were to be taken from her, she would become as nothing."

After a few moments of silence, during which he measured the effect of his words in my face, Isaac returned to his dead father's side.

I left the house. Several Jews had carried the Torah out of the synagogue into Calle del Barranco to pray for rain. They were blowing on horns, singing and wailing. And all the while a toothless old Jew at the window of his house moved his lips as if in prayer, repeating to each passerby, "There is no paradise save the market of Calatayud; there is no paradise save the market of Calatayud."

It was time for the grape harvest when I came to Teruel, the walled city upon a hill in the south of the Kingdom of Aragón, on the eastern bank of the Guadalaviar River.

I entered the city through the Saragossa Gate, I walked down the streets that lie beneath the soaring towers of San Salvador's and San Martín's churches, I left my mule at the White Horse Inn, and I set out for the house of Brianda Ruiz, which was behind the synagogue.

Leaning against the wall of the house in the midday sun, a ragged, barefoot man with unkempt beard and hair was eating a rabbit and spitting out the bones as if they were a fish's. A friar passing by saw him and began to admonish the fellow for devouring God's creatures in such a rude, greedy and sinful fashion.

"I know naught but my own hunger," the tatterdemalion answered.

"Jew or New Christian?" the friar demanded forthwith.

"Neither the one nor the other, but unfortunately only a man."

"That sounds like heresy," said the friar.

"It sounds like it, but it isn't," replied the man.

"Where do you come from?"

"From Cedrillos; my father used to work for Doña Catalina Bonet and he was born two streets away from her tavern."

"Do you relish the hares, partridges and other varieties of local fowl?"

"Very much so."

"And the pale red wines of these fields?"

"Even more so."

"Where do you spend the night?"

"In the big orchards just outside the walls of this city, not far from the river's waters."

"Take care you do not drown, like a certain Gil Ortiz who was returning from Saragossa and fell into the river, and as he could not get his feet out of his horse's stirrups, the current, which was swollen by the mountain snows, carried him away," said the friar.

"I shall be exceedingly careful, for it was I who first saw his horse emerge from the water and who searched for the fellow most diligently," the raggedy man answered. "Antón de Mesa, Martín de Huete and I found him halfway across the river, still wearing his turban and his sword, and we pulled him out with grappling irons a few days later."

"May God forgive him his sins . . . what are your garments made of?"

"Of the most humble cloth that is sewn in Teruel."

"Do you turn towards the wall when you pray?"

"I have already told you that I sleep in the big orchards close by the city ramparts."

"Do you observe the Sabbath?"

"Why yes, just as I do the other days of the Lord, out of doors," said the man.

"Do you eat meat in Lent?"

"If it falls from the sky."

"Then you are a Jew," the friar declared.

"When I was a boy, my mother used to say that our first parents were Adam and Eve the Jews, we obeyed the commandments of Moses the Jew, and we believed in the religion of Jesus the Jew."

"Do you know who I am? I am Don Francisco Bonfil, nuncio of the Holy Office charged with summoning and seizing heretics."

"Should I consider myself a condemned heretic on account of what I have said and for what I have kept to myself? When I was a boy, my mother also used to say that if my tongue was cut out I might reach old age and save my soul, but otherwise it would be pierced with thorns and I would be hanged from the gibbet at the outskirts of town, propped against a ladder with my hands bound behind my back, just like that lad from Cella brought here the other day by the King's assistant, accused of repudiating God and the cross."

"When you say 'King's assistant,' are you referring to Don Juan Garcés de Marcilla?"

"The selfsame one, who caused proclamations to be made, who had the lewd women trussed up and bandied about, who forbade gaming and who arrested the *Conversos* who later were burned," the man replied.

"Your words will make you wish you were never born," said the friar.

"Many is the time I have wished it, Señor Nuncio Don Francisco Bonfil, and I have no fear of death," the man said with a mute laugh that was more like a grimace.

"I don't know why, but you look like a murderer to me," said the friar. "Were you perchance the accomplice of a bawdy-house keeper by the name of Juan Navarro, who in the year 1480 beat to death with his sword pommel the wife of a certain Terol? Weren't you standing next to the cooper Juan de la Vega, when he killed Francis Besant outside the Valencia Gate? Wasn't it you who helped that man to hang himself from a tree after he got the idea into his head that no power on earth

170

could absolve him from a terrible sin he had committed? Didn't you take part in the great brawl near the Saragossa Gate on Shrovetide Tuesday, when Fernand Dobón stabbed Judge Francisco Navarro in the head?"

"You may stop counting, Señor Nuncio, for I have never been an accomplice to a crime nor have I helped any creature to lose his life; as a hungry and destitute man I have often erred in this world, but never have I been guilty of the sin of Cain," the man answered.

"If you make a timely confession of the sins you have committed against our Holy Catholic Faith, Mother Church will receive you with open arms," said the nuncio, stalking a peasant who was carrying bunches of grapes to a house. "Who dwells under that roof?" he asked the man.

"Four members of the Sánchez family, Your Worship, but none of them is at home, for they are all elsewhere fasting the fast of Kippur and will be back only when the star comes out," said the laborer, hanging his head.

"Do you know exactly where they went?"

"To the fair at Daroca, I think."

"Be careful not to lose one single grape, for your masters might scold you for it; I, too, will return when the star comes out," he promised.

Once the nuncio was out of sight I entered the house of Brianda Ruiz through a side door, which opened onto a corridor that brought me to a yard, another door and another corridor, as if I had entered two dwellings without going into any at all. In a clean, well-swept room I came upon four *Conversas* dressed in white, either barefooted or shod in cloth slippers, who were keeping the fast of Kippur until nightfall. Through a window opposite the synagogue I saw Rabí Simuel and the avowed Jews at their prayers. In the main room, towards the rear of the house, a white-clad damsel of some fifteen years stood facing the wall, her black hair flowing down her white back. It was the maid of Teruel, one of the twenty-five prophetesses who, according to their followers, roamed the earth announcing the arrival of the Messiah, the one who, after famines, plagues, earthquakes, widespread persecutions and false messiahs who would seek to confound the elect with portents and wonders, would finally come into the world.

She was the daughter of Juan Ruiz, a physician in the city, and the shoemakers, tailors, blacksmiths, dyers, goldsmiths and other disciples showered her with gifts, hearkened to her words and believed everything she said: that the Messiah had raised her up to the heavens to reveal to her the mystery of the Last Judgment and the exact day when He would come to save the Jews from the inquisitors' fire to carry them away above the clouds to the Promised Land.

In this whitewashed room were women, children and elders who belonged to the Gracián, Puigmija, Tristán, Pomar, Ram, Besante, Sánchez, Martínez de Rueda and other families; all had a live kinsman under arrest or being tortured or already penanced in the residences of the archbishop, or a deceased or absent one (exhumed or burned in effigy in the Plaza de Santa María) condemned for the same crimes as always, of keeping the Sabbath, eating meat in Lent, reading the Bible in Hebrew, bringing oil to the synagogue, praying turned towards the wall, eating partridges and pigeons that had not been strangled, giving alms to Jewish paupers, failing to kneel down when they heard the church bells announcing the Elevation of the Host, washing the bodies of the dead and bewailing them in the Jewish fashion, celebrating the festival of the unleavened bread and the Feast of Tabernacles; here were all those whose kindred had been summoned by the crier Juan Martínez, seized by the nuncio Francisco Bonfil and the *alguaciles* Miguel de Chauz and Juan Navarro, denounced by witnesses they had trusted—such as the servants Sevilla and Catalina Márquez, Angelina Tormón, María Valero, María Justa, Elisa Sánchez, Francisca Crespo, the hunter Juan Alcalá, the weaver Juan de Albarracín and other common folk—one day to stand in the Plaza Mayor of Teruel in the midst of a great throng of clergy and faithful, listening to the sentences passed by the tribunal of the Holy Office, sentences that condemned them as obstinate heretics and veritable apostates to perpetual prison, to burning at the stake, to the confiscation of their goods, to the disqualification of their descendants from public office and ecclesiastical benefice down to the second generation.

Surrounded by these people, Brianda Ruiz, the maid of Teruel, began to relate her adventure in the heavens: "One night as I lay in bed immersed in the profound mortification of my body, my dead mother appeared before me and said that God had sent her to show me the marvels of the hereafter and to reveal its secrets to me. The Messiah, whose wings were like rainbows, led us both through the air, and after a few puffs of wind we had left behind the sphere of souls in purgatory and entered the sphere of God's glory. We heard a surpassingly sweet canticle, and the Messiah said to me, 'Daughter of God, what you hear is the song of those creatures who perished in the flames for their faith and who are here seated in the eternal enjoyment of the Garden of Eden; they are the martyrs whose ashes were strewn over rivers and fields, but their souls were not scattered: although their dust remained in the dust, their spirits soared up to God. Their persecutions were my sufferings, and their shirts of fire became these garments of light which can no longer burn.' 'For Thee,' I said to Him, 'we would endure death daily.' 'It is better to die than to transgress the Law, for in death you will sanctify the Name,' He said, using the words of Maimonides the sage. 'Repentance is of no avail for whosoever has profaned the Name,

the day of Kippur does not bring absolution and affliction does not lead
to forgiveness, and only in death is there expiation—so wrote the wise
man of Córdoba,' I replied. 'Now, as proof that you have been in heaven
with Me, take this spike of wheat and this laurel branch, symbols of
celestial nature. But when you return to Teruel, be on your guard against
Death, which in the guise of a Dominican is scourging the Kingdoms
of Castile and Aragón, outraging divine justice and desecrating the peace
of cemeteries,' He added. 'I am an ignorant maiden living in times of
persecution and wretchedness, and my nights are filled with fear: there
are other masters in Spain far wiser than I am, whose strength is greater
than mine,' I answered. 'I will second your acts, I will inspire the words
you shall speak unto others,' He reassured me. 'Then so be it,' I said,
'and may the Eternal One watch over the innocent.' Afterwards, when
I found myself in bed again, I discovered that my body had not moved
a whit and that the house and the street looked the same as ever. . . .''

The maid of Teruel fell silent, her delicate profile partially hidden by
her long black hair. She turned her waxen face and flashing eyes towards
me, parting her lips, but she remained mute, as if waiting for the words
to emerge of their own accord from deep within her. And then she
spoke: "Dear brothers and sisters, men and women, children and elders,
let us fast the fast of Kippur in honor of the forty days that Moses spent
on Mount Sinai, with naught to eat or drink, waiting for enlightenment
and the forgiveness which God would grant Israel for the sin of idola-
try. . . .''

"Adonai, Thy dwelling is our fortress: from generation to generation,"
a man cried out.

"For in Thine eyes a thousand years are like unto the day of yesterday,
when it is past," another exclaimed.

"Leviathan is dead," said an old man behind me, as if the monster's
corpse lay before his eyes.

"It is a sign that the Messiah is nigh," said another old man, whose
shaggy white beard grazed the badge on his tabard.

"And that Torquemada will die, that the justice of the Lord will roar
over him like the roaring of the ocean," a youth chimed in.

"Even in life are the impious numbered among the dead, and even
in death are the righteous numbered among the living," the first old
man declared.

"They have hounded me since childhood, but I have never taken the
Name in vain," said the second old man.

"How much longer must we endure persecution and exile?" asked
the youth.

"It is ordained that all sufferings and exile will cease when the Messiah
comes," answered the maid of Teruel.

"In the morning stars I have seen the arrival of the Messiah; in all the confines of the earth I can already hear hymns of praise," said a toothless, grizzled man of uncertain age.

"Beneath this infamous mantle I am wearing my festive clothes; I shall set forth whenever the daughter of Juan tells me to," declared one woman, ready to travel the world at the maid's slightest hint.

"Take care, for it has been said that should a prophet or visionary rise up from within your midst and offer to perform a miracle as proof, you shall not heed the words of this prophet or visionary, for the Eternal One, our God, is putting us to the test," warned the youth.

"The Proverbs say that to speak without having understood is folly and a source of confusion."

"Saints of wood and stone, created by the hand of man, are forced upon us; are we to worship them?" asked the first old man.

"Maimonides the sage has written: 'In this persecution which we endure, we must not feign to serve an idol, but rather pretend to believe in what they tell us,' " said the maid.

"Don Fernando de Madrid, a Converso from Torrelaguna, has said that in the year eighty-seven there would be no justice in the world, and in the year eight the world would become a cattle yard, and in the year nine all laws would be as one. . . . And he said that after persecutions and evils have befallen us, then the Messiah will come whom we are all awaiting, and blessed will be he who sets eyes upon Him. . . . And he said that He will come to the city of Palos, which is Seville, but first the Antichrist will come to that city bringing a philosopher's stone, and if it touches a rod of iron, the rod will turn to silver, and if it touches a rod of steel it will become gold, and the sea shall reveal its treasures to him. Must I believe in this?" asked an old man on the other side of the room who had not spoken until that moment.

"Believe in the calamities you have before your eyes, for the future will be revealed to you one day at a time and there is no point in seeking it out," answered the maid of Teruel.

"They ravished my daughter," one man confessed, ashamed to admit it before the people assembled there. "What am I to do: cherish her, punish her, kill her?"

"It is written that you shall do no harm to a ravished maiden, for she has committed no crime deserving of death," answered the prophetess.

"I am looking for Isabel de la Vega," I said when it was my turn. "She disappeared from the city of Madrid, and I have no idea where to seek her. Tell me if she lives or dies."

"Isabel de la Vega is neither near to you nor far from you," said Brianda Ruiz in a barely audible voice, her face again turned towards the wall.

"What does that mean?" I asked.

"Exactly what you have heard, no more and no less," she said.

"Which road should I take to get closer to her?"

"The road to Toledo."

"Will I find her in Toledo?"

"On a street in that city you will hear a man telling you where to go next."

"How shall I know him?"

"When he shouts the name of another city at night."

"What is his face like?"

"You will not be able to see his face."

"Take this poor man to the kitchen to eat and drink his fill: he must be hungry and thirsty," said an old woman who found me too insistent.

"Away with him," said a burly, quarrelsome fellow.

Just at that moment a lookout who was posted at the door of the synagogue gave the alarm: "The *alguacil* and the familiars of the Inquisition are coming this way to arrest us!"

"Run for your lives!" another man inside the room shouted. "Hurry, take the backyard."

Everyone rushed out. Everyone except Brianda Ruiz, who stayed behind waiting for them, motionless and clad in white, as if death meant nothing to her. Calm and innocent, she stood enveloped in the serene light of her vision, protected by the image of the Messiah who had revealed Himself to her in the sky, perhaps unaware of the brutality of the inquisitors who were about to seize her, to accuse her of outrages against the Catholic faith and all manner of heresies, before condemning her to the stake after a cursory trial.

I wavered between remaining at her side or taking flight as well, and I finally fled, for I knew there was no divinity who was sheltering me, nor would it be a comfort to die for a belief I did not hold. Moreover, the need to find Isabel and my son was stronger than any temptation to sacrifice myself or than any person who might cross my path. That is why I felt no remorse whatsoever as I escaped through the yard, and after scaling fences, walls and roofs, I sought refuge in a hovel, which appeared providentially at the end of my race, hearing all the while behind me the threats and insults which the inquisitors hurled at the Jews and *Conversos* they were unable to catch or whom they already had in their clutches. I slammed the rickety door behind me so hard that the walls shook.

"You may come in, but you needn't throw the house down," called a woman's voice from an adjoining room.

"Help me, for the love of God," I pleaded, not knowing what person to address.

"Aren't those the *Conversos* who are running for their lives in the streets?" asked the voice.

"Yes, along with several Jews," I said as softly as possible, fearful of being heard from without.

"And are you a *Converso*?"

"I am a hunted man," I replied, "if that is what you mean by *Converso*."

There was a silence in the other room. The woman was trying to decide whether to give me shelter or hand me over to my pursuers. Outside in the street I heard footsteps, noises, voices; I was certain that many of the followers of Brianda Ruiz had already been arrested. Their capture left me shaken, as if it had been my own and I was now at the mercy of the *alguacil* Miguel de Chauz, about to be conveyed to the prisons of the Holy Office.

I went through a low, narrow doorway into a dark room which had a dirt floor and bare walls. The lone window framed the boughs of a tree. There sat a youngish woman with a pale face, lively black eyes, black hair and full lips, wearing shabby, threadbare clothes; she appeared to be suffering from hunger and privation. She scrutinized me as if she had not yet made up her mind whether to hide me or cry for help.

"Are you wounded?" she asked.

"No, I am only covered with dust," I replied.

"Who was that chasing after you?"

"The chief *alguacil* and the familiars of the Inquisition."

"Why?"

"They came to arrest everyone who was in the house of Brianda Ruiz, and I happened to be there as well."

"Did they take Brianda away?"

"Most assuredly."

"Then there is no doubt that she will be tried and burned," she said, lowering her voice so I could not hear the rest nor whether she uttered a prayer or a curse.

"She will be burned?"

"And what do you propose to do to save her?" she asked, looking me up and down.

"Why, nothing," I answered.

"Nothing? Won't you stand up to them, sword in hand, to rescue her?"

"I am not a man of arms, I am a man of words," I protested.

"So you conceal your cowardice with words?"

"I protect my life with them."

"What a pity you are a man of so little character," she remarked.

"It is by virtue of being so that I am still alive," I replied.

"Be that as it may, I shall hide you until you are safe from your pursuers. No one will ever suspect your existence in that room at the back, and you may stay there as long as you like," she said.

"I only expect to stay for today; I will depart tomorrow at dawn," I said.

"Do whatever best serves your own designs, but rest assured that no one will find you here. As far as the inhabitants of Teruel are concerned, this house is a tomb."

"And why is that?"

"I am Clara Santángel; my father was a wealthy *Converso* who was brought to ruin over the course of two years by the inquisitors Fray Juan de Colivera and Martín Navarro, with some help from the King's assistant, Juan Garcés de Marcilla, who took against him unmercifully and brought him to the stake in an auto-da-fé early this year. . . . My father owned land in the city and a house on the Plaza Mayor, but all his estate was confiscated to swell the coffers of the King, Don Fernando, and of the inquisitors. Using his influential position on the council of Teruel, he tenaciously opposed the establishment of a tribunal of the Holy Office in the city when the inquisitors sent by Fray Tomás de Torquemada came here to conduct investigations. The King, however, was implacable against the people's will, the tribunal was installed, and my father was arrested by the *alguacil* at the beginning of May in the year 1485. They accused him of imperfectly knowing the *Pater Noster*, the *Ave Maria* and the *Credo*, of reciting the Psalms and reading books in Hebrew, of furnishing dowries to marry off orphaned girls and of giving alms to Jewish paupers, of lighting candles on Friday and of eating meat in Lent, of having said one day, 'Blessed be the Lord for not making me a dog and for not making me a cat,' and for refusing to eat bacon or rabbit or conger eels, or partridges whose necks had been wrung.

"Unmindful of his advanced age, they emprisoned him in a chilly dungeon with shackles on his feet and repeatedly tortured him. No one knew where he was to be found until one Sunday, for not having confessed to his crimes, he was declared an unremitting heretic, his goods were confiscated and his descendants until the second generation were declared unfit to hold any sort of office or ecclesiastical benefice. He was relaxed to the secular arm and delivered up to Juan Garcés de Marcilla to be burned alive."

Her face clouded over and her voice choked as she continued. "My dead mother, Alba Besante, the youngest of seven sisters and the first among them to die, was accused after death of cooking Saturday's meal on Friday, in order to keep the Sabbath. María Barragán, who had been employed as her servant for the last twenty years of my mother's life, revealed under interrogation by the inquisitors that my mother was wont to celebrate the festival of the unleavened bread, that she habitually fried chopped meat with onions, that this and other meat from cows ritually slaughtered at the butchery belonging to Armesina Vilespisa was delivered to her, that she did not listen piously to the bells heralding the elevation of Christ during Mass, that she failed to utter the name of Jesus if someone fell down in her presence and that when anyone sneezed, she would say 'Saday.'

"Furthermore, the servant informed them that when my brother died, my mother washed his forehead, hands and feet with a damp cloth, that she ate hard-boiled eggs for the space of nine days and fasted on Kippur of that year in mourning. She reported how, when my mother was overtaken by death, we washed her body and wrapped it in a linen shroud, and that my father sent for interment in the Monastery of La Merced a doll which had been placed instead of her corpse into the coffin they hastily buried in the family vault, in front of the main altar, lowering it with ropes and stealing away without even shutting the doors; for once night had fallen, other men carried her genuine remains in secret to the cemetery of the Jews, without benefit of crosses or chaplains, while at home and elsewhere in town our kindred shattered pitchers and porringers as a token of mourning. It rained heavily that fourth day of August. Hailstones the size of walnuts fell from the sky, and the houses were flooded upstairs and downstairs. The Guadalquivir River overflowed its banks and covered the pastures. Mud walls and stone walls, vineyards, orchards and roads were devastated and destroyed. The inquisitors granted those men who pointed out my mother's grave, and those who dug her up and fetched the wood for the pyre, three years' pardon and indulgences."

When she had finished her tale, Clara Santángel looked at me intently, expecting answers, but I had none to give.

"If I were a man, neither the inquisitors, nor the King's assistant, nor the *alguacil* would be alive now! I would have killed them all long ago, with a noose or a knife or a lance or an arquebus or even with my bare hands!"

Wishing to turn her mind from her misfortune, I inquired if she was married and if she had any kin in Teruel or elsewhere in Aragón or Castile. She replied that not only was she unwed, but she had never known a man nor would she ever: why bring any more creatures into the world to be imprisoned or burned alive? Then I asked for a jug of water, as I had been burning with thirst for hours. She answered that the well had run dry, and that the only water in the vicinity of the house lay in puddles, but that she would give me fresh water nevertheless. She asked me the reason why I had come to Teruel. I briefly recounted to her my love for Isabel and my search for her during the past years.

Immediately, as if we shared the same evil fortune, she took my hand and gazed at me with something resembling love. I hastened to inform her that since there was nothing to hold me back in this city, I would be on my way at the third cockcrow, after spending the night under her protection and care. My words displeased her, for she had quickly taken to the idea of having a man in the house. So forlorn was the look she gave me that I had to avert my eyes.

"Isabel de la Vega is still alive, and I shall have no peace until I find her," I offered in excuse.

"It will be to your advantage to remain a few days longer hidden away in this house far removed from the world," she said plaintively. "No one will look for you in a cemetery."

"I can slip away from Teruel; shrouded in the shadows of dawn, I will be taken for one more shadow," I replied.

"By now the *alguacil* and the familiars of the Inquisition will surely have surrounded the *judería* and the city gates," she said, looking scared and bewildered.

"I cannot remain hidden forever in Teruel, I must go to Toledo and other places as well," I said, chafing at her insistence. "The informers in the employ of the Holy Office will eventually discover me if I stay here."

"This poor cottage has been forgotten by all. No one comes this way for fear of the inquisitors, and they know they can do me no further harm than they already have: they even carried off the key to the door!"

"It would be better if you came away with me; the Dominican friars never forget the kin of a condemned heretic, and they are only awaiting their chance to accuse them of the same crimes committed by the parents, the brother or sister, the husband or wife," I said.

"Where can we go?" she asked, her face ghostly pale.

"To anywhere far from here."

"There is no life for me far from Teruel; I shall die where my mother and father died," she declared.

"I advise you to leave this house, these people and this kingdom as soon as possible. Do not abandon yourself to your own downfall."

"At least I know my own misery," she answered obstinately.

"In Madrid you could lodge with a most honorable and discreet friend of mine by the name of Pero Meñique; you might stay in his house as long as you like," I said in a last attempt at convincing her.

She refused to leave. Before daybreak I was lucky enough to evade the sentries at the Teruel Gate, and I set off towards Madrid.

I reached Toledo by way of the vast plains and countryside of Sagra, stopping to rest at Getafe and Illescas.

From afar I could see the city where generations of Jews had lived, perched as it was on a hill of granite and girdled by three walls of stone and one of green water, the Tagus River.

Standing in the middle of the old Alcántara Bridge, which gave access to the city, I could see the *alcázar* to my left, its ramparts surmounted by towers, and the Gothic cathedral whose spire pierced the heavens like petrified time. Olive trees and poplars, willows and cypresses climbed the banks of the crystalline river, while the stream reflected the red-streaked clouds of twilight, as if dusk were floating upon the waters. The Tagus was reputed to abound in nymphs and golden grains of sand, but at that moment the tranquil flow of its waters only rippled the trees and the motionless stones.

Beneath the troubled sky, the city looked not merely strange but supernatural; it seemed to slant towards the waters, while its walls appeared to rise out of the rocks. There was a full moon. It hovered like a blind eye over the jagged horizon, amidst gray and livid, purple and silvery clouds. I entered through the Bisagra Gate. My long shadow and I traversed the steep and narrow streets, the slopes and naked rock, the unexpected squares.

On my way to the cathedral, I came across lanes occupied by bridle makers, armorers, chopine makers and goldsmiths; there was a great trafficking of trade in Toledo, especially in silks, velvets and damasks, well-tempered swords and daggers, gold purses, glazed tiles and colored glass.

In between the rows of tall buildings whose windows seldom faced the street I encountered monks, beggars, vagabonds, gentlemen and pale, oval-faced damsels with curly hair, dark eyes, snub noses, carnal mouths and gorges plump as doves'.

In front of the cathedral, which was served by forty canons, fifty prebendaries, thirteen chaplains and other dignitaries, as well as an archdeacon, the inquisitors were preparing to celebrate an auto-da-fé the following day, and the scaffoldings for the persecutors and their victims had already been erected. The green cross had been planted on the altar, and soldiers and familiars of the Holy Office were standing guard over it.

I walked down the *alcaná*, the exchange lined with dozens of Jewish shops. It was closed off by gates at both ends and bounded by the Church of Santa Justa and the scrivener's office on one side, and by the Cal de Francos, the Pellegería, or Hide Market, and the Espartería, or Matwork Market, on the other. I entered the *aljama* through the main portal, which is in between a tavern called Ojos de Vaca, the dyers' walk and the Jewish almshouse. Making my way through the parish of Santo Tomé, I reached the walls of the Montichel enclosure, the farthest boundary of the *judería*.

I emerged from a narrow street in front of the hermitage of Santa María la Blanca, the sober but handsome synagogue that Fray Vicente Ferrer had converted to a church at the start of the century, storming it with armed men from the Church of Santiago del Arrebal, where he had been preaching. Torches, candles and lanterns were being lit in the windows of several houses; in the distance the sun sank into the ocean of deep night as if it would never rise again.

In the sanctuary barefoot *Conversas* clad in clean shifts and black hooded cloaks were washing their hands in an aquamanile, lighting candles and giving alms. The lay brothers, *Conversos* to a man, under the leadership of a certain Fernando de San Pedro, took care of its maintenance, as constant repairs were called for. It was said to be the second Jewish temple after the one in Jerusalem and had been built with earth from the holy land. People complained of negligence during the past twenty years on the part of clerics, administrators and chaplains who had sold the synagogue's sacred vestments and ornaments, and the Jews had endeavored to purchase the inscribed parchment fragments of the Torah.

The main body of the building consisted of five naves formed by four arcades of horseshoe arches supported by thirty-two octagonal columns surmounted by elaborate carved capitals. There were Hebrew letters in many places, chiseled spandrels with geometric knots similar to lattices, and a gallery for the women. Its chapel, to the right of the altar, was shut, "for in the time of the Jews, when it was a synagogue, that was the Holy of Holies, and in truth it was a most holy place," as Fernando de San Pedro said. Nevertheless, in the blink of an eye, as if all the *Conversos* had vanished simultaneously upon being warned of some danger by means of secret unspoken signals, which I did not perceive, there was no one. The silence was all around me, and nothing moved except a cat prowling among the matte white columns.

The darkness of night was solidly entrenched as I emerged from the *judería*, walking between the blank walls of empty alleyways where fear appeared to have obliterated all signs of life. I arrived at the Hostal del Tajo, where the hostess, Débora Dorado, offered me a choice between a fancy bed fit for a gentleman or a person of consequence and one suited to a servant, which cost half the price, along with barley, straw and water for my pack mule. I chose the gentleman's bed to avoid sharing a room with drunkards or ruffians.

Later on, seated at a table, I gorged on hare, sheep's entrails and wine, with no further thought in my head than eating and drinking, until from another such table a lackluster fellow, whose sickly complexion suggested that he had just suffered some sickness of the soul or that he whiled away his days in a murky room, asked me if I was not a familiar of the Inquisition accompanying the penitents who were to be led forth on the morrow.

"A familiar of the Inquisition? Whatever gave you that idea?" I asked him with a laugh, for never had it occurred to me that someone might mistake me for one of them.

"Your discreet and honest appearance and the courteous and gracious way you carry yourself," he said, his eyes feverish. "But what are you laughing at?"

"I am laughing at myself," I replied.

His face became troubled, and he looked away, only to stare fixedly again into my eyes. I lowered my gaze.

"I am lately come from Segovia, from the Convent of Santa Cruz, the spiritual home of our father inquisitor, Fray Tomás de Torquemada, a zealous defender of the faith," he said, raising his cold hand from the trencher so as to wring the other hand with it. "*I* am a familiar of the Inquisition."

I remained silent. He obstinately sought me out in conversation, interrogating me about my origins, my name and my habits. I answered with straightforward explanations and good judgment and asked him in turn if he was not acquainted with a Señor Miguel Husillo, a friend of a friend of mine in Madrid. The smile froze on his lips, and he raised a ruby jug of wine as if to drink, but did not. Then he drawled, "Tomorrow we shall burn Señor Miguel Husillo as a heretic in an auto-da-fé. Do you have any dealings with him?"

"No," I hastened to reply, "it's only that someone told me he is a skillful goldsmith."

"We may say with no hesitation that Señor Miguel Husillo *was* a skillful goldsmith," he said in a mild voice that belied the fanaticism on his face.

There was something about his manner of speaking and staring that was wholly repulsive to me. Not wishing to look at him any further, I shifted my gaze to the fair and comely mien of our hostess, Débora Dorado.

He turned towards a man of some forty years who had a long, freckled face, lively azure eyes and white hair and whiskers that still had a faint reddish tinge; he was eating alone at another table.

"You over there, where do you come from?"

"From myself," the man replied.

"Are you a *Converso*?"

"By San Fernando, I am not."

"There are many criminals on the loose—you would not happen to be a murderer or a thief or a fugitive from justice?"

"No, señor, I am a navigator; I learned cosmography in Portugal from a brother of mine who makes charts for seafaring."

"What are you looking for in Toledo?"

"For our good Queen Doña Isabel, to propose a most grandiose undertaking to her."

"How to conquer the Kingdom of Granada?"

"How to reach the Indies by going west, señor."

"Take care you do not land in the heart of heresy."

"By San Fernando, no, for I only sail on the sea of faith."

"That is a cold, dark sea."

"I have sailed over seas colder and darker than death," the man replied.

"The generations of man succeed each other like the waves of the sea, and his dreams as well," said the familiar of the Holy Office.

"What I seek is but a stone's throw from my dreams."

"I hope it is not a stone's throw from the stake."

"There is no danger of that, señor, for I always call upon the Holy Trinity before taking any action; I begin all my letters with *'Iesum cum Maria sit nobis in via'*: 'Jesus and Mary be with us,' and I always carry about on my person a book of the canonical hours in order to say my prayers in private." He rose from the table to retire to his room.

"Are you leaving so soon?"

"I have many a league to travel before dawn."

"You must not go without telling me your name."

"Cristóbal Colón."

"Colombo?"

"No, señor, Colón."

The man went to his bed. Straightway I, too, rose from the table, meaning to get away from the familiar of the Inquisition.

"And where might you be going at this late hour?" he asked me.

"I wish to walk about the city."

"In the dark of night?"

"Yes."

"But it is raining," he added, as if by saying so he could keep me from leaving the inn.

"So it is," I said.

I ventured out into the damp and gloomy streets of Toledo, rendered even more narrow and steep by darkness and drizzle. I walked along them, glad they were deserted. The houses seemed like the stony fragments of some other city, long gone and legendary. The river sped into the shadows like a horizontal green flame, its verges merging with the night's. Soon it stopped raining, the sky began to clear, and the full moon was visible once more. From the San Martín Bridge I could see the boulders in the water and the trees rippled by the imperceptible flow of time in the river. I heard footsteps behind me and felt certain I was being followed.

"Am I being pursued by that ghoul from the Holy Office?" I wondered, turning with a shiver towards the sound.

There was no one in the dark alley, only my shadow drowning in a deep puddle. But no matter how fast I walked down other streets, trying to get away from the city itself and my own fear, the footsteps still followed. It started to rain again; the night acquired a greenish cast, like an underwater twilight. The trees climbing the riverbanks seemed to dissolve into mizzle, becoming liquid phantasmagories. The muffled voice of a woman cried out, as if from the depths of the Tagus, "You will mind me in Avila, you will mind me in Avila," which at first I mistook for "You will find me in Avila, you will find me in Avila." Stricken by an ineffable sadness, with my clothing and hair soaked through and my feet chilled, I started back to the hostel, resolved to sleep in my gentleman's bed until well into the morning.

At break of day Débora Dorado awoke me to recount how their final breakfast had been served to the condemned heretics; the familiar of the Holy Office had already left the inn and was officiating at Sunday Mass before the altar of the green cross in the cathedral square. I should be sure not to miss this Mass, for the town was teeming with the informers of the *Suprema*.

"The auto-da-fé is a specialty of Toledo, Your Worship," she said.

"Indeed! Yet they also celebrate it in other cities of these realms," I observed.

"Ah, but the fire is not stoked with the same zeal," she replied. "Hurry along, for it is not good for the hostel or yourself that you should appear laggardly in your faith."

A little later I found myself in the freezing street, jostled by the crowd bound for the square in front of the principal church to witness the ceremony. The procession of those reconciled with the Church had already set out from San Pedro Mártir's, following the route customarily taken on Corpus Christi. Flanked on either side by a familiar, the repentant heretics from the archdioceses of Toledo, Talavera, Madrid and Guadalajara formed a lengthy and somber human serpent of more than one thousand bodies, overwhelmed by humiliation and cold.

The men came first, holding snuffed candles, bareheaded and without cloaks, belts, hose or shoes, except for a thin sole under their feet to protect them from the icy ground. The women were next, cloakless as well, their faces exposed, feet unshod, also holding candles. Men and women alike were said to be leading members of the *Converso* communities. They had a large audience—the auto had been proclaimed eight days earlier throughout Toledo and its confines—which ogled them and jeered; many felt more aggrieved at being displayed in public in this fashion than by the vile words and insulting gestures of the rabble. Some were sobbing, tearing out their hair and weeping. As they reached the door of the cathedral two chaplains blessed them, passing their hands over the bare foreheads as they intoned, "Receive the sign of the cross, which you denied and abandoned when you were led astray." The penitents filed into the church towards a platform where the inquisitors were seated, and they heard Mass.

Barefoot on the cold pavement, they waited to be called by the notary of the Holy Office, who asked, "Is so-and-so here?" to which the person in question answered, "Yes," holding the snuffed candle aloft. He was then reminded how he had fallen into Jewish practices, and he declared that henceforth he desired to live and die as a Christian. After each article of faith he had to affirm aloud, "Yes, I do believe," swearing on the cross never to Judaize again, and to inform the inquisitors if he knew of anyone who did. He received the sentence to scourge himself on six consecutive Fridays in a procession, "his back laid bare, using hempen cords tied into knots, and wearing neither hose nor headgear, and to fast as well on the six Fridays"; to wear over his clothes each day a *sanbenito* of coarse cloth with a red cross front and back; not to venture out of the house without it, under pain of being relapsed; not to hold any public office, such as *alcalde, alguacil,* municipal councillor, juryman, public scribe or gatekeeper; if he had held any such office, he lost it from that moment on. He was informed that he was forbidden to work as a money changer or a spice merchant, that he was not allowed to wear silk or scarlet or any colored cloth or gold or silver or pearls or seed pearls or coral or any jewelry whatsoever; that he could not ride a horse or bear arms or act as a witness, or rent a house, under pain of being relapsed. Furthermore, as a penance he was required to donate a fifth of his estate to support the war against the Moors.

Behind the reconciled stretched a long line of those condemned to perpetual imprisonment: men and women, boys and girls, wearing *sanbenitos* and miters, barefoot and shivering from the cold. Some hung their heads low, staring at the ground, incredulous at their plight, aghast at the triviality of their offenses, which were atrocities in the eyes of the Dominicans. Others looked dumbly upwards as if expecting a miracle from the sky—an angel in flames to swoop down from the heavens and put a stop to the auto-da-fé. Still others, more pessimistic, dragged their feet leadenly as if the worst fears of their lives had been realized.

In the endless file, I noticed a man who seemed to require more space than the others because of his unusual size. From beneath his miter his long hair streamed over his broad back, and his bound hands clutched a yellow candle. As he drew nearer I could see his wounds and how the gashes on his feet left a trickle of blood behind them; the torture inflicted on his body was manifest. Ill-used to the light of day, his eyes glowed like live coals as he struggled to distinguish my features and suddenly recognized me.

"They arrested me in the Plazuela de la Paja during the first days of September of the year which has elapsed," said King Bamba in a hoarse voice that seemed to emerge from the past, from his memory, cleaving his chest. He walked on without looking at me as if he were talking to himself to keep time with the others. "They threw me into a dark dungeon and shackled my feet, and one day they brought me to the chamber in the church where the inquisitors were wont to hold audience at the hour of Terce. It was then I waxed wroth, I picked up a notary by the scruff of his neck and flung him on his back like a beetle onto his writing table, and I was about to do the same for the venerable Dominican fathers when, in response to the bawling of the prosecuting officer, upwards of fifty familiars armed with lances and swords burst into the chamber. They fell upon me, trounced me soundly and conducted me once again to prison. However, this time the chief *alguacil* ordered the keeper to bury me in an even darker and damper dungeon, a veritable ergastulum, reeking with noxious smells, to put me in irons hand and foot and wrap me in a chain weighing thirty *arrobas*. The keeper carried out his instructions to the letter. I staggered under its great weight, unable to carry the chain on my shoulders and my body for very long, so they threw it on the ground. Ever since then, the world has known naught of me, nor I of it."

He turned his face away, and his voice became inaudible. Suddenly his eyes bored into mine, and as if revealing a secret known only to himself, he said, "Do not repeat this, but many of those behind me who wear the insignia of 'Condemned Heretic' will be burned."

In that instant a mounted familiar jabbed him with his lance to silence

him. King Bamba shot back a look of mute defiance, bit his lips and
trudged on.

Several prisoners in the forefront complained of the cold, while others
declared they were very thirsty. The familiars pushed them forward,
shouting, "Keep moving, you heretics, for hell will be far worse!"

A few paces away from King Bamba, a discreet, fine-featured man of
some thirty years blushed scarlet upon receiving a number of lashes
across his back, as if his very soul were being flogged. But in lieu of
groaning, he glared disdainfully at his torturer, convinced of his own
superiority to his tormentors in whatever situation. In response to his
victim's scorn, the familiar whipped him even more vigorously.

King Bamba reached the portals of the cathedral, where the chaplains
continued to make the sign of the cross and repeat the same words as
before over each penitent: "Receive the sign of the cross, which you
denied and abandoned when you were led astray." But he turned his
back on them and jabbed his elbow into one prelate's stomach. Two
familiars forced him to turn around and kneel before the chaplains, but
when one of the guards tried to stick a knife into his back through the
yellow *sanbenito*, he ducked the gesticulating hands with a quick shake
of his head and freed himself from his captors. One of the friars fell flat
on top of a kneeling reconciled heretic. It took eight soldiers to subdue
King Bamba and bind him about his chest and back with cords that dug
deep into his hands, arms and neck. To prevent him from blaspheming,
they thrust a gag into his mouth. The head *alguacil*, the *alcalde*, the
familiars and the keepers of the Inquisition pitched into him, relishing
the injuries they dealt this corpulent man who seemed to grow bigger
with each blow. One diminutive rider in particular proved to be most
adept at harassing him, first tightening with all his might the cords
around King Bamba's leathery neck, then pricking him all over with a
sword, with the impunity of one who believes the man at his mercy is
unable to defend himself. King Bamba clenched his teeth and his fists,
until he gave an unexpected leap and, although his arms were tied,
succeeded in grabbing the manikin's whip and tumbling him off his
horse, to fall upon him with a vengeance. In a trice dozens of armed
familiars bore down upon him and so belabored him with their lances
that my friend was left lying on the ground looking very like an early
Christian martyr. Without further ado, all bathed in sweat and blood as
he was, they propped him on his knees before the chaplains.

"Accursed devil, we are going to throw you into a black hole where
you will have neither food nor drink and whence you will never emerge
alive, although I promise that all the air therein will be yours!" the
homunculus shrilled at him.

And then, enveloped by a swarm of soldiers and surly spectators,

King Bamba was plucked from the procession, to be taken to the prisons of the Holy Office.

The auto-da-fé resumed its solemn pace; hundreds of porters came forward carrying the effigies of the absent who had Judaized. On a scaffolding opposite the platform where the inquisitors were assembled, a catafalque swathed in black was uncovered. A notary recited the names of the dead as the statues of those he mentioned, wrapped in winding sheets in the Jewish fashion, were taken out of the catafalque. Once the trial of the deceased had been read aloud, he was invariably sentenced to burning in the pyre in the middle of the square, along with the effigies and bones that had been exhumed from churches and monasteries. Henceforth his chattels and estates would belong to the King, and his male and female descendants were disqualified from ever holding public office, being forbidden as well to ride on horseback, carry arms or wear silk.

The sorrowful troupe of men and women to be burned at the stake appeared, their hands tied to their necks with nooses, wearing the miters and yellow *sanbenitos* on which were written their names and the words "Condemned Heretic." A look of almost animal panic contorted their wan faces as they were lined up on a tiered scaffolding facing the other one on which the inquisitors and their notaries were ranged. The latter, after reading aloud the list of offenses, pronounced the sentences and turned the condemned over to the secular arm of justice, which was charged with conveying them to the Horno de la Vega, the Furnace on the Plain, where "nary a bone among them was left to burn and become ashes."

Finally, two clergymen dressed as if for Mass and holding chalices and breviaries were exhibited on the platform. Standing before a bishop, an abbot and a prior, they listened to a public reading of the trial in which they had been accused of observing the Law of Moses. While the bishop read from a holy book they were stripped of their priestly vestments down to their jerkins; then they were clothed in the yellow *sanbenitos*, miters were placed on their heads and ropes around their necks, and they were delivered to the secular authorities. Asses bore them to the Horno de la Vega, followed by a great throng avid to witness the burnings. It was four o'clock in the afternoon.

For some while I had had no news of Pero Meñique. Fearing he might be ailing or dead, I went one day to his house. The yard door was open and there was nothing in my friend's room but a bedstead and the basin from a washstand. On the ground, the wax from an enormous candle took up more room than before it burned down, as if hundreds of candles had melted over one another to form a mute white bell on the floor. The caldrons, earthen pots and copper pans in the kitchen were full of dirt, ashes and neglect. The grease and soot on the hearth had hardened into stone and silence.

After the tolling of Vespers, I found Pero Meñique in the midst of a large crowd in the Plaza de San Salvador, listening to a toothless crier who spat his words to the four winds. The blind man's hair and beard had grown long enough to hide most of his face, so that he nearly succeeded in disguising himself from himself behind the hairy mask. Clad in a patched doublet, threadbare hose—one leg was yellow and the other scarlet—and a hat so full of holes that the sun's rays shone through it, he looked more like a scarecrow than the prudent man of my acquaintance.

"Pero Meñique, it is I," I said, laying my hand over his cold one.

"Who is I?" he asked, pulling his hand away distrustfully.

"Juan Cabezón," I whispered, for I did not want other people to overhear my name.

"Sometimes when I feel the sun's warmth upon my face, I take myself for a god emerging from the night—but dawn has not yet broken; other times my face feels so cold that I imagine it is still darkest night, but the sun has already been up for hours and it is only a dismal morning," he said.

Wordlessly I took his arm and pushed him into motion, meaning to lead him far away from the square.

"Juan Cabezón, from the very first moment I heard you coming, I knew it was you; I recognized your smell, your breathing, the roughness of your hand, the sound of your voice, but in the crowd I deemed it wiser not to know you," he confided to me a few steps later.

"Are you afraid of informers?" I asked him.

"One-Eye and the Moor, after going off to Málaga to fight alongside of Hamete el Zegrí, were impaled for being turncoats by the King, Don Fernando, when he took that city," he said, ignoring my question.

"I hope that Don Gonzalo de la Vega was not so imprudent as to seek refuge in that town."

"Gonzalo is a most judicious man," he replied in a tone that dispelled my doubts.

"Speaking of people who are missing, what has become of our friend the Trotter?"

"She married a chandler, a boy from the suburb who fell madly in love with her; believing her to be an untried wench, he felt such remorse for having plucked her lily that he resolved to repair the damage with a hasty wedding, at which I was present," he answered, pressing his hands to his head as if it pained him.

"Does it hurt very much?" I asked.

"For some time now I have been uneasy. My nights are haunted by hideous dreams and my days by hobgoblins, phantoms and shadowy, fantastical figures; an odious creature constantly crops up before my eyes—his name is Tomás de Torquemada," he disclosed.

"I fail to understand what Torquemada has to do with your dreams and visions," I said.

"I shall never be quit of my nightmares and headaches until I have slain Torquemada," he replied.

"Have a care, for there is no sight more sad to the eye than a blind man in flames."

"This darkness of mine will make a dazzling corpse."

"It is impossible to kill Torquemada," I argued. "The Catholic Kings protect him with fifty familiars on horseback and two hundred on foot, all armed to the teeth. They say that when he is at table, he employs a unicorn's horn and a scorpion's tongue to detect and nullify any poison."

"I will know how to outwit the surveillance and foil the horn and the tongue, for I have already seen him die a thousand times over the most horrifying death from which a human creature may perish," he insisted, grasping my cold hand with his icy one. "We must kill him together."

"I wish to die from an excess of days, wrinkles and appetites," I protested.

"It is not death which kills us, it is we ourselves who cease to live," he pointed out.

"Perhaps."

A woman came towards us.

"There is someone approaching," I murmured.

190

"Don't think of me as a thirsty man,
cast out beyond this earthly span,
but picture me sitting by your side
drinking you up as my little bride,"

Pero crooned as she passed by.

"Faugh, what a nasty old blind man!" shrieked the woman.

"You are mistaken, I am the spirit of Enrique Cuarto groping along the walls of the city in search of youths to bed down in the bushes," he retorted.

"You foolish dotard," she snapped.

"I am not so old as that, but solitude makes me seem ancient," he said to me, once she had vanished. "Won't you go with me?"

"That I will, even if we do not come out of this business alive," I answered.

He thrust his face into mine, as if he would pierce the barrier of his blindness to tell me a secret he preferred to reveal with his eyes alone.

"Listen," he said, "a friend of mine who dwells in Avila told me that Torquemada is holding captive in that city a number of Jews and *Conversos* who are accused of the ritual killing of a Christian child and of profaning the consecrated Host. On account of the personal interest he is taking in the case, it is rumored that he is preparing a mighty blow against the Jews, for instead of putting the accused on trial in Toledo, to whose archbishopric La Guardia—the village where the crime was presumably committed—belongs, he first imprisoned the suspects in Segovia and afterwards had them transferred to Avila."

"I don't see what is so unusual about that," I objected. "He arrests *Conversos* if they so much as breathe in the Jewish manner."

"Hear on: At the beginning of the month of June in the year 1490, one Benito García, a *Converso* native to La Guardia and a carder of wool by trade, happened to be in the town of Astorga, where he was obliged to share lodgings with a pack of scoundrels who rifled the knapsack he carried with him and inside it found a consecrated wafer. 'The man's a heretic!' they exclaimed, and they tied a rope around his neck and brought him before Doctor Pedro de Villada, at whose behest the carder received two hundred lashes and was put to the water torture and the thumbscrews. Benito García confessed to more than he had ever known, enough to burn several times over. He admitted that he was wont to Judaize, having been encouraged to do so by Juan de Ocaña, a *Converso* also native to La Guardia, and by two Jews surnamed Franco, a father and a son, inhabitants of the village of Tembleque. The son, Yucé, a young shoemaker, was immediately seized by the inquisitors, and being taken sick in jail, he asked to see a physician. The inquisitors sent him a spy in the guise of a doctor, a certain Antonio de Avila, one of the friars who had compiled the work *Censura et confutatio libri Talmud, Censure and Refutation of the Talmud*, in the Monastery of Santa Cruz. Taken in by the ruse, Yucé Franco asked the impostor to send him 'a Jew who would say the words which the Jews were wont to say when they were on the verge of dying.' Fray Alonso de Enríquez, disguised as a rabbi, paid him a visit. When the spurious rabbi questioned him as to why he was being held prisoner, Yucé explained that it was on account of the *mitá* (death) of a *nahar* (boy) whom they had used in the same way as *otohays* (That Man), imploring him not to repeat this to anyone except Don Abraham Senior.

"Antonio de Avila was sent to him again eight days later by Fray Fernando de Santo Domingo, the inquisitor appointed by Torquemada for the trial; however, this time Yucé Franco was sorely afraid of him and refused to speak, upon which they locked him in a cell for three months, until he revealed that approximately three years ago, as he was on his way to La Guardia to purchase wheat for the festival of unleavened bread, he heard that an Alfonso Franco—who was no kinsman of his— had fine white wheat for sale, and on their way back from the square to his home, the latter had recounted how once, on Good Friday, he and his brothers had crucified a little boy in the same way that Christ had been crucified. Immediately the prosecutor of the Holy Office, Alonso de Guevara, accused Yucé Franco, along with several others, of having crucified a Christian child on a Good Friday, in addition to having profaned and defiled the consecrated Host, with the aid of divers sorcerers, in order to make Communion one day during Passover using the said wafer and the Christian child's heart, so that all the Christians might contract rabies and perish. The prosecutor asked the inquisitor to assign Yucé's goods to the Kings' exchequer and turn him over to the secular authorities to be burned alive.

"Yucé Franco protested that this was the biggest untruth in all the world and he denied everything. Martín Vásquez, who was acting as the young cobbler's defense counsel, confronted the inquisitors with a brief drawn up by the Bachelor of Laws Sanç disqualifying them from acting as judges in this affair, because it was common knowledge that their jurisdiction was limited to the bishopric of Avila, and there were inquisitors in Toledo to whose diocese the prisoner should be remanded. Furthermore, the prosecutor's accusation should not be admitted, since it was highly general, vague and obscure, and did not specify 'the places, years, months, days, times or the persons with whom the said Yucé Franco had carried out the transgressions imputed to him'; nor could it be affirmed that he had committed any crime of heresy or apostasy, since he was a Jew and not a *Converso*, a mere boy ignorant of even his own Law, who in plying his trade as a shoemaker was more concerned about earning his livelihood than about inducing and luring Christians to Judaism. The Bachelor Sanç asked that he be released immediately from prison, that the good name he hitherto enjoyed be restored to him and that the property taken from him be returned.

"One month later the prosecutor replied that the arraignment held, and that he was under no obligation to identify 'the day or the time or the year or the place' because the charge was the special one of heresy. Meanwhile, Fray Tomás de Torquemada formally petitioned Cardinal Pedro de Mendoza, the Archbishop of Toledo, to allow the trial to be conducted in Avila.

"Months went by. The inquisitors placed the *Converso* Benito García and the Jew Yucé Franco in adjoining cells, so they could engage in conversation through a hole in the wall; one day the Reverends Pedro de Villada and Iohán López de Cigales went down into the prison and entered Yucé Franco's cell. Under sworn oath he revealed to them that he had not remembered until then how this past New Year it would have been three years since Maestre Yuça Tazarte, a Jewish physician, had asked Benito García to procure for him a sacramental wafer to use in the manufacture of a rope with certain knots for performing witchcraft, and told him to deliver it to Rabí Peres, a physician in Toledo.

"On Tuesday, the eighteenth July, the inquisitors obtained an apology from Yucé Franco for not having divulged to them earlier all that he knew, and a plea for his own and his aged father's lives. He confessed that a matter of three years ago, being assembled in a cave near La Guardia, his father Ça and his brother, Mosé, Maestre Yuça Tazarte, David de Perejón, Benito García, Johán de Ocaña and Alonso, Johán, García and Lope Franco, Alonso showed them the heart of a Christian boy and a consecrated Host, while in a corner of the cave Yuça Tazarte cast a spell to prevent the inquisitors from doing them any harm, promising that should they happen to do so, they would go mad within one year's time.

"Compelled to testify yet again that evening of the eighteenth July, Yucé recounted how, while the accused were gathered together in the cave, he had seen them bring in a Christian child of some three or four years of age, whom they crucified on a pair of sticks, binding his arms with ropes of twined esparto grass and covering his mouth with a muzzle; he confessed that they had practiced the following abominations upon him: Alonso Franco had opened the veins in his arms, letting him bleed for upwards of half an hour; Johán Franco had thrust a knife into his side; Lope Franco had whipped him; Johán de Ocaño had stuck spiny furze into his back and the soles of his feet; García Franco had gouged out his heart beneath the nipple and sprinkled it with salt; Benito

García had slapped him; he, Yucé Franco, had yanked his hair; Maestre Yuça Tazarte had spit on him; his own brother Mosé had done the same. His father Ça, an old man of eighty years, did not remember having said or done anything to the child, aside from being present there, and the same was true for David de Perejón. Next they untied the child and carried him out of the cave, Johán Franco holding him by one hand and García Franco by a foot; and although he had not known then where they buried him, afterwards he had heard that they interred him in the valley of La Guardia, near the stream at Escorchón.

"Yucé Franco also confessed to them that Alonso Franco had kept the child's heart until they all reassembled in the cave, when Yuça Tazarte took it to perform the magic spell; that Lope Franco brought the hoe for burying the child along with the blood-filled caldron. And when he was asked whether the deeds had been done by day or by night, he answered by night, by the light of white waxen candles held aloft, the entrance to the cave having been covered by a cape. And when he was asked about when all this had taken place, he answered that he believed it was 'during Lent and before Easter Sunday,' and that he could remember no more, but if he did remember, he would certainly tell it to them. And when he was asked whether at that time there was talk of a child being missed in the region, he said that he had dreamed about a child who was lost in the hills and about another who disappeared in La Guardia, but that the aforementioned Franco brothers came and went to Murcia with wagons and barrels of sardines, some of which were empty, and it was possible they might have picked up a child from there or on the road."

"We should go to Avila," I said resolutely.

"We will start at dawn," Pero Meñique replied, still affected by the story he had told.

"How will we get pack mules for the journey?" I asked.

"They have been waiting in the yard at my house for the past several days; I also have victuals, so we need not tarry along the way to eat, for the taverns are usually smoke-filled and dirty."

"Then let us meet before second cockcrow," I said, taking my leave of him.

To tell the truth, while the particulars of the trial of the child of La Guardia filled me with horror, the person of the Inquisitor-General was relatively unknown to me. I was aware that he was born in Torquemada in the year 1420, that since childhood he had worn the habit of the preaching order, that he never ate flesh, and that he always wore a shirt of the coarsest weave. I knew that at the age of thirty-two he had been appointed prior of the Monastery of Santa Cruz in Segovia and, while acting as father confessor to the Catholic Monarchs, in the autumn of

1483 had been designated Inquisitor-General of the Holy Office for the Kingdoms of Castile and Aragón. His cruelty was more famous than his person; he was a man who had become known for his deeds. Countless fiendish acts were attributed to him, and popular fancy had it that each wrinkle on his face and each hair on his body stood for a burnt victim. To all appearances he lived solely to arrest, try, torture and burn those Jews who were unlucky enough to dwell in the kingdoms where he had established his tribunal of terror.

I imagined him in a cemetery, rummaging among the bones of the deceased in his presumptuous attempt to pursue the dead beyond the grave, affronting God's justice by his own as he competed with it, falling into the diabolical temptation of passing judgment on souls who already sat in the celestial courts, damning their repute and memory not only on earth but in the other world as well. I could see him presiding over the general assembly of inquisitors in Seville in 1484 during which instructions were issued for proclaiming the establishment of the Inquisition in every town and for publishing the Edicts of Grace in the churches; for commuting the sentences of heretics already held in the jails of the Holy Office, upon their reconciliation to the Church, to perpetual prison; for changing the sentence of perpetual prison to death at the stake if the penitent's conversion was found out to be feigned; for ensuring that two inquisitors would always be in attendance during the torture of a culprit; for condemning as a convicted heretic any absent person who failed to appear within the term of the edicts if he was summoned before the tribunal of the Inquisition; for drawing up a case against any deceased heretic discovered through records or testimony, even if he had died twenty or thirty years earlier, in order to condemn him as a heretic, exhume his bones to incinerate them and confiscate his property from his heirs, because, in accordance with the supplementary instructions issued in 1485, the prosecution of the living did not imply the neglect of the dead.

Over and over again as I wandered through the streets of Madrid, the image of this elusive man troubled me; in my fancy he was impervious to human weapons, and as I was convinced he could inhabit the bodies of people and animals at will, it seemed virtually impossible to wound, capture or kill him. What drove me above all was the desire to wrest from his clutches Isabel and my son, whom I already saw in my waking and sleeping nightmares in custody and burning in some square in Córdoba, Teruel, Saragossa or Guadalupe.

I was brooding on these cavils when I found myself in a long, steep and muddy avenue. Under cover of darkness, men and women relieved themselves in the street or emptied chamber pots out the windows. Four women dressed in black, their faces hidden, bosoms tightly bound and bodies veiled from top to toe, could easily have become the future mourners for my own funeral. The wooden rosaries hanging from their waists dragged over the ground as each one, in the privacy of her own garments, told the string of beads in commemoration of the mysteries of the Virgin, making no distinction in their devotions between church and street, between their dwellings and their own bodies.

Other women went by as well, women wearing coats over hooped skirts, loose flowing mantles, slashed sleeves, open kirtles, network caps and shirts of embroidered cambric; women with cloaks, clogs and kerchiefs, hennins, bonnets and turbans. Furtive, bareheaded maidens with painted faces who were adorned with rings and bracelets threaded their way among other maidens wearing habits, pendants and pious images of the Lamb of God on their sleeves and collars. All these women walked down the street with their feet scarcely moving beneath their trailing skirts and gazed dreamily into my face.

A young girl was bathing in the brook clad only in a smock, with her black hair covering her large breasts. Standing in the water, she saw I was watching her but neither hid her nakedness nor stopped staring at me, almost in defiance. I contemplated her in her entirety, not knowing whether she was a virgin or the figure of Death, or merely the proffered body of an ephemeral woman.

A female dwarf, whom I at first mistook for Don Rodrigo Rodríguez, appeared behind me. Her head was bigger than her body, her springy hair hung down to her hams, and her features were ugly and truculent. She walked so close to me that I could hear her breathing. Suddenly I was afraid of her, as if she were a goblin sprung from one of the looming buildings. I pressed against a wall; she trundled by and vanished into the distance.

The streets turned desolate and cold; the city seemed to sink into a gray sleep. I felt a great relief as soon as I had crossed the threshold of my house. However, the silent rooms made me think of Isabel and my son traversing solitary highways infested with murderers and thieves, suffering hunger and thirst, knowing not where to go or whom to turn to in their flight.

That is why there was nothing strange about my dreaming of her that night. She appeared before me naked in the room, flushed with the sweltering heat of a nameless city bleached by the noonday sun.

"Beware of the dog days, for a summer cold does more harm than two in winter," she cautioned, twisting her face into a contortion that spread over her entire body.

"I am, but I must be more wary of the Inquisition and the evil people who pullulate on earth," I replied.

"So minute are the pores of my skin that no human eye can discern them, nor can air pass through them; I am impermeable to warmth and cold," she said.

"You must muffle yourself in clothes from head to foot until no one can recognize you," I admonished her. "The inquisitors are searching for you throughout the Kingdom of Castile. They say that you are the one responsible for the rains and the wheat, for the birth of children and the greenness of trees, for the rising of the sun and the blue skies."

"Don't put those unmarked clothes on me; remember the ordinances of Queen Catalina and the Catholic Sovereigns which command the Jews to wear voluminous cloaks down to the ground, no scarf or head-dress, the head being covered only by folded cloths," she said, suddenly alarmed. "Where is your kirtle with the hanging sleeves, where are your red badges? Why have you trimmed your hair and beard? Can't you see they will kill you?"

"I am not afraid of them or of their ordinances. I have no fear of Torquemada or his inquisitors; the *alguaciles*, the *alcaldes*, the familiars and the notaries of the Holy Office make me laugh. I know of a future world where they are already dust, where they do not amount to a shadow, and if a place can be found for their souls, it will be among the Cainites," I blustered.

"I don't care a fig for your future world. Down here they are killing us every day. Did you not hear how the city council of Vitoria had it proclaimed in the squares and the streets that for the benefit of God and the Kings and the furtherance of the Catholic faith, no one may enter the *judería* to peddle vegetables or meat of any kind, and they must limit themselves to selling from outside the gate? Haven't you heard that in Gerona an ordinance was issued requiring Jews to wear badges and to brick up the doors and windows of their houses that face outside the Call, which is their *judería*?"

"I have heard and seen these things, and others far worse, but it does not matter to me," I answered.

"You must go away!" she cried. "Don't you know that a Christian may not visit a Jewess, and a Jewess may not enter the house of a Christian?"

With that all the bells began to toll, announcing an auto-da-fé that was to be celebrated simultaneously in many cities. Processions of prisoners filed through the streets of Seville, Saragossa, Toledo and other towns unknown to me. Hundreds of green crosses appeared, nailed to the breasts of hundreds of skeletons; thousands of black boxes sprang open, revealing the distinterred remains of deceased heretics. Down every road Death led a cavalcade of inquisitors. Someone shouted, "Run for your lives! Pedro the Ceremonious has melted down the church bells to give his enemies bronze to drink, and every man is his enemy!"

Isabel and I and the child, whose size, face and sex kept changing, hid inside an empty tunic, and we flattened ourselves against an immense wall, trying to disappear into it.

"Come towards me from the door, immure yourself with me," Isabel said, when the wall had swallowed her up along with the child.

I walked backwards and she reached out from the wall to embrace me from behind, pulling me towards her bed on the other side of the room, for she was hot to make love to me.

"I was sent back to you because God took me into His grace and because I am hungry for you; love will turn my ashes into flesh once more," she murmured.

"Hurry, come fast," I begged her, as she was on the verge of dissolving in my hands.

But she did not dissolve. In quick succession her face took on the features of the Trotter, of my mother and of Débora Dorado.

"It is not warm enough," she said, bringing candles to the bedside.

"We have fire enough in our veins," I protested. "Keep those flames away from my eyes."

"Stop rocking back and forth. Whoever sways like that has no firm foundation on earth or place in the firmament," she pleaded.

"It is only my lips moving when I speak to you; the rest of my body is elsewhere," I answered.

There was a knocking at the door.

"Who is it?" I called out.

"Nobody. It is dawn seeping into the cabbages; it is the wife of the simpleminded gardener who, when he laughed at something which waggled between her legs, told her husband that it was a fragment of night stirring among the cauliflowers," exclaimed a voice on the other side of the door.

Shepherded by Death, the procession of inquisitors crowded into the room to snatch Isabel out of my arms and drag her off to an auto-da-fé in which they paraded the skeletons of cobblers, doublet makers, tanners, goldsmiths, spice sellers, barber-surgeons, and physicians from Toledo. From a balcony facing the main street of the *aljama,* a Dominican friar gesticulated mutely at the Jews, *Conversos* and Christians, carried away by a sermon whose words made no sound.

We reached Avila towards dusk, when the last rays of the sun were wounding the mountains, pale with dust and almost invisible in the blue twilight, and shrouding the town in a golden veil. The swallows soared over the fortified towers of the surrounding walls, their trills and swift shadows swooping up and down the mountain crowned by a city.

We entered through the San Vicente Gate with the herdsmen who had gone out to graze their cattle on the common pastures, slopes and meadows of the city. They asked if we had heard about the local ordinance that no person was to drive cows or goats to sell outside Avila and its jurisdiction, under pain of paying the council a duty of ten *maravedis* for each head of bovine cattle, one *maravedi* for each ram or he-goat and one old-style *blanca* for each ewe, sheep, she-goat or lamb. Upon answering that we had come from Madrid to purchase woolens and other stuffs from a merchant in the Mercado Chico, we were informed that for every *arroba* of merino wool the council and its lessees would exact a duty of five *blancas* in the current coin of the realm, or two and a half *maravedis*. We were also forewarned of the council's directive that mules could not enter the Plaza del Mercado Chico or the Plaza del Mercado Grande on market or feast days, and that it was strictly forbidden to bear crossbows, fowling pieces or blunderbusses, much less discharge gunpowder with them, and if ever we were caught breaking this law, we would surely be put to death for it.

Armed with this knowledge of sundry city ordinances, we ventured inside, leaving behind us the Church of San Vicente, built on the spot where Vicente and his sisters Cristeta and Sabina had been martyred by Dacian. We made our way to the Mesón de la Muralla, not far from the Malaventura Gate, now closed as a sign of mourning, whence had sallied forth the knights whom Don Alfonso I boiled in oil.

In the courtyard of the inn, the hostess was chasing after a sow, her six sucklings, and a pair of geese, aided by a mastiff who was more wolf than dog. Upon seeing us she left off her pursuit to inquire whether we had brought raw meat for her to cook, as otherwise she would send to the butcher's for it; she did have on hand trout, hens, sardines, partridges, bread, eggs, and wine. As for sleeping, she could offer us two beds fit for gentlemen in a new and spacious room towards the rear of the rambling building, with a view of the Adaja River.

"Here, Your Worships, is my house; use it and me as you will. In truth, you have come to the finest city in all our Kingdom of Castile," she said, inviting us in.

And then, when Pero Meñique and I had eaten our fill of trout, stewed mutton, partridges, cheese, bread and wine from the local vineyards, the hostess sat herself down with us at the round table to make several suggestions of her own: we must never dare, either openly or in secret, in town or in the suburb, to play at dice or cards or to wager money or bream or other fresh fish or partridge or young pigeons or kids, under pain of paying a fine of three hundred *maravedis* for each offense. Next she told us of a law prohibiting the faithful of the city and the *alguacil* from laying hands on the Jews within their own quarters, even if they happened to observe them working at their trades and going about their business openly on Sundays, feast days and holy days, or if they walked about within the *judería* without the distinguishing badges, for there were many who profited from the rules laid down by the Cortes, or parliament, of Madrigal forbidding Jews to wear gold and silver and garments of silk, who sneaked into their houses during weddings to steal from them, "because the greater part of the population of Avila is made up of Jews, and for that reason considerable abuses, crimes and commotions often take place."

Questioned by Pero Meñique about the Jews of Avila, our hostess answered that she knew their history well. They had been led to the city about the year 1085 by David Centén, and now they lived in pitiful straits in two separate neighborhoods, one hard by the Adaja Gate, the other near the stockyard. Many had no house of their own but lived two or three families jumbled together under one roof. The *aljama* was cut in two by a door, which was never opened. There was not enough sun to dry the woolens, and because of the nearness of the river and the tanneries in its confines, it was always dank and malodorous. Even after Don Rodrigo Alvarez Maldonado had resettled the Jews in accordance with the decree issued by the Cortes of Toledo ordering their segregation into separate quarters, there were still a few Jews who lived among Christians in the Rúa de los Zapateros and in the Mercado Chico, where the Church of San Juan stood.

After taking supper, thanks to our weariness and the abundance of wine we had drunk, we could barely drag ourselves to the room at the rear of the inn. We slept well into the next day, when we were awakened by the hostess, who served us milk which she claimed was not watered down and clotted cream which she swore had not been thickened with flour, rennet or any other admixture.

"Should you visit the Fortress-Church of San Salvador to admire its granite roof and its tombs of recumbent knights, do not fail to go outside the walls to the Church of San Pedro on the Plaza del Mercado Grande, where Avila is celebrating San Gil's Day with a fair to which great numbers of traders flock to sell, barter and exchange cattle, clothing and the fruits of the earth. It is famous for many leagues round because of the important dealings that take place there," she said when she saw we were about to set foot outside the inn, passing the water carriers on their way in to sell her their wares in two-gallon pitchers.

As if familiar with the warp and woof of the city's streets, down which he had never walked before, Pero Meñique found his way with his cane, without the slightest hesitation, his cheerful face belying the reason for our journey to Avila.

Each movement he made fitted the place he was in, his sharpened senses mysteriously divining whatever lay in his path. And while I followed close upon his heels I often wondered whether an obscure certainty at the heart of his blindness did not guide him, impelling him to take the right direction in the labyrinth of streets of an unknown city which to my eyes was sprawling and filled with light.

Near San Vicente's, at the corner of Calle del Lomo and Calle del Yuradero, we passed in front of a butcher shop selling *tref* meat and a synagogue that had been transformed into a church now called Todos los Santos. At the entrance to the *aljama* we encountered blacksmiths, chopine makers, silversmiths, mattress stuffers and vendors of cloth coming and going through the gate. Farther on, in the parish of San Juan, near the Mercado Chico, a woman whom someone addressed as Vellida darted into a one-story wood and adobe building, leaving her shadow quivering on the threshold.

In the Calle de la Pescadería, men and women leaned out of their windows to watch us go by, as if a blind stranger in the street were a great novelty. Sea bream and other fresh fish were sold on Fridays and during Lent, except to Jews and Moors, who could not buy them on fast days until Vespers had chimed, and not at all during Lent. In the Plaza del Mercado Chico, the bells of the great Church of San Salvador and those of San Juan commenced ringing; in the midst of drummers and tambourine players Pero Gómez, the public crier of Avila, began to read a proclamation in a resonant voice. For our part, we walked away down the Rúa de los Zapateros.

And that is when I saw the Inquisitor-General, Fray Tomás de Torquemada, coming up the street, a rim of hair encircling his tonsured head. He was preceded by banners bearing the green cross. Fifty horse and two hundred foot, all armed, escorted him. The monk resembled a raven in the midday sun. His piercing eyes managed to look right and left while staring straight ahead, as if he had double sight. The tip of his tongue stuck out between his livid lips, testing the air. Perhaps it was my fancy that made him hover a span above the ground and gave him the fleshless hands of a corpse. And I'm no longer certain if his haunches, knees and elbows jutted out of his clothes as he walked, or if it was his funereal garments that made him seem a creature of the night, a devourer of the dead.

"God forfend that a judge such as this should ever rummage in my soul," I said to myself, wondering whether to dash at him and deal him a dagger blow, or stand still as he passed me by, on his face the supercilious sneer of one who feels invulnerable to any human design and knows that any hostile movement will be detected immediately by his guards or avoided by his own body, in the manner of a bat on the wing ducking stones thrown at it.

"Who is that going past us?" Pero Meñique asked when he heard the men and horses clattering down the street, making a great din with their weapons and hooves.

"It is the Inquisitor-General, guarded by two hundred and fifty armed men," I answered.

"Had you only told me, I could have killed him by now with this silver knife I always carry on my person," he wailed.

"The only dead man by now would have been you," I replied.

"I cannot forgive you for having hidden his presence from me. Swear that you will notify me the next time he crosses our path," he said.

"Very well," I promised halfheartedly.

By then we were walking in the midst of many people who were headed for the town fair; there was a great profusion of stalls representing silversmiths, tailors, fishmongers, cheesewives, fruiterers, clothiers, silk mercers, drapers, glaziers, cutlers, swordsmiths, braziers, ropers, purse makers, weavers, tinkers, jewelers, blanket makers; vendors of trout, wine, porringers, earthenware dishes and pitchers, seeds, greens, pins, knives, paper, frying pans, bells, onion, coal and tallow, as well as traders offering live sheep, she-goats, pigs, mares, mules, asses and cattle. In a tent, an assortment of jesters, tumblers and jugglers was entertaining a crowd of people while two fools traded quips as they made the rounds with an *alguacil* who policed the fair—for the performance of which service he extracted an armful of bread here, a melon or a scoopful of hazelnuts and walnuts there, three *blancas* from the dagger dealer, four *maravedis* from the saddlers, a basket from the basket weavers and a handful of oregano from the herbalists. A mountebank with blackened face and hands promoted an aged dwarf clad in brown doublet, brown hose and thick-soled brown shoes who carried an iron sword taller than himself: "You have before you Don Luis Montaña the

Abulense, who returned to Avila before setting out on a journey and came back after death to recover his body. It is common knowledge that he earned his living as a buffoon dressed as a lady, wearing a baby's bonnet that covered half his head and shoes four times larger than his feet. They say that at the age of ten he fell down, to arise at thirty-six no bigger than before. Moreover, such an amorous dwarf was he that he married three peasant girls, the triplets Ana, Juana, and Susana, who soon cut him down to size. By virtue of his great gift of mimicry, he is an excellent remedy for melancholy and a potion for any ailment."

Behind Don Luis Montaña stood three very similar she-dwarves, each holding a poppet in her arms: Ana, her face framed by big tawny curls, peeking out from among a heap of sheets, shirts and woolen stuffs; Susana, who wore a red cape trimmed with bells and a sagging petticoat; and Juana, fat and slovenly, boozy and bumbling.

The dwarf launched into his rigmarole: "These ladies are the same as that one over there, except she has a different shape, a different name and a different voice; a painter to the Kings painted her naked and fleshless, as if newly delivered and newly expired, although at night she weighed five *arrobas*, was as long as a two-league cough and could hold two *azumbres* of wine, four quarts of water and three sacks of air," he prattled, his chest puffed out like a rooster's as he pretended not to see the women. Then he interrogated his audience, "Have you seen Doña Ana, who stayed in bed because a fish bone stuck in her gullet? Or Doña Susana, who is married and owns three dwarves, three dogs and three stallions, gifts from the Kings of France, Rome and England? Or Doña Juana, who was cuckolding me with Don Toribio the Tepid and the cripple from the stubble field? All three of them are here, so they must be absent elsewhere. All three of them are mothers to my sons San Vicente, San Clemente and San Prudente: may they perform the miracle of making me grow up to heaven."

A mummer in parti-colored clothes exhibited a great lummox standing in a wagon; arrayed in green doublet, green hose and green hair, he teetered from side to side, holding a rock in one hand and a log in the other. "When we found him on the road to Santiago, this hulking lad of twelve summers was not yet able to talk. A bearded female dwarf gave birth to him one moonless night, after she was got with child by a male gnome who took a quick turn through her thicket. The enormous trouble it cost her to carry him and the pains she suffered during his delivery led her to abandon him in a meadow. When the little one saw us looking at him, he tried to run away and bumped into a tree, which he attempted to remove from his path; but the effort put him to sleep, doubtless in the belief that the tree would be gone by sunup."

We left the fair and proceeded to the Jewish graveyard alongside the

Adaja River, outside the walls, to meet a certain Martín Martínez, a friend of Pero Meñique's from the days when he aspired to be a Dominican monk. This was the same man who had confided to him the secret details of the trial of the child of La Guardia—which he himself had learned from a notary in the employ of the Holy Office.

As we drew closer to the graveyard, we were able to make out the funerary pillars—cylindrical shapes on which designs had been incised with a chisel—the graves whose heads faced east and feet faced west, and the tombstones of ordinary people who had died natural or violent deaths long ago: "Luna Cohen, thou art not alone." "Jaco Crespo, may his soul be bound up in the bond of everlasting life. He passed on to his eternal abode at the age of eighty-six, on Wednesday, the fourth day of Tammuz, in the year 575 of the new calendar." "Tombstone of the youth Cristino Curiel, son of Simuel, who passed on to his eternal abode on Thursday, the twenty-ninth day of Tishri, in the year 576 of the new calendar." "Tombstone of Yento Tamaño, son of Ximon, may his Rock and his Redeemer keep him. He died in the year 5066 after the Creation of the World." "This is the grave of Don Licio, who died by stoning in the month of Tevet, in the year 5092 after the Creation of the World." "Here lies David Ahumada, who treasured in his heart the book of medicine and the tree of knowledge. His ways were the ways of righteousness, until he was gathered up to his people on the holy Sabbath day, the second day at the beginning of the month of Heshvan, in the year 576 of the new calendar." And there was another one, with no name, like a voice astray in space and time: "My Lord found me in your company, my beloved; protect my house and keep my memory there."

In the very center of the graveyard, amongst the monuments sunk into the ground, a tall angular man leaning against a tombstone stared fixedly at us. So one was he with the peaceful sepulchers that at first he scared me. He stood there as if petrified; nothing stirred on his person, not a thread of his clothing or a hair on his head. His sallow face was of a waxen consistency that seemed to need only a flame to melt away. His pointed black beard jabbed at the air, indicating the direction in which his bulging eyes, very like two old, tarnished coins, were looking. But even when we were standing in front of him, he neither blinked nor altered his expression, so immersed was he in the silence of the stones and the dry clods of earth. Then, as if our bodies were disturbing the quietude, bringing human commotion into this landscape of dark green trees and soft shadows, his face slowly eased into a crooked smile, and he came towards us to clasp Pero Meñique's hand in his own.

"Martín Martínez?" my blind friend asked, almost in a whisper.

"Recollect, think back, for I am the same as ever," he said as he strode between the tombs towards some bushes where a skeleton with a ring in its mouth lay in an open pit. "I am brimming with bile, and I shall have no rest until Torquemada goes to his, buried in his own excrement, until the inquisitors in Castile cower in fear and the justice of God turns their putrid flesh into a feast for jackals and fodder for worms."

"Señor Martín Martínez, why did we have to meet in the graveyard?" Pero Meñique inquired, his face turned upwards as if asking his question of the wind or listening to the flight of swallows.

"Because it is the one place in Avila and its jurisdiction where we can avoid suspicion," the other man replied.

"Every day new trials are brought before the court and new fires are kindled in these godforsaken kingdoms," declared Pero Meñique. "We must put Torquemada to death."

"The Inquisitor-General will be excised from Castile and Aragón," Martín Martínez vowed resolutely.

"If we can find him, and if we can find the courage once he is found. The Dominican friar is so suspicious that he distrusts his own shadow and his hands which carry the food to his mouth," I said.

"Though he be wary of his shadow, his life is hanging by a thread; one day his feet will stumble and the hand of the Creator will turn him into excrement, for he is a savage beast and a plague on all the world," Martín Martínez exclaimed.

"We will scour the streets of Avila to find him," said Pero Meñique.

"And I will scour the night," the man added. "For years I beseeched the enchanters and soothsayers who mumble gibberish in the half-light to reveal his hiding place to me, but they merely mimicked the quavering babble of the spirits of the dead whom they evoked, and told me nothing."

"Take care, for you may forfeit your life in this enterprise," Pero warned him.

"I am the son of a lost woman and a father who was burned. Will I have less if I am dead?" replied Martín Martínez.

"Bethink yourself of the happy times," said Pero.

"When I remember my kind father, I grieve even more; when I think of my mother sitting in the dust by the roadside, I am filled with even greater melancholy," answered the other man. "God grant that thorns grow in Torquemada's soul instead of wheat, and deadly cheatgrass in lieu of barley."

"We must mind that the Inquisitor-General does not become our bane, for it is known that he spends his days casting evil spells over people," said Pero.

"I wonder which would be the best weapon: a lance or a spear, a crossbow or a slingshot," mused Martín Martínez.

"We must kill him with the silver dagger I always carry about on my person, which I inherited from my father, and my father from his father," said Pero, pulling at his beard.

"And then we're supposed to run away behind you?" Martín Martínez asked in astonishment.

"What do you mean by that?" asked Pero Meñique.

"So you honestly believe you will be able to kill him and make good your escape?"

"Kill him? I have already done so many times in my dreams."

"But now it is a question of stabbing him in the heart in earnest, not merely in your dreams."

"Wait and see, I shall burst from my lodgings swollen with rage."

"That is not enough. You must hit the mark and then fly for your life."

"I shall strike like a bolt of lightning and go galloping away like the wild ass," said Pero.

Martín Martínez stooped down to pick up a few pebbles from a grave, putting them, for superstition's sake, into the shepherd's pouch he had with him.

"I live in the Rúa de los Zapateros, in a squat house with an old door that has no knocker. Should you have need of me, inquire of the neighbors, for they know me well in that street. Say only 'Martín Martínez,' for I lost my Jewish surname when my grandfather was baptized in Salamanca after the miracle of the luminous crosses. If no one can tell you my whereabouts, know that I am such as you see before you in disguise," he said, pulling on a brown wig which fell over his forehead like a dog's pelt.

"I am sure to recognize you from afar by the smell you give off, by your voice and by the sound of your footsteps," said Pero Meñique.

"You will confuse me with another," Martín Martínez protested.

"Have no fear of that, for I can clearly discern the special smell of each person, even if peasants, monks, *alguaciles*, notaries, maidens, married women and swineherds are all massed in a square or in some church."

"I am most concerned," Martín Martínez fretted, "about how Pero Meñique will know that he is face-to-face with Torquemada and not some other Dominican friar, and if he does succeed in knowing that, how he will then know where to plunge in the dagger, that is, in what part of the bareness of his body, since it is common knowledge that the Inquisitor-General has a considerable tonsure on his head, which a blind man could easily mistake for his belly."

"How a blind man can tell the difference in this world between a wall and a rock or a tree and a human being is a mystery known to God alone," exclaimed Pero, greatly vexed, as if someone wanted to snatch out of his hands the enterprise he had taken upon himself.

"That is the mystery which ruins my sleep at night and my appetite during the day, so much that I can no longer enjoy the exquisite delicacies with which my wife Jumila daily regales me," muttered Martín Martínez.

"Obviously, I am a man in the dark, walking down a dark street in a darkened city," said Pero Meñique huffily, "but my path has eyes and feet answering to the name of Juan Cabezón, a trustworthy lad who at the right moment will guide my silver dagger to avenge the boundless evil committed by the monk Torquemada."

"Aren't you afraid of dying if the thrust into the hated heart goes awry?" asked Martín Martínez. "Don't forget that at Saragossa Pedro de Arbués was wearing a coat of mail beneath his soutane and a helmet beneath his hood; it will be difficult for you to find the most exposed spot on his body quickly."

"I have already told you that my path has eyes and feet called Juan Cabezón," Pero replied.

"As for you, never forget that it is nobler to die pierced through by the two hundred and fifty lances of the two hundred and fifty familiars who guard Torquemada than to burn in the slow fire of the stake," Martín Martínez admonished me, searching my face for a sign of fear.

"I can't forget it for one moment," I answered.

"I have no desire to fail in this business and lose our lives as well on account of a blind man's rashness," Martín Martínez said.

"When Pero Meñique rushes at Torquemada with his dagger, why don't you attack him as well?" I suggested.

"That is most reassuring," he answered.

"Let us speak of it no further," said Pero Meñique, determined not to relinquish the feat of murdering the inquisitor to anyone else.

"I have been astounded all my life, but nothing astounds me more than this man," declared Martín Martínez, looking him up and down.

"I have said that I will do it, and I will! This silver dagger shall not fail me," Pero cried out, wildly excited.

"Sh-sh-sh-sh," Martín Martínez cautioned him, as if the air were filled with spies and Torquemada were peeking over the rosy horizon.

"I can already picture myself standing in front of the Inquisitor-General. I strike him, and his cruel eyes go white, the blood drains from his lips, and his head empties of evil thoughts," exclaimed Pero in a state of blind euphoria, baring his teeth amidst the hairy tangle of his mustache and beard as his large, lifeless eyes unwittingly reflected the yellowy light of dusk, until he took a false step and tumbled headfirst into a muddy grave, his feet pointing skywards.

"Very well, if that's the way it is," said Martín Martínez resignedly as he helped Pero out of the hole, "I will have horses ready at all times outside the city walls for our escape, for a relentless pursuit will be launched against us, not only in Avila and its bailiwick but throughout the Kingdoms of Castile and Aragón. Now, mark you well that a very great friend of mine, an Old Christian by the name of Luz Pizarro, can give you shelter at her inn in Trujillo; you have only to say that Martín Martínez sent you. She will furnish you with a safe hiding place in exchange for a few *maravedis*. Thus, if we are separated by fate, we can meet up again at her inn. And if not, may God bless whichever of us reaches that hilly city safe and sound."

Just then we caught sight of a black cloud of men approaching the graveyard in somber procession. At first they looked like a mass of shifting shadows coming from the west through the pine trees, poplars and holm oaks, more remote than the twilight and more inscrutable.

As soon as he saw the men, Martín Martínez turned pale and began to tremble, as if the mere sight of them filled him with supernatural terror.

As the men came closer to us, their heads hidden inside their hoods and faces covered by masks, they proved to be more ordinary and insignificant than they had appeared from afar.

Oblivious to what was happening in front of his face, Pero Meñique asked us why we had stopped and why we no longer spoke. Elsewhere on the horizon, peasants were hunting hares and pheasants in the vineyards or carrying bunches of raisins and grapes in baskets and gunnysacks. Remote from humankind, doves and sparrow hawks flew at different levels in the scarlet sky.

The men came to a halt before a grave with their hoes and shovels; two of their number stood guard, weapons poised for an attack by ghosts. We spied on them from behind a funerary monument, which stood among rocks and bushes. Their grisly occupation made us shudder: they were exhuming the bones of the deceased, who had been tried by the Holy Office, in order to burn them during the proximate auto-da-fé.

Bathed in the day's most ethereal light, as the guards cast their long shadows over the tombstones, the body snatchers standing up to their waists in the grave brought to mind creatures out of hell in search of carrion to gorge on at a devil's banquet to be held that very night. All wore black and white, all heads were hidden from sight, all hands caked with earth, and they moved as one in a single direction, towards death.

Not much time elapsed before the diggers produced their first treasure: a skull, then more finds: bones and ashes, which they crammed into sacks and black boxes. But the dead, protected by the impenetrable

mystery of death, immune to the justice of Torquemada and his inquisitors, tried and burned on secular pyres in an infamous parody of
the Last Judgment, were not to be found in their bones or their graves,
they could not die anymore; they were immortal in their ashes.

"These are the Inquisition's spies. Rotten flesh from the cemeteries is
their fodder, and they snatch at death behind every blade of grass and
every clod of earth," said Martín Martínez.

"What if these stalkers of souls could see how big the dead really are;
wouldn't they fall down dead themselves? What if the so-called heretics
on earth were saints in the spirit world, and the inquisitors after their
death were to find themselves in a celestial kingdom where Hebrew was
spoken and they themselves were burned alive for having profaned the
Law of Moses? And what can it matter to a dead man whether his
skeleton is consigned to the flames or his ashes are strewn over the
fields or thrown into the stream of a river, if he is insensible to human
passions for all eternity? The inquisitors doggedly persist in pursuing
creatures who disappeared from their houses, mouths that dissolved in
the air, feet that were effaced from the street; they fight against the
nonexistent; they seek to grasp the ungraspable, to condemn what is
already out of mind. No matter how hard they try, they cannot inflict
the same torture on a soul as they inflict on a live body, for just as a
bat's flight is thwarted by the light, so does the beyond act as a shield
against them," I reasoned.

Pero Meñique listened, his movements arrested. Martín Martínez,
stupefied as he was by the sight of the men and their macabre booty,
may not have heard. The funerary monuments, the ramparts of Avila,
the diggers and we ourselves were soon enveloped by darkness, which,
along with light, is the most evenly distributed commodity in the world.

When we returned to the inn, the hostess was waiting at the door to
inform us that about two hours after midday our mules had broken loose
and subsequently been recaptured by some persons who had brought
them to the stableyard belonging to Pedro Manzanas, near the Church
of San Nicolás in the suburb. The said Pedro Manzanas would keep
them at our expense until the following day, providing for all their needs.
She sat us down forthwith at a large dining table, regaled us with meats
and fresh fish and a great quantity of wine and kept us company. Her
name was Orocetí Lunbroso, and she was a native of Segovia. Ten years
ago she had married Pero Dávila, also a native of that city, and six
months after the wedding she was left a childless widow. She had a
modest, open face, pleasant, lively eyes, dark hair and a full mouth.
Her body was shapely and well proportioned, and the soothing timbre
of her voice enthralled Pero Meñique.

By the light of the flickering candles, she began directly to tell us how her mother was descended from the family of María Saltos, the saintly Jewess from Segovia, who in the year of Our Lord 1237, being at that time a married woman, was accused by another woman of committing adultery with her husband, on account of which a secular judge sentenced her to be hurled live from the Peñas Grajeras, Jackdaws' Rock, the customary punishment in those days for miscreant Jews. On the fatal day she was escorted by her husband and the officers of justice, and by Jews, Christians and Moors, to the highest point, where they stripped her naked to the waist, bound her hands and forced her to kneel, then threw her over the side of the cliff.

Being innocent, she commended herself to the Virgin, crying out, "O Virgin Mary, favor a Jewish woman as you favor a Christian, and as you know that I am blameless, help and succor me." The Virgin appeared in the midst of her fall and caught María Saltos in her arms, setting her down unharmed in the lowest part of the valley, at the foot of a fig tree.

When the people who had watched from above as she was hurled into the air made their way down to see what had become of her, they found her kneeling unscathed, giving thanks to God and to the glorious Virgin for having delivered her from death. All she asked was to be baptized with the name of María Saltos, Mary the Jumper, and until the day of her death she dwelled in a church where, being imbued with the prophetic spirit, she served God and the Virgin.

After a pause during which the three of us drank several pitchers of wine, Orocetí continued with her story. "My father, Yucé Lunbroso, was buried on the slopes of the Jewish cemetery near the Clamor River, his arms crossed over his chest and his eyes looking eastwards. He died of melancholy when they bricked in his house's doors and windows that faced Christendom and he learned that the inquisitors Doctor de Mora and Licentiate de Cañas had burned at the stake a friend of his by the name of Gonzalo Cuéllar, a neighbor and former Regidor of Segovia, the same man who years earlier had escorted Doña Isabel from the *alcázar* to the town square when she was proclaimed Queen of Castile."

"Who did you say covered over the doors and windows of your father's house?" asked Pero Meñique.

"Don Rodrigo Alvarez Maldonado, who took it upon himself to enforce in Avila and Segovia the provisions of a letter issued by the Catholic Sovereigns in the year 1480, to the effect that Jews and Moors must be moved into separate quarters, and in all the courtyards situated between the houses of Jews and Christians, walls or fences were to be erected in which there were to be no holes or small doors through which they might speak or otherwise communicate with one another."

"And was this separation the cause of Don Yucé Lunbroso's death?"

"Yes, because he could not bear to see the doors and windows, which let the light of day into his room, covered up, and because in the depths of his soul he knew that this separation which the Kings had determined, like the trials of the Inquisition against the *Conversos*, were the warning signs of even more cruel measures to be taken against the Jews, and as no one moved a finger or opened their mouths, after a while my father grew sick at heart, and his heartsickness was so powerful that in a few months' time he had breathed his last."

Pero Meñique eagerly drank in both her words and the beakers of wine she set before him, and when she fell silent he promptly asked, "Think back on how it happened that you remained a widow."

"As a married woman I was never expectant, I never gave birth, I never fed sons or fussed over daughters, for I never knew a man; when my husband died the youths of Avila came in quest of my virginity, but I did not give it to them . . . perhaps because I knew that you would appear one day."

"Are you an easy woman?" he asked her.

"I am a hospitable woman," she answered.

"I asked if you are a whore, a harlot, if you have fornicated with many male friends," he said.

"I don't understand your meaning," she replied, flustered.

"I asked if you bared your bum and bartered your belly, if you broadcast your lechery on the wooded slopes and in the beds of night, if you made a painted couch for yourself and the seed of fornicators entered into you." He drew his face near hers.

"I still do not understand you," Orocetí said, pushing his face away.

"I shall ask you once more if you lavished your lewdness on every passerby, if you regaled him with your lust." He drew his face near hers again.

"I have made it plain, I never gave a fig for sly, shifty fellows," she exclaimed with annoyance. "I am a welcoming woman, or if you would rather, an untrodden woman, a female whose milk has never flowed, a winsome wench who is wholly virgin."

"Are you afraid of sinning? God blessed Adam and Eve, saying, 'Be fruitful, and multiply, and till the waters of the seas.' To man and woman alike He said, 'Be fruitful, and multiply, and replenish the earth.' "

"Thine is the body of the generations of Adam, mine is the body of the generations of Eve," she replied.

"So that we may be fruitful, and multiply," he added.

"Am I to know the throbbings of a man between my legs? Your scrabblings will not cause me pain," she cried.

"Inside you I shall experience the sufferings of the grave, the paroxysms of death," he exclaimed.

"Take me now as a gift that has fallen into your lap, for God took pity on you and willed that I should be yours entire."

"Take care lest I get you with child, and you give birth to a second Cain or bring another Torquemada into the world."

"May God forbid. Rather would I perish like the festering corpse of some snake or vermin," she hastened to say.

"I smelled the fragrance of your garments, and I said to myself, 'The fragrance of her body is like the fragrance of the fields after newly fallen rain; the perfume of her breasts is like the perfume of apples on the apple tree,' " he rhapsodized.

"I shall be for you like the tender mushrooms that sprout from the earth in the sunshine after the rain," Orocetí murmured.

"Then so be it. Now warm me as a mother warms her child's flesh, for I shall lay me down to sleep at the verge of your body as if under the dense foliage of a holm oak beneath the fierce heat of noon," Pero declared.

"This is the beginning of our love, and henceforth no part of my body will be forbidden to you," she vowed.

"Come into my arms, daughter of Babel; embrace me, daughter of the soothsayer, for my heart is dust and would warble; twine your legs about me, that I may devour you bit by bit," he crooned.

"Take me now, write on me with your virile quill."

But just as Pero Meñique was about to fold her in his arms, she wriggled away from him and scampered into the kitchen. He took advantage of her absence to empty three more beakers of wine and to assure me that he was very satisfied to have embarked upon the important business that had brought us to Avila, and as he drew his face near to mine, as if his cavernous orbs would plumb the depths of my eyes, for an instant I thought he saw me through a tiny slit.

"Should another opportunity like today's to murder Torquemada present itself, we must not squander it, for in the Kingdom of God one instant's imprudence can result in monstrous havoc for the next century or millennium," he said, squeezing his hands together around the wine beaker.

"Yes," I sighed, my drunkenness and his incipient amours flooding me with melancholy over the absence of Isabel and my son.

"We must agree on certain signs of our own, which only you and I can understand," Pero Meñique declared. "If you tap me on the right shoulder with the flat of your hand, it means I should keep quiet. If you jab me in the back with your fist, it signifies that I should hurry ahead. If you say to me, 'I see the light,' it means I must attack the inquisitor then and there."

Through the walls of the inn we heard some drunken men outside singing.

> *The king has only one daughter,*
> *and she is dainty and fair,*
> *he locked her up in a tower,*
> *to keep her in safety there.*
> *One day as she stood at the window*
> *to escape from the sultry heat,*
> *she espied a reaper down below*
> *reaping the barley and wheat.*

When the song was over, Pero Meñique staggered towards the kitchen in search of Orocetí, who was scouring the skillets. He tried to hug her, chasing her among the caldrons, earthen pots, water jars, bread paddles and fruit baskets. She pushed him away with an iron spit, and he fell into a large basin used for salting pork, from which he emerged only to step into some porringers stacked on the floor.

Moved to pity by his clumsiness, Orocetí took him by the hand and drew him to her breast; then she led him to her own bedchamber, the last and largest room in the house. I retired to the upstairs room facing the street, lighting my way with a modest brass candlestick. All of a sudden Pero shouted for me to come to him.

"You must surrender to this lady and put yourself in her hands," he called out to me as I entered the room, half smothered as he was beneath her breasts.

"This time I will leave the field to you," I answered.

"Do these buttocks and tits leave you cold?" he asked me, his blind bearded face peeking over Orocetí's right shoulder.

"Yes."

"Then you must not look at the wine while it ferments or a man while he is making love; turn towards the exit or towards the wall," he ordered.

"He has lost the scent, in his befuddlement he fumbles from one end of my body to the other," the hostess declared.

"We are already pitched," he said.

"What do you mean by that?" I inquired, keeping my eyes on the door so as not to see him naked on top of her.

"Anointed, oiled, don't you see?"

"I'm not looking," I replied.

"If I have found favor in your eyes, stop talking and take the gift of my body, for ever since you came into the inn, your face reminded me of my father's face, and you gave heart to me," she urged.

"You are like a spacious house, you throw open windows for me here, you shore me up with beams there, you paint me red all over," he murmured.

"Enough of words," she said.

"Think back, remember what happened in Segovia, the lonely nights of your widowhood in Avila, your body in the cold bed troubled by imaginary caresses and fantasies of men," he coaxed, immersed in the double darkness of himself and her body, grabbing at her flesh as if he meant to devour it, as if he could never be surfeited of her; meanwhile I crept out of the room, feeling heavy with wine and weariness and intending to sleep for days on end.

But a few hours later I awoke to find him sitting on the edge of my bed, holding a candle which burned brightly in the daylight.

"I love Orocetí, and once our undertaking is accomplished, I shall marry her and become an innkeeper in Avila de los Caballeros," he announced.

And then she came in, clad only in her shift, her thighs bare and hazel eyes shining.

"I love Pero Meñique, I'm going to marry him," she said.

She took him by the beard and led him to a room above the kitchen stove where we had never been before. After a few minutes she summoned me: "Juan, Juan."

My friend was standing next to the cresset, his face contorted into a smile that braved the void. She was taking her husband's clothing out of a large pine chest and giving it to him. She piled the clothes over his outstretched arms as if she wanted him to put them all on at once: a doublet of black cloth, a doublet of brown cloth, a cloak of red London woolen, a kirtle with gray fringes, a shirt of dyed Courtrai cloth. She gave him the weapons as well: two lances, three arrows, two helmets, a crossbow made of horn and a quiver, two shirts of mail and a gauntlet, a touchstone and a small copper pan.

She herself donned several petticoats of white camlet and a scarlet cloak. She put gold rings variously set with rubies, sapphires, turquoise and pearls on the fingers of her left hand. Then she bedecked herself in a gold necklace and a black coif shot with golden threads, scarlet stockings, a pair of well-worn chopines and a silver belt with eight medallions, four red and four white, with a gilded buckle.

She moved me to another room, an ample, airy chamber with a large window facing a luxuriant tree. A chipped mirror and a picture of the Virgin painted on a square of canvas hung on the wall. A cracked basin, the brass plate from a washstand, an alembic made of clay, the traces for two mules and a small glass jug were strewn about the room, left behind by a succession of past visitors.

It was Tuesday. From nine to ten o'clock in the morning the bells rang out from the Church of San Juan as the judges and aldermen summoned the inhabitants of the city in order to hear their complaints and grievances and to consider any other business that concerned the public weal of Avila and its jurisdiction. Orocetí had to wait at home until after midday for the peddlers who would bring to her inn the unsold fruit from the public squares and marketplaces.

After the hour of Nones, Pero Meñique and I searched for Torquemada from the Calle de Santo Tomé to San Salvador, then on to San Gil, down the public streets that led to the Cesteros and Papalúa quarters, and thence to the dunghills of San Vicente; from San Millán to the Plaza de San Gil and to the street where horses are raced, and from San Pedro to the torch market; from San Miguel to San Millán again and to the fish market, to the castle at the San Vicente Gate, to the Calle del Lomo, the Rúa de los Zapateros and the Grajal Gate, in the castle courtyard. I described to Pero Meñique all that my eyes could see and his were ignorant of, the neatly stuccoed walls, the wooden ladders by which people climbed to the lofts or descended to the cellars, the ramshackle roofs, the yards with wells ringed by edgestones, the poplars of Santo Tomé, the overhanging houses, the portals as wide as the houses, the houses which had neither door nor threshold, the narrow, shabby entrances, the towers and the churches, the fences and the shops and the markets, the rotten wood, the dilapidated walls, the dirt floors, the flimsy staircases, the splintered doors and the sagging timbers.

"Fray Tomás de Torquemada must be in Avila now to conduct in person the trial of the child of La Guardia, I'm sure of it," Pero Meñique said on the way back to the inn, tired of chasing all over town, his staff pointing towards the meager waters of the Adaja River.

Vespers having chimed, the woodcutters trundled by on their return from the mountains, their wagons stacked with timber and board, firewood and holm oak. Gilded by the setting sun, Avila made me think of a walled crown; in the streets, squares and private houses shining yellow water flowed from a great profusion of fountains. Something about Pero Meñique had been troubling me since he had begun to consort with Orocetí Lunbroso; his gait seemed awkward, his movements exaggerated, and he often mumbled to himself so softly that I could not make out what he was saying, although now and then he did confide in me.

"Orocetí is slender of body, fair of face, white of skin; she has a short upper lip; her eyes in their frame of delicate lashes are limpid and smiling. She is both diligent and discreet, witty of speech and a great friend of justice. Should I perish in this undertaking, it is my last wish that the monies and possessions I have laid up in Madrid be handed over to her."

"You must not think of death," I protested.

"A few gleanings are all that will be left of me; it will be like shaking an olive tree; two or three olives remain at the top of the highest branch, and four or five cling to the boughs," he said.

"I fear for you," I said.

"But I do not fear for me," he replied. "Let us return now to the inn, for I have little desire to walk the streets of Avila once the cold sets in."

A week went by. The courtship of Pero Meñique and Oroceti Lunbroso grew more intense, more urgent, more free and easy, acquiring an almost domesticated bustle. As I was always making the rounds of the inn, like a moth flitting about a candle, it was difficult for anything they did not to come to my notice, either through my own eyes and ears or through the secrets Pero confided to me, for he kept me abreast of Oroceti's amatory habits. Thus, unbeknownst to her, I soon knew which words and which caresses were most agreeable to her in the nuptial bed, and on what part of her body a mole, a scar or a black-and-blue mark was to found. He worked himself to fever pitch, feeling impelled to narrate to me his amorous encounters blow by blow, as if this afforded him a double pleasure, chewing the cud of memory. For my part, I lived in apprehension lest the inhabitants of Avila should begin to suspect their carnal couplings, albeit these took place at night in the utmost secrecy of the bedchamber.

A month had gone by, and I still had no idea whether we would ever kill Torquemada or even meet him again in the street. The very reason for our presence in Avila seemed increasingly vague to me, and I found myself constantly wondering whether we had not remained there solely for the sake of Pero and Oroceti's dalliance. She behaved more like an established wife than a future bride, availing herself of my friend's person as if he were a mule, a piece of furniture or any other object that belonged to her. Nevertheless, there were nights when her maternal fluxes could not stem the anxiety he felt upon remembering the purpose of his coming to Avila, and having no notion of the time of day, he wanted to rush into the street and fall upon the first creature who came his way, as if anyone could be Torquemada. Meanwhile the monk might easily be as far away from us now as he had been before or, even worse, at that very moment and unbeknownst to us, walking beneath our feet along a subterranean passage between the monastery of Santo Tomás and some church.

Pero Meñique had become superstitious, attaching great importance to his dreams and to casual signs which he took for auguries of our undertaking. He drank too much every night, and within the space of a few moments his face went from serene to wrathful, from prudent to lascivious, from quiet to boisterous. Moreover, as he could not endure the sadness of being blind or the solitude of being drunk, he would throw the heaving mass of himself upon Orocetí, to engage in grotesque copulation before my very eyes, for he kept falling, either naked or half clothed, off the bed of love. He would wander besotted among the inn's many rooms in search of only he knew what, until finally he sat down on the stairs, pressing his hands against his splitting head. Otherwise, he spent hours going back and forth between the windows and the door, listening to noises, waiting for a sign that we should begin our business. Sometimes wakeful at midnight, perched on the edge of my bed, he would mutter, "One demijohn of olive oil, two of watered wine." Or, "Then the Pope said, 'You must be Hilary the Gaul,' to which Saint Hilary replied, 'I am not the gall but *from* Gaul.' "

Conversely, there were days that he spent sunk in profound melancholy, in total silence; he became impenetrable as well as inaccessible, like a mythical beast isolated in its blindness. It was at those moments that he would send Orocetí to fetch me, because he wanted either to hear my voice or to tell me something urgently. He had kept his promise not to reveal to her anything of our plan to kill Torquemada, both out of discretion and so as not to compromise her, for if worst came to worst, the woman's ignorance would be her best defense against the inquisitors.

One day in November—I remember it well—Martín Martínez strode excitedly into the inn and, without pausing to catch his breath, began to tell us the latest events in the trial of the child of La Guardia. The inquisitors had put Benito García to torture and brought him to admit that in a cave on the flank of a hill on the road to Villapalomas, Yucé Franco, in league with the implicated Jews and New Christians, had crucified a Christian child on two sticks tied together in the form of a cross with a rope of esparto grass; that it was nighttime; that they had wax candles and the mouth of the cave had been covered with a cloak.

Johán Franco and Johán de Ocaña had also been tortured, confessing that the Jews had crucified a Christian child on some "olive wood sticks," the child having been brought from Quintanar to Tembleque on the back of an ass by the late Mosé Franco. Fray Fernando de Santo Domingo had traveled to the Monastery of San Esteban in Salamanca especially to ponder and resolve the case, with the help of Johán de Sanctispíritus, professor of Hebrew, Fray Diego de Bretonia, professor of Holy Writ, Fray Antonio de la Peña and other professors versed in heresies, the learned scholars from Salamanca having declared in their final verdict that Yucé Franco, found guilty of abetting and participating in the crime of heresy, should be turned over to the court of judicature and the secular arm and his property confiscated for the royal exchequer.

Upon being informed of the verdict, Yucé Franco had defended himself before the inquisitors, arguing that the witnesses who had accused him were incompetent to testify because they themselves were accomplices to the crime. Disregarding his defense plea, on Wednesday, the second November, 1491, Fray Pedro de Villada and Fray Fernando de Santo Domingo went down into the prisons of the Inquisition, ordered that he be brought before them, and "exhorted and admonished him lovingly and with the utmost humanity to tell the whole truth about those things he knew which were of interest to the Holy Office, and any other things as well; they especially and repeatedly bade him to reveal whence came the child whom they had crucified in the cave of La Guardia, and to indicate whose son he might be, and who had carried him thither, and who had been the first to propose this business of crucifying him and of doing what they had done to him. Moreover, should he prove willing to tell the truth, they would conduct themselves towards him as mercifully as good conscience and justice allowed."

But as Yucé Franco was unable to say any more than he had already said, they ordered Diego Martín, the officiating torturer, to convey him to the building where their reverences were used to administer torture, there to strip him naked and bind him on his back to a trestle with hempen cords wound about his arms and legs; and once again Pedro de Villada and Fernando de Santo Domingo enjoined him to tell them the entire truth about everything that he knew, for they were still prepared to show him mercy; otherwise, they had declared before a notary "that if injury, or spilling of blood, or mutilation of limbs, or death should ensue from the said torture, the blame would be laid to the charge of the said Jew, Yucé Franco, and not to their Reverences," this having been witnessed in person by Francisco Bezerra, jailer, and Diego Martín.

Under torture, Yucé Franco told how Johán Franco had conveyed the child who was crucified from Toledo in his wagon, after finding him outside a door shortly before sunset, that he had seen and heard the brothers Franco and Benito García discussing how all the Christians saw light shining out of the crucified child's anus, and how they had woven spells so that all the inquisitors and other officials and people who wished them harm would die foaming at the mouth of rabies. When the inquisitors had gathered the guilty together, "they all agreed as one and acknowledged what they had done conjointly, and each one acknowledged what he himself had done in particular," in accordance with the confessions that had been wrung from them. That day it was learned that Benito García and Johán Franco had met in Toledo in order to find a child and that Johán Franco had kidnapped him at the *puerta del perdón*, the portal of forgiveness, of the cathedral.

Martín Martínez had scarcely finished his tale when the news about the sacrilegious crime began to circulate through the streets; at the church doors, in the marketplaces and outside the Monastery of Santo Tomás knots of indignant men and women formed to demand quartering and burning at the stake for the guilty parties. Incensed common folk of all ages, sorts and conditions congregated in the squares and roamed the streets. An anonymous body bristling with thousands of heads and thousands of clenched fists, the mob was waiting for the slightest provocation, the tiniest sign, the smallest spark, to launch its attack with a blind fury that could easily mistake its victims. It was dangerous for us to go outside and cross its path at every turning, for we could arouse its suspicions by speaking too loudly or too softly, by walking too fast or too slow, by standing still or by shunning the commotion. Being strangers, any pretext would suffice to implicate us in the crime.

"A monk from Avila is saying that the martyrdom of the holy child of La Guardia had been foretold," muttered an old crone behind us.

"The little Christ's heart was on his right side, so the crucifiers couldn't find it when they cut open his chest to tear it out," a peasant affirmed.

"His Honor the Inquisitor-General dropped many important matters to come to Avila and take personal charge of the details of the auto-da-fé in which they will lead out the holy child's murderers," one woman declared.

"I have heard that Their Worships the inquisitors will send the criers throughout Avila and its bailiwick, to draw a great throng to the auto-da-fé," the crone added.

"If it is really true that Torquemada is in Avila, once the ceremony is over, he will doubtless depart in secret for Segovia or some other city in Castile," I conjectured. "The trial has come to an end."

"We must act immediately and kill him," Pero Meñique blurted out.

"I'm sure the dog has gotten away," I said, jabbing my fist into his back.

"With each passing day, the world seems more uncanny to me and I have less faith in what I hear but cannot see," he said, hurrying along.

"Where have you been?" Orocetí asked us distraughtly from where she stood at the door of the inn.

"Sniffing about the streets of Avila," Pero replied.

"Are you all in one piece, your clothes haven't been torn or your beard pulled?" she asked.

"Thanks be to God, I am untouched," he answered, "and my beard and clothing have come to no harm; it is only my soul that has picked up a bit of dust on the way."

"Well then, my friend, tell me now, what have you brought me back from your outing? What unguents, what fish, what rings, what necklaces, what shoes, what scissors, what frying pans, what pieces of glass, what lengths of cloth are you going to give me?"

"I have nothing like that, my dearest Orocetí, I have only food for thought."

"No matter, my dearly beloved friend, come in and rest," she said.

"I do feel weary, but it is not my body," he said, falling into a dispirited silence.

After Vespers had rung, he began asking Orocetí all manner of questions about Avila and its environs. With the natural surroundings, the white doves, the storks, the Church of San Salvador, the Mercado Chico, the city walls and other matters, she was well acquainted. As she talked, seated at the round table in the principal room and well supplied with jugs of wine and savory tidbits, we saw the sun set and night come on, without a moment's pause in our conversation.

Towards Matins Orocetí, either in her cups or much in love, asked Pero Meñique to marry her the following day, to which he answered with a laconic "No," swiveling his face towards hers as if to transfix her with his blind stare, the lusterless intensity of his eyes even more stunning than the unexpectedness of his reply. She received his stare with a scintillating look of her own, shot through with sadness.

"Let us stay as we are, gay and unfettered lovers," Pero added after a long pause during which he appeared to ponder the words he would say. "There is a great difference of age and intention in our lives, and who knows, perhaps we may soon be separated from each other forever."

She refused to understand. He explained further.

"Soon we will leave here, perhaps even tomorrow."

"I have told my relations that we would have a wedding. What shall I tell them now?" she moaned.

"When I am no longer here to explain to you the scandalous events which are about to take place in Avila, you will understand everything," said Pero Meñique enigmatically. "This way, the loss of my body and my soul will be mine alone, not yours."

"And will that make you happy?"

"If it doesn't make us happy, at least it will make us easy."

"You or I?"

"Both of us, but enough of that for today, lest we become even more sorrowful. Let us say good night to our good friend Juan Cabezón and share our bed as two lovers should."

"As husband and wife should," she corrected.

"If it pleases you, let it be so in our pleasure and in our hearts," Pero Meñique relented.

"So be it," I said, leaving them alone for one of their last nights of love.

Two days later, on 16 November, 1491, the eight prisoners charged with the murder of the child who never was, clad in the yellow *sanbenito* of the condemned heretic, and the three statues of the deceased heretics, carried aloft on poles by porters in the employ of the Holy Office, were led out of the Monastery of Santo Tomás—which Torquemada was building in those days with the properties and monies of the Jews who were condemned by the Inquisition, and which he would finish two years later using the slabs and tombstones from their cemetery in Avila, ceded after the Expulsion by the Catholic Sovereigns for the convent works—in solemn procession, until they reached the Mercado Grande, where the inquisitors in their black and white habits, accompanied by their entourage of civil judges, familiars, notaries and monks, took their places next to the Church of San Pedro to celebrate the auto-da-fé.

That very night we learned from Martín Martínez, who had followed the human sacrifice with close attention, that after being bound to the stake at the Brasero de la Dehesa burning place, Yucé Franco had been abandoned to the secular authorities and his properties confiscated, the inquisitors having recommended that the Corregidor Alvaro de Santiestevan "treat the said Jew Yucé Franco with compassion, and not proceed against him to the death, nor mutilate his limbs nor shed his blood, declaring, as they did declare, that if the opposite should occur and death ensue for the said Jew Yucé Franco, their Reverences would not be to blame."

"And then the said Corregidor answered that he was receiving and did receive into his keeping the said Yucé Franco, as an accursed and excommunicate person and limb of the devil who was deserving of being dealt with in strict accordance with the law." And so he and his father were torn apart with red-hot pincers and the pieces burned in a slow fire, both denying their errors and refusing to the end to "call upon God or the Blessed Mary" or to make the sign of the cross. Benito García, who died as a Christian Catholic, Johán de Ocaña and Johán Franco, "who died with the knowledge of God and avowing their sins," were strangled by the executioner prior to being burned at the stake. The others, along with the effigies of the deceased, were consumed by the flames.

After the auto-da-fé, Torquemada ordered the story of the child crucified by the Jews to be read from every pulpit in the realms of the Catholic Kings, and an outraged mob clamoring to attack the *aljama* stoned a Jew in the streets of Avila. From Córdoba, Isabel and Fernando were obliged to send a letter of protection to the officers of justice of Avila and elsewhere in their kingdoms, instructing them to safeguard the lives and estates of the Jews. Subsequently the imaginary child acquired a name, Cristóbal, a legend, akin to the Passion of Christ, and performed many miracles, amongst which was the expulsion of the Jews from Spain.

As a consequence of the auto-da-fé it became very difficult for me to restrain Pero Meñique's fury; imprisoned in his blindness as if in a cage with no bars, he spent his days immersed in anguish and gloom. In vain did Orocetí do all in her power to console him.

It was, I recall, a cold morning in December when, at the hour of Terce, Pero Meñique, Martín Martínez and I left the inn and headed for the Monastery of Santo Tomás, determined to accomplish our enterprise that very day. Pero Meñique, erroneously believing he had overheard the words "Torquemada, Torquemada," from the lips of a porter of the Holy Office who was chatting with his fellow at the monastery gates, rashly followed a Dominican monk into the first room where he heard voices and addressed himself to the first person whose proximity he sensed, to ask the whereabouts of the Inquisitor-General, neither Martín Martínez nor I nor the friars themselves having any idea of what the bold blind man's intentions might be. He had already outwitted the watchful eyes of the myriad familiars of the Inquisition who guarded the entrance with great zeal and inexorability, but who had not even asked him where he was going. The person having answered that His Honor the Inquisitor-General was without and not within, Pero Meñique immediately rushed out of the convent and, colliding with a notary of the Holy Office whom he took for Torquemada, in his eagerness to execute the act of justice drew his silver dagger from amidst his clothes and with great mettle and dispatch stabbed the man in the arm so deeply that it was almost fastened to his ribs, shouting all the while, "Die, die, die!"

At that moment another notary happened to pass by, whom Pero Meñique also attacked, slashing at his beard and bringing about the loss of several hairs and a quantity of blood, which spurted over his chin and chest.

At once the familiars of the Inquisition came running, to fall upon him en masse with drawn swords and couched lances, and hack at him ruthlessly. And while Pero Meñique fell moribund to the floor the face of Martín Martínez shattered against the desperate knowledge that not only had the enterprise failed but our lives were in danger to boot. For my part, as I stood looking from the first notary, who lay in the dust exaggerating his wound, to the second, who never let up bewailing the ruin wrought on his shredded beard, I wondered if there was not something I could have done to warn my friend of his mistake and stay his hand in time, but any answer was beside the point.

"It is now or never," Pero Meñique mumbled from the ground, as if it were all a game between the familiars, the notaries and himself. As he was unable to sit up, he turned his blind face towards his executioners and was on the verge of speaking when four familiars grabbed him by the arms and legs while a fifth, a froggy-eyed, apple-cheeked hidalgo as yet unfledged, who was working his way up in the Holy Office, effortlessly plunged his sword into Pero Meñique's chest.

"Run for your lives!" he managed to shout, deathly pale, his voice seeming to abandon his body along with his spirit. As he tried to raise himself he opened his eyes wide, as if God in his infinite goodness had granted him one single glimpse of the world before he sank into eternal darkness.

A terror-stricken Martín Martínez, taking Pero Meñique's warning cry to heart, in a moment of fatal indecision wavered between running away and unsheathing his sword to join battle with the familiars, who, when they observed his fright, ran him through so many times that in the blink of an eye he looked more like a bleeding sieve than a human body. The same pop-eyed, rosy-cheeked hidalgo smote him again, and ten more familiars of the Holy Inquisition did likewise, leaving him lying on the ground like a dying dog. Just before he succumbed, Martín Martínez gave me one last look between his murderers' legs, on his face the pessimistic frown of a man about to die who knows he still has the worst ahead of him.

Once both of them were dead, I judged any assistance or resistance on my part to be pointless: there were upwards of two hundred and fifty familiars, guards and soldiers, weapons in hand, not counting the curious spectators who had gathered around I shall never know from where. What is more, to my own shame and in spite of myself, as I looked at them lying lifeless in the dust I felt boundless joy at being alive beneath the light of day. All around me, for a few crucial moments the familiars and the armed rabble stood stiff as statues in contemplation of the interlopers—moments in which the air and time itself also were stilled, as if suspended in God's imagination. In that interval I heard the mute, posthumous cry of Martín Martínez bidding me, "To horse, to horse." "Horse?" I wondered. "Yes, for you must leave here immediately, before the arrests and interrogations begin."

While he was telling me this, I noticed a man in the crowd who was watching me: it was the dwarf Rodrigo Rodríguez in the garb of a familiar of the Inquisition, who, as a good little hidalgo, was making his career and his fortune on the corpses of the *Conversos* and other victims of the Holy Tribunal.

Beneath his implacable gaze I suddenly realized that he hadn't taken his eyes off me all the while I was staring at the inert bodies of Pero Meñique and Martín Martínez. Either he did not recognize me or he was so overcome by the death of his friend Pero Meñique that he neglected to give me away, saving me from certain death by his silence. In any case, with the urgent words of Martín Martínez buzzing in my head, I hurried away from the Monastery of Santo Tomás, keeping within the shadow of the city walls of Avila until I reached the place where the horses were.

I galloped off on what looked to be the swiftest of the three steeds, thinking all the while of Pero Meñique and of Orocetí waiting for him at the inn, her ignorance of our conspiracy perhaps protecting her from the inquisitors, though they would surely find a way to drag out of her mouth crimes she had never dreamed of.

The afternoon mantled the great wall of Avila in its scarlet rays, and the encircled city glowed like a bloodstained jewel. Soon the reddish patches of houses and towers grew smaller and darker, shrank and faded, and I, feeling sad and hungry, was swallowed up by the night.

The year 1492 was dawning when Granada fell. Clad in his royal vestments, the King, Don Fernando, rode towards the castle and the city, followed by his armed knights, the Queen and their children, and the grandees of the realm. As they neared the Alhambra King Muley Boabdil, "the little King," came out on horseback to meet him, escorted by fifty Moorish riders. When he made as if to dismount to kiss the hand of the conquering king, Fernando did not allow it, embracing him instead. Then Muley Boabdil kissed his arm and with averted eyes, humbled body and mournful countenance gave him the keys to the castle, pronouncing these words, "These, my lord, are the keys to your Alhambra and your city. Go in, my lord, and receive them into your possession."

King Fernando handed them over to Queen Isabel, saying, "I entreat Your Majesty to accept the keys to your city of Granada and to appoint a governor." Bending her head, the Queen replied, "All this belongs to Your Majesty," upon which she gave the keys to the Prince and said, "Take these keys to the city and the Alhambra and appoint in the name of your father the governor and captain who shall have Granada in his keep."

The Prince gave them to Don Iñigo de Mendoza, the Count of Tendilla, who dismounted from his horse and knelt on the ground while the Prince said to him, "Sir Count, it is the wish of your Sires to bestow upon you in their presence the governance of Granada and its Alhambra." And then the Count of Tendilla and the Duke of Escalona, who was also the Marquis of Villena, accompanied by other noblemen, with a suite of three thousand cavalry and two thousand musketeers, entered the Alhambra and took charge of the castle.

The King Don Fernando went in, followed by the prelates of Toledo and Seville; the Grand Master of the Order of Santiago, Don Rodrigo Ponce de León, Duke of Cádiz, the captain who surpassed all others in the battle for Granada; Fray Hernando de Talavera and other gentlemen and ecclesiastics. The royal standard and the standard of the Order of Santiago were flown from the principal and homage towers. The King knelt down before the cross to give thanks to God for the victory achieved. The archbishops and the clergy sang the *Te Deum laudamus,* and those already within flourished the banners of the Apostle Santiago and King Fernando as they shouted, "Castile, Castile!" After the prayer, the grandees and nobles clustered round the King to offer their congratulations for the new kingdom and one by one fell to their knees to kiss his hand, the Queen's and the Prince's. After eating they retired in hierarchal order to the encampments hard by the nearest city gate. Boabdil, the Little King, was given the valley of Purchena, and five hundred Christian captives were set free.

I arrived in Trujillo one chilly morning in the midst of a dense fog after winding my way over mountains and crossing stone bridges, after walking many a mile for days on end, with only the holm oaks and the cork trees among the gray rocks for company.

I arrived on foot, my horse having died near the escarpments of the broad Tagus River beneath the flight of eagles reflected in the stream as if they were swimming among the liquid branches of the oak trees. I had journeyed day and night, slowly making my way through a forest in which silence seemed to have put down roots and dark greenness to have sprouted leaves in the air.

There is a saying that goes, "No matter which way you approach Trujillo, you must first traverse a league of granite boulders," and indeed on every side the boulders lie embedded in the earth like so many placid turtles nestled among the sparse grass, the ashen rocks clambering over each other like gray veils metamorphosed into stony animals or broken skulls.

Shrouded by the fog, I entered the earth-and-stone-hued city with its walls, its castle and its towers which dominated the countryside—the pale blue mountains, the blurry roads, the hazy streams, the dusty horizon.

A pale sickle moon still hung in the sky as I followed the narrow twisting streets to the square in search of the tavern owned by Doña Luz Pizarro, who proved to be an ample, thickset woman of peasant stock.

"All pilgrims are welcome within," she called out from the doorway of her house.

"You would not happen to be one of those landladies who venture out on the highways to invite travelers to their inns, and once they are safely inside, make them pay through the nose for candles?" I said in jest.

"Our Lord has said in his Gospel, 'Whosoever shall receive you, receives me as well,' " she answered.

"Would you happen to be Doña Luz Pizarro?" I asked.

"I have answered to that name ever since I was born, and I never changed it," she said.

"I have been sent by your friend Don Martín Martínez."

"How is that man I loved so much that years ago I almost married him?"

"He lives in the utmost tranquillity of his soul," I replied.

"A renegade priest hindered the wedding, but there will be time to tell you the story after you have rested and taken refreshment. Come into my inn now, for you have arrived in an admirable city which has not its equal in the entire world."

"I am not very rich," I warned her. "Martín Martínez told me you would give me a room at a good price for several weeks."

"Enter, and leave that for later; all the poor who come here receive their pittance, especially a friend of my friend Don Martín Martínez," she said, giving me the room in her inn which was most sheltered from the wind and then feeding me a piece of meat so full of fat that my shriveled stomach could not digest it for a long while.

I lay down after Vespers and did not awaken until the hour of Terce the following day. There was only one other guest in the house, a merchant about whom it was impossible to say whether he was young or old, clumsy or spry. His face was neither handsome nor ugly. In short, he was exactly the sort of man one sees a thousand times in a lifetime and forgets a thousand times as well. But notwithstanding the vagueness of his appearance, he always went straight to the point when he spoke, saying just what he intended and nothing further; it was like having two people before you at the same time, one who looked you in the eye and another who was always hiding something, one who seemed pale and sickly, as if he had just emerged from a lengthy illness, and another who was shifty, enterprising, blunt, rapacious. Day and night he scurried about the hostel, making ready to buy, sell, barter or depart, although in fact he was not in a hurry at all, and neither bought, sold, bartered nor departed, but stood instead in the doorway staring at the tower of the Chávez palace, the belfry of the Church of Santiago, the city walls, the castle, the horizon. Doña Luz Pizarro always became flustered when she bumped into him, thinking that he wanted something he didn't want, that he was about to say something he didn't say, or that he was going to leave, but he never did. He would rush at the woman, falling all over himself, without a moment to lose, only to stand idly becalmed in front of her, as if he had nothing else to do but stare into her eyes. What fascinated her about this man, Doña Luz used to say, was the precise way he pronounced each word, the measured,

nearly perfect ordering of his thoughts, his tact and his total incapacity
for laughter; for since the day he arrived, many months ago, this two-
faced fellow had never once been heard to laugh.

"I have visited all the fairs in these realms," he said to me one night
when, to my surprise, he sat down to keep me company at the round
table, "the fairs at Badajoz, at Santiago, at Talavera de la Reina, at Seville,
at Cádiz and at Avila, but never have I seen one so crowded as the fair
at Medina del Campo, where merchants from Flanders, Genoa, Florence,
Milan, Alexandria, Burgos, Seville, Granada, Toledo, Segovia, Valencia,
England, France, Ireland and Portugal congregate, and where there is
such an abundance of silks, brocades, cloth of gold and silver, weavings,
pearls, cattle, fish, meats, wines, oils, honeys, spices, woods, seeds,
fresh and dried fruits, doors, windowpanes, leather, candles, earthenware and glass. I have mingled safe and sound with Christians, Jews
and Moors, always paying my entrance fee, my tithe and my ground
rent when it was required of me."

Long-winded in his description of the fairs, he proved to be knowl-
edgeable about the weights and measures in use at the time, drawing
out his conversation until midnight with accounts of eight-gallon wine
jars, bushel baskets of twelve pecks for bread and Castilian ells for
measuring lengths of cloth; in the course of his interminable trafficking
he had bought and sold horse and donkey hides to be turned into
shields, hats from Segovia, clear and colored soaps from Seville, saffron
from Saragossa, crockery from Málaga and glass from Alhama; he had
journeyed with his wagons, pack animals and muleteers over highways
and mountains at great risk of his life and goods, up until the day when
the Santa Hermandad had peopled the fields with footpads armed with
bows and arrows. He discoursed on countless subjects but finally with-
drew into himself, as if some other part of his being had suddenly
realized that he had revealed too much to a stranger, informing him
about not only the fairs but his own merchandise and monies as well.
He bid me farewell with the air of a man who, after babbling on about
himself to an unknown person, regrets his familiarity and runs off to
hide what is still left unsaid. The very next day he left the inn, never
having mentioned whence he came or what his name was.

With the merchant gone, I was left alone in the tavern with no further
employment than to submit to the cosseting of my landlady, who was
far from repulsive, and no other occupation than that of strolling to the
castle, whose walls resembled an earthen serpent basking in the sun. I
also walked in the parish of Santa María la Mayor, down the Calle de
las Palomas, past the Escobar family's house and as far as the San Andrés
Gate.

In the Plaza Mayor, I was told, there had lived not too long ago a wealthy Jewess by the name of Doña Vellida, a widow and the mother of three sons, who had been hanged in 1491 by the Corregidor of Trujillo, Diego Arias de Anaya. Several years earlier, after she had been accused by the local *aljama* of having carnal relations with Sancho del Aguila, chief jailer, and Corregidor as well, who had been discovered many times sleeping by her side in the commission of adultery, Fernando and Isabel had dispatched Alonso Contreras of Valladolid to arrest them bodily and sequester their goods. Two months afterwards, when the same *aljama* accused her of having dallied with the *alguacil* of Trujillo, Gonzalo de Herrera, the Sovereigns again ordered the aforesaid Alonso Contreras to take the guilty parties into custody and confiscate their properties. Six years later, Diego Arias de Anaya arrested her for committing adultery with a Christian called Juan Ruiz. This time, however, she was tortured and made to ride through town on a donkey; half her property was confiscated for the royal treasury, and she was banished forever from Trujillo.

Doña Vellida addressed a petition to the Monarchs explaining how Juan Ruiz had repeatedly made love to her with pretty words and cozening, until he had finally taken her by force, which she had never told in order to avoid dishonor. As she had not been able to oust him from her house, the Corregidor had seized them both and put her to torture. The Kings ordered Diego Arias de Anaya to lift the embargo from her property and vouchsafe her to return undisturbed to the city and remain in her house for the space of fifteen days, at the conclusion of which she would go into exile. But the remorseless Corregidor apprehended and hanged her, seizing all her chattels and *maravedis*.

In the Plaza Mayor I would often encounter Abraham Barchillón, who was crier for the *aljama*, *shammash* of the synagogue and in charge of keeping the lamps lit. He was reputed to be crazy, a buffoon and a drunkard, a one-eyed fellow up to all sorts of tricks, a coarse man impaired in his understanding, who slouched about the streets bantering and making jests, forever cadging gifts and ready to forfeit his life for a glass of wine. He used to run around the square wearing a casque and carrying a truncated shield and a lance in full view of most of the townspeople, who would lash him with their belts, laughing at him as he hurled curses from the Law at a certain Gonzalo Pérez Jarada, a former Regidor of Trujillo who had been tried by the Inquisition and who, once upon a time, had locked him up in the synagogue, together with several other Jews, forcing him to exit by way of the roof.

Sometimes *Conversos* and Christians came to dine at the tavern on Sundays. The *Conversos* would sit at the head of the table eating their own food from their own plates, in accordance with their own rites and ceremonies, after having heard Mass at the Church of San Martín as faithful Catholics. The Christians would eat rabbits, partridges, lamb, hens, fish, eels, pork and bacon, a great quantity of which Doña Luz had hanging in the house.

In the afternoons the foremost Christians of Trujillo strolled about the square: the Chávez, Hinojosa, Pizarro and Vargas families, as well as other inhabitants of lesser prominence, such as the painter Alonso González, the shield maker Alfonso Rodríguez and the master mason Alí de Orellana. One would also see such Jews as Delgado, Cohen, Follequinos, the physician Cetia, the future majordomo of the synagogue Samuel Barzilay and the sons of Ysaque Saboca, who had been brought to ruin and put in prison by the Regidor Gonzalo Pérez Jarada. Isaac del Castillo, his wife Jumila and his daughter Azibuena, all spies for the Inquisition, and Alvaro and Francisco de Loaisa, "with their homicidal henchmen of evil repute," also took a turn around the square, perhaps under the watchful eye of the ubiquitous specter of the *Converso* García Vázquez Miscal, who one day had pursued Gonzalo Pérez Jarada through the four streets of the town, trying to stab him, and who had been burned by the Holy Office.

Quasimodo, or Low Sunday, which fell on the twenty-ninth of April in 1492, was different from other Sundays. Between twelve and one o'clock in the Plaza Real de Santa Fé, with three trumpeters, an officer of arms, two local judicials and a pair of *alguaciles* in attendance, before a great throng of men and women, a public proclamation was made of the edict signed by the Catholic Kings in the city of Granada on the thirty-first of March of that same year, which commanded "all Jews and Jewesses, of whatever age they may be, that live, reside, and dwell in our said kingdoms and dominions, as well natives as those who are not, who in any manner or for any cause may have come to dwell therein, that by the end of the month of July next, of the present year 1492, they depart from all our said kingdoms and dominions, with their sons, daughters, manservants, maidservants, and Jewish attendants, both great and small, of whatever age they may be; and they shall not presume to return to, nor reside therein, or in any part of them, either as residents, travelers, or in any other manner whatever, under pain that if they do not perform and execute the same, and are found to reside in our said kingdoms and dominions, or should in any manner live therein, they incur the penalty of death, and confiscation of all their property to our treasury, which penalty they incur by the act itself, without further process, declaration, or sentence. And we command and forbid any person or persons of our said kingdoms, of whatsoever rank, station, or condition they may be, that they do not presume publicly or secretly to receive, shelter, protect or defend any Jew or Jewess, after the said term of the end of July, in their lands or houses, or in any other part of our said kingdoms and dominions, henceforward for ever and ever, under pain of losing all their property, vassals, castles, and other possessions; and furthermore forfeit to our treasury any sums they may have, or receive from us.

"And that the said Jews and Jewesses during the said time, until the end of the said month of July, may be the better able to dispose of themselves, their property, and estates, we hereby take and receive them under our security, protection, and royal safeguard; and ensure to them and their properties, that during the said period, until the said day, the end of the said month of July, they may travel in safety, and may enter, sell, barter, alienate and dispose of all their movable and immovable property, freely and at will. And that during the said time, no harm, injury, or wrong whatever shall be done to their persons or properties contrary to justice, under the pains those persons incur and are liable to, that violate our royal safeguard. We likewise grant permission and authority to the said Jews and Jewesses, to export their wealth and property, by sea or land, from our said kingdoms and dominions, provided they do not take away gold, silver, money, or other articles prohibited by the laws of our kingdoms, but in merchandise and goods that are not prohibited."

After the General Edict of Expulsion had been promulgated in the customary public places—and in Trujillo near the cisterns, where the inhabitants were wont to hold their council—and overseen by the officers of justice, the magistrate of the Hermandad and the public brokers in every town throughout the realms and dominions of Fernando and Isabel affixed the royal coat of arms to the main gates of the *juderías* and to the principal dwellings of all the Jews, which dwellings "were seized by authority of the court of His Highness." After which, they proceeded to take inventory of, sequester and put into deposit all their movables and immovables, ordering the King's commissary and notary, subject to His Highness's wrath and under pain of excommunication by the inquisitors, to dispatch trustworthy persons to stand guard over the Jews and the *juderías* in order to prevent the Jews from selling, transporting, giving in trust, divesting themselves of or hiding their possessions before the inventory and sequestering of the same had been concluded.

One by one the inhabitants of the *aljamas* were brought before the commissary of the Holy Inquisition to swear an oath, in the presence of the officers of justice and the magistrate of the Hermandad, and to make a declaration of "all and whatsoever goods, tributes, rents, titles, rights and shares belonging or owed to you in whatever form and of whatever kind, nature and condition," for "should it be discovered that you or any other persons . . . had transported, hidden, put aside or given in trust any of the aforesaid or any other thing that was owing to you . . . and you had not made mention of, imparted and declared it to the said commissary, know that in accordance with the aforesaid, from that moment on you will be surrendered to the Holy Inquisition, to be sentenced as a recalcitrant . . . for being an impostor and a defender of heretics."

In the Kingdom of Aragón, Fray Pedro de Valladolid and the Grand Master Martín García admonished and exhorted the Christian faithful, on pain of excommunication and sentencing at the discretion of the inquisitors, to refrain "either on their own or through the interpolation of any person or persons, directly or indirectly, or under any pretext, from receiving or taking by way of a loan or in charge or in trust, or in any other fashion, any goods whatsoever . . . which have been, or are in their possession or in any way or manner belong to or may belong to the aforementioned Jews and Jewesses." Taking an active part in the expulsion of the Jews and in the confiscation of their property, Fray Tomás de Torquemada made it known that once the last day of July and the first nine days of August had gone by, all the Christians were forbidden "to converse and communicate publicly or in secret with Jews, or receive them into your homes, or befriend them, or give them nourishment of any sort or victuals for their sustenance, or have dealings with them in the way of bartering or selling." Since the properties of the *aljamas* and of several private Jewish citizens in Aragón, Valencia and Catalonia "were mortgaged to the King, and to monasteries and churches and divers towns, the order was given to make a general sequestering of all the properties of the Jews, so that satisfaction and indemnification might be afforded to the parties who claim they are owed annuities and other debts."

As I walked along the streets of the city on my way back to the inn, feeling as if I, too, had been banished, I glanced with indifference at the buttresses, the stones, the granite rocks and the flight of the garrulous swallows amidst the rooftops. The castle high on the hill seemed more inaccessible, more remote and alien than ever, as if it were the symbol of the sovereign power that was casting the Jews out of Spain and somehow turning me adrift by expelling Isabel and my son.

A pale moon shone in the middle of a limpid sky, storks clacked at the top of a tower, and the sun was setting over the distant mountains. The two gates to the *aljama* of Trujillo had been closed for good, and as of the last day of July, it would no longer be necessary for the Jews to be locked inside when the bell rang for the nine o'clock watch, or to investigate the complaint against the *alcalde* who, in order to rob and extort from them, had caused it to be proclaimed earlier on that any Jew or Jewess found abroad after dark would forfeit his or her clothes and

have to pay a fine of two hundred *maravedis*. Many measures and ordinances would no longer be necessary: the General Edict of Expulsion
put an end to everything else.

The door to the inn was closed but not bolted, and I sought out Doña
Luz Pizarro to discuss with her this afternoon's proclamation. However,
as she was not in, I repaired to my room. The hostel had only three
bedchambers for rent and a large room with a round table for eating,
conversing and doing business. After the merchant's departure the silence had become nearly total, interrupted only occasionally by the barking of a dog or the whistling of the wind. Grime, smoke and the passage
of time had blackened the rafters in the public room, and the frame of
the window facing the rocks looked as if it had been ripped out, leaving
a forlorn hole in its place.

The upstairs rooms had been closed off for mysterious reasons, the
evil tongues in town averring that the men who had disappeared without
a trace from my landlady's life slept in them their eternal sleep. I gave
some credence to the gossip, for the woman did look like a man-eater.
Everyone knew she had borne children by a Jew, a Moor and a Christian,
for which reason she was known as "the Spain of all three religions."
Her bedroom, in a corner next to the worm-eaten staircase, was so small
and dark that one passed by without noticing it, as if she deliberately
intended to conceal her wantonness.

Another kitchen lay three steps from her room, its hearth forever cold;
no meat was dressed in the copper pans, no bread was kneaded in the
basins, no water was heated in the caldrons, and the tablecloths, napkins
and wine jugs were always ranged in a pinewood chest.

The fowls, goats and cows in the courtyard were subdued, and night
fell in silence over the holm oak, while the dawns receded in a hush
from its dark green leaves.

"Did you hear the crier at midday making public proclamation of the
Catholic Kings' decree that all the Jews, with their people and their
belongings, have from this day hence until the last day of July to quit
these kingdoms, under pain of death and the confiscation of their property for the royal fisc and exchequer?" she asked me through my slum-
ber, for I had just begun to sleep.

"I have heard it," I said, my eyes half closed, uncertain as to where
she was in the room, "but I do believe that other persons of much
erudition and conscience were of the opinion that the King erred in
wishing to cast out of his dominions such a profitable people who are
so good at the farming of taxes."

"They say that when this business of the Expulsion was brought
forward at court, Don Abraham Senior and Don Isaac Abrabanel offered
a considerable sum of money from the *aljamas* to tempt the greed of

King Fernando, but that the Queen was against it and then Torquemada
stormed in holding a crucifux aloft and cried, 'Behold the crucified one
whom Judas sold for thirty pieces of silver; do you purpose to sell him
for a larger sum?' '' said Doña Luz, now plainly visible in the doorway,
holding a candle in her hand.

"That, and even worse, have I overheard in the streets," I replied,
sitting up in bed.

"You would not be defending the heretical depravity?" she rebuked
me angrily.

"I do not defend the Jews, but neither does my heart rejoice at their
sufferings," I answered.

Days went by. The bad news traveled faster than the wind. In the
same square where the edict had been announced, a letter issued by
the Catholic Kings in Santa Fé on the fourteenth of May was read aloud,
giving the order to proclaim in the squares and marketplaces of all the
towns and villages throughout their realms and dominions that they
hereby granted permission for the Jews to sell their movable effects,
lands and houses and their livestock, and to give away, barter, exchange,
transfer and otherwise dispose of whatever debts were owing to them.
On that very same day also in Santa Fé, the King had appointed Martín
de Gurrea, from Argavieso, to oversee the removal of the Jews, young
and old alike, in his name, making certain that they carried away with
them only those belongings that were permitted, within the time limit
established by the royal edict, and to escort them, by whichever road,
mountain pass or seaport in his realms and dominions, by land or by
sea, towards whatever part of the world they should desire to go to,
provided it was beyond the bounds of the said realms and dominions,
protecting and defending them from any person who might do them
injury or harm, at the risk of incurring the King's wrath and indignation
and a penalty of ten thousand gold florins to be taken from the property
of the transgressor.

Yet another edict ensued. It was issued in Córdoba and proclaimed
in the presence of notaries public in the squares and marketplaces of
the towns and villages ruled over by Isabel and Fernando. It called for
those Christians and Moors to whom Jews were indebted and those
Jews to whom Christians and Moors were indebted to appear before the
magistrates of the localities where the debtors had their abodes, in order
to furnish proof of and settle the debts which each was owed by the
others, proceeding to payment in a simple, straightforward manner
without recourse to the law, only sifting out the truth so that all such
debts might be reckoned, adjudged and settled by mid-July. The Christians and Moors were coerced, compelled and constrained to take and
receive in payment for whatever was owing to them yet other debts that

Christians and Moors owed to the Jews, or land appraised at its fair value and price by the aforementioned magistrate and two other persons with an understanding of such matters. As for those debts owed to Jews by Christians and Moors which were not due for settlement until after the time allotted for the Expulsion, the Jews were obliged to cede or sell them as best they could to Christian or Moorish proctors who would collect them as they fell due in whatever manner the debtors had engaged to pay them.

Meanwhile, there was a rumor abroad among the Jews of Trujillo that the venerable Rabbi Isaac Aboab, accompanied by thirty other rabbis, had been commissioned to negotiate with the King Don João II of Portugal for admission into his kingdom of the Jews expelled from Spain, the King having demanded one *cruzado* for each Jew who remained for six months, at the end of which time each household would be obliged to pay one hundred *cruzados*. The Jews of Trujillo began to depart for Portugal almost as soon as the Edict of Expulsion was proclaimed, leaving an assortment of properties behind—houses, vineyards, and other possessions. Once the Jews had gone, the synagogue was to be given by the Kings to the nuns of the Convent of Santa Isabel, and the bricks and tombstones from the Jewish cemetery to the Monastery of Santa María de la Encarnación, which belonged to the Order of Santo Domingo.

When another month had passed, one midnight Doña Luz Pizarro, all barefoot and in disarray, carrying candles and red in the face, burst into my room at the inn and, surreptitiously placing my hand on her stomach so I could feel whether it was cold, asked me, "What are you doing there in the dark?"

"I was standing by the window looking at a very bright star," I answered.

"Make love to me, and nobody will ever know," she blurted out.

"For years I have been seeking my lost love in every town and city," I countered.

"I can cure you of your melancholy."

"The hand that made the wound must apply the salve."

She took off her shift. "Then give me some of your salve, for I am plagued by the stinging of these creatures which they call teats, and my backside is burning with the prickly heat of lust; for many a day I have been looking for a friend to sin with."

"You are too big for the two of us to fit into a single grave and too passionate for a single bed to suffice us."

"Tomorrow we will die; today we must hasten to make love," she importuned.

"We never stop dying," I replied.

"Death will fill our bodies with ugliness."

"Death is an empty shape."

"I prefer King Croesus, for he was mute."

"Then make love to him."

"I want to love you passionately."

"You constrain me overmuch," I said, twisting out of her grasp, for she had laid hold of my arm.

"Am I not to your liking?"

"If you were sufficiently to my liking you would be my wife."

"I implore you to show me how I should love you," she groaned.

"I have already told you, the one I love is lost."

"Come with me, I shall lay the table for you."

"I have no appetite for uncooked flesh, or for the love of a woman whom I do not hold dear," I said, "and I have no wish to be the cause of your damnation."

"I damn myself by lusting so on my own," she answered. "You and your reflection in the mirror bear a great likeness to Proveto and Jacinto, who were castrated."

"There may be two of me now, but we both have a lost love, be we geldings or stallions, faithful Christians or heretics."

"I, too, have a lost love," she declared, "a backsliding friar who is no longer alive. He was a whoremaster where women were concerned, overly fond of maidens and a glutton for food and drink."

"How is that?" I asked.

"He traveled the highways with a pilgrim's staff in one hand and a shell in the other, doing battle with the bees for spoiling the flowers, and making miracles in the stomachs of virgins, for he was a great cropper of maidenheads and made prophecies of babes in their bellies. He even lay with a mother and daughter together, and with ladies whose natural disease was upon them, and who had banished their husbands to another room."

"Was he young and handsome?"

"He was a cherub somewhat the worse for wear, who hid his baldness under hair smoothed over his forehead, and covered up his wrinkles with face paint. Every night when he returned from his forays he would scrape his shoes clean in a chapel close by his house, rend his garments and turn his back black-and-blue by dint of scourging himself, and then he would ask for a nail to gouge out his eyes on account of having fallen into the sin of adultery, and he would spend the whole night long in prayer, his knees pressing against the cold stone, or walking barefoot to and fro over some thorns he scattered upon the ground."

236

"And you gave your love to a man like this?"

"When he heard my confession he used to make me dishonorable propositions, exclaiming that he yearned to lie with me, and on one occasion when he came to this inn, he led me into such temptation of the flesh that I coupled with him, and he got me with child. . . . In the months that followed, my stomach swelled day by day with his fruit, and it was as if I had eaten a sheep which bleated at every turn; wherever I went people would ask me if I was pregnant of a man or a beast. To allay my doubts, I asked an astrologer whether my child would be a boy or a lamb, to which he replied that I would give birth to an arrogant mule who would repudiate his father the ass and his mother the mare . . . or else I would bring into the world a creature resembling the hippopotamus, a wild beast with the cloven hooves of an ox, the neck and mane of a horse and the tusks of a boar, which when it is full-grown seeks to mate with its own mother and, if its father stands in the way, is capable of killing him. . . . He only knew for a certainty that it would be born in a field by the wayside, like the sainted Don Fernando."

"What happened next?"

"I lost the child in a fall I took when I rolled off a big rock at the entrance to Trujillo, and no one asked me ever again who had made me pregnant."

"And what did he do?"

"He waylaid the girls in town to take his pleasure with them whenever he was able, and many a one became suspicious and jealous of him for having had carnal knowledge of her only to deceive and abandon her afterwards. . . . It came to pass one day, after he had left me at the inn to go confess a damsel who stood in grave danger of losing her life on account of being pregnant by him, that the girl's parents and four uncles, kinsmen every one of Don Diego García de Paredes, laid an ambush for him among the granite boulders and shot him through with arrows from their crossbows, wrenched the eyes from his sconce, yanked a span of tongue out of his mouth and broke his feet, whereupon he began in vain to bray and cry out, until he gave up the ghost."

This chat had a calming effect on Doña Luz, and after Lauds were rung she betook herself to her bedroom and left me to sleep. But another day as I sat at dinner with her she tried again to inveigle me into her bed that night.

"Do not disparage the rose because it springs from thorns, nor the beauty of a woman because she is the daughter of peasants," she said.

"Put an end to your wheedling, for I am married and the face of a beautiful woman who happens to cross my path is no more to me than the wind," I said.

"You may make love to me and no one will accuse you of ravishment."

"The female who bridles her lust spares herself many charges and chagrins."

"Should you change your mind, come to my bower and I will show you many things withheld from those men in this world who do without women," she said, going off to her room.

But soon she called for me, and I hurried to her side to find her sprawling on the floor, intent on luring me to her body with promises of pleasure, threats, reproaches and vile hints.

"What are you doing there on the ground?" I asked her.

"I am stretched out in ecstasy, having a dream," she replied.

"It looks more like the seething of lewdness than ecstasy," I said.

"The truth of the matter is, as I was lying on my bed a troop of ants came to eat me up alive and I had to take refuge on the floor."

"What's that?" I asked when I noticed she was all bloody between the legs.

"I was wounded down the middle by some demons who came into my room after sunset, but ask me no more questions, for my voice is going."

"Put an end to your sorrowing and put behind you this love which brings you nothing but bitterness."

She arose slowly, as if weighed down by her body; she muttered something unintelligible, a sob or perhaps a curse, and she went to the kitchen, where I could hear her through the wall furiously smashing several pitchers.

One Friday after Nones, close upon the twentieth of July, it was bruited abroad in the town of Trujillo that there were countless Jews outside the walls on their way into exile, some of them heading for the Kingdom of Portugal and others towards the sea. In hopes of seeing Isabel and my son amongst them, I walked down from the Church of Santa María la Mayor, along the Calle de las Palomas, past the Escobar house and the Church of San Andrés, until I emerged from the city through the Triunfo Gate. I continued walking beyond the city walls, followed by the clucking of hens and the bleating of an orphaned lamb.

There, beneath the Espolón, the banished had gathered, looking as if they had been locked out of the world and were being held prisoner amidst the granite rocks and the manure heaps, the ants, wasps and thistles. Crossbowmen kept an eye on the crowd from the towers of the Espolón and the twin-towered Alcázar of the Bejaranos. Closer at hand, the sentries and familiars of the Inquisition stood guard over them. It was three hours past noon; beneath the crushing heat, with their shadows splayed to the right of their bodies, they had halted to rest. They had come from all corners of the Kingdom of Castile and they would take up their journey presently.

I quickly scanned the faces of a multitude of women disheartened by hunger, thirst, weariness and the sun, but Isabel was not amongst them, although I was scrutinized in turn by the eyes of the outcasts, who sought in mine the reason for their exile, and I turned to leave.

Suddenly I noticed a man who was laying his hand on the shoulder of a maid of some twelve or fourteen years, who had wide shining eyes—his companion, perhaps.

"Gonzalo de la Vega?" I asked hesitantly, approaching him.

He stared as if he had never seen me before in his life, his face paler and more aloof, his gestures harsher and more abrupt than before. Finally, he assented with a nod.

To my great surprise, once he was standing before me I realized I had forgotten nothing about his looks, probably because he was the image of his sister.

"Juan Cabezón?" he asked in turn, before embracing me and smiling, as if the past had come rushing over him all at once.

"In the flesh, but a few years older," I replied.

The fear that I would give him bad tidings was visible on his face when he asked me what had become of Isabel. I led him a few steps away from the others and began to recount my fruitless search; he hung anxiously on my words, as if at any moment I might deal him a fatal blow.

When I had finished my story he wondered aloud whether they should not have contrived a way of learning each other's whereabouts in Aragón and Castile, thus sparing themselves the anguish of knowing nothing about one another since his departure from Madrid, for he had pictured his sister in the midst of the flames a thousand times over.

"If you ever see her again, tell her that I have gone to Portugal but not to search for me in that land, as I hope to move on within the time allotted to the Jews by King Don João Segundo."

The initial excitement of our meeting having passed, we noticed how many people were listening to our discourse and we moved farther away from them to continue, followed only by the maiden who seemed to be his friend.

"Do you see this young girl next to me? Her name is Judith, and she is but twelve years old. I have taken her to wife, for before our exodus began, all the Jewish fathers decided that their daughters of twelve years and up should travel 'in the shadow and company of husbands.' Her elder sister was ravished by Moors on a mountainside while her helpless parents looked on. It was midnight, and under cover of darkness the villains sprang out from behind the pitch-black pine trees, slitting open the bellies of other unarmed Jews, in their search for the gold they believed the Jews had swallowed."

The girl glanced at me as Gonzalo, his head held high, made his way among the exiles. Suffering and the passage of time had left their traces on his face, but he wore his rags as artlessly as he might have worn a king's robes.

"Where have you come from?" I asked him.

"From out of the night."

I looked at him in puzzlement.

He added hastily, "What I mean is, the city gate is closed to us, and since last night we have advanced no farther than the place where we are now halted."

"They did not allow you to enter Trujillo?"

"No, for in every town in these kingdoms we are looked upon as people who are no longer there. These wagons and these beasts of burden are laden with a lifetime's labors, with the memory of centuries of existence in these lands; but our choicest possessions have been left behind, because we are unable to take them with us."

"I am thirsty," whimpered a little girl whose cheeks were dry and sunburned.

"I am hungry," complained a little boy.

"And I am nothing, neither hungry nor thirsty, nor desirous of living—nothing at all," an old man despaired.

"Back in my village I would have sold my house for a song, but no one wanted to buy it, so I left it empty and the first person to go inside is welcome to live there," said a man with curly black hair.

"I burned mine, along with all my memories of the town where I was born," declared a buck-toothed man.

"That's a lie, the commissaries of the Expulsion had to drag him out of it," said a woman at his side. "He didn't want to leave Avila, he didn't even want to leave the house; the best he could do was blacken the walls with smoke."

"Don't you recognize me? I am Abraham Costantín from Calatayud, brother of the physician Mossé, who was forced to abandon his library, with all his Bibles and treatises on medicine," asked a nearsighted gray-beard who stuck his face into mine, the better to see it.

"You old fool, you're confusing your own life with tales other people have told you," an old woman chided him.

"It all gets jumbled together inside my head; no matter, when we look back, all our memories will become one single story," he replied.

The storks made a great racket with their clacking, and several people turned to look at them.

"The Hebrews call storks *chasidah*, merciful," the old man explained, "because they say that when the storks' parents grow decrepit, their offspring fly them on their wings and bring food to them in the nest."

"They are pilgrim birds; we have no idea where they come from or where they're going," said the curly-headed man.

"It is a well-known fact that, having no tongue, they make a loud noise with their beak," the old man added.

The little girl picked up a trampled butterfly from the ground and showed it to him. High above on the hill was Santa María la Mayor with its two doors and its cool interior. Down below, a solitary figure dressed in black was standing still on a granite rock.

"Hearken to me," began a man whose face was reddened by the sun. "As the Jews traveled the royal road which stretches from La Bóveda to Zamora, on a mountain along the way certain scoundrels built a hut where they charged twelve *maravedis* for each wagon that went by and half a *real* for each person and twenty-three *maravedis* for the pregnant women, taking the money by force without having any right or leave to do so."

"When the Jews passed a place belonging to the Order of San Juan which is called Fresno de los Ajos, they were obliged to pay a tax and a toll of twelve *maravedis* to every house along the road and, on top of that, half a *real* for each of their number," said a short man.

"Where I come from, in León," recounted a grizzled, bearded man, "the Corregidor Don Iohán de Portugal, acting in violation of the law and against royal provision, has done the Jews many wrongs. In particular, under the pretense of protecting and defending them he stole some thirty thousand *maravedis*. Moreover, in order to make his own even more of their riches, just prior to their departure, and in connivance with his *alcalde* Juan del Corral and his *alguacil*, he had attachments made of the Jews' property although no judgments were passed or deeds of surety presented, taking into account only those suits that happened to be brought against them. Even before a debt falls due they seize the goods the very same day that a suit is brought, without inquiring further into the truth, even seeking out plaintiffs to bring suit against the debtors so as to provoke more attachments, in order to pocket the fees and keep the goods for themselves; and when goods are seized at the request of the Jews, he and his officials receive the money and keep it, giving only as much as they choose to the Jews."

"I heard that the King Don Fernando impounded the property of the Aragonese Jews as advance payment for the tribute which the *aljama* of Saragossa used to pay him every year, and that he confiscated eighty thousand *sueldos* that were owing to Jucé Chamorro to make up for the renting of the *aljama*," said the buck-toothed man.

"In Saragossa, the King appropriated the entire Jewish quarter, between Calle del Coso and Calle San Miguel, for himself; they say he will sell, lease or give the houses away in reward for services to the Crown," a woman next to him declared.

"In Huesca the King seized some houses that were part of the main synagogue," an old man with a straggly beard noted.

"In Daroca the commissary Domingo Agustín sold all the houses that used to be our synagogue and our hospital," sobbed a little boy.

"The townspeople in Ejea and Magallón forced the Jews to hand over the five thousand *sueldos* which the *aljama* used to pay the King every year in January," said the red-faced man.

"In Saragossa, after the Edict of Expulsion was proclaimed, the twelve men who were sent to guard the gates of the *judería*, the two painters who painted the royal coat of arms four hundred and seventy times on the doors of the Jews' houses, the notaries, commissaries, assessors, *alguaciles*, collaborators and couriers were all paid their wages at the Jews' expense," reported the woman next to the buck-toothed man.

"I was in the synagogue of Exea de los Caballeros when Iohán de Peramán, an official of the Inquisition, burst in brandishing the staff of the Holy Office to announce to the congregation that by order of the father inquisitors the Jews were obliged to deliver up within the space of one day to the commissary sent by them all the texts of the Talmud, all the commentaries on the Bible and all the Torah scrolls. From there, Iohán de Peramán went with a notary to the house of Maestre Jucé Almerecí, a Jewish doctor, in whose study he confiscated sixty books. These were identified by Maestre Jayme, a doctor from Taust, and the official carried them away in a sack which he tied tight. From there they proceeded to the house of Rabbi Jucén, where they found forty books, which were also identified by Maestre Jayme, and put into another sack, and it too was tied by the aforementioned official himself," a man who was wiping his face with a bit of cloth told us.

"When the lord of Argavieso was granted the royal preferment to guide and accompany the Jews of Aragón into exile, for which he was allotted two thousand *sueldos*, he designated Johán de Fabara, a citizen of Saragossa, to escort them towards the sea, but upon his arrival in Exea, Johán de Fabara discovered that nine Jews were being held prisoner by the commissaries until they paid to the King Don Fernando all the monies owed by the *aljama*. One of the prisoners was Mossé Alcolumbre, who had little time left to reach the sea, so the other eight gave themselves and their estates in guarantee so that he might be on his way," yet another man disclosed.

"In Huesca, when the day came to depart, we left behind the *aljama*, which had always been our abode, and went out from the city by the road to Puendeluna, emerging onto the Sotonera plain after we had passed the groves of holm oaks; we slept in a place called Ortilla, where that night we were robbed of a wagonload and a half of clothes, the very best we had brought away with us," the old man with the scraggly beard said plaintively.

"Once the edict had been proclaimed in the synagogues and the *aljamas*, in the squares and in the churches, in the streets and in the fields, many clergymen and learned Christians took to preaching the Gospel to the Jews, haranguing them on the doctrines of the Church, the coming of the Messiah and the falsehood of the Talmud," said the toothy man in a voice loud enough for everyone around us to hear.

"On the very same day the edict was made public, Rabbi Yucé of the *aljama* of Teruel was arrested in his own house to enable the Franciscan friars to go about their proselytizing undisturbed, which they did, obtaining the baptism of one hundred men, women and children in a single morning. Several rabbis preached that the banishment was God's will, because He wished to take the Jews out of captivity and lead them into the Promised Land, and to that end He would perform miracles for them and would bring them out of Spain prosperous and with much honor, and that He would shepherd them over the seas as He had done for their forefathers in Egypt," the woman next to him affirmed.

"The rich Jews have borne the cost of the poor Jews. All have used one another with the utmost charity in this departure, so that they have staunchly refused conversion, save a very few of the most impoverished," added an old crone.

"This past thirty-first of May, the physician Abraham in Córdoba became a Christian, and on Friday, the fifteenth of June, in the afternoon the aged Abraham Senior, rabbi to all the Jews of Castile, and his son were baptized in Guadalupe, the King, the Queen and the Cardinal of Spain having acted as godparents; their names now are Fernando and Juan Nuñez Coronel," said the short man. "At the same time Abraham Senior's son-in-law, Rabbi Mayr, and his two sons took the names of Fernando, Pero and Francisco Pérez Coronel."

"Even though three of the four heads of Spanish Judaism turned Christian, Don Isaac ben Yudah Abrabanel did not convert. However, he did pardon the Catholic Kings the monies which he and his brother had advanced to them against the revenues from taxes they had not yet farmed, in return for which each brother was granted a license to take out of Spain one thousand ducats and gold and silver jewels, which they did, setting sail from the port of Valencia at the beginning of July," recounted the old man with the straggly beard.

"Being desperate to dispose of their properties and patrimonies within the time allowed them for abandoning these kingdoms, many bartered a house for a donkey, or a vineyard for a bit of cloth or linen, and there were others who tried to smuggle out gold and silver, *cruzados* and ducats, swallowing them down to carry in their stomachs through the mountain passes and ports where they are searched, and this is done especially by the women," the man with the sunburnt face informed us.

"In Segovia, after the proclamations are made in the Plaza del Alamo, near the San Andrés Gate, as it was customary to do when the Jews had articles for sale, when the term of the edict has elapsed, many Jews will quit their houses and go to the burial fields on the Cuesta de los Hoyos, near the Clamores brook, to make their dwellings in the tombs of their dead and the caves on the mountainsides. Inhabitants of the city, both religious and lay, will venture out to preach at them, scolding them for their blind incredulity in the light of so many proofs and dire calamities throughout the long centuries. In honor of those who accept baptism, the place will be known ever after as the Holy Field, the Prado Santo, and the remainder will depart from the kingdom," said one woman as if reading the future.

"Remember, remember: Medina Tarkuna, which lies upon the sea, is a city with an *aljama* and walls of marble, just as Echisi said about Tarragona," a toothless elder thrummed.

"Already I seem to see in my dreams a man of another time who stands in front of the *judería* of Sagunto, where I was born, and says, 'This gate was called the Portal de la Judería,' but behind it my house is no longer there, nor even a trace of its existence." said another old man, his beard trembling.

"I can see, as if in a congregation of shadows, a man who is unknown to me in a time yet to come, standing in the humble *aljama* of Valderas and saying, 'These are the Jews who lived here in this town at the time of the enclosure: Belloci, a shearer of cloth; Lazaro Jucé; Buenavida Simuel; Doña Sara; Jucé Rojo; Doña Vida; Isaque, a weaver; Avelloci, a cobbler; Jacá, a bellows maker; Leví, a shoemaker; Salomón, a dyer; Fadaza; Mosés de San Felices,' but not a one of us is left to hear him, the very enclosure is no longer there . . . only ruins on the ground where the synagogue stood," a woman lamented.

"I have listened to all these people bear witness as if with a single voice to what they have seen, heard and suffered, but I have yet to hear your history since that dawn when you left Madrid until today. I am desirous of being acquainted with your adventures, unless there is something so terrible you would conceal it from me," I said to Gonzalo de la Vega.

"Listen closely, for I have naught to hide," he replied. "Early that morning I set out for Guadalajara, where Mosé Arragel, the sage of the

Law of Moses, had lived when he translated the Bible into the vernacular, between the years 1422 and 1430, at the behest of Don Luis de Guzmán. The kabalist Selomoh Alhabés and Rabbi Isaac Aboab still dwelt there, and under the name of Diego Díaz I went to work for a printer of Hebrew books, rendering them into Spanish, and writing down the Psalms of David on parchment scrolls for whoever employed me to do so.

"I made perilous journeys, such as driving a pack mule laden with books to be hidden away in Toledo and other towns in Castile. But after the tribunal of the Holy Office had been established in the residence of Don Pedro de Alarcón, a knight of the Order of Calatrava, many *Conversos* were burned alive or managed to escape from Guadalajara. Being suspect in my faith, to avoid the accusation of heresy I passed myself off as the Jew Moisés Zacuto and busied myself with teaching such things as would be useful to the children whose parents had died at the stake or were languishing in the jails of the Inquisition.

"Abroad at night and in hiding during the day, I came and went in secret between the main synagogue and the old synagogue of the Matute family, the synagogue of the Toledans and the house of María Alvarez, making my abode with Guiomar Fernández, a young woman who as a Jew was known as Clara and who fed me on fruit and stews. I also spent some days with a dresser of goatskins, a certain Pedro García Torrillo, who used to make the peasants of Robledillo laugh when they would ask him, 'How do the Jews teach their children to read?' for he would answer, '*Shin, sin, ayin, zayin, vav, tav, het, bet, tet.*' The townspeople addressed me variously as Zecut, Zecuth, Zecute, Zacudo, Zacut, Zacuth, Sacut, Zakut, Zacuto and even Zancudo (which is a kind of long-legged gnat), but some of the better-informed asked whether I was related to the astrologer from Salamanca, Abraham bar Samuel bar Abraham Zacut.

"It became difficult to sustain myself, and Pedro García, the baker Yucé Amarido and a woman known as Fat Elvira took turns feeding me. I was shod by the shoemaker Juan de Chinchón and clothed by the tailor Pedro de Benavente, and in a darkened room I was nursed through the quartan fevers by Mencia Rodríguez de Medina, called "the Simpleton," because it was recounted of her that in the belief that she was serving Jesus Christ, she took her niece to the wedding of a Moslem woman in the Moorish *aljama*, and when her son fell sick, she went barefoot from church to church and caused many Masses to be said, and on another occasion she sent a porringer full of oil for the lamps to the synagogue. And thus I lived in Guadalajara until the day I met with a *Conversa* by the name of Juana García who perpetrated all manner of tricks against the Jews of the town. She became suspicious of me and denounced me to the Inquisition.

"I left and wandered here and there, sometimes on foot, sometimes on a pack mule or a donkey, making a fire at night with the dung of animals to cook whatever dinner offered itself, sleeping but little and dressed in the garb of a shepherd or the clothes of a dead man I had stumbled upon in the fields. Through heat, wind, lightning and rain I did not always choose the shortest way, indeed often taking the one steepest and most difficult of access. I did not always head for the safest village or the most trustworthy house, and whenever I arrived in a place, I pretended I was going on to the next, as fugitives do to avoid capture. Thus I reached the walled city of Huesca, where I lodged with Doña Toda, the widow of Pedro Sellán, who fell madly in love with me and who had great difficulty letting me go at the end of the twelve months we spent together, for each time I tried to bid her farewell she announced that she was with child and would give birth to my son in a matter of months.

"She, who had never traveled farther than Valencia, where she went as a young girl with her father, and where she had been much struck by the Valencian women, who strolled the streets at night with painted faces wearing low-cut gowns that showed their nipples, was convinced I had come from the ends of the earth. And yet, I confess to you that her stratagem of promising me fatherhood delayed my departure from Huesca for longer than I would have wished, until one evening as we were walking down the public thoroughfare of the Cosso, near the principal synagogue, it occurred to me to leave the city, which I did forthwith, never once turning around even to look at her face.

"Tonsured and clad in a habit, I roamed the highways, masquerading as a pilgrim or a beggar. One day a Hieronymite monk whose path crossed mine on a mountain pass happened to mention that a good friend of my mother's from Ciudad Real, Beatriz Núñez, who had taken care of me as a child, had been accused of heresy and arrested by the inquisitors in Guadalupe, near the monastery of the Order of San Jerónimo. Without a second thought I hurried thither in the hopes of helping her to escape, or at least being useful to her in some way. After walking through ravines, skirting precipices and scaling rugged mountains, I reached the village with its monastery at the foot of the craggy sierra. There they worship the wooden statue of a dark-skinned Virgin holding a child in her arms which, as legend has it, had been carried in a procession in Rome during an epidemic of the plague by Pope Gregory the Great, who had then given it to San Leandro, the Archbishop of Seville, who placed it in the cathedral of that city; but at the time of the Moorish domination it had been removed to a mountain next to the Guadalupe River, dubbed "River of Wolves" by the Arabs, and hidden there in a cave with the remains of San Fulgencio and Santa Florencia for the space of six hundred years.

"About the year 1330, a cowherd by the name of Gil, who had lost one of his cows, found the statue when he obeyed a voice which said to him, 'Go to such and such a place, and you will find your cow dead; but delve into the ground where she lies and you will uncover my statue: place it upon the cow and she will revive.' A church was built at the Virgin's request, and in celebration of her miracles a monastery was erected, and she appeared to the masons in the guise of a young girl and handed them the stones. Ever since then, in the center of the high altar of the church—which never closes day or night, for pilgrims sleep inside it on the bare flagstones, and it is perpetually lit by sixteen lamps of silver and parcel-gilt donated by the shepherds of the district and the members of the Mesta and by kings and gentlemen—the statue found by the cowherd Gil is venerated.

"Within the church are many iron fetters which were worn by Christians held captive by the Moors, who had vowed to the Virgin that should they be set free, they would make a pilgrimage to bring their shackles to Guadalupe. In the sacristy the monks have stored the treasure in upwards of twelve massive chests. They say the statue has a wardrobe of more than eighty robes fashioned from brocade, gold tissue and silk, as well as jeweled ornaments, necklaces and crowns, and when the prior and the sacristan dress her for her birthday, in September, they dare not look at her directly in the face, but only sideways.

"The Catholic Kings have their own palace within the monastery, with many rooms and courtyards, for they are very devoted to the statue. In the two cloisters, monks wearing white sackcloth, scapulars and gray capes walk amongst the fountains, orange trees and cypresses; on the tables where they take their meals, on their seats in church and above the beds where they sleep, is written the inscription 'Thou must die.' However, they have a cavernous cellar hollowed out of the mountainside which is filled with great earthen jars of wine, in the kitchen there are vessels so vast you might boil an ox in one, and at the foot of the mountains there are orchards of citron, orange, lemon and olive trees; bakers, shoemakers, tailors and menders labor daily in their service. But such strict vows of silence are observed in the refectory that any monk who utters a word while at table is put into the stocks for several hours.

"Not far from the monastery there is a hospital with a large number of beds and a room where bread is distributed to the poor. That is where I arrived, wearied and hungry, to eat supper and spend the night, under the name of Pedro Selaya. Going into the village early the next morning, I took lodgings at an inn where I saw a woman standing in the doorway holding a loaf of bread and a jug of wine in her hands.

"The three inquisitors in charge of the tribunal of the Holy Office in Guadalupe—the elderly Fray Nuño de Arévalo, prior of the Convent of the Hieronymites; Doctor Francisco de la Fuente, who had been transferred from Ciudad Real to assist the inexperienced old man; and the Licentiate Pedro Sánchez de la Calancha, or Calle Ancha—had as their mission to cleanse the village of the Judaic heresy, which they accomplished with such zeal that in one year they celebrated seven autos-da-fé in the cemetery, burning fifty-two men and women and one monk, Fray Diego de Marchena, whose fifty-two disciples had joined him in his recantation.

"The inquisitors had also exhumed and cremated the bones of forty-six dead persons, burned the effigies of twenty-five fugitives, condemned sixteen souls to perpetual prison and countless others to lifelong banishment and the galleys. They ordered it publicly proclaimed that the obstinate adherents to the Judaic superstition must abandon Guadalupe under threat of the most severe penalties; they also determined, in honor of Our Lady, that not a single Jew should henceforth make his home in that town, by virtue of which the property of any Jews still living there was confiscated on the spot and granted as alms by the Kings to Nuño de Arévalo, to be employed in the building of a residence to receive the Monarchs whenever they visited the sanctuary.

"Beatriz Núñez, who when she came to Guadalupe was already married and the mother of several children, had been accused on the thirteenth of January of 1485 by the Bachelor Tristán de Medina, one of the Inquisition's attorneys, of having gone to the Jewish baths when she had her monthly courses, of having laved the body of her dead son, of lighting candles on Friday evenings and of performing other Hebrew rites as well. The prosecutor asked the inquisitioners to relax her to secular justice—in plain words, to burn her alive. An attorney by the name of Juan de Texeda undertook her defense, arguing that she had been and continued to be a faithful Christian, and that if she had fallen into errors, she was now fully repented of them and grieved for having done so, imploring Jesus Christ for pardon and forgiveness and the inquisitors for a salutary penance.

"The prosecuting attorney presented witnesses, the defense attorney asked for mercy, 'for the living who desire to serve Our Lord are more worthy of praise than the dead,' but another prosecutor, Diego Fernández de Zamora, argued against her being shown mercy because her act of contrition came too late, at the conclusion of the trial and lawsuit, and because in the house of torture, although she had repeatedly been called upon by the inquisitors to tell the truth, she had always protested her innocence. And so, at the hour of High Mass, on the last day of

July of that year, she was condemned to confiscation of her property and burning at the stake.

"On the same day that Doña Beatriz Núñez was consigned to the flames, her stepson Manuel González, the innkeeper at the Mesón Blanco, the tavern where I had taken lodgings, was also burned on the pyre. The *alguacil* Antón del Castillo had taken him into custody two days after his stepmother and compelled him to testify at her trial that the second wife of his deceased father, who had been a scrivener, 'used to keep the Sabbath and prepared the meals on Friday for Saturday and fasted all the fasts of the Jews.' The witness himself was accused of eating meat on proscribed days, of working on feast days, of having dealings and conversation with Jews and showing them overmuch respect, providing them in his own house with the wherewithal for their meals, and of profaning the sacrament of baptism by allowing himself to be circumcised. The virtues he had shown as a hosteler, when he welcomed Christians, Moors and Jews who came to his house, his charity towards an orphaned girl by the name of Teresa and his generous almsgiving to the poor, churches, hermitages and hospitals became offenses in the eyes of the inquisitors, just so many proofs of heresy and apostasy punishable with fire.

"On the morning when the auto-da-fé was celebrated in which they led out Doña Beatriz Núñez and her stepson, while the townsfolk were busy watching the conflagration in the cemetery across from the portal of the Hieronymite Convent, I took my leave of the inn where I had been staying, not without first giving assurances of my compassion to the family of Manuel González, which at any moment was about to be despoiled of its possessions to swell the coffers of the Kings.

"The Edict of Expulsion took me by surprise in San Martín de Valdeiglesias, where for some time I had been living in the Calle Ancha of the *judería* with a *Conversa* named Aldonza Alvar. Ever since childhood my companion was used to observe the Sabbath and fast the principal fast of the Jews, and celebrate the Feast of the Tabernacles with other maidens, by erecting in the patio of their houses huts made with the green branches of leafy trees and weeping willows, and by eating sweetmeats and fruits. I had made her acquaintance one day in Diego Martín's tavern when she came there, holding a booklet in her hand, to dine. While the host was showing her to a seat at a table near mine he inquired whether the booklet had anything to do with the Bible or the Law of the Jews, contrary to our Holy Catholic Faith.

"Aldonza Alvar replied that it had been given to her years ago by a Jewish youth by the name of Yucé Funes, a native of Los Pradejones, where her father had vineyards, but a few days afterwards a cousin of hers, a friar, had tried to fling it into the fire, which she prevented by explaining that it contained a Jewish prayer which the *Conversos* used to say when they were being held in the jails of the Inquisition, in which they begged God to save them from prison and the stake. Then she had asked the innkeeper what advice he could offer for the salvation of her soul, to which he replied that she should not trouble herself overmuch about it, for her good works would recommend her to God at the hour of her death. Satisfied with his answer, she turned to ask me where I came from and what my name was, and I answered that I came from Tarazona, my name was Alfonso Nunca (Never), and I was a carpenter by trade in search of houses in this town where I could ply my trade.

"She seemed worried as she began to tell me how every night she said a prayer for her father, a *Converso* as well, who had been arrested by the inquisitors in Cadalso one day in October of the year 1487 and accused by the prosecuting attorney of having turned his house into a synagogue, because he had given hospitality to the chief *alcalde* of Escalona and its bailiwick, who was taken gravely ill one Thursday at midnight and requested him the next day to send to his village for a Jewish physician named Rabbi Jacob so he might minister to him. As the physician arrived quite late that Friday, the *alcalde* asked her father to procure some hens for his supper, and in order to ensure he did not leave his bedside, begged her father to allow Rabbi Jacob and other Jews who were in Cadalso into the garden of his house to do their praying. That was sufficient. As her father denied the charges of heresy brought against him, he was tortured twice, having been bound tightly with sharp cords which cut into his flesh and forced to drink two gallon jars of water, although he had nothing to confess. Her sister María was put to the question as well, though all she knew was that her father had gone out to the patio of their house with the physician Rabbi Jacob and the other Jews and had come inside again forthwith. Despite his innocence being proved, absolution did not come until the year 1490, and he was sentenced to refrain from practicing his trade for the space of one year and to abjure *de vehementi* the sin of heresy.

"As a consequence of these persecutions," Gonzalo de la Vega went on, "it was not unusual to see matrons, young girls and old women doing penance in the streets of San Martín Valdeiglesias, dressed in *sanbenitos* emblazoned before and behind with the cross, their clothing stripped of gold, silver and jewels, while their houses served as jails and they themselves were obliged to go to Mass every Sunday wearing the *sanbenito*, with no dawdling allowed on the way. An acquaintance of Aldonza Alvar's, a certain Pedro Rodríguez, who afterwards became a friar, used to wax wroth at the sight of the *sanbenitos* hanging from the rafters of the church, one among them having belonged to his grandmother Beatriz González, alias Queen Serrano, who had been burned alive by the inquisitors; so that one day he exclaimed angrily, 'What on earth is that thing doing there?' 'You needn't bother yourself about it anymore, the person who wore it is in hell!' a voice said from behind. 'In hell, in hell! May it please God to send my soul where hers is and not where the soul of whoever sent her there has gone!' replied Pedro Rodríguez.

"I was enamored of Aldonza Alvar, but I lived in constant fear that the officials of the Holy Office would find me out; I clearly foresaw that one day they would lay hold of me, and I felt an evil noose tightening around us. When I lay in bed at night I often wondered whether the immobility of sleep was not a foretaste of the tomb, and if I was not postponing the moment of my death with cunning subterfuges which ultimately would be of no avail, for when I least expected it they would catch me, either in the street or in Aldonza's house.

"These were my worries when Sunday, the twenty-ninth of April, arrived, the day on which the criers read out the General Edict of Expulsion in which the Catholic Kings also conferred on Don Iñigo López de Mendoza, the Duke of Infantado, all the possessions, be they chattels, real estate, or movables, of the Jews who lived in his lands. Wasting no time, Don Iñigo ordered an inventory taken of all the properties in the two *aljamas* and the Christian town—above one hundred houses, a dozen mansions, two burial grounds, one synagogue, one butcher shop, one hospital, together with vineyards, orchards, meadows, fields of flax, pastures, watering places for cattle, mills, warehouses, crockery, bee-hives and cattle grazing in the field of San Martín de Valdeiglesias and elsewhere. And thus did the estates of the Ocañas, the Calvos, the Castros, the Funes, the Adaroques, the Navarros, the Rosillos, the Robledos, the Caros and the Pardos pass into the hands of Diego Ruys de Sepúlveda, Gonzalo Xexas, Abrahén Gavisón, Diego de Alva and others. Diego Ruys de Sepúlveda got more than thirty houses, either claiming they were his in settlement of trifling debts or because he was owed monies, impounding the houses of the Jews just as they were abandoning them, or drawing up counterfeit bills of sale even if the owners were not in his debt and he had not paid a single cent for the houses. It was robbery, pure and simple. In their desperation the Jews exchanged a vineyard or an orchard for a donkey to carry the children, the ailing or the aged; some paid one thousand *maravedis* for an ass, or gave away their houses for a handful of coins, as did Abraham Agí or Ruy Sánchez.

"Be that as it may," said Gonzalo de la Vega in conclusion, "the Jews of San Martín de Valdeiglesias left within the allotted term, many heading for San Pedro de las Arenas with the intention of reaching Plasencia and thence going on to Portugal. Others of us went by way of Talavera,

Puente del Arzobispo, the Ibor Valley, the mountain pass at Rebata-capas, Guadalupe and Trujillo. Aldonza Alvar decided to remain in San Martín in hopes of being enlightened by the grace of the Holy Ghost; after abandoning the rites and ceremonies of the old Law and receiving instruction and indoctrination from special prelates in all those things she must needs know and believe in order for the holy water of baptism to bear fruit in her, perhaps the venerable inquisitors would have no further cause to send her to the stake."

"The preaching friars are still lighting fires in Valladolid and Cór-doba," said a man who looked like a notary, who was standing behind Gonzalo.

"Stake or no stake, whatever Torquemada believes, I disbelieve; what-ever his order of monks affirms, I deny," declared an old man who was standing in front of him.

"Over and above the sentence of banishment weighing on your head, you have just earned the right to one month of prison in Castile," observed the man who appeared to be a notary. "The Catholic Kings recently dispatched a strict ordinance from Valladolid commanding the authorities of the realm to suppress blasphemy, and henceforth it is forbidden to say 'I disbelieve in God' or 'I despair of God' or 'God's pox on you' or 'God willing' or 'Goddamn,' or say such things of His mother, the Virgin Mary, or utter similar and like words, under pain of a month's imprisonment the first time, of banishment for six months and a fine of one thousand *maravedis* the second time and of having one's tongue pierced with a nail the third time."

"You have a good memory for punishments, but the fire will be amply sufficient for me," the old man retorted.

"Move on there, we must reach Cáceres before nightfall! Get on your way, or else I shall leave you to your fate at the hands of the commissaries of the Expulsion and the *alguaciles* of the Holy Office," shouted the guide who was leading them into exile.

"But you may stay, for you are a *Converso*," I whispered into Gonzalo's ear, as he made as if to rejoin the others.

"Do you want me to deliver my body to the stake?" he asked bluntly, astonished at my words.

"Is there anything I can do for you?"

"Tell my sister, if you ever see her again in this world, that I am strong enough to brave hunger and exile. Tell her that one day I will find her . . ." he said as the crowd, huddled together into a single, weary, disconsolate animal, prepared to be on its way.

Young and old, men and women, they all began to march along the walls beneath the rocky Espolón, encouraged by the rabbis, who urged them to sing: "Then the Lord said unto Moses: 'Go in unto Pharaoh, and tell him: Thus saith the Lord, the God of the Hebrews: Let My people go, that they may serve Me.' 'And Pharaoh will say of the children of Israel: They are entangled in the land, the wilderness hath shut them in.' " "And the children of Israel cried out unto the Lord. And they said unto Moses: 'Because there were no graves in Egypt, hast thou taken us away to die in the wilderness?' " "And the angel of God removed and went behind them."

And other voices sang: "Sing to the Lord who made marvels, proclaim it all over the lands . . ." "Our God will open up a way in the midst of the sea, He will make paths for our lost feet on the land . . ." "He will make rivers in the mountains, in the midst of the fields He will make springs and will confound the thirsty earth . . ." "Trust in Him whose hands work marvels and whose eyes fill the earth with light . . ."

"You, what are you carrying there?" an official asked an elderly Jew who lagged behind the others, stooping under the weight of a great sack as if he were loath to lose its contents.

"As I have nothing to give the guards at the border, I have filled this sack with sand so they will allow me to leave," replied the old man.

"God be with you," I said to Gonzalo de la Vega.

But he did not hear me, or he chose not to look back, his shadow blending with the departing shadows, one more shadow amidst the troop of crestfallen shadows. The Jews were leaving the Kingdom of Castile with a heavy step, as if bound for the other world rather than a new life. Uprooted from the places of their birth, they had no tree-lined paths to shield them from the sun, which shone down leadenly and caused the distance to shimmer, making it all seem a hallucination, a delirium brought on by the feverish heat and not a nightmare visited upon men by other men. The castle on the hilltop, the inaccessible walls, the incandescent afternoon, seemed more like products of human cruelty than features of an inanimate landscape. It was four hours past noon; like a wound opening slowly across the dry fields, or a long serpent of dust, the line of exiles trudged westwards between the faint paths and gray granite rocks towards the Kingdom of Portugal, growing ever smaller in the distance until only the low, dark hills were visible. In Trujillo, the storks clacked under the white skies, glided pointy-beaked over the towers on their black and white wings and abruptly flew off in flocks, filling the air with a great noise.

"Christian or Jew?" a rough voice asked behind me.

"Christian," I replied.

"What were you doing outside the walls?" continued the voice, which belonged to a soldier on horseback.

"I came to see the Jews leaving the Kingdom of Castile," I answered.

"You were conversing with one of them for a long time."

"I was endeavoring to convert him to our Holy Catholic Faith, entreating him not to go into the Kingdom of Portugal still clinging to the heretical depravity."

"What is your business here in Trujillo?"

"I intend to spend the night at a tavern in town, for I am on an errand for a sister of mine, a devotee of the Blessed Virgin, who aspires to admittance in one of the religious houses here: to wit, the Convent of Santa Isabel, of the Dominican nuns who, ever since the Edict of Expulsion was promulgated, and by order of their prior, have locked themselves into and remained in the synagogue, hoping to force the granting to them of all the goods and chattels, furnishings and land belonging to it, and I have not been able to speak with any one of them no matter how hard I have tried," I explained.

"Very well, you may go, but have no further truck with these Jews unless you have permission from the commissaries of the Expulsion or the father inquisitors," said the soldier, galloping off towards the west, in the direction taken by the exiles.

I returned to the inn without stopping on the way. The door to my room was open, as if someone had come to occupy it or make a search. The hostess had gone out, and from the neighboring room, whose door was also open, a familiar voice remarked on the heat beating down on the city that day. I answered absentmindedly. The man came out of his room and into mine. I suddenly realized who he was: Agustín Delfín, Babylonia's brother, dressed as a familiar of the Holy Office.

"What are you doing here?" he asked me.

"I am on my way to Seville," I quickly replied.

"I have just come from there, from the rejoicings over the taking of Granada. I took part in the procession to San Salvador, which was held to give thanks to God for the enjoyment of conquest this victory has afforded Their Highnesses. We carried out Nuestra Señora de los Reyes amidst all the richly appareled parish crosses, with a great many waxen candles and the standards of all the confraternities, exiting the church through the Puerta del Pardón, then going down the Cal de Génova, the Cal de la Sierpe, the Cal de las Armas and the Cal de San Vicente, until we reached the Cal de Santiago," he said importantly, just as if I counted for nothing compared to him. "Now I am on my way to Cáceres bearing a letter from the Catholic Kings to Sancho de Paredes, cautioning him to keep watch at the confines of his district to prevent the Jews who are leaving these kingdoms from carrying gold or silver or other forbidden articles into the Kingdom of Portugal."

"And I am seeking my fortune," I admitted, "for I am growing old, and I have no place in the sun in this world. These have not been good times for me."

"Have you heard tell of the great undertaking which Don Cristóbal Colón is preparing in Palos, at the behest of our Queen Isabel?" Agustín Delfín asked me. "He proposes to reach the Indies by sailing west and to discover the fabled palaces of the Great Khan."

"No," I answered, feeling myself the most insignificant of men.

"If you tell Don Cristóbal Colón that I sent you, perhaps he will take you on one of the three ships he is equipping," he said.

"When does he set sail?" I asked.

"Early in August, with many mariners and provisions for an entire year, but he is so in need of men that he has asked for royal pardons in order to secure the release from jail of four criminals who are guilty of murder, to take them along with him," he said. "So if you are a homicide, a thief or a fugitive from justice, and you want the proceedings against you suspended until two months after your return from the voyage, you are in luck: go and find him."

"I am no murderer, or thief or fugitive, but if fate takes me to Palos I will be honored to join Don Cristóbal Colón in his undertaking," I replied.

"Did you know that in Badajoz the chief customs officer has been commissioned to ascertain which persons receive money and other payments from the Jews in exchange for smuggling out of these kingdoms their *maravedis*, gold, silver, sheepskins, coins, cattle, wheat, barley, animals, gunpowder, weapons and other things, which are strictly forbidden in the royal decrees?" he continued, paying me no attention, for he was interested only in himself and whatever might concern him.

"They say that at the city limits of Plasencia two shepherds found a leather pouch filled with gold and silver, the which supposedly had belonged to some Jews who were killed when they were taking it clandestinely out of these kingdoms," I said.

"I have heard tell that in Puerto de Santa María, off the shores of the Guadalete River, on Conejos Islet, a rich Jew was observed burying a coffer filled with Moorish doubloons, Sicilian doubloons and coins from Venice, Pisa, Florence, Ferrara, the Vatican and elsewhere, in the foolish belief that one day he would return to these Catholic kingdoms," said Agustín Delfín.

"And did you dig it up?" I inquired.

"In due time the officials of the Catholic Kings will delve into all the suspicious places where the Jews used to dwell," he declared, turning his back on me as he went towards the door.

"You haven't told me whether the man you are going to see in Cáceres is a kinsman of the Samson of Trujillo, Don Diego García de Paredes, whose strength and corpulence are notorious in this town and its environs," I said.

"I have no interest in the kindred of people who are unknown to me, nor in the history of village Samsons," he answered testily, crossing the threshold.

"The townspeople say that one night when this Diego García de Paredes was in the countryside next to a tree, a black horseman rode up and they battled all night long until sunup, when he felt a great chill all over his body and realized that he had been fighting with the devil," I recounted, to impress him.

"The devil will lead you to the stake, if you continue to consort with fugitive heretics," he said coldly.

"I do not consort with any sort of heretics, be they absent or present," I retorted.

"Where have you been all these years?" he asked without looking at me.

"I told you, I have been seeking my fortune here and there in these kingdoms of God, but I haven't had much luck," I replied.

"Judging by how skinny you are, I would say you have had none at all," he sneered.

"Little enough, in truth," I conceded, careful not to appear offended.

"Your fortune has dwindled to the point where you look poor and disinherited," he added.

"But I am rich in experiences and memories, albeit slender of means."

"If you cannot gratify your bodily appetites, you must nourish your soul and your hungry nights on wise counsels, contemplation and mortifications, which, though they may not win you a place in the world to come, will at least make patent to you your own wretchedness," he said, clutching his belly, which shook with laughter.

"Your advice is clear, but your reasoning is murky," I parried.

"And now, tell me," he said, turning towards me threateningly, "did you not frequent the Rinconada, where, so they say, the wealthiest Jews in Trujillo lived, and where the worthies who visited the city were wont to lodge?"

"I knew it by name alone, for my walks took me only as far as the Church of Santa Catalina to say my prayers," I replied.

"Then perhaps you heard about the commotion and brawl that occurred last year in the synagogue when the Jews fought amongst themselves with swords and stones in the presence of the *alcalde*?" he asked, looking at me out of the corner of his eye.

"I heard nothing of any commotion," I answered, staring straight at him.

"Doubtless you didn't know either that before the Expulsion, most business dealings were in the hands of the Jews, and that during the winter months, when meat became scarce in the Christian butcher shops, it was necessary to buy it in theirs," he said, looking out the window.

"I am newly come to this town and shall depart ere long, but the short time I have been here sufficed for me to know that even the churchmen and the nobles bought at the Jewish butcher's, because the meat was better there," I responded.

"You seem to know too much; perhaps the Jews also taught you how to clip the gold and silver coins which are in circulation in our kingdoms; I can easily find witnesses who will swear to it," he said.

"Beware of false witnesses and rumormongers who give testimony from hearsay and baseless beliefs; there is no rhyme or reason to what they say," I declared.

"Beware of your own words: many have gone to the stake for telling too many truths," he growled, on the point of leaving the inn.

"May you have a good journey, Señor Familiar of the Inquisition," I called after him.

"May Your Worship have a bad journey on the undertaking of Don Cristóbal Colón," he muttered, without looking back at me.

As soon as I was certain that he had disappeared down the road towards the setting sun, I returned to my room to ponder what had happened that day and what still lay before me.

In the penumbra of night everything seemed clear and muddled at the same time. A nightmarish scene, in which I was included, took shape before me, without my being able to tell whether the figures I saw were the others or myself. And it was not until a door slammed that I awoke with a start, as if a decision had made itself inside me. I would depart at dawn for Puerto de Santa María in a last attempt at finding Isabel and my son among the exiles who were leaving by ship. Afterwards, perhaps, I would go to Palos.

Doña Luz Pizarro came into my room; upon seeing my belongings readied for the journey, she began to revile me and make up a reckoning of everything I had eaten and how much I had slept, lest I should get away without paying.

"These varlets and wenches do not live by bread alone," she complained. "Each year I must pay the steward manservant one thousand five hundred *maravedis* and the ploughboy one thousand; I must give the maidservant, over and above her salary of five hundred *maravedis* and all my discarded hose, the use of one of the finest pieces of land in all Trujillo; she has enough to buy herself a cloth petticoat, two pairs of lambskin shoes and many other items of clothing. As for you, you owe me thirty *maravedis* for the brace of hens you ate, eighty *maravedis* for the four capons, six *maravedis* for the dozen eggs and ten *maravedis* for the small goose. And don't forget, I loaned you two *maravedis* to pay the blacksmith who shod your mule, thirty *maravedis* to give the shoe-maker for the cordovan shoes you bought from him and fifty *maravedis* for the doublet maker. Add to that sum the price of the room in which you have slept, loafed and dreamed, and—"

"You shall be paid every single *maravedi* that I owe you," I said, putting the money into her hand, and I closed the door in her face.

But that night I was unable to sleep. Hours went by while I sat on the bed staring at the rafters, the holes in the wall, the chinks in the door, turning over and over in my mind that four *arrobas* of white wine cost six hundred *maravedis*, that a pound of white waxen candles costs forty-two *maravedis*, that one hundred silver *reales* had been given to Antonio de Ludueña, a lackey in the service of the Count of Cifuentes, as a reward for a letter he brought to Seville which recounted the surrender of Granada to the Catholic Kings. In my drowsy state I was apprehensive lest Agustín Delfín burst into the room brandishing the green cross of the Holy Office and a knife to stab me in the chest; I was afraid that Doña Luz Pizarro would throw herself upon me in quest of passionate love, and I saw myself setting sail on a wooden nag, rocked by the waters beneath the vast ocean of a night where dawn was breaking, reminding me of the calm that precedes the sun's appearance or the eclosion of a new world.

In the midst of my insomnia I heard the world that is run by church bells, as if waking, eating, working and sleeping were done at their command and according to the ecclesiastical timing of life. I finally fell asleep at Lauds, awakening at Prime to quit the inn, traverse the streets at daybreak and encounter the town's early risers. At the city gate I came across an obese man wearing sumptuous vestments; as he was suffering from gout, he was unable to ride on horseback, and so four of his servants carried him on their shoulders, followed by a horde of solicitous menials.

I reached Puerto de Santa María one day before dawn towards the end of July. The morning promised to be limpid, and the air smelled of flowers and the sea. Across the bay rose the silhouette of Cádiz out of the dark waters, gleaming above the rocks like an effluvium of the starry night, the Gaddir of old, founded by the Phoenicians before Carthage, the Gades of Hercules in Roman times, the Moorish Kadis. Like an island girdled by waves, little by little the city braved the splendor of the nascent sun, a dream barely anchored to the mainland by its narrow isthmus. This spot had been the ends of the earth for the ancients, and the memory still lingered of the epitaph of one Heliodorus:

I, Heliodorus, a madman who was born in Carthage, left instructions in my testament to bury me in this sepulcher, here at the end of the world, to see if there was anyone more mad than I who would come to pay me a visit.

It was in this *ne plus ultra*, this ultima Thule, that the real exile began for the Jews. At the sight of the sea, they began to lament in great wails of anguish, imploring God for mercy, still hoping that He would again open a path for them amidst the waters and bring them safe through the thousands of tribulations that lay ahead of them. I searched for Isabel and my son among the crowd waiting to embark, my eyes darting over each woman and child. Suddenly, I noticed one woman whose face was hidden from my gaze; a small boy clung to her dress. Drawing nearer, I gently laid my hand on her head and turned her towards me. It was Isabel de la Vega. My heart leapt and I clasped her so violently that she nearly fell.

"How is it that you are here?" she asked, casting me an affrighted look.

"I have been searching for you in every corner of Castile and Aragón; each day I thought to find you on a street, in a village, on a road, in a town. Now that the Jews are being expelled by the Catholic Kings I came to Puerto de Santa María hoping to find you alive."

"You should not be here. The inquisitors will arrest you as a heretic

259

for having communication with Jews," she said in a faltering voice, raising her hand in a gesture of protection and rebuff.

"I will leave with you."

"The sentries would prevent it and you would only put my life in danger. Even in the midst of the Expulsion, the officials of the Inquisition are still hunting for fugitives amongst the outcasts," she replied.

"Then stay here with me."

She looked at me hard, hesitating briefly, then with a shake of her head rejoined the other women; the boy followed her. I caught up with them.

"You will bring us all to ruin," Isabel said to me.

"I will defend you with my life; no one shall do you any harm."

Her face, formerly smooth and bold, was lined and faded; her large almond eyes, though they had their old brightness, seemed melancholy.

"They may have sentenced me to death, but despite all their efforts they could never catch me. Now they are banishing me, with all the Jews, from the land where I was born and where my fathers' fathers were born for generation upon generation. The names of those who are to blame for this edict will live on in the history of mankind, to be honored and extolled in memorials, chronicles, annals and legends, but injustice will always be injustice, a crime will never stop being a crime, no matter if the words of praise are inscribed in gold on marble," she said.

One of the guards pushed me, reminding me that my feet had crossed the invisible line separating the living from the dead, the Old Christians from the *Conversos*, the Catholic faithful from the stubborn practitioners of the heretical depravity, those who remained from those who had to leave. An insignificant line for some, a fatal one for others, sharply drawn with fire and blood.

I slipped a gold coin into the sentry's hand to keep from being bothered, and in a welling up of tenderness I kissed my son; my emotion made him laugh.

In an instant Isabel had thrown her arms around my neck, pressing against my body as if she would transmit to it in a few moments the long years of love, sorrow and fear. I kissed her dusty cheeks, her parched lips, her disheveled hair. And then, her grief transfigured into pride and valor, with a tremulous smile she pulled away from me.

"It is time for us to go on board; there are many people waiting for the boats, which will set sail at dawn, and if we do not embark in time, they will leave us behind."

"I will not let you go," I cried, as if I were addressing a remote figure on the other side of a dream.

"We must be on our way," she said once more, her eye upon the maneuvering of the boats and the anxious bustle of the exiles trying to board them.

"Ever since you fled Madrid I have searched for you: in Saragossa, in Calatayud, in Teruel, in Toledo, and wherever else my feet have taken me; not for a single moment did I cease combing the roads and the hours," I said.

"I, too, have looked for you everywhere we have been, but always with the fear of finding you, of not knowing what would become of me when I saw you," she replied.

"Tell me about my son," I begged her.

"Your son was born in Saragossa one night while the inquisitors were ransacking the homes of *Conversos* in search of concealed Jews. A midwife friend of Doña Blanca helped me to give birth at my Aunt Luna's house. My aunt had lost her wits and kept coming up to me to sing softly in my ear;

> '*The river flows on,*
> *the sands remain,*
> *love is burning,*
> *ah! your heart feels the pain.*' "

"And then what did you do?"

"Early one Sunday morning my Aunt Luna's maidservant Oro passed us through the Angel Gate and we made our way to Calatayud, where we sojourned for a time. From thence we proceeded to Teruel, forever in flight, forever in dread of capture."

"It was in Toledo that I lost all trace of you and no longer knew which way to turn; tell me what happened afterwards."

"From Toledo I went to Burgos, purposing to get as far away as possible from the inquisitors of Ciudad Real. A friend of my father's was living in Burgos, the physician Rabbi Samuel. Notwithstanding his advanced age, he received three thousand *maravedis* every twelvemonth from the town council to carry on the practice of medicine with science and scruples, attending above all to the poor of the city, with the assistance of his son Abraham. But as in other parts of the realm, although the city had need of its Jewish doctors, this had not hindered the issuance of an order, in the year 1481, that the Jews 'must wear badges the size of a doubloon openly and uncovered and affixed to their shoulders,' and in the year 1484 the same council had ordered the segregation of the *juderías*, locking the gates at certain fixed hours and keeping them shut entirely on Saturdays and Sundays, which drastically limited the Jews' activities, commerce and communication with the Christian part of the city.

"My son and I made our home in Burgos in an old house on the Cal Tenebrosa, a narrow, dark street inhabited by merchants. There, close to the principal butcher's shop, we scarcely went out of our dismal dwelling all winter long, as the sun was hidden behind rainy clouds for days on end. Nevertheless, one day I chanced to observe and marveled at the worship in the Monastery of San Agustín of a Christ that had been found on the bottom of the sea in a chest very like a coffin. The statue had the height, girth, sinews, hair, beard, nails and pliant flesh of a recently dead man. Whenever the faithful touched the head, hands, feet and joints, the monks would chant and ring the bells, and great miracles were ascribed to this Christ, such as raising children from the dead and healing the sick.

"But well before the Jews were driven out of Burgos over the Laredo pass, in compliance with the Edict of Expulsion, we had set out for Hita, a city built on the slopes of a hill, whose walls climb from the lowest point to the fortress on its summit.

"We dwelt in that town with a matronly Jewess known to all as 'the Old Mother,' who owned a vineyard, and in my life there I experienced no greater grief than my own fears nor greater misfortune than the uncertainty of my own tomorrows. My days were spent between the San Pedro quarter and the Sancha Mártinez Gate, venturing from the Mercado as far as Jorge's Tower, walking down the streets leading into the main square or the lanes in Huda de los Puntos, calling at the butcher's or at the bakery belonging to the *Conversa* Francisca López. The Jews of Hita lived not only in the *aljama* but in the main square as well, along Calle Real, and near the city gates. The community had nine rabbis, two physicians, several surgeons and one butcher. They owned houses, cattle yards, building lots, warehouses and vineyards. But to me the tranquillity became monotonous. No one urged us to leave save my own feet, and nothing haunted my nights save my own dreams. Nevertheless, one day my son and I set out on the road to Buitrago, a walled city in the arms of the Lozoya River, with a castle, stony fields and dark holm oaks.

"Glimpsed from the plain, Buitrago looks like a dream come true on the slopes of the Somosierra, but the arid interior of the town is revealed as soon as you pass through the Arco de la Guarda Gate. My son and I arrived on San Lucas Day, when the yearly fair begins at which Christians, Jews and Moors buy and sell their wares for two weeks. We had scarcely entered the city when I was reminded of Don Iñigo López de Mendoza, the former lord of Buitrago, who was made Marquis de Santillana by the King Don Juan Segundo, at whose behest he compiled a collection of old wives' sayings and fireside adages. But above all, he was a great poet who loved the mountain girls and wrote poems to his

three daughters, as well as a gallant knight who was wont to say, 'If
we wish him well who does well by us, we must do well by him who
wishes us well.'

"We went down Calle de la Escalera and, by asking our way, reached
the house of the Alfandari family, where we could stop for only several
months, as the Edict of Expulsion was proclaimed on the twenty-ninth
of April. The life of centuries came tumbling down in a day, and we
who had no houses to sell had no need to linger until the end of the
term allotted for leaving the Kingdom of Castile, and so we set off one
day at dawn while the stars were still shining, for we wanted to get to
the sea before the end of July; I hoped eventually to reach Flanders,
although this lengthy detour took us even farther away from our des-
tination.

"We took with us a shepherd's pouch stocked with a few days' provisions, an ass on which my son rode and a dagger that I carried hidden
beneath my tight-fitting corselet. That whole first day, we walked up
and down mountains and untamed valleys, skirting a stream, which
flowed amongst the stands of pine, encountering no one on the way
but peasants bundling fagots and cows grazing. As the afternoon drew
to a close we chanced upon a shepherdess sitting in the bushes who
was the image of that woman described by Don Juan Ruiz, the Archpriest
of Hita. And just after sunset we saw two men standing next to a hut
with their shepherd's crooks and dogs. Farther ahead, a cowherd who
had no cloak walked among the boulders in his patched clothes. When
it was night we slept outdoors, never once awakened by fear. But the
following day at noon a man on horseback who had been hiding behind
a tree blocked our path.

" 'Where are you going at this unseemly hour? Why not tarry a while
with me. . . . Life is so short,' he said.

" 'Do you not see, sir, that my young son is with me?' I answered.

" 'You should not ford this river alone, for the place is swarming with
bandits,' he said.

" 'You are the bandit, if you do not let me and my child pass unhindered,' I replied.

" 'I have a yen for early fruit,' said he.

" 'I am not one of your mountain wenches, but a married Jewess,'
said I.

" 'It is all the same to me, for as the saying goes: A warm heart may
hide beneath a worn jacket, and a lusty drinker lurk under a lowly cape,'
he said as he dragged me into a coppice and tore at my clothes.

"While he was trying to possess me my son hit him on the head with
a stone and left him stretched out on the grass. We hurried away without
so much as a backwards glance, until we found the road and upon it a

great number of Jews who were marching towards the sea, guided by several officers of justice who were removing them, at their expense, from the kingdoms of Isabel and Fernando, with leave and license to protect and defend them, for it was feared and expected, despite the royal safe-conduct, that while they were passing through some towns or villages or barren lands in these realms and dominions persons on foot or on horseback might attempt to wound, rob, extort, seize or kill them as they went by with all their goods and chattels; or they might be charged customs duties at mountain passes, or tolls, imposts and tithes, or even levies for crossing bridges; or, upon their arrival at certain places, they would be denied entry or even the right of passage. Food and lodging would be refused them; they would not be sold the beasts or wagons which they might require for transporting their women and children, and would be condemned to endure hunger and spend the night in the fields, at the mercy of thieves and murderers.

"Be that as it may, we joined up with the men and women who, having made a bad sale of their possessions, were carrying into exile, either on their backs, loaded onto donkeys or in wagons, whatever they had received in exchange. To hearten and console themselves, they strove to believe that God would lead them beyond the mountains, rivers, hungers and sweltering heat into the Promised Land. Young and old alike took sick; pregnant women gave birth; people died or fell behind and returned to their birthplaces and converted, while Christians who took pity on us appeared on all sides to exhort us to be baptized. The rabbis kept our spirits up and made the boys and girls sing songs and play timbrels and tambourines to lighten the hardship and toils of our long march into exile. The people said to each other, 'We come from God, our strength is in the Almighty! If we are to live, let us live; if we must die, let us die; but let us not violate our covenant, let our hearts not look backwards, let us go in the name of the Lord, our God.' Or they quoted Scripture: 'And the Lord said unto Moses: "Stretch out thy hand toward heaven, that there may be darkness over the land of Egypt, even darkness which may be felt." And Moses said unto the people: "Remember this day, in which ye came out from Egypt, out of the house of bondage." '

"We trudged on in this fashion for several days until one evening, before we were out of the mountains of Gredos, the guides attempted to divide us into two groups, shunting to one side the comeliest maidens and those they took to be the wealthiest men, alleging that they had heard rumors of armed Moors from the host the Kings had defeated in Granada who were now on the loose with their scimitars, attacking Jews on the way to Portugal and Cádiz, for everyone knew that some of them were carrying a great deal of money hidden inside their bodies and their clothes. However, someone warned us that the López brothers from Illescas along with other kinsmen and cronies of theirs had pacted with Jews from an *aljama* to escort them, their wives, their children and their chattels as far as the Kingdoms of Fez and Tlemcén for the sum of four hundred *maravedis* per person over the age of eight and one florin for those eight years and younger, amounting to some six thousand Castilian doubloons in all. But they had not carried out their bargain with the Jews, causing much wrong and injury, ignominy and harm to their persons and possessions, and even robbing those rich men who had entrusted them with a quantity of gold and silver *maravedis* and other forbidden things to be taken to the boats in exchange for a payment of money. And so, we refused to be separated.

"Beneath the fierce July sun we resumed our journey towards the sea, some of us hoping to take ship at Cádiz and Puerto de Santa María and others at Málaga. Infants and ancients, pregnant women, nursing mothers and maidens, walking on foot or riding on donkeys, dragging their belongings in wagons or carrying them on their backs, we left behind us Toledo, Orgaz, Consuegra, the Guadiana River, untilled fields, steep paths, squalid taverns where the beds were harder than the ground, Calatrava, Almagro and the Sierra Morena, which separates Castile from Andalusia, and every hour of every day the heat became more unbearable. Some people veered towards Jaén, while the rest of us went on to Córdoba, which we glimpsed from afar, amidst its palm groves and olive trees. Under the scorching sun we passed Ecija, which they call 'the little frying pan,' because of its climate, and Carmona la Blanca. We tarried one day outside the walls of Seville and then continued on to Jerez de la Frontera and thence, finally, here to Puerto de Santa María." Isabel paused.

"Stay here," I pleaded. "You must both be very weary."

"The expulsion of the Jews is mine as well, their death is my death," she replied. "I must go with them."

"But you are a *Conversa*, you are allowed to stay," I insisted.

"Shhh, the sentries who guard us believe I am Jewish; they would arrest me and send me to the stake if they knew I am a fugitive *Conversa*," she whispered.

"We could leave behind all persecution and fear."

"My parents' faces are written across my own, and my body casts their shadow. I cannot dissever myself from their flesh and blood; their exile is mine."

"We three could live together, start a new life under a different name in some forgotten hamlet of these kingdoms."

"For want of my body, the inquisitors have burned my effigy: I no longer exist in these kingdoms," she answered.

"But the soul of a living creature cannot be burned up; you will be alive forever," I argued.

"Rather than live in a village and feed on infamy, I prefer to follow the example of that comely young Jewess from Calahorra who, when the French were looting the city and five of them broke into her house, hid with her eight-year-old daughter until nightfall, then emerged, dagger in hand, and slit the throats of all five, who had fallen into a stupor after drinking the fine wines that were in her cellar," she recounted proudly.

"Will we ever see each other again?" I asked.

"I cannot foretell the future," she replied.

The little boy stared at us; he was wan and tired. Then he turned his gaze on the sea, near at hand but unknown. All of a sudden I became aware of the sun beating down on our heads, of the shadows jutting to the right of our bodies, of the pebbly dust shining in the light of day. The green curve of the bay and the silhouette of Cádiz sharpened in the distance; closer by lay the mouth of the Guadalete River, golden glints on the green water.

"What news do you have of my brother? Tell me in a word if he lives or is dead," she demanded, looking hard into my eyes.

"He lives."

"In freedom, jailed or under torture?"

"He is free and on his way to Portugal. I met him a few days ago, and he asked me to tell you that his body is robust and strong and can survive hunger and exile, and that he will find you one day."

"Hurry up, we have to get on board the boats while there's still room for us," the child said, suddenly anxious.

"Where will you go?" I asked, realizing that she was set upon leaving.

"To Flanders," she replied. "Look for me in Flanders."

"I give you my word, I will," I promised.

And they slowly began to walk away among the others, as if they, too, bore on their backs not merely the weight of a handful of belongings, the remains of a lifetime, but the sorrows of generations and generations of Jews on their way into exile.

"Wait a minute," I said to my son. "What is your name? How do they call you?"

"Juan, my name is Juan, like my father," he replied.

"I am your father. One day I will come to get you in Flanders, but first I must make my fortune elsewhere."

The men and women were singing as they boarded the boats: "And the Lord said unto Moses: 'Wherefore criest thou unto Me? speak unto the children of Israel, that they go forward. And lift thou up thy rod, and stretch out thy hand over the sea, and divide it; and the children of Israel shall go into the midst of the sea on dry ground.' 'And the children of Israel went into the midst of the sea upon the dry ground; and the waters were a wall unto them on their right hand, and on their left.' " "And the Lord said unto Moses: 'Stretch out thy hand over the sea, that the waters may come back upon the Egyptians, upon their chariots, and upon their horsemen.' " "The Lord is a man of war: The Lord is His name."

The ships began to leave, furrowing the green water in an inexorable procession, as if setting out on the voyage of death.

Early that morning they set sail, one by one, towards the left side of the bay, rocked by the waves. Their passengers did not look at the marine horizon but at the beach, at the land that was left behind. They soon vanished over the horizon, beyond the green line where the waters and the whitish sky came together. Cádiz and the farther shore turned brighter, seemed closer.

I took the road to Palos, in search of fortune. I went to sea with Don Cristóbal Colón, as mastman on the ship *Santa María*. We left port by way of the Saltés River, half an hour before sunup, on Friday, the third day of August, in the year of Our Lord 1492. *Deo gratias.*

Trial of Isabel de la Vega
and Her Brother Gonzalo de la Vega
Natives of Ciudad Real
Absent
Transcribed by the Scriveners and Notaries
of the Holy Inquisition

In the noble city of Ciudad Real, this fourteenth day of November of the year one thousand four hundred and eighty-three after the Birth of Our Savior Jesus Christ, the Reverend Inquisitors Pero Dias de la Costana, licentiate in holy theology, canon of the church of Burgos, and Francisco Sanches de la Fuente, doctor of canonical decrees in the church of Zamora, presiding in their residences in the said city, in the lower hall where they are wont to give audience at the hour of Terce, in the presence of the hereinafter undersigned notaries and witnesses, the Honorable Ferrand Rodrigues del Barco, cleric, chaplain to our sire the King, prosecuting attorney of the Holy Office, appeared before the said father inquisitors, summoned to the audience by the said gentlemen. Thereat he declared and denounced to them that many inhabitants of this said city, men as well as women, who were suspected and defamed of heresy, had removed and fled from this said city in fear of the said Inquisition, that Isabel de la Vega and her brother Gonzalo figured notoriously among the fugitives, that their whereabouts were unknown, and that he intended to accuse them of the said crime of heresy and of having Judaized; consequently, he was asking and did ask the said father inquisitors, after having heard his evidence demonstrating their notorious absence from this city, to issue a subpoena summoning the said Isabel de la Vega and her brother Gonzalo to appear within a certain term to answer in person to the complaints and charges against each and every one of them in reference to the said heresy and having Judaized and followed the Law of Moses, which he intended to present and bring forth and prosecute, employing all his powers to do so. After having heard the prosecutor's plea, they commanded the witnesses to appear before them in order to hear their depositions concerning the absence from this city of the said Isabel and Gonzalo de la Vega. Upon which, the prosecutor presented before the said inquisitors the witnesses Juan Gomes, potter; Juan Peres, lime burner; Juan de Soria, ragpicker; and Ferrand Falcón, Converso, each and every one of whom was enjoined by the inquisitors to swear an oath in due form, placing their right hands on the cross and promising to say

truth in the present case. Each one of the said witnesses answered: Yea, he did
so swear, and at the conclusion of the said oath they all responded: Amen. And
as the said inquisitor asked them whether they knew for certain that the said
Isabel de la Vega and her brother Gonzalo were absent from this town, and that
they had departed on account of the Inquisition, and how much time had elapsed
since they had removed themselves, the said witnesses replied and affirmed that
it was public knowledge that the said Isabel and Gonzalo de la Vega were absent
from the said city, and that it was more or less a matter of fifteen days before
the arrival of the father inquisitors in the city that they had fled, and that their
whereabouts and present abode were unknown. Upon which, the said inquisitors
declared that it had been established that the said Isabel and Gonzalo de la Vega
had absented themselves from the city and the houses where they had lived and
dwelt, and that it was not possible to say with any certainty where they were
to be found, on account of which they were ordering and did order that a citation
in the form of an edict be issued against them and each one of them allotting a
term of thirty days divided into three fixed terms, the final term being peremptory,
by means of which they were commanded to appear within the said terms to
answer to the charges and accusations of heresy and Judaizing to be drawn up
against them by the said prosecutor. After which, they commanded that the said
citation be notified at their domiciles in the said city and be promulgated in the
square and notified in the Church of San Pedro, of which they were parishioners,
on a feast day, when the populace was assembled at Mass and the Divine Office,
also commanding that the edict be affixed to the doors of the said church, to
remain there during the entire aforesaid term of thirty days. Witnesses to all
the foregoing who were present: Juan de Coca, Juan Zarco, Juan Lopes, and
Ferrand Falcón, and the notaries Juan Sanches and Juan de Segovia.

Then, on Sunday, the sixteenth day of the said month of November of the
aforesaid year, the said citation was read aloud and made public in the Church
of San Pedro by Juan de Segovia, notary of the said audience and of the Holy
Office, in the presence of a considerable part of the populace of the said city, at
the hour of High Mass on the day when the penitents were making their act of
contrition, in the presence of the virtuous gentlemen Juan Peres, corregidor of
the city, mosén Lope de la Tudia, prefect of Malagón, and many other gentlemen
and aldermen of the said city. Witnesses who were present: the licentiate Juan
Bastante and Teresa the lime burner, among many others.

Then, the following Monday, the seventeenth day of the said month of November of the aforesaid year, in the public square of the said city, the said citation
was promulgated loudly and clearly by the said notary and by the crier Juan de
Lorca, official of the said city and commissioned to perform such tasks. Witnesses
who were present: Juan de la Gallina, scrivener; Christóbal, tailor; Pero Peres
de las Peras, stutterer; and Gonzalo Grillo.

• • •

Then, on the said day, before the door of the domiciles of the said Isabel and Gonzalo de la Vega, in the said city in the precinct of San Pedro and Barrio Nuevo, in the street known as Calle de la Torre, the citation was notified and intimated in person by the honorable gentleman Juan Peres, corregidor. Witnesses who were present: Pero Zebrón and Christino de León, inhabitants of the said city.

Then, on the aforesaid day and year, the said citation was affixed by the said prosecutor to the door of the said Church of San Pedro, being nailed to it by the said notary. Witnesses who were present during the said affixing: Pedro Gomes, Ferrand Alonso, Pedro Ferrandes, clerics of the said Church of San Pedro.

Then, on the twenty-fifth day of the said month of November of the aforesaid year, the said inquisitors being in their said residences, in the lower hall where they are wont to give public audience at the hour of Terce, the prosecutor of the Holy Office appeared before them. He declared that on the said day the first ten days of the term of thirty days allowed to Isabel and Gonzalo de la Vega had expired, a term allotted to them in the citation for appearing and presenting themselves before their reverences, which they had not done, and therefore he was accusing and did accuse them of the first instance of contumacy. And the said inquisitors replied that the complaint was admitted. Witnesses who were present: Miguel Morales; Antón Gomes, cobbler; and Gonzalo Martines.

Then, on the fourth day of the month of December of the aforesaid year, the said inquisitors being in their said residences, in the hall where they are wont to give audience, in the presence of the notaries and witnesses herewith appended, the said prosecutor appeared and declared that on the said day the second term of the said thirty days allotted in the citation and edict issued against the said Isabel de la Vega and her brother Gonzalo expired, and they had not appeared, and therefore he was accusing and did accuse them of the second instance of contumacy. The reverend inquisitors replied that they acknowledged the fact. Witnesses who were present: Pero Peres de las Peras, stutterer, and Juan Sanches, chaplain to the said licentiate de la Costana, inquisitor.

Then, on Monday, the fifteenth day of the said month of December of the said year, while the inquisitors were giving audience at the hour of Terce in the lower hall of their residences, as was their wont and custom, the prosecuting attorney appeared before them and declared that on the said day the final and peremptory term expired, the which had been granted to Isabel and Gonzalo de la Vega in the citation and edict, summoning them to appear, and they had not appeared, and therefore he was accusing them of the third and final instance of contumacy, and asking their reverences to declare them to be rebellious and condemn them

271

as such. And the said inquisitors replied that they accepted the prosecutor's complaint and they were prepared to act in accordance with their duty. Witnesses who were present: Mencio Mendes, stonecutter; Urraca Núñez; and Pedro de Yepes.

Then, on the fifth day of the month of January, in the year one thousand four hundred and eighty-four after the Birth of Our Savior Jesus Christ, the inquisitor Doctor Francisco Sanches de la Fuente being in the said hall giving ear to those persons who appeared before him, the prosecutor appeared and announced that he was presenting and did present the accusatory petition against the said Isabel de la Vega and her brother Gonzalo, the import of which is as follows:

Most Reverend and Virtuous Judges and Inquisitors of the heretical depravity: I, Ferrando Rodrigues del Barco, chaplain to our lord the King, prosecuting attorney of the Holy Inquisition, do hereby appear before your Reverences to denounce and bring charges against Isabel de la Vega and Gonzalo de la Vega, her brother, natives of this city of Ciudad Real, absent at the present time, for being rebellious and contumacious towards the apostolic commandments and to your convocations and summons issued in their absence, which should be considered their presence. I say this because the said Isabel and Gonzalo de la Vega live under Christian names and enjoy the benefits of such, committing an offense against Our Lord and our Holy Catholic Faith, with no fear of the punishments and censures which, on account of Judaizing and keeping the Law of Moses and performing Jewish rites, they might well expect, practicing heresy in the following particulars: First, that they did kindle and caused to be kindled lights in clean lamps on Friday nights in honor of the Sabbath ceremony, in accordance with the Jewish custom. Item, that they did cook and caused to be cooked viands on Fridays to be eaten on Saturdays, to avoid cooking them on Saturday, a feast day, arraying themselves in clean garments of fine cloth and linen more so that day than on any other during the week, and going to take their ease on such days in the houses of their kinsmen. Item, that the said Isabel de la Vega and her brother fasted the fasts which the Jews are wont to fast by not eating until nightfall, when the stars come out, then to sup upon meat in a ritual manner, making a blessing over it as the Jews do and holding a goblet of wine in their hand. Item, that the said Isabel and Gonzalo de la Vega ordered the kneading of unleavened bread and did partake of it on the holidays which the Jews call the feast of the Lamb. Item, that during the said holiday the said Isabel and Gonzalo de la Vega ate only out of porringers and dishes and pots and pitchers and other vessels which were all new, as is the wont and custom of the Jews. Item, that following and in keeping with the said Law of Moses, they did not eat flesh from animals which were not killed and their throats slit according to Jewish ritual or at the hands of a Jew, and when they were unable to obtain it they ate no other meat, nor did they eat the fish which are forbidden by the said Law of

Moses, saving fruit or eggs or suchlike, all in the Jewish fashion. Item, that the said Isabel and Gonzalo de la Vega partook of meat during Lent and on other days when it is proscribed by Holy Mother Church, in violation of our Holy Catholic Faith, and deliberately purposing to offend the Faith they washed their dead after they had died according to the Jewish fashion, making a funeral repast in their honor at the death of their parents, eating seated upon the floor for the space of seven or nine days, and only such things as fish or eggs, and even burying their kinsmen as the Jews do, with those selfsame ceremonies. Item, that the said brother and sister de la Vega agreed to make a hadas ceremony on the seventh day after the birth of a son who was born to the said Gonzalo, persisting in the offense to and disdain of our Holy Catholic Faith, for the said Gonzalo had been circumcised when he was nearing fifteen years old. Item, that the said Isabel and Gonzalo de la Vega denied the advent of Our True Redeemer and Savior Jesus Christ, our Messiah, and that they assembled with other male and female Conversos on the roof of a tower and when a star seemed to give off sparks they all clamored: "He who shall save us is born! Our Messiah is born!" Item, that the said Isabel and Gonzalo de la Vega listened to and went to hear Jewish prayers in the house of Alvaro the linen draper, who read the lesson in lieu of a rabbi, wearing a pointed cap set upon his head, and they did so on Saturdays as well as other feast days of the Jews, putting their entire faith into these beliefs, straying from our Holy Catholic Faith and sinning against Our Savior and Redeemer Jesus Christ. Item, that the said Isabel and Gonzalo de la Vega Judaized and practiced heresy in other ways and circumstances and fashions and occasions, which, should it prove to be necessary, I am prepared to enumerate for the business at hand. By virtue of which, most worthy sirs, as the said brother and sister have practiced heresy and apostasy both notoriously and publicly in the aforesaid particulars, and have refused to appear before Their Excellencies, to be received once more into the fold and humble themselves before Holy Mother Church, whom they so grievously offended ere they fled this city on account of the Inquisition, I say that the said Isabel and Gonzalo de la Vega should be considered as notorious heretics and apostates, thereby incurring the ecclesiastical censures and other civil and criminal punishments established by the law and the holy canons. For which reasons, Reverend Sirs, I do ask and require it of you to declare and pronounce them to be notorious heretics and apostates who have incurred the said punishments, thus imploring the holy and noble office of Their Excellencies for the execution of justice. And I do swear, by the orders I have received, that had the said Isabel and Gonzalo de la Vega appeared before you, I would have made this selfsame accusation. That is why, Reverend Sirs, I ask and require you to proceed against them as if they were present, as befits the gravity of this affair and the contempt evidenced by the said Isabel and Gonzalo de la Vega, always remaining within the confines of the law in such circumstances, up to and including the definitive sentencing; and I am prepared to justify my plaint and accusation to whatever extent may be necessary.

• • •

And once the writ of denunciation against Isabel and Gonzalo de la Vega was presented, the prosecutor answered that he did receive it, and he ordered the two defendants to answer the said petition within the three subsequent days. To which effect, the notary was bidden to summon them to an audience in their domiciles, the which he did straightway, by virtue of the said commission and order, summoning them aloud in the said audience in the presence of those who were there. Witnesses who were present: Juan de Hoces and Juan Ruys de Cordova, master of holy theology, and many others as well. And then he proceeded immediately to the domiciles of the said Isabel and Gonzalo de la Vega, demanding before their door that they appear within three days to answer the said accusation and plaint which had been brought against them. Witnesses who were present: Pero Peres de las Peras, Martín the Blind Man, and Juan de las Higueras, inhabitants of the said city.

Then, on the seventh day of the said month of January of the said year, the inquisitor being in the said audience, the said prosecutor appeared and declared that, insofar as the said Isabel and Gonzalo de la Vega had been summoned at his behest and by order of His Reverence to appear in person in that audience to answer to a denunciation and plaint brought against them by himself, and they had not appeared, and that on this day the term expired, he was accusing and did accuse them of contumacy. The inquisitor declared that he admitted the accusation. Witnesses who were present: Martín de Cepeda and Christóval de Burgos, familiars in the service of the said inquisitor.

Then, on the seventh day of the month of January of the aforesaid year, the said inquisitors Pero Dias de la Costana and Francisco Sanches de la Fuente giving audience at the hour of Terce, the prosecutor Ferrand Rodrigues del Barco appeared in order to present his witnesses: Juan de las Mozas, Marina Lopes, Juana Ruys, Alvaro de las Parras, Antonia Mexía, Diego de los Olivos, Antón de Murcia, Rodrigo Núñez, carpenter, Juana Torres, Ferrand Falcón, Juan Barva de Santo, María Bastante, Elvira de Jaén, Pero Peres de las Peras, and Gonzalo Grillo, all natives of the said Ciudad Real, from each and every one of whom the prosecutor received an oath in due form, causing them to place their right hand upon a cross and upon a book of the Holy Gospels open at the words in principium erat berbum, *and he asked them if they did swear on that cross and those words of the Holy Gospels, which each one had corporally beneath his right hand, to tell the whole truth in the present case wherein they were cited as witnesses, and to tell it regardless of money or self-interest or love or kinship or any other reason. And each one of the said witnesses answered and they all answered and declared aloud: Yea, I do so swear. And the said gentleman told them that God would help them if they uttered the truth, but otherwise they* would be struck dumb in this world and the next, as befits bad Christians who perjure the Holy Name. And each one of them answered: Amen. Witnesses who were present: Martín de Cepeda and Pedro de Villacis, familiars of the Inquisition.

And what the said witnesses averred, upon being examined and questioned each one individually by the said masters Juan Ruys de Córdova and Juan de Hoces, clerics, is as follows:

Firstly, being duly sworn in and interrogated by the said assessors, Juan de las Mozas declared that, as a witness under oath, he knew as a fact that approximately five years ago, when he had made the acquaintance of Gonzalo de la Vega, one day when walking down a road with him, the latter began to talk and say things against our Faith, purposing to turn him, Juan, into a Jew and adherent of the Law of Moses. And this witness declared that on several occasions he had climbed to the tower of Gonzalo's house to ask him divers things concerning his farm, and he had been obliged to wait until Gonzalo had finished speaking with his God, turned to the wall in the manner of a Jew, and that he had not been able to understand what he was saying. And he also declared that upon going to Jahén with Gonzalo de la Vega on one occasion, they had reached Linares on Friday afternoon and the following day, Saturday, he had not wished to continue, because he was keeping the Sabbath. And he avowed that the sister Isabel de la Vega also kept the Sabbath and ate meat during Lent, and that both of them celebrated the feasts of the Jews, and that he had seen them fast many times, one day each week, until nightfall, and then they would taste meat. They never went to Mass, he had never seen them make the sign of the cross, and they ate no flesh from the Christian butcher, and when they did not have meat they ate grapes and eggs instead. They kneaded and baked unleavened bread in their own house and ate of it in season. This is what the first witness declared under oath.

Marina Lopes, wife of Pero la Pelegrina, miller, who lived in the precinct of Santa María at the doors of the said church, after being duly sworn and interrogated, declared that one Sunday as she was passing by the door of Isabel de la Vega and her brother Gonzalo, she saw soapy suds issuing from a drain in the house into the street, and that she believed they were washing clothes on the Lord's Day in the house of the said brother and sister so as not to honor the Sunday. She also noticed that they observed the Sabbath and donned clothes worthy of a holiday and took their ease that day and went out to visit kinsmen, and others came to pay them a visit. As for the food they cooked, she vaguely remembered that Isabel had eaten flesh during Lent and her brother did so as well. This is what she said, and it is the truth, by the oath that she swore.

. . .

Juana Ruys, serving maid and aforesaid witness, declared that some five or six years ago, when she was dwelling in Isabel de la Vega's house, their neighbor was a cousin of the said Isabel's by the name of María, who having just given birth, this witness went to see the son who had been born to her, and as the witness entered the house shortly before they brought him back from being baptized she saw the said Isabel removing a caldron of water from the fire, after which she sent for the child and removed his coverings and asked for others and she washed his entire body with warm water. This is what she knows and saw, by the oath that she swore.

Alvaro de las Parras, aforesaid witness, when interrogated and examined by the said assessors, declared that he had been the owner of the butcher shop of the said city for some ten years, and that Isabel de la Vega had not purchased meat from him for upwards of three years, for it was public knowledge and notorious that the said brother and sister de la Vega lived the life of Jews and not of Christians, and he told of selling sheep on the hoof to the Conversos *in the city, and that he had heard tell that Juan Panpán would slit their throats, as did another man who called himself Garsía Barvas, and then they shared out the flesh among the other* Conversos. *And this is what he knew, by the oath which he had sworn.*

Antonia Mexía, being presented and duly sworn in by the said assessors, declared that some two years ago she had taken up residence in Ciudad Real, in the house of Juana de la Torre, wife of Diego, the scrivener, and that while she was living there Isabel de la Vega had come to the house and she, Antonia, had heard them praying through a closed door and afterwards had seen them reading out of a large book which lay on the table, which they told her was the Bible, and she had seen them eat unleavened bread. And this is what she knew, by the oath which she had sworn.

Diego de los Olivos, being duly sworn in, was questioned and examined by the said assessors, and declared that for the past ten or eleven years he had been wont to go out selling partridges, and once Gonzalo de la Vega had asked him, in fact, now that he thought of it, several other times as well, to bring him live partridges. And Ramiro the coppersmith said to him: Do not bring them to him, for he wants them to perform Jewish practices. And this is what he knew, by the oath which he had sworn.

Antón de Murcia, husbandman, duly sworn in and upon being questioned and examined by the said assessors, declared that some four years ago he had seen Gonzalo de la Vega in a wagon at his father's farm in the act of praying

276

and singing, and that the witness did not understand his prayers and songs and thought it was wrong for him to be praying all alone as if God were there in front of him. And this is what he knew, by the oath which he had sworn.

After duly swearing an oath and being questioned and examined by the said assessors, Rodrigo Núñez, carpenter, declared that one day when this witness was at work in the house of Isabel and Gonzalo de la Vega, he happened upon several small books containing Jewish rites, and that he read somewhat in them and discovered that the name of Jesus Christ was nowhere to be found, nor was there any mention of the cross, but only of Adonay and the Merciful One. And that he took them away with him, and afterwards the said Gonzalo offered to give him enough cloth for a gown and wine to drink if he returned those books to him. And he declared that one day while conversing with this witness the said Gonzalo de la Vega had assured him that this world would be everlasting, dawning and growing dark, the moon following the sun, to which this witness replied that this contradicted the Psalm of David which said that the heavens were the work of God's hands, and that He could change them as easily as changing clothes, but that He and His years would never perish. But Gonzalo declared that it would only come to pass as he had said. And this is what he knew, by the oath which he had sworn.

Juana Torres, having appeared before the said assessors, declared that some six years ago this witness had resided in the house of Catalyna, the wife of Rodrigo de la Vega, mother of the said Isabel and Gonzalo, who was a widow at the time and had her two children living with her. While she was in their house she observed how mother and children kept the Sabbath and dressed in finery on that day and arrayed themselves. Starting on Friday at noon they would shut themselves up in a room and all read out of a book, their heads covered, in the Jewish fashion, and the only word she understood was 'Adonay.' She also saw how they cooked food on Friday to keep for Saturday, and kindled clean lamps, and that they celebrated the feasts of the Jews, ate fowl slaughtered by Pero Gonzales, the wax chandler, and kneaded and ate unleavened bread in their house. She declared that the mother had never taught Isabel and Gonzalo to say the Pater Noster or the Credo or the Salve Regina, and that she did not take her children to church, and that one Sunday she surprised the said Catalyna in the act of spinning, just as if Sunday was a day like any other in the week. And this is what she knows, by the oath that she had sworn.

Ferrand Falcón, of the parish of San Pedro's, near San Francisco's, husband of Briolángel, and a Converso, after being sworn in and questioned by the said assessors, declared that one Saturday this witness entered the house of Catalyna, wife of Rodrigo de la Vega, mother of the said Isabel and Gonzalo, when she

*was a widow, after knocking on the door, and he heard the murmur of people
in a room and after climbing a staircase he came upon the old Catalyna and her
two children praying from a Jewish book which they called* cidur, *and that the
said Gonzalo was sitting on a small chair, his face turned to watch how they
were praying. And the witness had understood, because his own father had been
a Jew and had taught him the Jewish rituals. And he added that once the family
de la Vega gave him a dish which had been prepared with many spices and they
had called it* adafina, *and unleavened bread as well. And this is what he knows
and it is true and he affirms it.*

*Juan Barva de Santo, a resident of the blind alley called Torre de la Merced
in the Santa María precinct, was duly sworn in and under oath declared that
some fifteen years ago he had been hired as a peon to lay tiles in the house of
Catalyna, wife of Rodrigo de la Vega, mother of Isabel and Gonzalo, and one
Friday while bringing some tiles to the overseer, he had been obliged to pass
through the kitchen and had seen a pot on the fire, and when he took off the lid
he saw there was meat in it. The mother of Isabel and Gonzalo had been about
to put away the pot when she was called outside to speak with several* Conversas.
This is what he knows and saw and he affirms it.

*María Bastante, wife of Juan Merlo, shoemaker, was duly sworn in and
declared that some fourteen years ago, her next-door neighbors had been Catalyna,
wife of Rodrigo de la Vega, and her children Isabel and Gonzalo, when they
lived on Calle de la Torre, and at the time when the said Rodrigo de la Vega,
physician in Ciudad Real, passed away, his wife and children had bathed him,
shaved him all over, wound him in a shroud, keened over him, and buried him
in the Jewish fashion in the cemetery of San Francisco. She added that they had
made a funeral repast and eaten fish and eggs while sitting on the floor for the
space of nine days, and during that time had drawn no water from the well,
only setting out a lamp and a water-filled porringer to bathe the soul of the said
Rodrigo therein. And on another occasion, she peeked between some boards
separating her garden from the house of the said Catalyna and her children Isabel
and Gonzalo and saw them reading a Bible written in Romance which their
father had hidden away in a hole in the wall before the pillaging of that city so
it would not be discovered, and she had also remarked that they fasted the fasts
of the Jews, not eating until nightfall when the stars came out, and then supping
on meat, reciting prayers which she could not understand as they were in Hebrew,
and she saw that they ate no other meat save that slaughtered by slitting the
animal's throat and that they had a separate pot in which they prepared food
and they would carry with them a small kettle out of which they drank when
they went to their beehives, drinking a beverage called* Gibada, *which was
prepared by Juan Gonzales Panpán, an inhabitant of Ciudad Real who had been
burned in effigy as a heretic. This is what she knew and she ratified it.*

• • •

Elvira de Jaén, a Conversa, declared that she had heard Gonzalo de la Vega praying from a Jewish book one day when she went to his house for some pots the said Isabel was lending to her, and that upon entering a room she overheard the said Isabel saying she did not believe the Messiah Our Savior and Redeemer Jesus Christ had already come, nor did she believe in the virginity of Our Lady the Holy Virgin Mary, and that she knew no Christian prayers, but could recite one which went like this:

> Adonay, thou hast made thy dwelling amongst us
>> from generation unto generation.
> Before the mountains were born, before thou
>> createst the earth and the world,
> thou wert God forever and ever.
> Thou makest the man turn to dust, and the children of man,
> for a thousand years are to thee as the day of
>> yesterday which is past, and thou watchest in the night.

And this is what she saw and heard and she affirmed it.

Pero Peres de las Peras, stutterer, and his brother, Gonzalo Grillo, sons of Martín the Blind Man, aforesaid witnesses, being duly sworn in did declare that one day when they were at work in the house of the said Isabel and Gonzalo de la Vega, the said Pero Peres de las Peras saw the said Gonzalo kindling the lamps and causing them to be kindled one Friday night; Gonzalo Grillo saw the said Isabel cooking and causing to be cooked certain foods on Friday to be eaten cold on Saturday in honor of that day; Pero Peres de las Peras saw that the said Gonzalo was wont to keep the Sabbath by ceasing all work on that day and not receiving money and giving himself over to pleasures, as on a feast day; Gonzalo Grillo saw that the said Isabel de la Vega and her brother put on clean clothes of fine cloth and linen on the said Saturdays and holidays; Pero Peres de las Peras saw that the said de la Vegas did eat and cause to be eaten unleavened bread and meat slaughtered in the Jewish ritual fashion: Gonzalo Grillo saw and heard the said de la Vegas affirm that our Messiah had not come, scorning Our Redeemer and our Holy Catholic Faith; Pero Peres de las Peras heard them agree one Friday night to light the lamps and prepare the cold stew to eat on Saturday in honor of the Sabbath. And this is what they saw and heard and they affirmed it.

Then, on the third day of the said month of January of the aforesaid year, the said prosecutor appeared before the said doctor inquisitor, who was giving audience at the hour of Terce in the hall where he was wont to do so, and the prosecutor said that, inasmuch as he saw no need to present any further witnesses *aside from those who had already testified, he hereby asked that ratification be made of the testimonies given. And the said inquisitor admitted his request and ordered that the parties be summoned to the audience tomorrow in order to hear the ratification of the testimonies. Witnesses who were present: Juan el Cojo (the Limper), Pedro el Mudo (the Mute), and Ramón el Ciego (the Blind Man). And that same day the said notary called upon the said Isabel and Gonzalo de la Vega before the doors of their domiciles to be present the following day. Witnesses: Yñigo Ruys and Juan de Ciudad.*

Then, on the fourteenth day of the said month of January of the said year of 1484, the said prosecutor appeared before the reverend inquisitor who was giving audience at the hour of Terce, and he declared that the said Isabel and Gonzalo de la Vega had been summoned to the audience to appear before His Excellency and be present at the ratification of the testimonies of the witnesses, and they had not appeared, whereby he was accusing and did accuse them of contumacy, and he was asking and did ask the said inquisitor to order that ratification be made and published by the said notary. And the said inquisitor commanded that copies be made of the said testimonies and delivered to the said Isabel and Gonzalo de la Vega, only concealing the names of the witnesses but publishing the facts, so that three days hence they might appear to answer as they saw fit and say whatever they would in rebuttal. Witnesses who were present: Santiago el Tullido (the Cripple), Ferrand Falcón, and Diego Dias, carpenter.

Then, on the sixteenth day of January, the said inquisitor being in the said hall at the hour of Terce giving his audience, the said prosecuting attorney appeared and was accusing and did accuse the said Isabel and Gonzalo de la Vega of contumacy, inasmuch as he had given them until that day to come forward and contest the allegations of the witnesses. And the said inquisitor answered that he admitted the prosecutor's request and commanded that the parties be summoned to appear three days hence, warning that if they failed to appear, he would hold the case to be closed. Witnesses: Pero Peres de las Peras and Ferrand Falcón.

Then, by order of the said inquisitor, the notary once more summoned Isabel and Gonzalo de la Vega at the doors of their house to appear on the third day hence before their reverences for the conclusion of the proceedings and trial in which they stood accused by the said prosecutor. Then, on the nineteenth day of the month of January, the said inquisitor being in the lower hall giving audience at the hour of Terce, the prosecuting attorney appeared and declared that Isabel and Gonzalo de la Vega had been summoned to appear that same day to answer to the charges against them, but that they had not appeared. Consequently, he was accusing and did accuse them of contumacy and was asking and did ask the said inquisitor to bring this trial to an end and pronounce the sentence. Witnesses: Toribio de Torres and Briolángel de Padilla.

Then, this said day in the afternoon, the said inquisitor ordered that the following examiners be summoned to hold a consultation about the trial: the superior of the convent of San Francisco, the prior of Santo Domingo of the Order of Preacher Friars, the licentiate Juan del Canpo, the licentiate Jufre de Loaysa, the bachelor Gonzalo Muñoz, and the bachelor of Camargo. And after they took counsel and deliberated, each one of them gave his vote, and they all were unanimous and in agreement in their opinion and vote and counsel that the said Isabel and Gonzalo de la Vega should be inculpated as heretics and relaxed to the secular arm.

Then, immediately thereafter, in the said audience and in the presence of all those who were there, the notary Juan Sanches did loudly and clearly summon and call upon the said Gonzalo and Isabel de la Vega to appear on the third day hence to hear their sentence in the trial for heresy of which they stood accused. Witnesses: Miguel Hidalgo, glover, and Ysabel de Monteagudo.

Then, this said day, at the hour of Vespers, the said notary, by order of the reverend inquisitors, summoned and called upon the said Isabel and Gonzalo de la Vega at the doors of the house where they were wont to dwell, admonishing them to appear before the inquisitors on the third day hence at Terce, in order to hear their sentencing at the trial for the heresy in which they had incurred, according to the complaint brought against them by the prosecuting attorney. Witnesses who were present: Antón, lime burner; Juan, mason; Luys Tenbleque, carpenter.

Then, on Friday, the thirtieth day of the said month of January, of the said year, the said inquisitors being in the lower hall of their residences giving audience, as was their wont, at the hour of Terce, the said prosecutor appeared and declared that at their behest, Isabel and Gonzalo de la Vega had been summoned and convoked to this audience to hear their sentencing for the heresy of which they were accused, and that they had failed to appear. Therefore, he declared that he was accusing and did accuse them of contumacy and consequently requested that the sentence or sentences be pronounced. Then the said inquisitors asked the notary Juan Sanches if he had in truth summoned and convoked the said Isabel and Gonzalo de la Vega to this audience in order to hear their sentencing, as he had been ordered to do. And he replied that he had done so and affirmed that he had summoned them publicly in the audience as well as afterwards at the doors of their house. Upon which, the said inquisitors declared that they were satisfied that the summons and convocation to hear sentencing *had taken place, and that they admitted the accusation of contumacy brought against the said Isabel and Gonzalo de la Vega, and adjudged them to be contumacious, and that they were ready to pronounce their sentences in the presence of the said prosecuting attorney. Witnesses to the aforesaid: Beatris Gomes and Pero Peres de las Peras, and the notaries Juan de Segovia and Juan Sanches.*

Then, with no further delay, the reverend inquisitors did give and pronounce the sentence, which was read aloud in their presence and at their behest by the notary Juan de Segovia. And each and every one of them said at the end of the reading, 'Thus have we pronounced and declared.' The import of the said sentence, de berbo ad berbum, *is as follows: We have seen for ourselves, Pero Dias de la Costana, licentiate in holy theology, and Francisco Sanches de la Fuente, doctor in decrees, inquisitor-judges by virtue of apostolic authority, and I myself, the said licentiate Pero Dias de la Costana, as vicar and general official to the most reverend Don Pero González de Mendoza, cardinal of Spain, archbishop of the Holy Church and of the archbishopric of Toledo, that it is public knowledge and notorious in Ciudad Real that many of those who were going under the name of Christians were practicing heresy and solemnizing and keeping the Law of Moses, performing the ceremonies in accordance with the ancient Jewish rites. And wishing to show clemency and mercy to each and every one of them, we issued and made public our letter and edict of grace, so that all the persons in this said city and its bailiwick who had fallen into and incurred the said heresy of following the Law of Moses might come forward within the term of thirty days to appear before us and confess their errors and abjure and renounce and break away from the said heresy, and embrace our Holy Mother Church in harmony and union with the Christian faithful, and we would receive them using as much pity and compassion as we were able. And we would wait for them not only for the said term of thirty days, but for yet thirty days more, and we would receive all those who were desirous of coming forward to confess and recite their sins pertaining to the said heresy. And once the said term of the said sixty days had passed, and even more time afterwards, acting against those who did not come forward or appear, in particular against those who fled in fear of our said Inquisition, about whom we had information and testimony had been made to us, being required by our prosecuting attorney, the honorable cleric Fernando Rodrigues del Barco, chaplain to our lord the King, we commanded that our summons and edict of convocation be issued against the suspicious and incriminated persons who had thus absented themselves. And because it was evident that among them Isabel and Gonzalo de la Vega were notorious and public heretics who did and do publicly follow the said Law of Moses, we commanded that our said summons and edicts be issued against each of them, by virtue of which we ordered them to appear in person before us within thirty days, divided into three terms, allowing them ten days for each term, the last one being peremptory, to defend themselves and answer to the charges of heresy and of Judaizing of which they were notoriously and publicly defamed and accused. And seeing as how our said summons was proclaimed at the doors of the houses and domiciles of the said Isabel and Gonzalo de la Vega, and in the parish church of which they were parishioners, and promulgated in the public square of this said city and afterwards affixed to a door of the said church; and as their contumacy to the terms and times allotted in the said summons was denounced before us by the said prosecuting attorney, thus it was deemed necessary to accuse them, inasmuch as the said Isabel and Gonzalo de la Vega, being Christians by name and benefits did practice heresy and Judaize, following the Law of Moses, observing it solemnly, whether by keeping the Sabbath, lighting lamps on Friday night, donning clean clothes on Saturday, keeping the holy days of the Jews, fasting their fasts, eating unleavened bread on the day and at the time when they do eat it, praying the prayers of the Jews in the manner that they do pray them, and receiving many male and female Conversos into their house on the said Saturdays and feast days to pray and listen to the reading aloud of Jewish books. On account of which he declared and denounced that the said Isabel and Gonzalo de la Vega notoriously and publicly had sundered themselves from our Holy Catholic Faith by following the Law of Moses in the aforesaid fashion, and that they were deserving of being proclaimed and denounced as notorious and public heretics and for having incurred the punishments and censures stipulated by the law, and as such to be proclaimed and declared, requesting that this be done for the accomplishment of justice. And having seen the said accusation and the proofs presented by the prosecuting attorney by means of abundant witnesses, by reason of which it appears and is evident and proven that the said Isabel and Gonzalo de la Vega did commit and consent to perform the excesses and crimes of heresy and apostasy contained in the said accusation, and did follow and solemnly celebrate the ceremonies and honored the Law of Moses; and inasmuch as it has been proven that they absented themselves and fled from this city in fear of the Inquisition, leaving by the Toledo Gate, forsaking their houses and properties, and that they took shelter and went to places and dominions where they could not easily be had by us nor by our command. Heedful of the notoriety of the crime and of its gravity, and taking into consideration above all our counsel and deliberation with both religious and learned secular persons with whom we held communication and consultation concerning the said trial, in accordance with their opinion and shared determination, and keeping God before our eyes, we have reached a verdict which we must and do declare, condemning the said Isabel and Gonzalo de la Vega, together and separately as public heretics and apostates, for having sundered themselves as they did from our Holy Catholic Faith, and for following the Law of Moses, incurring the sentence of major excommunication and all the other punishments, spiritual and temporal, including the prohibition and the sequestering of their goods, which have been established by law against such heretics and apostates, and consequently we must relax them and we do relax them to the virtuous gentleman Juan Peres Barradas, corregidor of this*

Ciudad Real and its bailiwick, by grace of our lords the King and Queen, and to their alcaldes *and* alguaciles *and officers of justice of any and all cities and towns and villages within and without these realms, so that they may be burned at the stake as heretics. And because the said Isabel and Gonzalo de la Vega are absent and it is not possible to apprehend them now, we command that their statues be relaxed and we do relax them, the which are here present, so that the said punishments may be executed on them and they may be burned in effigy. Thus do we pronounce and command in these writs and by them. This said sentence was given and pronounced by the reverend inquisitors in the said Ciudad Real, in the place where they were wont to give audience at the hour of Terce, being seated before us the said gentlemen Juan de Segovia, clergyman chaplain to our lady the Queen, and Juan Sanches Tablada, scriveners and notary publics in the employ of the said Holy Inquisition, on the thirtieth day of the month of January in the year one thousand four hundred and eighty-four after the Birth of our Savior Jesus Christ.*